The Messiah

Books by the author

The Book of Abraham (1986)

The Jester and the Kings: A Political Autobiography (1989)

The Children of Abraham (1990)

*Stories of Deliverance: Speaking with Men and Women
Who Rescued Jews from the Holocaust* (1998)

The Wind of the Khazars (2003)

Sarah: A Novel (2004)

Zipporah, Wife of Moses: A Novel (2005)

Lilah: A Novel (2006)

alter

THE MESSIAH

TRANSLATED BY

Lauren Yoder

The Toby Press

The Messiah

The Toby Press LLC

First English Language Edition, 2008

POB 8531, New Milford, CT 06776-8531, USA

& POB 2455, London WIA 5WY, England

www.tobypress.com

First published in 1998 as *Le Messie*

Copyright © Editions Robert Laffont, Paris

Translation © Lauren Yoder, 2008

The right of Marek Halter to be identified as the author
of this work has been asserted by him in accordance
with the Copyright, Designs & Patents Act 1988

Cover image, *Portrait of a Man with a Turkish
Hat* by Maurycy Gottlieb (1856–1879)

ISBN 978 1 59264 216 8, *hardcover*

A CIP catalogue record for this title is
available from the British Library

Typeset by Koren Publishing Services

Printed and bound in the United States

Chapter one

Barukh Haba

The rumor started in Egypt and was now spreading all over Europe.

Trustworthy travelers, among them merchants, rabbis, and learned men, brought it to Italy where many penniless Jews had found refuge. During those fateful years of 1492 and 1496, they had been forced to flee Spain and Portugal, where they had been persecuted and where some had been massacred and even burned at the stake. They were still horrified by the pogroms and could not shake the memory of the tens of thousands among them who had perished. Homeless and without a country to call their own, those who left Spain and Portugal had gone to Italy, France, the Netherlands, and even as far as Denmark, traumatized by so much injustice.

About thirty years later, they were still living in make-shift camps outside cities. Their situation remained precarious and there seemed to be no obvious solutions to their problems.

Sometimes the difference between misery and great hope is quite small. Here in Italy, during the winter of 1523–1524, that is during the year 5284, after the creation of the world by the Eternal (blessed be His name!), the news had spread like wildfire. From the Marche to Puglia and from Venice to Rome, people spoke about nothing else as they left their synagogues, met in the town markets, and dreamed at night in their desolate camps around glowing fires.

A man was going to appear, a Messenger of hope.

Rumor had it that Israel was his inspiration.

People said that he would lead the children of Israel back home.

Everyone was whispering the name, David.

David was going to come.

One day, one day soon, he would appear. He would be coming by sea, and Venice would be his port.

In those days the City of the Doges was the center of the world. Their clothes decorated with pearls from the Orient, its noblemen boasted, not without reason, that they governed the most perfect of republics. Venice was a true maritime power, and its ships, strange vessels with raised prows, reigned over every sea, from the Adriatic to the Aegean, and the Mediterranean all the way to the coasts near Alexandria and Joppa.

Venice was also a city filled with intrigue and crime. There were plots against the local potentate, but also against Charles v, Francis i, the pope, and Henry viii. It was in Venice, on the Murano Islands or on San Michele and Torcello, where brigands, pirates, and other ruffians would come to find refuge before returning to their devious ways. And it was in Venice where disoriented adventurers, preachers, eloquent demagogues, and all sorts of false prophets would turn up. At the time, the City of the Doges was an immense gambling den. Casinos, attractive buildings offering rooms for lovers and for clandestine gambling, crowded up against the cathedral. And to the great displeasure of the rabbis, they even extended out into the Ghetto's tiny streets and squares.

In those days, a traveler arriving in Venice never failed to visit the Ghetto, attracted first of all by gaming tables, but also in hopes of making some rare acquisition or applauding the most famous actors. Sometimes ecclesiastical dignitaries or counselors of foreign princes would come to Venice hoping to learn how to solve the problems raised by their own Jewish populations, which though intelligent and inventive, were often recalcitrant and obstinately refused to follow Christ.

In the Calle del Forno, unleavened bread was being baked, and on the wide, brightly-lit Piazza del Ghetto Nuovo, there were groups of people, including rabbis, debating the news. Was the Messenger really going to come? Or was the rumor just another one of those baseless chimeras that stirred up people's imaginations from time to time? All around the square, multi-story buildings stood tall above the passageway leading from the Ghetto, their massive facades uniform but not completely identical. There were many different-shaped windows of various sizes, small terraces, gables, oriental-looking domes, and long rows of arcades that added interest to the facades. A few one or two story buildings, designed to complement each other, were leaning up against their more powerful neighbors for support. Who was the expected Envoy? Some people were doubtful, some were hopeful, but no one knew exactly what to think about that unknown person arriving with a plan who could be little more than a mirage, a dream, or just the centuries-old nostalgia of returning to Jerusalem.

So, during that winter of 1523–1524, inside the Ghetto as well as around flaming campfires in the miserable camps near the city, everyone was discussing the pending arrival of the stranger, David. It was said that he would liberate the Jews and lead them back to Israel.

All those Jews who were locked up each night behind the Ghetto walls, as well as the others, ignored and as much as locked away themselves, away from cities, work, and society, were talking about the man who might come, the man who was perhaps already on the way to lead them to salvation. Here, there was no thinking or doubting. People waited expectantly, dreaming and praying. Their psalms brightened the winter night, and their fires flickered through the fog.

In his large workshop at the entrance to the Ghetto Nuovo, near the bridge crossing over Rio San Girolamo, the artist Moses de Castellazzo was deep in conversation with his friend Titian. He was showing him the wood engravings he had just completed at the request of the Marquis of Mantua to illustrate the Pentateuch.

A massive man with thick red hair, Moses turned from discussing his own work to the current situation:

"Just try to understand this paradox and the iniquity of it all," he said to Titian. "It has been almost eight years since March of 1516, when, for the first time in history, the city set aside a neighborhood for Jews, this Ghetto Nuovo in which we find ourselves now, the old foundry quarter. To protect the Jews, it was said. What a false pretext and what a sad precedent!"

"We mustn't exaggerate," Titian interrupted him gently. "You know that in Venice it has always been customary to congregate in religious and cultural groups according to one's country of origin."

"That is true," Moses admitted. "But what is different about the Ghetto is that it has been imposed upon us. There are unprecedented legal constraints! And yet, there are educated people who learn Hebrew, and a Christian marquis comes to ask me, a Jewish artist, to illustrate the Bible."

"Moses, my good man, for us Christians your Torah, that we call the Old Testament, is considered to be the source of the Gospels! So it is not at all strange for the marquis to want to refer back to it."

"Fair enough," grumbled Moses de Castellazzo, "but at the same time those good people never lose any sleep over the misery of the Jews expelled from Spain and of those who continue to flee Portugal!"

"Don't give up all hope of charity," his friend chided affectionately. "How about a drink? We should be paying more attention to that nice little grey wine you have just poured!"

Moses shrugged his shoulders and raised his glass. They lifted to their lips a wine that only artists can enjoy without grimacing, drinking to the health of the stars. A fire was crackling in the huge fireplace, giving off sparks that disappeared up into the soot-darkened chimney.

"It seems that the Jewish Messiah is about to appear," Titian said, setting his glass down.

Moses didn't answer immediately. He carefully stepped across a canvas that had slipped off his easel and stood before his friend.

"Cursed be the bones of those who try to calculate the end times!" he shouted.

And, theatrically lifting his index finger toward the sky, he continued:

"For they will say: 'Since the predetermined time has come and He has not arrived, He will never arrive…'"

He brushed back the long strands of red hair hanging down over his forehead and sat back down on the bench beside Titian.

"Those are words from Samuel ben Nahman found in the wisest of Jewish books, the Talmud," he explained.

"It is wise indeed," said Titian. "But, men need to keep up hope. That is how we are made. So, in spite of the wisdom that comes from your books, I can understand those Jews who continue believing, who keep hoping, and who think that he is perhaps here among us already."

They stared at each other quietly for a while and then both broke into a smile. Moses stood up, cracked his gnarled fingers, and placed the painting back on his easel.

"Indeed, my dear Christian friend, it is true that in Jewish tradition every man carries within himself a portion of the Messiah. Just between you and me, if the Messiah should appear in Venice, I would say to him: '*Barukh haba*,' welcome."

Chapter two

The Man Who Resembled No Other

I t was February 7, 1524, a Sabbath eve, and the moon was full. In the middle of the night in Venice, waves were rocking the ships anchored at the juncture between the Grand Canal and the Canal de la Geudecca. And a large ship was just entering the port.

The *Alfama*, a galleon belonging to the rich Venetian Santo Contarini and sailing under the orders of Captain Campiello Pozzo, docked near customs, where the Dorsoduro began. The ship was arriving directly from Alexandria after a two-month trip, loaded with dyes, spices, and silk.

On board the ship, on the bridge near the mainmast, a man was standing. His white figure stood out in the shadows. He was watching alone, looking out over Venice as he waited for the dawn. As if, by staring out over the ducal palace and its ghostlike lacy stone-work, barely perceptible through the mist, his eyes were trying to penetrate the obscurity.

Little by little, as dawn broke and its vaporous light reflected over the water like numerous mirrors, Venice began to spring to life.

7

The man standing on the deck of the *Alfama* could not help but be fascinated by the power of the aquatic ballet spread before him, charmed by the grace of those palazzi inspired by Byzantium, and moved by the harmonious simplicity of the bourgeois dwellings lining the Grand Canal as well as the majesty of the Gothic palaces. The golden structures of stone on water shimmered in the early morning mists. Venice was beginning to wake up and conform to the legends surrounding it.

In turn, on the quays, life began to teem in the morning's coolness. Suddenly stands appeared, attracting more and more people, as if every house had emptied of its occupants. The whole lagoon was buzzing with sounds.

When the man, along with a companion, climbed into a skiff that the galleon's captain, Campiello Pozzo, had provided for him, it already held three other people. They were all wearing similar white woolen tunics. Each tunic bore a Star of David embroidered with gold thread, and the group's simple garments conferred on them an aura of ceremony and mystery.

The skiff began to move along the quays, and soon it attracted attention, drawing all eyes to it. Normally nothing could surprise Venetians, for they were used to seeing travelers from far-off lands dressed in the strangest attire. Were they not accustomed to seeing visitors from all over the world? From Cyprus, from Muré's three kingdoms, from Sidon, Acre, and Thessalonica, and even from the Ukraine and Ethiopia. But this tall forty-year-old with his tanned face and his short black beard was unlike anything they had seen before. Everything about him spoke of the unusual, including the way he held his head and his turban from which a few strands of his hair appeared, the color of petrified lava. Standing there on the platform in the little boat that flew a white silk flag with Hebrew symbols, he looked like no one else. Not like a French merchant dressed in his loveliest velvet, not like a Turk in his multicolored clothing, and surely not like any of those Jews living in the Ghetto, any German, or anyone from the Eastern or Western Mediterranean.

And yet the man was clearly Jewish. Rather than trying to hide his origins, he displayed them for all to see. The way he was dressed, his swarthy skin, his armed guard, and the flag waving its stars above his head all bore witness to his background.

The man surely came from some far-off land, from a place people could scarcely even imagine.

Even before the skiff drew up along the steps of Captain Pozzo's residence, a simple palace located near the San Marcello di Canareggio church, away from the Ghetto, the news of his arrival had spread throughout the city. People already knew that he would be staying with the captain. Scores of people wearing yellow berets, identifying them as Jews, were gathering around the captain's residence.

"Master," one old man shouted, "welcome to Venice!"

The stranger wearing the white turban didn't even glance at the old man who greeted him with such fervor. His sharp features did not invite familiarities, and his thoughts seemed to be turned inward. Captain Pozzo, embarrassed at how the old Jew was being treated, whispered to the stranger:

"The man is a bookseller, a respected scholar. His name is Elhanan, Elhanan Obadiah Saragossi."

The stranger did not reply to his host's comments. Without a word, he entered the captain's house. They walked through the patio, a garden filled with plants and exotic flowers, and then through a round room to one of about twenty meters long with a high ceiling. There, the guest indicated that he wanted to be alone.

He thanked the captain for his hospitality and then sent away the four men accompanying him, once they had set down the ivory-inlaid ebony chest that never left his side.

Chapter three

Memories of Makhpela

Once home from a sea voyage, Captain Pozzo liked to stay a long time. His "sea room," as he called it, was spacious. It had high windows and all sorts of woodwork, almost as much as one would find on board a ship. On the walls hung paintings and drawings that indicated his fixation with life at sea. Forests of oars and masts danced over the waves, along with sails, shrouds, breaking waves, and flashing lightning. Diffused light reflected from a few places onto two well-preserved but rusty anchors hanging on the far wall. There were ropes and ship's equipment everywhere. On a heavy long table in the center of the room lay a copper pulley, a spyglass, and a compass, and all the colors of the rainbow that were reflected off the compass rose near the candlesticks.

At the captain's request, one of his servants began to explain the objects in the room to his mysterious guest, when another servant entered to announce a visitor.

Soon thereafter a tall, thin man with thick blond hair, about fifty years old, was introduced into the sea room. He was a member of the Counsel of Ten that helped the Doge govern the Venetian

Republic, and was none other than the owner and outfitter of the *Alfama*.

"Welcome to my home, Magnifico Santo Contarini!" the captain exclaimed. "Our guest and his followers are here as you requested. He has withdrawn to meditate, and I'm afraid you won't be able to see him until this evening. But here is our friend Joseph Halevy, his right-hand man."

A man in a white tunic stepped forward. He was also about fifty years old, heavy-set and of medium height. His square face was framed by a thick, salt-and-pepper beard. Count Contarini greeted him effusively, disregarding their different ranks in society.

"Ah, Joseph!" he said. "How happy I am to see you again!"

"Likewise, Count, likewise!" Joseph answered.

Clearly pleased for them to have met, Captain Pozzo announced that he wanted to celebrate the occasion with a bottle of that famous grey Venetian wine that he loved to open whenever he returned home.

Campiello Pozzo was a tall man, weathered by the wind and the sea. Although younger than his guests, he seemed older. He was only forty-two years old, but the wrinkles on his face betrayed long night watches, storms, and adventures. He served his two companions unhurriedly with a half-smile on his face. Then he raised his glass:

"To David's success!" he proclaimed.

"To his mission!" Joseph added.

"To his success!" the count repeated.

The captain took a swallow and clicked his tongue. Count Contarini's smile broadened.

"I will be pleased to see the prince again," he said to Joseph. "Since that day in Hebron, I have often thought about him."

"David, my master, is indeed an unusual man," answered Joseph laconically.

All three were clearly thinking about the same man. Indeed, they could not help but reminisce about their first meeting. The count pulled himself up out of the armchair he was sitting in and allowed his thoughts to revert back in time as he walked back and forth with his wine glass in his hand.

"Do you remember the Cave of Makhpela, Joseph?" he asked.

"Do I remember!" the man replied. "As if it were yesterday! However, sometimes it seems that it was years, or even centuries, ago!"

"It was only four months ago. I've only known David and you for four months, my dear Joseph. I had gone on a pilgrimage to the Holy Land, following the path of our Lord and Savior Jesus Christ. After visiting Jerusalem and walking along the Via Dolorosa, I left for Hebron. I had been told that there I could find the Cave of Makhpela, the cave of the Patriarchs. It was guarded by Turkish janissaries who kept everyone away. However, someone else wanted to visit the caves that day. Thanks to the authority of the Prince of Chabor, whom I was meeting for the first time, I was able to follow him into the sacred site. Do you remember how he confronted the guard who tried to block his path? But how about you, Joseph? As his confidant, how did you meet him?"

"It was near Israel, at Jeddah," Joseph murmured.

"Tell the count how you ended up in that Red Sea port running away from a woman," the captain chuckled.

"Quite so, Captain. Quite so. You haven't forgotten any of my secrets, have you? You see, my dear Count, I was born in Naples, in Italy. My parents were Jews who had been exiled from Egypt. In late adolescence I became a cook on a merchant ship. Several years ago, in Istanbul, I got married, thinking I was done with sailing, with the rolling sea, with pirates. Fatal mistake! Worse than a failure, our marriage was a disaster. It was as if I was in prison, being ordered around my 'home sweet home' by a shrew. Soon I was missing the rolling sea and the waves. Rough seas would suit me better than marriage! I had to get back to sea, I finally admitted. I signed up on a ship and sailed all over the Red Sea. That's how I met the prince in Arabia, in Jeddah. He was in difficult straits. Galla pirates had robbed him of everything he possessed, and his group of followers had almost been wiped out. Yet in spite of his misfortunes, he insisted on completing his mission. I was impressed by his fervor, his stubbornness, and the nobility of his soul. So I immediately joined his service, and we began to travel together. Soon he began to trust me with his thoughts, hopes, and concerns. And he plied me with questions about the different political powers in Italy, about influential people at the Vatican and in the Jewish communities in Venice, Pisa, and Rome. Of course, I was able to answer. But really, it was more as if he had the power to draw information out of me. Truly, I quickly began to admire my master's intellectual qualities. Though he had never set foot on European soil, he could already analyze Venetian society brilliantly, and he could already imagine all the intrigues and rivalries."

In turn, Captain Pozzo began to reflect on his own first moments with this David, who seemed to hold such fascination for them all.

"Two weeks after our meeting in Hebron he used his sword to save me from a perilous ambush in Jericho. Count Contarini and I have talked again and again about the mysterious Jewish prince whom we both had reason to esteem so highly. He gave the count access to the Patriarchs' Tomb, and he saved my life! Then the count left for Venice. Six weeks ago, in Alexandria, David and I met again."

"But this time, you offered him help," said Contarini the Magnificent. "You offered to bring him to Venice, as I had suggested."

As he listened to the two men, Joseph was filled with nostalgia. Time can be both a nurturing mother and an evil stepmother. Only six months before (or six years, or six centuries), he and his master had left Jeddah. The time since then seemed more fleeting than a dream.

"The Jewish prince," added Count Contarini, "confided in me the nature of his mission after we visited the Cave of Makhpela in Hebron."

His mission! David's mission! They had drunk to its success just a moment before. Joseph, made thoughtful by the grey Venetian wine, didn't say a word. He was lost in thought regarding the most recent travels in his master's company.

It had taken them three days and three nights sailing on the Red Sea before reaching Suakim in Ethiopia. Then, joining a caravan, they had reached King Amrah's palace in Lamuel Province. But fate follows its own laws. The king was charmed by David, and he offered him four handsome male slaves and four female slaves of great beauty. The king had grown angry when David refused his dubious gift, and they had been forced to flee to Egypt with the queen's help. There, they had joined up with a caravan carrying precious cloth to the Holy Land. Ten days later they were in Gaza. Then, they traveled to Hebron by donkey. That's where they met Santo Contarini the Magnificent, and that's where David had intimidated the janissaries and visited the Cave of Makhpela, containing the remains of the patriarch Abraham, his son Isaac, his grandson Jacob, and their wives Sarah, Rebecca, and Leah. In Hebron, it was said that nobody had entered the cave since the time of Caliph Omar. Once, four old Arabs had ventured in. Three of them had died on the spot, and the fourth had lost the ability to speak.

In the Galilean town of Safed, the kabbalist Salomon Halevy Alkabetz had told Joseph about a strange event that had taken place ten months earlier. As the Jewish prince was leaving the synagogue after evening prayers, three old men sitting on the ground with their legs crossed had spoken the following words to him:

"Go tell the Ishmaelites to leave this country so that our children can come home."

"And what if they don't obey?" David had asked.

"Tell them that Abraham, Moses, and Elijah the prophet have so ordered!"

When Joseph had asked his master about those words, about the mission he was supposed to accomplish, all David had done was quote Ecclesiastes:

"Trying to cling to dreams is like grasping at shadows or binding up the wind."

From that moment on, however, he had devoted himself to his mission.

As he evoked those memories, Joseph gave a sigh. David's mission was like the perfume of some tale or the wings of hope. And yet, it was above all a political question, and it needed to be undertaken logically and with intellectual rigor.

"You are dreaming, my friend. You are dreaming," the captain grumbled. "You've forgotten we are here."

Joseph looked up. Count Contarini was smiling. The captain was serving another round of the Venetian wine. Within the past few months a true friendship had begun to develop between Joseph Halevy and Campiello Pozzo.

"And then," the captain continued, speaking to the count, "David is indeed a prince, the brother of the Jewish king of Chabor, but he is a master strategist as well, and an excellent military man. I have discussed the art of war with him, and I admit that his knowledge far surpasses my own. Furthermore, I don't know any other generals who are as pious as he, nor any who would always try diplomacy before declaring war!"

"That's right," Joseph said.

"There is something I don't quite understand," said the captain. "You, Joseph, as his counselor as well as his confidant, how do you interpret the rumor that is making the rounds all over Italy and that I heard again today? That he is a savior, a prophet? I have even heard people call him the *Messiah*."

Joseph made a gesture of exasperation.

"You know me, Campiello. You surely are aware that I have little respect for such madness. David's mission is political above all else. His action must take place on the solid ground of reason, not on hysteria's quicksand or on sentimental fabrication."

"After all," the count added, "giving the Jewish people back their rightful land has been one of religion's ambitions throughout the centuries. So what is so astonishing about these poor folks referring to him as the *Messiah*?"

"Re-establishing the Kingdom of Israel is a matter of justice and strategy," replied Joseph. "Mystical exaltation in such business could be dangerous and even harmful! In any case, I keep telling my master to remain a general, to act like a politician and not a magus. He must not let himself be tempted by the crowd's acclamation. Besides, there are only false messiahs. And that, basically, is what I allow myself to point out to him. But I know that he sees things in much the same way. '*Israel*,' he said to me, '*will be created not by divine decree but thanks to human will. More than a promised land, Israel will be a return, a return to dignity.*' Did you not notice how irritated he was this morning? He, too, heard the word 'messiah' spoken as he passed. And don't think that he finds the word flattering. I was walking right beside him, and I heard him mutter under his breath: '*They are blaspheming.*'"

"And what if he were truly the Messiah? Without him or anyone else realizing it!" the count retorted.

Joseph made a grimace, and then, with a forced smile on his face, he said:

"Well, if that were the case, it is better that nobody knows! Let us understand each other, Count, and you too, Campiello. The hope of the masses is touching, but it is often hope without foundation. David cannot be hampered by foolish expressions of feeling."

He said no more. Thoughtfully, the three men clinked their glasses together before drinking one last round.

Chapter four

A Judeo-Christian Pact

In the room in which the Jewish prince had taken up residence, he opened up his ebony chest by the light of a candle and took out a thick manuscript. As he looked over the first page filled with a tight, angular, uneven Hebrew script, his eyes took in the first sentence, and he repeated it aloud as if to be sure that it sounded right:

"I am David, son of King Solomon, blessed be the memory of his Justness. My elder brother, King Joseph, reigns over the Chabor desert and governs the three hundred thousand souls of the tribes of Gad, Reuben, and a part of the tribe of Manassas."

With a brusque gesture—brusqueness was part of his nature—he grabbed a bottle of ink and a goose quill. He sharpened the point, and sitting down at the massive table in the middle of the room, scratched out the word *desert* and corrected the sentence so it read: *King Joseph reigns over the Kingdom of Chabor.* As he waited for the ink to dry, he studied with great interest the tapestry covering one of the walls. It illustrated a Biblical scene, the sacrifice of Isaac. The anonymous artist had carefully portrayed in great detail the instant that the angel held back Abraham's knife. He remained lost in his dreams for a moment, and then, picking up a blank sheet, began to write.

"When I reached Venice, I moved into Captain Campiello Pozzo's house. I am preparing to spend six days and six nights fasting, in order to pray and meditate without interruption, and also to note in this journal matters related to my mission."

He lifted his hand from the page. From beyond the walls, though he could not make out their words, he could hear Count Contarini, Joseph, and his host conversing. His face broke into a smile. He had become quite attached to Captain Campiello Pozzo. The captain had guaranteed the authenticity of his credential letters and had even made an effort to arrange additional such letters for him. David would have liked to accept his gracious dinner invitation, but he didn't have the right to do so. During the years of wandering in the Arabian wilderness, his fatiguing marches along African rivers, and his retreats in the Judean hills, he had forged his plan, constructed his character, and decided on a plan of action. Yes, he wanted to succeed. He had to overcome his human weaknesses, just as his ancestors had done in the Sinai desert. He had to become strong, master his desires, and dominate his servile habits. He needed to learn how to live like a free man if he expected to be able to liberate others. It was hard for him to be seen as insensitive when he failed to respond, for example, to a feverish greeting by an old bookseller. But the world was a difficult place. And a slave could never expect to experience luxury. Charity, according to the Holy Book, has the power to redeem all of our mistakes. Does it also have the power of preventing humans from making mistakes in the first place?

Unwinding his turban, he ran his fingers through his lava-colored hair and began to chant:

Rise up, Lord. May Your enemies be scattered before You, and may Your adversaries flee before Your face.

He looked down again at the first pages of his journal. Mechanically, he reread the passage written a year and a half earlier relating to his stay in Safed. His time there had been instrumental.

"After hearing the mysterious injunction of the three old men, I went back to Chabor to join my brother, King Joseph. I told him about the words spoken by those ghost-like men sitting in the dust outside the Safed synagogue. We talked for a long time.

"It seemed to us that a challenge had been forged for us as forgotten Jews, distant descendants of the tribe of Reuben, who in the old days had accompanied Moses on the road to Sinai before choosing a different path. Then Moses had given to the children of Israel the land promised by the Eternal, blessed be His name! But that land had since been lost, contaminated, delivered over to iniquity, and Israel, scattered to the four corners of the earth, had no fatherland and knew only His Book, the Holy Torah. And now, today, the charge was being given to us, the descendants of Reuben, to return that land to its people, to our scattered family, to a people from which we have been separated for so many centuries, a land that had been ours, just as the Holy Torah is ours!

"I had to accept the challenge. More than a duty, it was truly a mission. To be carried out successfully, we needed a three-fold mission: political, diplomatic, and military. We decided on a strategy, and I would be the messenger to the Jews regarding their return to Israel.

"The strategy for our mission can be summed up in few words, but putting it into practice will be a delicate operation. It will be a *Judeo-Christian pact*, and it is something I must propose to Pope Clement VII."

He paused and looked around for a moment at the large room in which he was seated. A fire crackled, glowing red in the semi-circular fireplace. Engravings and paintings lined the wall opposite the tapestry. On the table before him lay not only his writing material, but also a candlestick and a large copper tray on which were piled maps, multicolored beads, and odds and ends from various places. In the middle of the pile David noticed a tiny silver crucifix. He picked it up, looked at it for a moment, and then laid it back down. A little smile came to his face, and he continued reading:

"With this pact, Joseph, the Jewish King of Chabor, is proposing an alliance with the pope and the different kings of Christendom. According to the pact, Jews and Christians will unite to face Soleiman the Magnificent and put an end to Islam's expansion on both shores of the Mediterranean. The King of Chabor asks the pope to help me, his brother and messenger, arm European Jews and create a Jewish navy. That navy, with the help of the army of Chabor from the south, must liberate the land of Israel from Ottoman control in order to establish a Jewish kingdom with Jerusalem as its capital. In exchange, the king will cede control of the holy places to the Vatican."

He stopped reading and picked up the page on which he had written his first sentences that evening. He dipped his quill in the inkwell and continued his story, summarizing the current situation.

"After various incidents that were as trying as they were inevitable," he wrote, "I now find myself in the famous City of the Doges, a few days from Rome by horseback and therefore within hailing distance of the leader of the Christian world. It is on him, on Clement vii, that the destiny and future of Israel depend. I must convince him without offending him. I have carefully prepared the speech I plan to make. I am sure about every word, about every gesture.

"But here now in Venice, so near my goal, I am filled with doubt. What is happening to me? Is it the strong moldy stench coming from the canal? Why am I weakening? And at the same time, why do I suddenly also feel so calm and relieved? The devil take my doubt!

"I owe it to myself to give some thought to the Jewish community here in Venice. I will need its help, and especially the support of the *Va'ad Hakatan*, the little assembly that represents the community. To go meet the pope in Rome, I will have to cross an Italy wracked with armed conflict between Charles v's troops and those of Frances i. I will need funds, and a powerful armed escort as well. As they consider my plans, what will be the attitude of those worthy men who make up the *Va'ad*?"

David lay down his quill and rose to his feet.

"Let us now glorify the Lord with our songs," he murmured under his breath.

He thought of Salomon Halevi Alkabetz, the master kabbalist he had met on that far-off day in Safed, in that fateful city of Galilee, and the lovely hymn he had written:

Come, dearly beloved, to meet your fiancée,
Sabbath is coming, let us welcome it!

The Sabbath was indeed coming, and he, David, like all Jews, would know how to welcome it properly.

All the noises in the house had died away. Hearing some fleeting laughter in the night, he went to the window. The moon added a bluish tint to the lines of rooftops, pillars, facades, angles, and arcades. A few boats lit up with dim lanterns slid by noiselessly on the almost black waters of the canal.

He slept no more that night than on the preceding nights at sea onboard the *Alfama*. The next day, he would once again refuse all food and drink. He said his Sabbath prayers, repeating one verse several times:

When the Ark of the Covenant was under way, Moses said: "Rise up, Lord. May Your enemies be scattered before You, and may Your adversaries flee before Your face."

Chapter five

Turmoil among the Worthies

From high in Saint Mark's Basilica, the Marangona bell greeted the dawn, and the guards removed the heavy padlocks that locked the wooden panels every night on the two gates that closed off the Ghetto. And then the Venetian crowds from every religion and every origin poured, pushing and shoving, into Piazza del Ghetto Nuovo. They had been waiting for more than an hour in the nearby streets, from Rio Terra all the way to the bridge lining San Marcuola Parish to the Jewish enclave. For it was market day, and as usual, all of Venice was coming to the Ghetto to buy the best spices and the finest silks, to borrow money at the most favorable rates, to pawn a family jewel, purchase some used clothing, consult a famous doctor, discover a rare book, or ask about the latest news.

It was a cool morning, and the light fog that was beginning to lift still hung near the tops of the five-story ocher houses that surrounded the Campo. They were the tallest buildings in the city. Their owners kept building them higher in order to house the Jews who continued to arrive after being expelled from France or from

Northern Europe, who came from Italian cities from which they had been sent away, or from Spain and Portugal where people were trying to convert them by force.

All dressed in various ways, each according to his native country, the Ghetto crowds, ordinarily so noisy and boisterous, today seemed unusually calm. Even serious. David's arrival was on everyone's mind. Who was the man? Where did he come from? From the Kingdom of Chabor, it was said. But was it a kingdom with any territory? In those days of exploring America, of opening new routes to the Indies, of discovering new countries in Africa, was it thinkable that the Kingdom of Chabor really existed when no known traveler had ever been there? People were whispering, however, that the unknown kingdom could be from the tribe of Reuben, one of the ten original Jewish tribes whose traces had been lost over the years. That is how the rumor began to spread that David's name was *Reubeni*.

Even the women washing and mending laundry near the fountain were worried. What mission had the Envoy been charged with? Who had given it to him? What was the message he was to deliver to the pope? Might not all the uproar be detrimental to the interests of the community?

This David, to whom they gave the surname Reubeni, managed to stay holed up by himself inside Captain Campiello Pozzo's house, and except for the old bookseller, virtually no Jew had seen his face up close. But fortunately, his servants came daily to the Ghetto to purchase kosher food, and they were always ready to answer the questions asked by the curious people. But what did they really know about their master? Was he not too secretive to confide in his servants? However, since they had accompanied him across Arabia, Africa, and the Holy Land, and since they had sailed with him from Alexandria, the tales of their travels were fruit for conversation. But they did little to calm peoples' minds or dispel their doubts.

On the far side of the Campo, at the base of an ocher building whose fourth floor held the Scuola Tedesca, the synagogue of the Ashkenazi Jews, an especially dense crowd of onlookers had gathered to greet the members of the *Va'ad Hakatan* as they passed. Today, the little assembly responsible for the Ghetto was meeting expressly to discuss the *matter*. David Reubeni's appearance had come to the attention of the Venetian authorities, and the Doge, through his chief of police, had asked the *Va'ad* what position the wise men of Israel were taking concerning the Envoy from the Jewish Kingdom of Chabor. News of his arrival here in Venice had set in motion an unheard-of messianic movement in the Marche region, where many Jews expelled from Spain and Portugal had gathered to await their Deliverance.

On that particular day, a study commission was supposed to present its findings. The members of the *Va'ad* eagerly arrived, more promptly than usual and almost all of them at the same time. The crowd was even more curious, commenting on every gesture and every word. The first to appear was the banker Shimon ben Asher Mechulam del Banco. Wrapped in a large wine-colored cloak, he was well-known among Ghetto Jews. "The richest and most charitable man," people said of him. And some added: "Wealth has wings, and like the eagle, it flies to the heavens." But the banker was not flying. He could scarcely walk, leaning on a dark wooden cane. He was closer to the ground than to the heavens.

Then came representatives from the different corporations and Jewish associations in Venice, grouped according to their country of origin.

The attentive onlookers recognized all the dignitaries of the *Va'ad*. Sometimes they would call out greetings, and sometimes they would even applaud, as they did for Moses de Castellazzo the artist, a huge man with long red hair and a grey beard, renowned for his frescoes on the Fondaco dei Tedeschi on the Grand Canal. Commissioned by Giorgione, he had created the frescoes with his friend Titian. The last to arrive, as usual, was Rabbi Giacobo Mantino, a famous doctor and president of the *Va'ad*. He was a stocky man without a beard, and he wore a black beret like all Venetians. He was very proud of that unusual privilege, for in those days Jews were required to wear yellow berets.

He was the one who opened the discussion.

"Rabotaï, my masters, we are responsible for the community. Not only for its well-being, but also for its very existence. So it is our duty to remove any danger without delay. And this man David Reubeni presents a mortal danger for the people of Israel!"

The members of the *Va'ad*, seated around dark wooden tables forming a square that took up almost the entire space in the back room of the synagogue, looked up. A ray of light poured in through one of the four windows looking out over the canal. It furtively crossed the room, lingering over the marble columns and caressing the golden woodwork, before it reached the veiled blue eyes of the banker Shimon ben Asher Mechulam del Banco.

The banker shaded his eyes with his gnarled fingers and grumbled:

"First let us listen to the study commission's report."

He was not fond of Giacobo Mantino. He mistrusted his intelligence and envied his privileges.

Every head turned toward the three individuals seated facing the windows. The eldest among them, a slightly stooped fifty-year-old with thick eyebrows, rose to his feet. Joseph Pugliese was a doctor like Giacobo Mantino, and in some ways his competitor. But although he had many clients, even more than the president of the *Va'ad*, he was not nearly as famous. Joseph Pugliese's voice was calm and collected, and his report was precise, embellished with Hebrew sayings.

According to the commission's detailed report, there was no proof that the Kingdom of Chabor and its king Joseph even existed. On the other hand, David Reubeni's travels across Africa and Asia were real, and so were his meetings with the princes and kings of those regions. His letters of credentials had been verified and they were authentic.

The commission had been unable to determine David Reubeni's native country. Was it Yemen? Or Ethiopia? In any case, the investigators were convinced that in one or the other of those two countries the man had served in the army as a commanding officer, perhaps even as general. David Reubeni's knowledge of military matters was indeed considerable. As for his objectives, the commission had been unable to decide, because it had been unable to question him directly.

When he reached that point of his presentation, Joseph Pugliese paused. Staring out at the crowd from beneath his huge eyebrows, he said:

"People claim…people claim that David Reubeni…"

He paused once more.

"I don't know if I should go on. These are not solid conclusions from our investigation, but rather reports, rumors, and gossip…"

"Come now!" Giacobo Mantino cried out impatiently. "May my honorable colleague not keep us waiting!"

Joseph Pugliese smiled in satisfaction. For once he was the center of attention of the whole *Va'ad*, and he was not at all displeased.

"People are whispering…People are saying that David Reubeni is carrying a credential letter from his brother Joseph, King of Chabor, to His Holiness Pope Clement VII. In that letter the king is proposing to the supreme pontiff an alliance of Jews and Christians to take back Judea from the Ishmaelites. So that a Jewish kingdom can be established…"

Giacobo Mantino leaped to his feet.

"That is sheer folly! It's madness!"

And the president of the *Va'ad* pounded the table with his fist to stress his point.

"Why do you say that?" Asher Mechulam del Banco, the banker, asked quietly. He remained seated and went on:

"The news should at least be checked out. And if it were true, it does not seem to me to be inconceivable…

He coughed and continued:

"The situation lends itself to such a measure. Islam, carried along by the armies of the Sublime Porte, has already reached Rhodes, Bulgaria, Naples, and is moving toward Vienna. It is in the best interest of the pope and Catholic kings…"

Giacobo Mantino couldn't hide his impatience with the banker's words and interrupted him, shouting out once more:

"Folly, sheer folly! That's crazy!"

The banker was unimpressed. He smiled and calmly went on:

"Is it madness to re-establish a Jewish kingdom in Judea? Sheer folly? When Moses had the idea, was he crazy?"

It was the old banker's attitude more than his words that seemed to irritate Giacobo Mantino. He tugged on his doublet and shouted:

"If we let this stranger carry on, the Sublime Gate will learn sooner or later that Jews are preparing for war, and hundreds of thousands of our brothers who now live happily and safely in Istanbul, in Salonika, and all over the vast Turkish Empire, including those living in Judea, will be in mortal danger. Our duty is to think of them as well!"

He placed both hands on the table and leaned forward.

"As for our Christian princes, I admit that some might be attracted by David Reubeni's plans, but for most of them—and they are not my friends—his actions are one more proof, perhaps the deciding one, that Jews are different from their other subjects. At the first opportunity, Jews are quick to leave, people will say. And why not betrayal?"

Giacobo Mantino paused for a moment. Taking the silence that greeted his comments as support, he continued, his voice calmer:

"And finally, my friends. Do you really think, my friends, my masters, that a navy made up of Jewish sailors and outfitted by Christian kings would have the slightest chance of victory in a battle against the world's greatest military power? Even Venice itself has lost several battles and has had to come to terms with the enemy. Unless…unless…"

Giacobo Mantino paused once more and looked insistently at each member of the *Va'ad* as if he were putting them to the test.

"Unless you think, rabotaï, that this man is a very special envoy. As our brothers in the Marche province believe."

No one dared take a breath. It was time for prudence.

"And if such were the case," Giacobo Mantino went on, "then remember that man Asher Lai'mlein, may his name be cursed! Twenty-four years ago, right here in the Venetian province of Istria, he claimed to be the One we have been expecting since the first destruction of the Temple. Remember, rabotaï, the misfortune this man caused for our community. Also keep in mind our holy Talmud. Remember that it warns energetically against those who dare to announce the arrival of the Messiah, because…because if He did not appear, or if it were not Him, despair would not fail to swoop down on all of mankind…"

Giacobo Mantino raised his fist as if he were going to pound the table once more, but this time stopped before his fist struck the table. To relieve the tension, he moved over to the window and pretended to watch the boats and gondolas gliding over the slate-colored waters of the Grand Canal.

The members of the *Va'ad* sat motionless, as if they feared that one word, one gesture—may God protect us!—might be the origin of humanity's despair. Asher Mechulam del Banco coughed. Once. Twice. He kept coughing, and everyone waited until he finished.

"Well said," he remarked, without looking at Giacobo Mantino who turned toward him. "Our honorable president has been persuasive as usual. He has given solid, intelligent arguments, except that…"

The old banker coughed once more.

"Contrary to what we believe, my friends, the subject we really need to be discussing is we ourselves, and not this David Reubeni, some petty king of an unknown country called Chabor."

With great effort, the banker raised his hand with its two jade rings and looked around the room as he spoke.

"Have we forever abandoned all hope of returning to the land of our ancestors? Are we content forever to remain subjects who are persecuted, or at best, tolerated?"

Under the weight of the old banker's gaze, Giacobo Mantino was about to reply when Rabbi Shlomo da Costa shook his turbaned head several times and quickly spoke, as if he was afraid of being interrupted.

"The people of Israel will go back to the land of Israel when the Eternal—blessed be His name!—so decides."

His words were like a signal of alarm. Everyone began to speak at the same time. Moses Zacuto, the young secondhand clothing dealer, ignored the rabbi and leaned forward toward the banker. Pointing his index finger accusingly, he said:

"It is easy for you to talk! You are rich—rich even among the rich. You still have your palace Ca'Bernardo in San Paolo. When we are persecuted because of this David Reubeni, thanks to your money, you'll get off easy. As usual. As for us…"

Asher Mechulam del Banco sadly shook his head.

"No, no, young man. Not at all. Wealth generally protects everyone, but not Jews. No more than charity protects Christians. Among Gentiles, sometimes people kill rich people because they are rich. As for rich Jews, Gentiles kill them because they are Jews."

The banker again raised his trembling hand.

"Perhaps you have no love for me, and that is your right. But you must realize that—like it or not—we must all share the same fate. In Spain, the Inquisition affected poor and rich alike."

His voice grew fainter.

"All of us belong to a people who are simply tolerated. On the other hand, in the land of Israel, when we are finally a people like others, the difference of wealth that you are indicating will perhaps mean something."

"Words, just words," the clothing seller replied irritably.

Theatrically, Giacobo Mantino spread his arms as if to announce that he wanted to speak again, but he was interrupted by Moses de Castellazzo the artist. Moses stood up quickly, knocking over his chair as he did so.

"Enough!" he shouted. "Enough! We are not here today to settle differences among us, but rather to talk about David Reubeni."

He ripped off his yellow beret and threw it down on the table.

"Look at my beret! Do you see what color it is? The question Asher Mechulam del Banco asked sums up all our questions. Are we going to accept for all eternity our situation as persecuted foreigners who are barely tolerated? Do we not have the same rights as the Venetians and the French who are now camping at the gates of Cremona and Como? Or even the Turks? Rights to our own country?"

The painter ran his fingers through his mass of red hair, and then, dropping his voice as if he were about to share a secret with the members of the *Va'ad*, he said:

"And what if the vow that we pronounce every year at Passover, '*next year in Jerusalem*,' were indeed within our grasp? Just think about it! At this very moment Christian kings are organizing expeditions to discover and conquer new continents. The old world is opening up. A request by Jews might find support and sympathy."

He paused, and then stated as if he were repeating a universal truth:

"David Reubeni is right."

Then, pushing back the hair hanging over his forehead, he waited until Giacobo had gone back to his place at the table before he continued.

"Here, in Venice, we are thought of as competitors. In the land of Israel we will be considered allies."

Rabbi da Costa had barely been able to restrain himself while the artist was speaking, and finally he exploded:

"But who in heavens are you talking about? Your David Reubeni is nothing but an imposter! A liar!"

Moses de Castellazzo burst out laughing.

"Since when are political leaders expected to tell the truth? Just read *The Prince*."

"It so happens that the author is not Jewish," Giacobo Mantino remarked.

"Unfortunately for the Jews," replied Moses de Castellazzo. "David Reubeni realizes that to attain his goal he needs a strategy. And his strategy seems sound to me. For you have to admit, without his story about the Jewish Kingdom of Chabor, would we have ever spent this much time talking about *Israel*?"

Giacobo Mantino placed his large hands on the table one last time.

"Rabotaï, it is getting late. We were not chosen to liberate the Jewish people, but rather to organize our daily life here in the Ghetto. To protect it. This David Reubeni represents a danger to the fragile equilibrium we have fought so hard to achieve. That is clear. Therefore, I propose that we denounce him to the Doge's Council as an imposter."

Moses de Castellazzo leaped to his feet.

"Is that how we should expect a translator of Averroes and Avicenna to be speaking?"

His voice became ironic.

"I thought we were dealing with a scholar, and what do I discover but a *profiteer*!"

Giacobo Mantino turned pale, and with surprising agility for a man of his corpulence, he leaped on the artist.

"You bastard, you son of a bastard!" he shouted. His voice was harsh, and with his left hand he grabbed Moses de Castellazzo's emerald-colored cloak. With his right hand, he tried in vain to strike the painter's face. Moses de Castellazzo, taller and stronger than the doctor, was able to hold him off with one arm. There was a sound of tearing cloth. The members of the *Va'ad* got to their feet and tried to intervene. A scuffle followed. People began throwing chairs, and one of them crashed through a window.

Asher Mechulam del Banco stood up.

"Rabotaï, please! You are the Ghetto's chosen ones. Rabotaï!"

Giacobo Mantino was the first to back off. He turned his chair back upright and sat down. His cheeks were red, and he was breathing heavily. When finally everyone was seated, he simply said:

"Let us vote."

The *Va'ad* voted three times, by secret ballot, as usual. Each time the result was the same: eight votes in favor of David Reubeni, and eight votes in favor of disavowing him. Asher Mechulam del Banco finally came up with a compromise formula that everyone accepted. The *Va'ad* would invite David Reubeni to come in person and explain himself. Moses de Castellazzo offered his services to transmit the message.

"If you insist," grumbled Giacobo Mantino.

Chapter six

The Veiled Portrait

I n spite of the rain that had resumed, the artist set off on foot. He loved Venice, and he loved to stroll along the narrow *calle* that inevitably opened up onto a *campo*, the true centers of collective life in the city. He loved the walkways bordering the sinuous canals and the tiny paved streets that linked them. As he walked through the city, he would happen across strange scenes and unexpected gatherings of people that would later burst onto his paintings, drawings, or engravings. Moses de Castellazzo never left his studio in the Ghetto without charcoal and paper in his portfolio. "Like a doctor's instrument case," he would say.

So, when he arrived at Captain Campiello Pozzo's palazzo, he had his portfolio under his arm, protected from the rain by a large green cape. In spite of the horrible weather, many people had gathered. Moses de Castellazzo pushed his way through to the door, but there, to his great displeasure, he was blocked by the Doge's guards. The Doge's personal secretary had come to speak with the Messenger. Moses explained who he was and that he had been sent by the *Va'ad Hakatan* to meet the Prince of Chabor as soon as possible. Finally, the guards and the secretary left, and the artist was led in to meet David Reubeni.

David was standing motionless near one of the French doors. A lantern was hanging outside, and on his dark skin it cast the reflection of the raindrops coursing down the windowpanes. When he learned that Moses de Castellazzo could speak Hebrew, the man from the desert dismissed the servant who was to serve as their interpreter.

There was an awkward silence. How should they begin their conversation? Not without a little malice, David Reubeni suddenly asked:

"Are you shocked by the way I look?"

"No, not at all," replied the large red-headed man. "I knew that you were dark-skinned. It's not that at all. But I am a painter, you see, and I am fascinated by your features and by the intense look in your eyes."

And, after a brief hesitation, he added:

"I would like to sketch your portrait."

The Jewish prince smiled.

"Indeed. Well, what are you waiting for?"

Moses de Castellazzo was already opening his portfolio.

"With pleasure," he said as he pulled out a large white sheet. "However, we must not forget that I have an invitation for you."

"I know," said the man from Chabor. "But can the invitation not wait?"

Caught up in anticipation of the sketch he was about to undertake, the artist, charcoal in hand, replied:

"Of course."

"Well then, go ahead."

Moses de Castellazzo was a quick worker. Sketches with various degrees of detail began to accumulate. He would always start with the nose. And then, he would drag his thumb over the charcoal lines and transform them into thin wrinkles that extended down to join the beginnings of a beard. Then he would draw the lips and move up to the forehead. He always left the eyes for last, waiting until they began to show impatience, or vexation, or even submission. *The artist always ends up dominating his model,* he was fond of saying. *Except,* he would add, *when it's a bad portrait.* And that is precisely the feeling he had when suddenly David asked:

"Do you like Venice?"

The big red-headed man nodded and added:

"It's really the only city that's truly livable. Perhaps because it is cut off from land…"

David laughed.

"Then why have you stated that you would like to go to Jerusalem?"

In astonishment, the artist lifted his pencil from the paper and glanced questioningly at him.

"How do you know that?"

"I know a great deal about my brothers in Venice."

And after a short pause, he added:

"You haven't answered my question."

"I don't see any contradiction."

"There will be a contradiction when I ask you to help me rebuild a Jewish kingdom in the land of Israel, won't there?"

The artist abruptly closed his portfolio and pulled off his beret, leaving his hair rumpled. He was able to regain his aplomb.

"Even during the time of the kings," he said, "most Jews did not live in Judea. Just as many of today's Venetians don't live in Venice."

He got to his feet and began to pace back and forth:

"And yet these Venetians have the right to have their own republic. *Res publica,* belonging to everyone equally, right? That doesn't prevent some Venetians from preferring Florence to Venice. But Venice will always be their homeland. And that is only just. I would like for the same justice to apply to the Jews."

As Moses spoke, David watched him attentively. He showed little expression, but there was a half-smile on his lips.

"If the Jews who have been expelled from Spain and Portugal could return to the land of their ancestors," the artist went on, "today they would not have to wander back and forth from city to city at the whims of kings…"

Finally David Reubeni's face brightened, and he walked briskly over to where Moses de Castellazzo was standing, leaned forward, and kissed him on the forehead.

And then he calmly asked:

"And about that invitation?"

Near the end of the afternoon on that same day, David Reubeni said goodbye to Captain Campiello Pozzo and moved in with Moses de Castellazzo in the Ghetto Nuovo.

The painter's studio was located in a large warehouse behind the Banco Rosso, one of the three Ashkenazi "banks for the poor." A large beam spanning the room rested on three grey stone pillars. Large windows opened out upon the canal, letting in the light. The light beams spread out over the floor, then seemed to climb up the easels holding paintings protected by white cloth. Everything in the room seemed hidden, secret, as if it were expecting something. Not a single sketch or a painting was visible. Even the leather-bound books were almost hidden away in the shadow of a tall, massive armoire with columns, and only their spines could be seen. David Reubeni made no comment, but as he was sitting down in an armchair near the door so he could take in the entire studio with one glance, Moses de Castellazzo said a few words as if to justify himself:

"Contrary to my friend Titian, I can't stand nakedness."

The stranger's arrival in the Ghetto had not failed to inspire unusual, dangerous gatherings. A crowd of curious people had assembled in front of Moses de Castellazzo's studio. David Reubeni's four servants had quickly realized they couldn't control the crowd, and it had been necessary to ask the *Va'ad* to send some sturdy fellows to help maintain order.

The Envoy from the Kingdom of Chabor refused to meet with anyone that day. Nor did he accept the meal the artist prepared. After saying his evening prayer, the *Ma'ariv*, he was content with a glass of water and began to ask his host about his background, his family, and his art. He didn't ask a single question about the conflicting political currents in Venice, nor about the debate he had involuntarily initiated that was now rocking the Ghetto. It was as if he were already aware of all that, or perhaps simply indifferent. Nor did he speak about his plans. Little by little, as if both men had come to a tacit agreement, silence settled in. Suddenly, a gust of wind from the sea carried a downpour that pounded against the windows. The studio grew dark. Standing on a ladder, Moses de Castellazzo lit, in turn, each of the twelve fat wax candles set in a grandiose chandelier made of spun sugar in Murano. Shadows began to dance and then grew still. Moses de Castellazzo smiled. David's interest grew.

"You are impressive," the artist said with true admiration. "The way you walk, the way you look at things. A different kind of Jew! A Jew who has never known the Ghetto."

And then Moses abruptly asked:

"Does the Jewish kingdom truly exist?"

"Do you doubt it?"

"Yes."

"But you would like there to be a Jewish kingdom?"

"Yes."

"Well, then it does exist. And I am its messenger."

"Some take you for the Messiah."

"They are crazy. Worse than that, those who say so are blaspheming."

"Will you say that tomorrow before the *Va'ad*?"

"That depends upon the questions."

"They say you have traveled through Judea, that you have gone to Jerusalem, to Bethlehem, to Safed…"

"That is true."

And as if compelled by sudden hope and pleasure, David Reubeni told Moses about his adventures and encounters in the Holy Land. Enthralled, the oversize man listened until dawn.

Chapter seven
Before the *Va'ad*

After *Shaharith*, the morning prayer, the Jewish prince drank a glass of water, washed his hands and face, and donned his white woolen tunic. He then went to the *Va'ad* along with his four servants and Moses de Castellazzo. One was carrying a flag on which, sewn in gold letters, were the Hebrew words, *Who can match Your power, O Lord?*—just as they had been written on Judas Maccabeus' victory flag.

The wind had died and rain had ceased, and the puddles of water remaining in the Ghetto square reflected a pale sky. In spite of the early morning hour and the chill in the air, the Campo del Ghetto Nuovo, the largest public square in Canareggio, was jammed with people. As they walked through the square, a murmur rose, sometimes in worry, sometimes in admiration. There was no shouting or singing; the crowd remained serious. Here and there, an old man would slip through the human wall to bless David Reubeni. But David kept walking straight ahead, his head high and his thoughts seemingly turned inward, as if the gathering of people had nothing to do with him, as if he were alone. Twice, however, he slowed his pace. The first time was near the fountain, near the center of the square, when a Jew with a turban, a Jew from the Levant if one were to judge by his purple caftan and the scarf of the same color wrapped around his waist, stepped out toward the little group and cited the Mekhilta (xiv, 10): Tefila, *prayer, is more powerful than any weapon*. And on the second occasion, just as he reached the door of the Scuola Tedesca, a beggar with no legs hurled himself out to meet David, rocking on his hands and chanting Psalm lv (17–18) in his high, childish voice: *I cry out to God and the Lord delivers me. At dusk, at dawn, and at noon I shall grieve and lament. He will hear my voice.*

As the little group climbed the synagogue's narrow wooden staircase, Moses de Castellazzo heard the Messenger murmur:

Who is like you, O people of Israel?

David Reubeni's meeting with the *Va'ad* took place in the same back room of the synagogue where the earlier meeting of the community's chosen leaders had been held. At Giacobo Mantino's request, they had simply removed tables so the room would seem larger and more spacious.

Shimon ben Asher Mechulam del Banco, the dean of the assembly, introduced each of the *Va'ad*'s members to the Messenger. He then laid out the reason they had invited him to come.

"When a stranger arrives in Venice, when he claims to be the Envoy of a Jewish kingdom, and when he undertakes political measures in the name of the people of Israel, the community's representatives, especially if they are linked to such measures in spite of themselves and without their knowing it, have the right to learn his true intentions and goals. And if necessary, express any objections they might have."

"A common prayer is always granted," David Reubeni answered in Hebrew.

And he added: "*Sha'alou*—Ask," according to the ritual expression used in rabbinic schools and cited by the Talmud.

Everyone was standing. On one side of the room, the sixteen elected members formed a semi-circle. On the other, facing them, was the Messenger. His four servants stood a few steps behind him. Moses de Castellazzo was halfway between David Reubeni and the members of the *Va'ad*, like a necessary link in an uncertain chain.

Giacobo Mantino did not appreciate the stranger's words. He believed that the stranger was acting like a master of the Talmud speaking to his disciples. Thus, his voice more aggressive than usual, he asked:

"Who are you?"

"My name is David, the son of Solomon and the brother of Joseph, who reigns over three hundred thousand Jews in the Chabor Desert."

"Are you a prince?"

Sarcasm dripped from Giacobo Mantino's voice.

"*All Jews are princes,*" replied David Reubeni, citing Rabbi Akiba.

"Have you any proof of what you are saying?"

"That we are all princes?"

The members of the *Va'ad* tried to repress their smiles. David Reubeni's answer irritated Giacobo Mantino even more. Color rose in his newly-shaven cheeks.

"Do you have any proof that the Jewish Kingdom of Chabor really exists?"

"Yes."

And, after a brief pause, David added:

"My word."

"They say that you are carrying a letter from your brother."

"That is true."

"Might we see it?"

"No."

"Why not?"

"Because it is not addressed to you."

"To whom is it addressed?" asked Giacobo Mantino.

"To the head of Christendom, Pope Clement VII."

"What does the letter say?"

"I am not authorized to reveal that."

Giacobo Mantino made a tired gesture with both arms, as if asking his colleagues to bear witness, and grumbled:

"There is nothing to be gotten out of him, nothing to be gotten out of him."

Rabbi Shlomo da Costa nodded his turbaned head:

"Are you a rabbi?" he asked.

"No, I am a military man," David replied.

"Have you been a student?"

"As all Jews have been."

"It is said that you would like to free the land of Israel from Turkish occupation…"

"And you do not?"

"And that you want to create in its place a Jewish kingdom."

"And you do not?"

"Do you know that the Jewish kingdom will be created only when the Eternal—blessed be His name—has so decided?"

"Who is to say that the One Who Is has not so decided?"

"When the decision is made, every Jew will know it!"

"You must allow them time to learn the news."

During the rapid give and take, Giacobo Mantino studied the visitor. The man's face had regular features, as if they had been carved in dark marble by a Greek sculptor, and his expression remained impassible. The calm self-control and mischievousness of the man made him more dangerous than expected. Mantino looked around at his colleagues. Though some seemed to have already made up their minds, many appeared perplexed and uncertain. No, he couldn't count on them. But he knew as well that the meeting could not become simply a verbal joust between the stranger and himself, a kind of personal quarrel, or then even those who had voted with him the first time might change their votes. Although he could not count all the members of the *Va'ad* among his friends, he did have a number of friends among the Gentiles, including some church dignitaries like Ghiberti, the Bishop of Verona. He reflected that he, better than anyone else, understood the fragile equilibrium in which the lives of the Jews in Venice rested. The equilibrium was so fragile that it was now at the mercy of a simple misunderstanding, to say nothing of a reckless adventure, especially if the adventure was led by a spirit such as that man's. That military man was too knowledgeable, Giacobo Mantino could feel it, and he lacked neither charisma nor intelligence. Therefore, Mantino had to disavow him and denounce him as a false messenger. Did he not need to save the Jews who had elected him to the head of the *Va'ad*? Save them in spite of themselves, and if necessary, even from themselves? For he was sure of it. David Reubeni's plans had no chance of succeeding, and would bring about nothing but new persecution. In the meantime, Giacobo Mantino needed to play the game. To appear open and tolerant. To avoid any obvious animosity.

He vaguely heard the scribe from Ancona, Joseph Luzzato, ask a question, and then, deep in thought, didn't even listen to the answer. The sun broke through the clouds and suddenly lit up the room with its raw winter light. The president of the *Va'ad* stepped forward once more, rocking lightly back and forth on his feet like a fighter in the arena, and then, trying to keep his voice neutral, he asked:

"Are you sure that the pope will receive you?"

"Yes."

"Do you have someone to introduce you?"

David Reubeni did not answer the question immediately.

His silence, the first since the meeting began, caused an uncomfortable stir in the audience. Giacobo Mantino sensed that the tide was beginning to turn, that the representatives were finally ready to express their opposition more openly and directly. So he took another step forward. Now he was practically in the middle of the semi-circle, in the sun's halo. His purple doublet took on the color of blood.

"Have you considered those thousands of Italian Jews whom your plans put at risk? Have you given any thought to those thousands upon thousands of Levantine Jews living in the Turkish Empire, whom your plans are putting in harm's way? Why so many lies? The Kingdom of Chabor…King Joseph…an introduction to the pope. If you had a means of meeting the pope, you would already be in Rome instead of wasting your time here in Venice!"

Moses de Castellazzo watched the Envoy. He saw him clench his fists, but not one muscle in his face had moved. Moses admired his ability to remain so calm. He was about to come to his new friend's aid when David Reubeni began to speak. Calmly and deliberately. His Hebrew took on a more guttural tone, like sounds from the desert.

"If I had been foolish enough," he said, "I would have asked the Creator to give men two mouths, one for eating and speaking, and the other for studying the Torah! But upon reflection, the idea is not a good one."

He paused and looked at Giacobo Mantino. Mantino's face tightened, and he looked hatefully at their guest. David Reubeni realized that the president of the *Va'ad* had recognized the words of Rabbi Shimon bar Yochaï in the Talmud. And that he knew what followed.

"Why is the idea not a good one?" Moses Zacuto, the clothing seller, asked innocently.

Giacobo Mantino stepped backward, as if a greater distance between him and the Messenger could protect him from the words that would follow, words that he knew by heart.

"The idea is not a good one," David Reubeni continued, "because already men devote their one mouth to such malicious gossip that it places the universe in peril. What would become of humanity if men had two mouths?"

The bitter irony of his comments visibly made everyone uneasy. Shimon Zarfatti d'Avignon bravely asked:

"What do you expect from us?"

"Nothing."

"Then why did you come to see us?"

"Because you asked me to!"

"And did you not wish to see us?" asked Moses de Castellazzo.

"Me?"

David Reubeni smiled. His face brightened.

"I am always pleased to meet Jews, and…"

He looked at the artist.

"And if, by chance, I can find a friend among them, then I am the happiest man alive."

And then he turned back to Giacobo Mantino.

"No, I did not come here to insult you, but rather to learn. That being said, please be reassured that I am simply passing through."

The stranger's words stupefied the assembly. The offense given to one of their members, the most important person among them—

even if deep down some were pleased—had the result of provoking a wave of sympathy for Mantino. Nothing authorized some stranger to come and insult a Venetian Jew.

It required all of old Asher Mechulam del Banco's rhetorical talent and Talmudic skill to calm the assembly's irritation.

"The words of our guest," he explained for those who might not have realized it, "are quotations from the Talmud. They were written by the famous Rabbi Shimon bar Yochaï, author of the *Zohar*, the Book of Splendor, and father of the Kabbalah. Those words, my dear friends, were spoken during the time of the Roman occupation of Jerusalem, when every Jew was subjected to careful surveillance and when many were victims of denunciations. In short, by virtue of that reference, the Prince of Chabor has firmly established his spiritual qualities. The reference vouches for his perfect honorability and makes it impossible to suspect him of attempting violence on any member of this august assembly."

The banker's explanations brought calm to the proceedings. David Reubeni did not say a word.

"Well then, what do you expect from us?" Shimon Zarfatti repeated.

"Nothing," David replied once more.

Then, when he saw the annoyed reaction on their faces, he dropped his voice and added in a confidential tone:

"Yes, it is true. I have indeed been eager to meet Jews in Venice. These famous Venetian Jews, protected by the Doge, matchless bankers, universally admired scholars, travelers, artists, inventors. In short, the best of the best."

He paused, and everyone could hear the bells ringing on the other side of the canal.

"No, I did not come to insult you. Nor to be insulted," he added. "And surely not to quarrel with Jews. I love them too much. I love them as they are: not always handsome, not always courageous, not always honest, but always alert. They are like good sails that pick up every wind, all knowledge."

He paused, waiting until the bells finished ringing.

"But I would like to see them free! Finally free! Free on the land of their ancestors after fifteen centuries of exile."

Since he had remained so still since his arrival, his first step forward surprised the circle of dignitaries and made them move back. He smiled once again. Then, suddenly serious, he addressed those members who had not yet opened their mouths.

"And how about the rest of you? Have you nothing to say? Only three of you have spoken. Do the others not have an opinion?"

Giacobo Mantino was about to intervene when David Reubeni's voice took on new tones. It became melodious and captivating, with the pitch, rhythm, and seductive quality of an oriental storyteller.

"I have a story to tell you. It comes from the Talmud."

The members of the *Va'ad* glanced at each other in surprise. The Messenger's four servants waited attentively.

"Rabbi Ishmael said: 'Job was part of Pharaoh's court. When Moses came to Pharaoh to ask for the Jews to be freed, the Egyptian king questioned his three counselors. Jethro said: 'Let the children of Israel leave.' Bil'am contradicted him. And Job? Job remained silent.' Hence the suffering he had to endure later. Neutrality's silence never works in favor of the victims, but always to the benefit of the oppressors."

A murmur ran through the back room of the Scuola Tedesca. Undeniably, David Reubeni had a talent for putting people at ease and charming them with his words. After he had spoken, the unsettled atmosphere in the room was filled with uncertainty and deep questions alternating with feelings of reprobation. Then David smiled, and his charm again worked its wonders. The smile freed the members, and they all began to chatter at the same time, like birds that have just escaped from an aviary.

The session lasted more than four hours. The man from Chabor withdrew early, saying that he wanted to let the chosen ones deliberate without undue influence from him. Their conclusions were mixed. Since the Messenger was not requesting help or support, they didn't need to discuss his plans. On the other hand, taking Giacobo Mantino's lead, some claimed to be concerned about the foreigner's activities. Were not the people in the Ghetto already beginning to agitate? Did not the Doge show too much interest in the man's actions, and were not the Jews' enemies beginning to raise their heads? So it was imperative to get rid of David Reubeni. But it might be useful to recognize the importance of his mission. For one never knew, perhaps the pope would respond favorably to his request.

They consequently agreed to provide David boat passage to Pesaro along with an armed escort, given the unsafe conditions in the region, to accompany him from Pesaro to Rome.

Once in Rome, it would be wholly up to him.

Chapter eight

An Impossible Dream

David Reubeni and his retinue left the Ghetto's densely populated labyrinth the next morning. Along the Riva degli Schiavoni there were crowds of people. The only members of the *Va'ad* who had come to see him off were Asher Mechulam del Banco and Moses de Castellazzo. Before boarding a large red galleon, David Reubeni shook the old banker's gnarled hand affectionately and once again quoted the Talmud: *You too console the afflicted.* Then, he turned to the artist.

"In the Chabor desert," he said, "I learned something important: No man can live without God, without friends, or without love. To survive, he needs at least one of these three gifts. How fortunate is the man who has all three!"

The galleon raised its anchor a few minutes later. The bells of San Marco announced its departure. It was the tenth day of the month of Shevat in the year 5284 after the creation of the world by the Eternal, blessed be His name, January 15, 1524.

Moses was upset by the *Va'ad*'s decisions, for he felt they revealed how cowardly the assembly was. When he returned to his studio, he spread out the sketches he had made of the Messenger onto the floor. He studied them for a long time, feeling displeased with various details. Then, after noting his criticisms in a little notebook he always kept with him, he tore up the sketches. Methodically, calmly, and with no regrets. He kept only one. It showed an ebony face built around unusual eyes. The water droplets had been reproduced, God knows how, on the Messenger's face. Moses marveled at how he had inexplicably managed to include them.

He decided to keep that particular sketch, reminded that chance governs more than half of our actions, and that without chance, art could not exist.

He picked up a pair of scissors and trimmed the sheet of paper. With smaller margins, the sketch seemed more powerful still, and the look in David Reubeni's eyes even more intense. A strange look indeed. "Do eyes truly reveal what is in one's soul?" he wondered. He hesitated for a moment. Perhaps he should get rid of the disturbing portrait. But his love of art and the certainty that he must keep a record of the Messenger's visit to Venice convinced him that he should keep it. Carrying the sketch, he walked through his studio. His eyes fell upon the cabinet full of books. He pulled out a book and inserted David Reubeni's portrait between its pages. When he placed it back on the shelf, he glanced at the title. It was a commentary of Dante's *Divine Comedy* written by Cristoforo Landino Fiorentino.

Once he knew the portrait was safe, he began to reflect, almost regretting that he had not followed the Messenger.

A Jewish kingdom in the land of Israel. He smiled, scratched his chin through his beard, and then abruptly pulled off the cloth covering a painting on the easel in the center of the room. It was another portrait. Or, rather, just a sketch. The top of the head was not yet finished. It was impossible to say whether it was a woman or a child. Moses de Castellazzo looked critically at his work. He was obsessed by the memory of the man from the desert. No, he would not be able to work today.

He draped a piece of white cloth back over the painting and decided to go see his friend Titian to discuss the mirage of the man

with lava-colored hair, the man who had come from the depths of
Fortunate Arabia with a dream almost impossible to believe in, and
yet Moses found himself believing.

Chapter nine

Tomorrow, Pesaro

T he first stage after Venice was Pesaro, a day's journey by sea. David was eager to get there. His stay in the City of the Doges had been too long—longer than he had planned. Truly, he had stayed because he had hoped to get some help. He would not have been able to undertake a trip across Italy at war without financial support or an armed escort.

Yes, he had secretly hoped for more from the Venetian Jews, more enthusiasm and money. But he had forgotten how stubborn Jews could be. Their suspicions were understandable but paralyzing. And some were miserly. In his disappointment, he had been tempted to quote the words of the Prophet: *Why do you weigh out money for things that are not nourishing? Why do you work for that which fails to satisfy your hunger?*

But he did not want to offend them. And he could even understand them. In the Ghetto, money was the key that could open the gates of freedom. But what kind of freedom? He grimaced at the thought.

"An illusion!" he muttered. "An illusion, nothing but an illusion."

He, David Reubeni, had offered them an opportunity that would not likely come again soon. To gain collective freedom, real freedom in the land of their ancestors. The play of political and military forces in the world at the time presented a favorable opportunity. But men are cowardly, cowardly by nature, and Jews are like all men.

Some seagulls flew past the boat. He admired their effortless flight, but found their grating cries unpleasant.

Many questions were running through his mind. Was the lack of enthusiasm for their own deliverance among some of the Venetians Jews due to his own failure to explain things properly, to get his message across? Had his plans been sufficiently prepared? Was his project even manageable? Giacobo Mantino remained at the center of his thoughts. The doctor was intelligent and influential. And above all, he considered himself to be perfectly integrated in society. So it was useless to try to show him the absurdity of his own situation, accepted as he was by the most important men of his day, yet still forced to live in the Ghetto like all other Jews. By accepting the situation, Giacobo Mantino surely saw the solution to the Jews' problems. David Reubeni did not question the doctor's sincerity, but his very sincerity made him even more of an obstacle. The Messenger from Chabor had no choice but to recognize that his own actions had so far produced few real results—a great deal of curiosity, a few apparently implacable enemies, and few friends. But do leaders truly need friends?

He heard someone walking quickly toward him. A sentence from the Talmud came to his mind: *He who leads others toward the Good will never fail.*

He smiled as he noticed a small grey serpent slipping over the ropes. He raised his foot to chase it away, but the serpent lifted its head proudly, like an offended woman, and disappeared between two planks, like a match flame blown out by a gust of wind.

Joseph appeared.

"Do you need me, Master?" he asked in Hebrew.

He was standing near the mast. He was short of stature, and the shadows made his white tunic appear dirty and wrinkled. He was holding a thick notebook in his hands, and under his arm was a bag with shawls and phylacteries.

"Excuse me, Master," he said. "I thought for a moment that you had called me."

His protruding eyes made him look unusually cheerful. It always seemed as if he had just celebrated some festival or birthday all by himself.

David Reubeni's only answer was to stare at the implacable sky. A hawk was circling, a silent witness from on high. The two men stood still for a long time, and the minutes flowed by. The shadow from the mast grew a few inches longer in the direction of the open sea. Like a dark hand on a clock, the hawk flapped its wings three times and moved on.

"Tobias," Joseph said hesitantly.

"What about Tobias?"

"I don't trust Tobias."

David Reubeni's face brightened into a smile.

"Trust and mistrust are both the ruin of men."

And then he lowered his voice and added:

"Why?"

"I believe...I believe he is betraying you, Master."

"Do you have any proof?"

"No. I came just to..."

He cleared his throat and spit out over the wooden rail.

"I'm afraid he is in the pay of Giacobo Mantino."

David Reubeni drew back in surprise when he saw the look on his servant's face. Showing his concern, he asked:

"Giacobo Mantino? Do you have any proof?"

Joseph was totally devoted to his master.

"No," he admitted. "Just a feeling, some doubts. I saw him speaking with Giacobo Mantino. And since then, he has been spending money freely."

Two sailors walked by on the deck, laughing loudly.

The master and servant grew silent. David Reubeni motioned to Joseph to move away. He wanted to be alone. Was there no way he could stop thinking about Giacobo Mantino on this trip?

As the ship pitched in the waves, David Reubeni reached out gracefully to grab a rope for support. The long sea voyage was relaxing. He knew his plan was sound. It was incumbent upon him to impose it onto others. He was sure that the time was right. And how about the Jews? Let the devil take them! To succeed, he first had to attract Gentiles. And then he could force the Jews to follow him. Like Moses.

He could feel the breeze caressing his cheek. He looked up at the mast and noticed the filled-out sails. The ship was moving rapidly. Off in the distance, on the starboard side, he could almost perceive the coast. He felt overwhelmed by the serious side of life. A memory came to mind, as if something alive, something in distress had begun to stir in his thoughts. He looked out to sea, and something unusual happened. He thought of his mother. He could not remember her very clearly. He could remember only the ocher scarf she wore, and her eyes. Her sparkling eyes, dark as jade, that were always studying, God only knows why, the sterile mountain, ocher like her scarf, that protected the village where he had been born.

He heard a ship's bell ringing on the portside, a galleon from Ancona on the way to Venice.

No, he had no right to doubt. Rabbi Ben Azzaï claimed that there is no man whose time does not come. The Envoy knew that his time had indeed come. It was inevitable. Little did it matter for which David Reubeni it had come—the son of Tamar whose father was killed by one of King John's guards, or the brother of Joseph, king of the Jews of Chabor.

The day was gently drawing to a close. In Pesaro, as the *Va'ad* had promised, an escort would be waiting. An escort, along with Rabbi Moshe da Foligno, head of the local community with whom he had corresponded since arriving in Venice. He had decided to leave Pesaro on that very day, taking the road toward Fano, Fossombrone, Foligno, Spoleto, Narni, and Castelnuovo, where he was hoping to spend the Feast of Purim. And then Rome, where his destiny would play itself out. He was afraid, and at the same time could feel a sense of pride rising in his throat.

But suddenly the ship was enveloped in shadow. A thick fog had swept in. On the upper deck, a human form quickly lit an oil lantern. David leaned against the railing and looked down at the sea, contemplating the incessant movement of the waves. Watching the moving waves allowed him to think more clearly. Could Tobias, the servant he had hired in Alexandria, a man he had trusted, be a traitor? Had Tobias agreed to spy on him for Giacobo Mantino? If so, had money been his only motive?

A fight between two Maltese sailors drew him out of his thoughts. One, tall and thin, was lying on the deck, trying to protect himself as best he could from the violent blows the other sailor was giving him. His attacker was short, squat, and rippling with muscles. Twenty or so sailors had encircled them and were egging on the attacker with their shouts and clapping. Shadows were dancing around from the torch one man was holding up. The cries and moans of the beaten man were getting weaker and weaker. Blood gushed from his face and covered his hands and shirt.

David Reubeni grew angry. He leaped through the noisy circle, making his way to the two combatants. To everyone's great surprise, he picked up the heavy-set man as if he were a bundle of straw. He walked all the way around the circle with the man yelling and gesticulating, like Hercules holding up the sky, and then he dropped him. The man fell heavily to the planks and lay still. Several sailors bent over to look at him, not sure what to do. One, braver than the rest, reached out to touch him. The heavy-set man rolled painfully to his side. The Messenger watched the scene for a moment, then shrugged his shoulders and returned to his followers. He motioned to them to relax and said gently, as if to justify himself:

"You can't reason with people in the heat of anger."

His servants did not utter a word. Who could have thought that a man as thin as David could be so strong?

The short struggle had calmed his mind. He prepared to say the evening prayer, *Ma'ariv: And He, full of mercy, forgives our sins. He does not accept destruction; He holds back His anger; He does not unleash all His wrath. Lord, come to our aid! May the King answer our prayers on the day we invoke Him!*

Chapter ten

The Ways of the Eternal

Davidavid Reubeni did not remain long in Pesaro. He quickly left the little city, as if he were afraid that some potentate might send him back by boat to Venice. Rabbi Moshe da Foligno was waiting for him on the quay with an affable smile. A large portion of the Jewish community was also waiting. A twenty-man escort, heavily armed, accompanied the rabbi. They were Swiss mercenaries, mostly from Basel. But what pleased the Messenger the most were the horses—seven lovely animals with beautiful saddles. He chose one of them, the only white horse of the seven, an animal with long graceful legs that kept its velvety-grey ears pricked up. As soon as David felt the horse's warm, trembling flanks between his legs, he cheered up, and to the great surprise of his servants, he broke out twice in laughter.

The road followed the coast, and they galloped all the way to Fano. It was a little town with many fountains and a silted-in port. Nothing seemed out of the ordinary, and they were able to ride through Fano without incident. But when they reached the other side of the town, David was surprised to find an immense crowd waiting for him. It was made up of Jews, many Jews who had come from Ancona to meet and touch the man they venerated. The majority of them were refugees who had been expelled from Spain. When he saw them, the Messenger's face darkened. He slowed down his horse, and keeping a tight rein, he walked slowly through the crowd that opened up ceremoniously to let him pass. He could feel that these people didn't understand his attitude, but he could not approach them. He had not come to Italy to attract them, but rather to liberate them, to find them a homeland.

"It's him! It's him!" cried a poor old man dressed in rags. "The Eternal has sent him to deliver us!"

"Did you hear that?" Joseph asked his master. "There's the danger. You want to liberate them, but all they can do is call for the Messiah."

He suddenly heard the shouts. Up until then he had been deep in his own thoughts and memories, and his ears had remained deaf to all the noise. Everyone was begging for him to bless the old man. "Give him a blessing!" People were shouting on all sides, "bless him!" David felt humiliated. They didn't understand anything at all! But had he even tried to explain? Had he even had the opportunity to explain? No. Rome was waiting for him. And then he remembered his mission, and only his mission could justify his attitude: When a man is hoping to set an entire people free, it is vain to waste time with individuals.

Finally, the road to Fossombrone and Cagli opened up. The old man still clung to the white horse, but David Reubeni, with pity on his face, kept moving roughly forward without a word. His goal was to discourage individual hopes and inspire collective hope. Without even seeming to notice what he was doing, he dug his heels into his horse's flanks and trotted off. The old man stumbled in surprise, then took a step backward and slipped into the ditch beside the road. David's escort set out after their leader, for he had already broken into an impetuous gallop. Behind Joseph floated the banner on which the people could read Hebrew words written in gold letters: *Who can match Your power, O Lord?*

They rode until nightfall. Exhausted, they stopped to rest and feed the horses in the town of Fossombrone, a few miles from Urbino. Fossombrone was a little town of eleven thousand souls, backed up against a mountain slope, with no Jews living there. The arrival of any strange horsemen made people nervous. They found the Swiss guards especially frightening. Since the great battle at Marignano a few years before, Swiss horsemen had been mercenaries in the service of some of the most prestigious masters of Europe: Frances I, the king of France; Charles v, the emperor of Spain and Sicily; the League, Alphonse de Medici, the pope.... For that reason, in the eyes of the people living in Fossombrone, the arrival of Swiss mercenaries presaged nothing good. A good hour of negotiations were necessary before Gianiacomo de Casena, the owner of a large inn set in the shadow of the Cardinal of Urbino's garden, agreed to lodge them.

David Reubeni and his companions were greeted, however, by Vincentius Castellani, a famous scholar and Bible commentator. His ocher-colored house stood opposite a stone bridge that crossed a stream, the Metauro, and led to the Flaminian Way, the highway that led to Rome.

When word had been brought to the venerable Vincentius Castellani that the Messenger had arrived, he had expressed his desire to meet him. The white-haired man stood there nobly in his purple robe, and he was eager to exchange thoughts with the brother of the King of the Jews concerning the holy book, and to tell him about his own scholarly work. But David Reubeni was eager, above all, to rest and say his evening prayer.

So he withdrew into a dark, damp room on the second floor of Vincentius Castellani's home.

"Master!!"

Someone was pounding at his door.

"Come in," he responded.

It was Tobias, the servant whom Joseph suspected of betrayal. He was chubby, jovial, and talkative, and he seemed to be perfectly open. He could speak several languages. With David, he always tried to speak Arabic.

"The Swiss guard wants to know when we will start out."

"At dawn," David replied.

As Tobias turned to leave, David called out to him.

"Tobias!"

"Yes, Master?"

Tobias placed his chubby white hand on his protruding stomach in a gesture of resignation, but the Messenger thought it seemed more like a gesture of annoyance.

"Do you know that any friendship based on gain evaporates as soon as the gain is gone?"

Surprise filled Tobias's pudgy, clean-shaven face.

David went on: "Remember Amnon's friendship with Tamar. But selfless friendship endures forever. Remember David and Jonathan."

Tobias's eyes widened. He didn't seem to understand. The Envoy from the desert felt discouraged and leaned against the wall for support. Appropriate words did not come to mind. Clearly, he had forgotten how to speak with people such as Tobias. In times gone by he would have known exactly what to say. Without feeling the slightest pity, he would have found some formula or some harsh words. But now he could see how useless such a conversation was. It was useless to try to urge a confession out of his valet. It would have been better to let him presume that David still trusted him. Either Tobias had betrayed him and he needed to be sent away, or Joseph's accusation was false and he should remain in David's service.

"Do you still intend to follow me?"

The servant's face lit up. Finally there was a question he could understand. And he grunted "yes," from deep within, like a deliverance. He seemed perfectly sincere.

"And how about Giacobo Mantino?"

"Yes, Master?"

"Did you meet alone with him?"

"Yes."

"Why?"

"Because he asked me to."

"What did he want from you?"

"He wanted to know more about you, Master."

"He did not ask you to spy on me?"

"No, Master."

"Did he give you any money?"

"Yes."

"Why?"

"For the trip," he said. "In case you didn't have enough."

His answers were clear and straightforward. It is easy to avoid a lance, but not a hidden sword.

"Why did you not speak to me about it?"

"You never gave me the opportunity, Master."

David was reminded of an Arabic proverb: *You catch a bird with another bird.*

"Giacobo Mantino told me that you promised to keep him abreast of what we were doing, so that he could help if necessary. How did you expect to accomplish that?"

Tobias hesitated. His smile disappeared, and with his chubby hand, he brushed back a strand of black hair from his forehead before answering:

"I don't understand your question, Master."

"Lies are like sand. Sand seems soft when you lie down on it, but hard when you try to get back up."

"What are you trying to tell me, Master?"

David realized that Tobias would not admit anything. Perhaps there was nothing to admit. But even if there was, he would cling to his lies. David must either send him away or live with doubt. He opted for living with doubt, until he reached Rome. In the meantime, Tobias would either confess or give himself away.

David Reubeni slept little that night. Vincentius Castellani loved to talk. He started out using a quotation from Genesis (1:26): *Let us make man in our image, after our likeness.*

They conversed in Hebrew. His host had learned the language of the Bible in order to read the Kabbalah in the original. For the Envoy from the Kingdom of Chabor, the answer to Vincentius Castellani's question was to be found in the Book itself: *To walk in all His ways* (Deuteronomy 11:22)... What are the ways of God? As it is written in Exodus 34:67–: *The Lord, the Lord God, merciful and gracious, longsuffering, and abundant in goodness and truth. He keeps His mercy for a thousand generations, forgiving iniquity, transgression, and sin, but that will by no means clear the guilty.* And, as can be found elsewhere, in Joel 2:32: *Whosoever shall call on the name of the Lord shall be delivered. But how is it possible for a man to call on the name of the Lord? Just as God is merciful and gracious, you also must be merciful and gracious and give to anyone in need without expecting anything in return. Just as God is called just, you too must be just. Just as God is called loving, you too must be pious.*

David pointed out to his host that for Jews, God was not a body but an essence. Therefore, likeness was not limited to form but to substance. And God's qualities led to normative standards for the actions of human beings.

Then they spoke about the state of the world. The old scholar was enthusiastic about inventions and progress. "Printing allows us to disseminate knowledge," he said. Knowledge of a world that was expanding and widening, both in space and in time. He quoted Columbus, Amerigo Vespucci, and Magellan, and he spoke at great length about Aristotle, Alfarabi, and Avicenna, whose writings were being rediscovered, and about Homer's *Iliad* and Plato's *Republic*, which people were finally able to read. He also mentioned Jewish writings: the Bible, the Talmud, the *Zohar*, Abulafia, and especially the Kabbalah, which the pope was especially fond of. Vincentius Castellani remembered fondly a remark made by Rabbi Moses de Burgos, a famous 13th-century kabbalist, concerning philosophers whose intellectual prowess was praised: "Those philosophers whom you praise end up where we begin."

David Reubeni was less optimistic than his host about the state of the world. It seemed to him that the fortunate era of discovery and new knowledge was beginning to run out of steam. He could even sense the end coming. A bloody end. Printing disseminated not only knowledge but also hate. People were studying ancient texts searching for ways not only to establish peace, but also to create war with each other. Islam was making advances, and even though Soleiman himself was a sovereign open to new ideas, his military leaders were proving to be as intolerant as Catholic or Huguenot generals. And finally, in the confrontation with Islam, Christianity was displaying all sorts of internal rivalries. The Church had splintered. Religious wars were raging in Germany. Empires were collapsing. Tiny kingdoms were appearing here and there, and they too were often at war.

"Do you believe in the coming of the Messiah?" Vincentius Castellani asked David point-blank.

"I believe in the responsibility of men," the Envoy from the desert replied.

"Have you read Machiavelli?"

"Yes."

"Is he the kind of man you expect?"

"Yes, though the man I expect would be more ethical."

"Would you like to meet him?"

"Yes, very much."

They continued talking until dawn. When they parted, the old scholar from Fossombrone offered to give David a letter of introduction to his friend Cardinal Egidio di Viterbo, who was close to His Holiness, the pope. The stranger's personality and dark lucidity had greatly impressed Vincentius Castellani, and he wanted to do what he could to assist him. As for David Reubeni, he said his morning prayer that day more fervently than ever. He had been hoping for such a letter ever since he learned that Vincentius Castellani knew the cardinal.

Such a long conversation between their master and the famous Bible commentator astonished the Messenger's servants. Joseph, however, had already seen his master engage in long debates with kabbalists in Safed and Jerusalem, and he was not surprised by his brilliant remarks.

Time had come for David to leave his host. He thanked Castellani warmly for his hospitality and for his precious letter of introduction. As he climbed back on his horse, his eyes met Joseph's, which were full of silent questions. But the dark pupils of the man from the desert remained impenetrable.

Chapter eleven

Escaping One's Destiny or Being Swept Along by It

T he little group started off down the Flaminian Way toward Rome. When they reached Cagli, they had to make a detour through Fabriano. Near Cagli there was a battle being waged between the horsemen and archers of Frances I, King of France, and the horsemen of Charles V, Emperor of Spain and Sicily, supported by those faithful to Charles de Bourbon who, for personal reasons, had betrayed his own camp.

David Reubeni watched carts loaded with wounded men roll by him. "Wounded men, but from which side?" he wondered. "The world is breaking into smaller and smaller pieces, and an individual's value is growing less and less." He went on, talking to himself, though his faithful servant Joseph could hear the words: "People forget that every time they kill a man, God is wounded."

An echo from a far-off cannon caused the horses to whinny. The captain of the Swiss escort pointed to the road to Fabriano, where he thought they could resume on the Flaminian Way. However, he had surmised without considering the passionate outpouring occasioned by the presence of the man from the desert.

Fabriano was only a couple of dozen miles from Ancona, in the middle of the Marche region. There, with the pope's authorization, thousands of Jews from Spain had taken refuge. As soon as the rumor of the Messenger's arrival in Venice had reached the area, carried by well-meaning couriers, thousands of people had gathered from near and far. Now that he was there, the gathering was so dense just outside Fabriano that David and his escort were blocked. There was nothing to be done about it. Neither his servants' appeals nor the Swiss escort's threats had any effect. The Jews formed a living wall. So the captain proposed that instead of trying to go through Fabriano, they should take the Camerino road and then start toward the mountains and Terni. So much for the Flaminian Way.

David Reubeni knew that raising the expectations of men who were so eager for hope was as dangerous as giving too much water to a man dying of thirst in the desert. So he was pleased that their maneuver would allow him to slip by those poor penniless creatures who had been awaiting the Messiah ever since they had been expelled from Spain. The Envoy was fully aware, however, that people sometimes end up coming face to face with their destiny even when they do their best to avoid it.

And indeed, after two hours of intense riding had put a good distance between them and the motley crowd that continued to follow, an unpleasant surprise awaited them. It happened in a clearing, near the Potenza River, just a few leagues from Camerino. To which army did those men wearing red berets with white feathers belong? Were they soldiers of Frances I? Of Charles V? Or just the private army of some condottiere who needed money, taking advantage of a war-torn Italy's problems to seek easy prey. Little did it matter which army it was, for the armed men burst out of the woods. Without any complicated maneuvering, counting on the element of surprise, they bore down on David and his men with their pikes lowered.

Even before David could draw his sword, their assailants had broken through the first line of Swiss guards. One scar-faced man, as tall as a beanpole, wearing an iron corset and a chain-mail skirt, galloped toward the Messenger with his lance outstretched. Joseph was quicker, blocking his path. He grabbed his weapon and pulled it so hard that the man fell off his horse with a horrible scream.

As a tactical plan, the attack was absurd. An ambush should come from both sides at once. David, his mind racing, quickly evaluated their situation. His face hardened. He was no longer the peaceful meditative man whom the artist Moses de Castellazzo so admired in Venice, but rather an efficient, determined military man.

"Off your horses!" he shouted. "Force them to lie down and get behind them!"

While his escort went into action, about thirty harquebusiers emerged from the woods and lined up in two rows, one standing and the other on one knee. But before they could fire their first salvo, David's guard had already taken shelter. The bullets flew over their heads and struck a number of those mysterious soldiers who continued to advance from the river. The second salvo dispersed the survivors. The harquebusiers realized their mistake. Things were not going according to plan. David Reubeni's men weren't playing by the rules of a game the attackers had thought they were controlling. With their harquebuses raised, they rushed forward in a confused, disorganized assault. That was their second mistake and the moment David was waiting for. He leaped to his feet, screamed something in an unknown language, and ran to meet them, brandishing his sword. Joseph, holding the Messenger's white banner high and ardently swinging his saber, also rushed forward with a yell, as did his other companions. Galvanized into action by such bravery, the Swiss guards also leaped into action, their blades at the ready.

The fight was intense, but brief. In their flight, the assailants dropped their weapons, leaving a score of dead behind them. Two Swiss guards would never rise again. Three others were wounded, one of them seriously. He had to be treated on the spot. By now the crowd following from Fabriano had caught up with them, and people were spreading the news of the fight throughout the region. And the story kept growing. "A Jew who wins battles! Like Moses, he must surely be aided by the Eternal!" Even the skeptics and the incredulous were shaken by the story of his exploit, for it was quickly taking on legendary proportions.

When David Reubeni's little band climbed back on their horses, once again the crowds tried to follow. More and more Jews appeared at every turn, at every crossroad, joining the swelling crowd.

In Camerino, more people were waiting for David. There were Jews from Ascoli, Fermo, and Macerata, the little town where the papal legate for the Marche region resided. Some had nothing but the rags on their backs, and others had hurriedly piled all their belongings on wobbly carts. Many had come empty-handed, as if they believed that the Messenger would be giving them not only a country of their own, but also food and ointments.

When night fell, David and his men stopped in Visso. It was a small town, but since it lay at a crossroads, between Ascoli and Foligno, Visso did have two inns. The master and his servants took lodging in one of them.

David summoned Joseph to his room. Since the morning's events they had exchanged only a few words. Yet, only few words were necessary for them to understand each other. To their minds, it had not been a chance ambush.

"What do you think, Joseph?" the Messenger asked.

"I can feel the hand of Giacobo Mantino in all that, Master."

"Do you think so?" David replied, with an innocent look. "Could a scholar, a rabbi, and especially a Jew have sent a band of murderers to kill a Jewish prince?"

"It would not be the first time," said Joseph with a grimace.

After his evening prayer, David went out onto the terrace. Off in the distance, he could see campfires flickering. He could hear music. The crowds must be singing psalms. He leaned against a stone pillar, trying to understand the shouts and calls, parts of which reached him, as if they were in pieces. The translucent sky seemed to be alive and glowing. The pale world lay spread out before him: fields, grey-green like two-way mirrors; the trees were dark, moving masses; clusters of clouds were enigmas carried by the wind. And then darkness fell, drowning everything and everyone. From time to time, he could hear the rustle of wings in the shadows.

He sat down on the steps and made an effort to reconstruct the verses of the psalm he could hear in the distance. Suddenly, at dawn, he woke up. He was chilled to the bone, though his mind seemed like a blazing inferno of jumbled words. The low winter sun was shining on his face. Dew covered his clothing. Like a madman, he leaped to his feet. Opposite, the cool blue mountains stood majestically along the river. Here and there, smoke from some campfires was still rising lazily. In the courtyard at the inn, people were beginning to go about their morning activities. A cock crowed. It was time for the morning prayer.

Immediately thereafter, as it began to grow lighter, David Reubeni and his servants set out on the road to Terni. Though he hadn't turned around to look, he knew that the crowds were following them. The road was about to leave the forest. At the forest's edge, he stopped. In the valley, and as the day grew brighter, he could see thousands of people, carried away by their dreams. They were massed together like a swarm of bees. What honey were they seeking? Where was their hive? An old man praying beside the road noticed David. Immediately, he pointed at the Messenger.

"There he is! There he is! Look! The Eternal has sent him to deliver us!"

David winced. He had recognized the voice of the old man in Fano. He watched as small groups pulled away from the mass of people and began to dance. His horse stomped its feet nervously. David closed his eyes and prayed to the Lord. "Adonai, Lord!" he murmured, "this is not what I wanted."

His horse whinnied and began to toss its head. He let it trot off. When he reached the mass of people, he stopped.

"I have brought no message for you," he said in Hebrew. "I bring you nothing more than the desire to return to the land of your ancestors!"

"He is just and modest," shouted the old mystic from Fano.

For a moment, David Reubeni struggled to evaluate the situation. He had planned for everything except the madness of men, except for their despair. "How can I keep him quiet? Maybe kill him?" The idea crossed his mind, but he rejected it immediately. He thought: "Being carried into Rome by crowds might frighten the Christians. But it might also give them a reason to listen to me."

He turned around. His servants were ecstatic. Even his Swiss guards seemed impressed. Once again, he looked out at the people, who now, in their exaltation, were singing Psalm XXIV:

Who shall ascend unto the hill of the Lord?
or who shall stand in His holy place?
He that hath clean hands, and a pure heart;
who hath not lifted up his soul unto vanity, nor sworn deceitfully.

"Lord," he murmured. He looked up at the sky. The sky was perfectly, transparently blue, and nothing more. And then he realized that reaching out to embrace his destiny was the best way to soften its rigor. And he set off at a gallop.

The band stopped once in Terni and then again in Rieti, and they reached Castelnuovo on the eve of Purim.

Several hundred Jews had reached Castelnuovo before them. Included among them were prostitutes, merchants, and vivandieres. Soon a makeshift town was standing there, out on the plain near Castelnuovo, a little citadel hidden in the hollow of the mountains. David Reubeni was invited to stay with Marcello Cesarini, who prided himself on being a descendant of Caesar's. Now David was no more than a half-day's ride from Rome, but he couldn't go there immediately. It was important to celebrate the Feast of Purim, the anniversary of the time the Jews were saved from an extermination plot in the Persian Empire. Rabbi Schemuel, from Castelnuovo, had organized a great celebration, and David was eager to participate.

Chapter twelve

Arrival in Rome

The Messenger arrived in Rome on the sixteenth day of the month of Adar in the year 5284, after the creation of the world by He Who Is. According to the Christian calendar, it was February 20, 1524.

The day was crisp and clear. Gardens and fields were already beginning to show new growth in those first spring-like days. Not a single cloud hovered over the city's hills. Not a sound, except the haunting tolling of the bells. David Reubeni wasn't fooled: the bells were not ringing in his honor, but rather summoning the faithful to prayers. Would anyone come to meet him? Had the Jews in Rome been alerted?

The papal city lay spread out at his feet. Sant'Angelo Castle stood before him, an imposing cylindrical mass raising its crenellated towers to the sky, as did Saint Peter's Basilica, surrounded by immense scaffolding during its construction phase. On the other side of the river, the hillsides covered with houses, the city ramparts, and all the spires and domes sparkled in the ocher light.

The long-expected moment had come.

Rome and David Reubeni's destiny were waiting.

His horse balked, rearing up and whinnying. David pulled back on the reins to calm it, and then rode forward toward the Porta del Popolo, a huge dark gate topped with crenellations. The papal guard, dressed in purple, forbade entry to all those Jews who had accompanied David all the way from the Marche, and who had reached the gate before he did.

When they saw David and his escort, and especially when they noticed the famous white banner with its Hebrew letters fluttering in the wind, the crowds quietly moved aside, leaving the way into Rome free. The Messenger motioned Joseph forward. He seemed calm, as calm as he had been in Venice standing before the *Va'ad*. David Reubeni had worked long and hard to tame his natural tendency toward impatience, excitement, or anger. How great the effort had been, how many appeals to reason, how many secret struggles, and how much constant attention had been necessary before he could remain calm and restrained no matter what the situation! Joseph reined in his horse when he reached his master. Then, from his bag, he pulled out a ram's horn, the *shofar*, and blew a long blast. A strange sound, like the final notes of a dying trumpet, echoed out over the plain. The papal guard was duly impressed and stepped aside to let them pass. The gate was open, and beyond it the Envoy from Chabor could see a huge crowd that filled the entire Strada Onina.

He was concentrating so much, trying to understand what was happening inside the walls, that he didn't even notice a small group of men moving toward him.

"Welcome, Rabbi!"

The words were spoken with an obvious Italian accent. The unexpected sounds nearly took David by surprise. There before him stood a delegation of Roman Jews.

"They must be the Fattori," he thought, "the three leaders of the community who represent the eleven Roman congregations. But who can the others be?" He looked at them almost tenderly. His face radiated joy and interest, as if he had never been in such agreeable company, but also as if he had known them for a long time.

Everyone seemed surprised by the Messenger's reaction. Surprised and flattered. An almost imperceptible murmur rose from the milling crowd massed impatiently below. The delegation seemed to be waiting for some gesture or word from David. They were all dressed as typical Romans: padded hose, high-necked doublets from which the turned-down collars of their linen undergarments extended, and light slippers. Their clothing displayed an obvious Spanish influence. Seven men dressed in black and wearing yellow hats stood behind the three Fattori. One man was dressed differently. He was wearing a robe, similar to the long cloak that priests in the medieval church wore, or university professors, as David had seen in Salamanca. He was a tall man, much taller than his companions. His face was very pale, and his blue eyes expressed little curiosity. He was simply waiting patiently. So was the Envoy. But who can know the true duration of a second when you are waiting, a second filled with anguish? A life, or an eternity!

The city's church bells drew him abruptly from his thoughts. He broke into a smile. Encouraged by the smile, one of the three Fattori, an old man with a black beard and a large ruby on his finger, took a step toward David. But the Messenger paid no attention to the dignitary and spoke in Hebrew directly to the man dressed in the long cloak. And in his Hebrew words, one could hear the guttural accents of the desert.

"Please come closer, honorable Doctor Joseph Zarfatti!"

The delegates looked at one another in surprise. How did the stranger know the doctor's name? And how had he been able to recognize him? Since the doctor did not move, David Reubeni pushed his horse forward.

"I am pleased to meet you," he continued, "for you are the man who will suffer the most from my presence in Rome. But did not the Ecclesiast say: *The man who increases his knowledge also increases his pain?*"

The man raised his blue eyes in astonished admiration, and made a gesture of welcome. The Messenger, his voice solemn, continued speaking to the doctor:

"Because of your knowledge, you became doctor to the pope. He is the one to whom, I, David, the son of King Solomon and brother of King Joseph who reigns over the Jewish Kingdom of

Chabor, am bringing a message. I would like to ask you to be my intermediary, and with your permission, I will stay tonight in your home."

"But Rabbi!" the old man protested. "We had planned, for you and your escort…"

David set aside those considerations.

"But Rabbi!" the man went on. "We thought…Tell us what we can do for you."

Then the Envoy leaned toward the dignitary, and whispered, as if he were going to let him in on a secret:

"Tell the guards that these thousands of Jews who have been following me for days must not be allowed into the city."

Then, seeing the indignation in the old man's veiled eyes, he added, in a louder voice so that the man's companions could hear him:

"It is not I who can free the Jews, but rather the pope. That is why I have come from so far away, so that I can meet him. As for those people…"

He gestured toward the crowd waiting below.

"They are wild and impatient, crazed with waiting so long in their great love for Israel. But they fail to understand!"

Once again, he leaned down toward the old man.

"Master Obadiah da Sforno, you at least understand me, don't you?"

The old man's face brightened. The Messenger knew who he was, too! He, too, had been recognized! But, along with his escort, David Reubeni was already moving toward the center of the city.

The doctor's house was in the Sant'Angelo neighborhood, between the Marcellus Theater and the Tiber. There, among fishermen and rope makers, lived more than a thousand Jews, confined like Bohemians in narrow streets. The most well-to-do part of the Jewish community had settled elsewhere, on the right bank of the river in Trastevere.

Joseph Zarfatti had preferred remaining with ordinary people, for one could encourage them to follow principles of justice and reason without forcing them to understand why.

His house was the largest and the most beautiful in the neighborhood. The windows on the ground floor and the second story opened up onto an alley graced with grape arbors, but the windows of the third story, where the guest rooms and kitchen were located, looked out across red-tiled roofs onto the shimmering Tiber. That is where David was given a room. His servants were housed on the ground floor, in a room which opened out onto the courtyard. As for the Swiss guards, now that they had fulfilled their contract, they had gone on their way.

Rome was disappointing. David thought he would find a grand city like Alexandria or Venice, but what he found was a conglomeration of towns with magnificent palaces separated by fields, vineyards, or piles of garbage. His path had even been blocked by a herd of goats near the Sant'Angelo Bridge. And even the ancient city offered a desolate spectacle. People were selling swine or making yokes and two-wheeled carts. And on the Palatine, one could hear oxen bellowing.

The Roman Jews who had shown up in such great numbers at the Porta del Popolo silently accompanied David Reubeni all the way to the house to which he had invited himself. And they were not the only ones. According to Obadiah da Sforno, completely won over by the stranger, there were also many Christians in the crowd that followed David through the twisting, narrow streets. The old man was afraid, in fact, that among them there might be some followers of the monk from Wittenberg.

"Martin Luther and his friends are not seen in a good light here in Rome," he explained, his beard bobbing as he looked up at David Reubeni. "The German monk continues to defy the Church and to criticize the pope. Therefore…"

His Hebrew was melodious and pleasing to the ear of the man from the desert.

"Therefore," he repeated, "if Vatican spies, who are surely among the crowd, think there is a connection—may God preserve us!—between Luther and yourself, a rabbi, the brother of the Jewish King of Chabor, then…"

David realized that Obadiah da Sforno's reasoning was indeed quite relevant. However, he made no response. He was unable to. He did not have a right to his own opinion, but only to his own goals. David regretted that his silence might offend the old man. He felt responsible for all those Jews following him, and he was obliged, as in Venice, to hold back, to restrain his naturally open and generous tendencies and refrain from speaking.

He walked over to the window and stood for a long time, watching the boats on the river and the crowd on the bridge over to Trastevere. Suddenly, his eye was caught by a female figure making its way in his direction through the carts and the crowds. At that distance, he could not make out any of her facial features. But her dress, with its wide brown and red stripes, set off her svelte, graceful form to full advantage. The way she walked displayed her vitality and love for life, and for a moment David forgot his duty and his worries, smiling at the sight of a woman who could not see him and whom he would perhaps never meet.

Sounds of a short, violent skirmish, followed by the shouts of a street vendor, quickly brought him back to reality and his need to act. He was in Rome. Now he must see the pope.

Chapter thirteen

An Unexpected Encounter

The next day, after his morning prayer, David Reubeni once again felt the need to write in his journal. He took the sheets, already filled with his compact writing, from the ebony chest. Then he sat down at the edge of the small oval table opposite the bed, took the time to trim a goose quill with care and to lay out his inkwell, and then began to write, almost as if in anger.

"I, David, son of King Solomon whose equity is to be praised, have finally reached the gates of Rome, followed by an innumerable crowd of Jews. I arrived yesterday afternoon, that is on the 16th of Adar in the year 5284 after the creation of the world by the Eternal—blessed be His name!"

The pen scratching on the parchment helped him think more clearly. He was about to continue when a rustle of cloth in the corridor made him look up. His door had been left slightly ajar by the servant who had brought him water. He could see a female figure glide by gracefully, the spiral of a green dress, the silky flight of a black shawl. When he got to his feet to close the door, he was struck by the sweet perfume that the apparition had left in its wake. And then he found himself face to face with his host, Doctor Joseph Zarfatti, who was coming to inquire about his plans and wishes. He greeted the doctor and welcomed him into the room.

The doctor had on a long cape similar to the cloak he had been wearing the day before, except that it had a red hood and a clasp decorated with fringes. He was pale and calm, and his eyes were deep blue. Good will was written all over his face.

"May the Eternal, God of Israel, bless you," he said gently. "Will the year 5284 be a good year?"

David Reubeni was not expecting such a question.

"Yes, it will be," he replied, almost in a whisper. And then, speaking a little more loudly, he added: "It will be!"

Joseph Zarfatti walked over to the window and noticed the Messenger's ebony chest.

"Are you transporting books?"

He also saw the sheets spread out on the oval table, along with the inkwell and the quill.

"You are writing?"

David's eyes had followed the doctor's. Energetically, with three sweeping movements, he picked up the papers, quill and inkwell, put them back in the chest, and closed the lid with its squeaky hinges. The room was once again as clean and orderly as if no one had spent the night there. The Messenger leaned against one of the columns rising up from the canopy bed. The impeccable bed clothes gave silent witness to how David had spent the night. He had meditated in the middle of the room and had never lain down on the bed. Finally, he answered the doctor's questions about books and writing.

"No," he said simply.

After David had gone to such effort to put away his material, his simple answer brought a smile to Joseph Zarfatti's face. He sat down on a stool made from exotic wood, not far from the bed, and asked:

"For today, what plans does the brother of the King of Chabor have?"

"To see the pope."

The doctor was surprised and studied the Messenger's face. David seemed disengaged and stared out the window. The cold winter sun caused tile roofs nearby to glitter. Clouds of pigeons took flight. "The days of man are more rapid than the weaver's shuttle," he murmured, before turning back toward Joseph Zarfatti.

"For my mission to be successful, it is essential for me to see the pope as soon as possible," he said gently but firmly.

And then his gentleness evaporated, and the sentences poured out feverishly.

"You must, you must arrange a meeting for me! As quickly as you can! Today, if possible! You can do it. I know you can."

Joseph Zarfatti raised his arms heavenward when he saw David's excitement. His natural impulsivity had won out over his deference and reserve.

"I am the pope's doctor, it is true. But he summons me only when he is sick, that is all! Or when he wants to discuss the Kabbalah! Is the meeting you want so urgent?"

"Do you think it's not?"

David Reubeni had unwound his turban. Like agile little ash-colored serpents, his silvery curls hung down over his forehead. In his eyes glowed great resolve.

Joseph Zarfatti got to his feet. Though taller than the Messenger, he appeared more frail.

"The pope does listen to me," he admitted. "But he will do nothing unless the Fattori approve. They are the institution that represents our community. And institutions always respect other institutions."

The doctor smiled awkwardly, with the distressed look of someone who asks for forgiveness in advance for something unpleasant he will have to say. He did not enjoy being the bearer of bad news.

"The Fattori are not on your side," he continued. "Why not? Because two days ago a messenger from Giacobo Mantino, the president of the *Va'ad* in Venice—you know him, don't you?—brought the Fattori an account of your stay in the City of the Doges. It was a very critical account, and not at all flattering to you personally, as you might imagine. In his letter, Giacobo Mantino tells the Fattori to be on their guard, warning them about anti-Semitic reactions that your activities might set off."

Before continuing, Joseph Zarfatti cleared his throat in embarrassment and gave a little cough.

"You must understand. Here in Rome, Jews enjoy great respect and security."

David Reubeni cut in:

"For the moment!"

"That is true," the doctor admitted. "In the past there have been difficult periods. We must accept that. When Gregory ix had the Talmud burned in Rome, or when Boniface viii…"

David interrupted him again.

"Exactly! I want to protect Jews from just such things! I would like to see them happy and free! Do you understand?"

And he repeated forcefully:

"Free!"

Joseph Zarfatti once again raised his arms heavenward.

"Only the Eternal is free!" he exclaimed.

And then, changing his tone, he said: "Here in Rome, we Jews are not slaves, you know."

A gust of wind filled out the curtains. Joseph Zarfatti gave a start, and with a kind gesture, he took a step closer to the Messenger.

"That being said, I did defend you. I supported your plan. The Fattori are quite confused. They are not sure what to think. At first they believed Giacobo Mantino. He is a famous doctor, and everyone respects him. On the basis of his letter, they at first believed that you were one of those wild-eyed mystics, perhaps an imposter, a charlatan, or a swindler. In short, just another one of those false prophets that sometimes appear in our markets and public squares. And then, you arrived. And they discovered a skilled politician with a sense of responsibility, a leader. Instead of riding into the city at the head of an immense crowd, something that would have greatly impressed the Gentiles—though in the worst way—you discreetly asked the papal guard to keep those thousands of Jews, who had followed you all the way from the Marche, from entering Rome."

The doctor was silent for a moment, almost overcome with emotion.

"The Fattori were relieved and delighted," he went on. "But I, myself, was hurt. All those poor people who believed, who still perhaps believe that…"

David walked over to him. His leg brushed against the doctor's leg. He laid his hand on the doctor's arm. One would have thought they were two brothers or two friends in deep conversation.

"At that moment, what did you think of me?"

Joseph Zarfatti shrugged his shoulders.

"What I thought is not important," he said.

"It is very important to me!"

"If you insist. I thought that you were acting like a politician, not as an ethical being."

David Reubeni took a few steps backward and leaned once more against one of the baldaquin bed's twisted columns. The conversation between the two men was taking on the character of a ballet written by Ariosto, the sharpest pen in Italy. Ariosto particularly loved to see two dancers mimic each other to the sound of a flute.

"Well then, why do you support my project?"

"Because it is just and because it comes at an opportune time!" the doctor replied, looking the Messenger in the eyes.

David was about to reply when they heard a light feminine step just outside the room. Joseph Zarfatti walked over to the door.

"That must be my sister, Dina," he explained, and once again, as the young woman passed, they could hear cloth rustling in the corridor.

Joseph noticed the turmoil in the Messenger's face.

"Dina has a passion for books. She reads constantly, especially the Kabbalah. She even reads Cicero, in spite of his anti-Semitic diatribes."

But David was barely listening. He was thinking about the young woman. This time he had caught a glimpse of her. She was the one, he was certain. He would have recognized her anywhere. She was the one crossing the Trastevere bridge while he was observing the activity in the street from the window of this very room.

A woman in his life. That was the last thing he needed!

"Does the Kingdom of Chabor truly exist?" Joseph Zarfatti asked with real affection in his voice.

David answered firmly.

"Yes!"

"In that case," the doctor said, "we need to try to convince Cardinal Egidio di Viterbo, the pope's closest advisor."

David Reubeni ran his long fingers through his unruly hair and murmured:

"I have a letter of introduction for Cardinal di Viterbo. From Vincentius Castellani, the man who creates books in Fossombrone."

Joseph Zarfatti raised his arms and exclaimed:

"Why did you not say so right away? The cardinal highly esteems the old scholar Castellani!"

He started toward the door.

"I'll send a servant immediately to alert the cardinal. We'll go see him this very afternoon in Sant'Angelo Castle!"

Chapter fourteen

The Cardinal

On the Sant'Angelo Bridge, there were no stalls, shops, nor dwellings as there had been on the Rialto in Venice. It was a solid, wide bridge with a covered colonnade to protect it from the rain, and it led over to Borgo de San Pietro, closing it off and isolating it from the rest of the city. Four large square towers stood high over the ramparts of Sant'Angelo, that is, over Hadrian's old mausoleum, frequently renovated and modified. Sant'Angelo Castle's imposing mass, the symbol of the pope's secular power, dominated the river.

David Reubeni was on his horse, accompanied by Joseph Zarfatti and his servants, all dressed in that unusual white linen tunic marked in its center with a Star of David. When they reached the area around the bridge, the esplanade that separated the river from the castle was already filled with an enthusiastic crowd. Among the crowd were Jews from Rome and some from the Marche, who had managed somehow to escape the vigilance of the guards and slip into the city. Some had been waiting for hours, ever since the rumor had started that there was to be a meeting between the Messenger and Cardinal di Viterbo. Everyone was eager to witness such an unthinkable event.

The brother of a Jewish king, leading an armed contingent, was going to be received into Vatican City!

Cardinal Egidio di Viterbo led David Reubeni into his library, one of the most prestigious libraries in Rome. Although his face was pale and he was of only average height, the cardinal was an imposing figure. He was about sixty years old. His corpulence, his full face dominated by a wide, high forehead, his dark, penetrating eyes, and indeed everything about him radiated the benevolent power of a lion. But there was nothing more refined, more civilized, or more disconcerting than the man who, when David arrived, stepped forward to meet him, saying in perfect Hebrew: "Welcome to Rome!" And who then burst out laughing.

The cardinal's good humor was contagious. Two men standing beside him, clearly Jews, also broke into laughter, followed by David's servants and then David himself.

"The situation is indeed amusing, is it not?" Egidio di Viterbo explained as if to justify himself. "The Messenger of a Jewish kingdom greeted in the language of the Bible at the very heart of Christendom!"

The cardinal loved paradoxes and situations that offered some humor. But the real reason for his good humor was this secret reversal of roles. Seeing the Messenger and his followers, all armed with swords and looking very much like a delegation of French or Spanish nobles, he himself felt Jewish, like one of those "archivists of memory," about which Saint Augustine spoke.

Had David Reubeni been able to read his thoughts? After nodding a greeting to the prelate, he said:

"The cardinal certainly is not used to receiving Jews like us. But in the country we come from, Jews are armed..."

And then, after a brief pause, he added:

"In the country we come from, there are no ghettos."

Joseph Zarfatti, standing beside David, held his breath. The cardinal's two advisors looked nervously at each other. As for the cardinal, he let his smile disappear before noting:

"Nor are there ghettos here in Rome."

And then he invited David and Doctor Joseph Zarfatti to sit down on a bench covered with a brocade that was lined with sable and hemmed with gold fringes.

The room was lavishly decorated. Precious carpets were spread out on the floor, a magnificent historical tapestry covered the wall behind the cardinal's seat, and near the other walls stood credenzas on which books were piled all the way to the ceiling. Once the prelate was seated in his armchair with its velvet upholstery, he immediately began to speak to his guests.

"Why was the land given to Israel already occupied by depraved people? Why was Israel not given an uninhabited land? Would not that have prevented so many divergent claims?"

David Reubeni smiled, and with his pebbly voice, he replied without delay.

"King David himself said: *He gave them the land of depraved people so that they might fulfill His laws.*"

"Well put," murmured one of the cardinal's close advisors. He and his companion were still standing on either side of the prelate.

The man from the desert gave a start. From the two words he had just heard, he surmised that the man speaking was the venerable Rabbi Barukh Askenazi, the cardinal's Kabbalah teacher.

"Is that why you would like to take back the land of Israel?" Egidio di Viterbo asked, his dark eyes staring intensely.

"No. Not for that reason alone."

"I believe I understand your plans," the cardinal continued. "Doctor Zarfatti, your friend, told me that…"

"That I am the bearer of a letter addressed to His Excellence by Vincentius Castellani," the Messenger cut in, holding out the missive to the cardinal.

A servant rushed up like a shadow, took the folded paper from David's hands, and handed it to the cardinal. Egidio di Viterbo, after removing the wax seal, unfolded the paper and read it carefully. Then, laying the letter down on the little table beside his chair, he looked the man from the desert in the eyes, spread his arms, and exclaimed once again in Hebrew:

"Our welcome then to David! Welcome to David, brother of King Joseph of Chabor! Welcome to David, son of Solomon!"

The Messenger nodded his turbaned head three times in thanks, and then, in a firm voice he excitedly presented his plan: The return of the Jews to the land of their ancestors had to be guaranteed by creating a Jewish kingdom in Israel with the help of the pope and the Christian kings. A Judeo-Christian alliance of that kind would be able to contain the expansion of Islam on both shores of the Mediterranean.

"And how about Jerusalem?" the cardinal asked, his dark eyes narrowing.

"Jerusalem will be the capital of the Kingdom of Israel, of course. And it is also obvious that the Holy Places, and in particular Jesus' tomb, will have to be placed under the authority of the sovereign pontiff—much like a second Vatican City."

Egidio di Viterbo nodded his agreement.

"Do you have a letter expressing those details? A letter from your brother, King Joseph of Chabor, for His Holiness the pope?"

"Indeed."

The cardinal's eyes swept over the rows of books that climbed all the way to the ceiling. He had a smile on his face.

"*Before building the tower, one must calculate the cost,*" he murmured.

"I am ready to discuss the matter with His Holiness," the Messenger said. "But allow me to not agree completely with the sentence from the Gospels you have just quoted. It is too much like a thought from the Talmud, which says: *Stretch your feet out according to the length of the blanket.* However, if we were to think about such things constantly, we would never sleep…"

Rabbi Barukh Askenazi could not keep from applauding. As for the cardinal, his eyes were sparkling with delight. He would gladly see this David Reubeni again. He made no attempt to restrain his natural love of speaking.

"You have won us over, Prince," he said, getting nimbly to his feet with surprising ease in spite of his weight. "You have a good plan. Now all you need to do is convince the pope. I shall try to help you."

Chapter fifteen

Rendezvous with a Fever

Back from Sant'Angelo Castle, the Messenger was prey to a deep foreboding. Neither the success of his meeting with Cardinal di Viterbo, nor Joseph Zarfatti's compliments, nor the hurrahs from the crowd could dissipate the feeling that was overcoming him as he neared the goal, making him fear the worst. He knew from experience that what we fear is more likely to happen than what we hope for. He was grateful when the doctor, guessing perhaps how worried he was, reminded him that the cardinal had promised to let them know the following day when his audience with the pope would take place.

The way back to Joseph Zarfatti's house seemed long to David. A heavy weight of fatigue had taken him by the shoulders, and he had to make a real effort at times not to simply collapse onto his horse's neck and its long white mane. He no longer even noticed the applause, the shouts of joy, and the blessings that accompanied them. In his mind, a burning imagination was making one last effort to give him access to that secret music the world was trying to discover and that was almost impossible to hear: the music of peace.

Joseph Halevy, David's servant, pulled his own horse up closer to David's.

"Along the way we don't only have friends," he whispered.

David quickly came back down to earth. He looked over toward where Joseph had pointed with his chin. Following them were armed horsemen wearing black capes. They were riding up from the river, pushing their way roughly through the crowds.

The man from the desert brought up the incident with the armed horsemen that same evening with the doctor. The doctor once again flung his long arms heavenward, exclaiming:

"Has not Rome always been the prey of factions? Periodically, there are internecine wars opposing the Colonnas and the Orsinis, the Borgias and the Medecis. A man like you, a courier from a Jewish kingdom, welcomed to Sant'Angelo Castle by one of the pope's most trusted advisors, who is himself from the Medici family. Do you see what I mean? And when I add to that picture that you are a man proposing war against the Ishmaelites…"

Then, after a short silence, Joseph Zarfatti sighed.

"You are making people uneasy, aren't you? In fact, many people have reason to mistrust you, and even more, to wish you ill."

"Including the Jews," added Joseph Halevy, who was respectfully standing at some distance near the door.

The doctor turned toward him.

"The Jews?"

"Some of them, in any case," the Messenger's servant continued. "I have heard that the honorable Giacobo Mantino has arrived unannounced in Rome."

Joseph Zarfatti seemed surprised by the news.

"Strange," he said. "That is contrary to general practice. He alerted no one that he was coming."

His blue eyes turned toward David. Once again he raised his eloquent hands above his head and in his indignant voice, deep and raspy, he said:

"I know that there is no love lost between the president of the *Va'ad* and you. But to think that he might make an attempt on your life! One Jew threatening another! There is no way that I can believe that! However, I shall go immediately to see if the Fattori can send us a few trustworthy men to reinforce your guard."

Once the doctor had left, David Reubeni loosened his turban, allowing his unruly silvery hair to cascade down over his ears and forehead. He turned to his servant.

"Tell me, Joseph. Where did you hear that Giacobo Mantino is now in Rome?"

"Tobias, Master."

"Tobias?"

"Yes. I have had him followed ever since we reached Rome."

"By whom?"

"By Francesco, a young Christian I met while he was begging along the Ripetta road."

"What did he tell you?"

"That this very morning, in an inn located between the Arch of Constantine and the Lata road, Tobias talked for a long time with a man whose description corresponds without a shadow of a doubt to Giacobo Mantino."

"Was he able to listen to their conversation?"

"No. He was unable to get close enough. He would have been noticed."

"Why did you not speak to me earlier about this?"

"I didn't want to worry you, Master. Your mission is to think about the Jewish people. And my duty is to watch over you."

The Messenger's eyes grew more forgiving.

"May the Eternal—blessed be His name—protect you."

The evening was lively at Doctor Zarfatti's house, once he returned from talking with the Fattori. Rabbi Barukh Askenazi dropped in to say how much Cardinal di Viterbo had been impressed by the Messenger. He had scarcely left when Samuel ben Nathan appeared. He was the president of the small Jewish community in Ostia, an affable man and generally aware of what people were saying in the Christian community. And then, unexpectedly, Rabbi Obadiah da Sforno with his little black goatee showed up, accompanied by three other Fattori.

They had spoken only briefly with Joseph Zarfatti earlier when he had come to ask for added security for the Messenger, and they were eager to learn the tenor of the conversation between David and the pope's advisor. At this point, were not the activities of this man from the desert the business of the entire community?

The doctor, after obligingly answering some of their questions, thought he should go inform David, who was resting in his room, that the delegation had arrived. He said that it would be desirable for the Messenger to spend some time talking with Obadiah da Sforno and the three other Fattori. David was still overcome by the great fatigue that had befallen him as he was leaving Sant'Angelo, and he was not enthusiastic about the prospect of seeing the Fattori. As was the case in Venice, he had not come to Rome to justify himself before a few Jewish dignitaries. He was acting first of all on behalf of those thousands of homeless people, those people without a country, who were waiting for him outside the city gates. Yet their destiny depended above all on the good will of the masters of the Christian West. Joseph had to beg him several times, because David was beginning to feel feverish, and his head, arms, and legs felt heavy. Was it the same fever that always seemed to strike when the time for action drew near? Or was it a fever that resembles worry and that always, according to the Ecclesiast, speeds up the aging process? The Messenger forced himself to agree to go talk to them. Joseph Zarfatti was right: It would have been unacceptable for David to turn the only institution recognized by the pope against him. So he followed the doctor out into the large living room on the ground floor, brightly lit with its ten oil lanterns.

The discussion with the Fattori took place in an atmosphere of mutual respect. The dignitaries asked David all kinds of questions, and he responded with great rigor and concision. The Messenger was completely exhausted, but he decided to listen, to listen very attentively to what the Fattori had to say, what they thought about the events, and what value they placed on them. The quality of his own comments was greatly appreciated by his interlocutors, and soon it was clear to them that the Messenger was nothing at all like the sinister portrait Giacobo Mantino had drawn of him. During their exchange, one man among them, the old rabbi, stood out in his verve and his intellectual curiosity.

The rabbi was a short man, wrinkled and sinewy like an old grapevine, and he was hardly visible beneath his long black coat. His profile was like that of a bird of prey with black piercing eyes. Though he was more than seventy years old, his goatee was still black, and it bobbed as he spoke, as if to emphasize his points. Rabbi Obadiah da Sforno also spoke with his hands, and as he did, the enormous ruby on his right hand sparkled, conferring on his words a majestic aura. He was not at all boastful, and was pleasant to be around, and he had a true gift for various facial expressions and comic contortions as he spoke. Loquacious and lively, he asked his questions and gave his answers with the agility of an ever alert mind. It was he who suddenly changed the subject, just as David had already said goodbye and was about to take his leave.

"Tell me, honorable Prince of the Jews, do you not fear offending the Lord?"

The Messenger turned back toward the old rabbi and looked at him with his steely eyes. The old man went on:

"You see, and don't take this incorrectly, many rabbis around the world are unable to look with a favorable eye upon an operation like yours. In their eyes, any political action taken with the intention of establishing a Jewish kingdom in the land of Israel could only be risky, even blameworthy. Only the Eternal—blessed be His name!—can, when the moment is right, take the Jewish people back to the land of their ancestors. Proceeding otherwise, trying to force His hand by forcing time, is that not defying God?"

David listened patiently to the old man, who now, rocking back and forth from one leg to another, was unstoppable.

"I can hear you from within, O reckless David! Allow me this familiarity, but you are still young, and this is something I know about. When you hear arguments like these, you restrain yourself, you remain impassible as is appropriate for the just—but inside you are boiling with rage, are you not? You rebel each time anyone proposes, rather than an individual action like your own, the idea of a collective destiny that lies beyond the will of mankind! Of course, to you the Eternal seems present at every moment of a man's life, even in His most unimportant choices. But I can see that you are convinced that He has long since ceased getting involved in those diatribes, quarrels, and conflicts that set kings and priests against each other. And you would be able to find support, to bolster your point of view, from the fact that after freeing the Jews from slavery, the Eternal—blessed be His name!—in His infinite wisdom, separated religion from politics. You could also say that in fact, whereas Moses was the one planning the conquest of Canaan, Aaron was placed in charge of being vigilant about the Law."

While the old man went on tirelessly, David, who understood and accepted the rabbi's intentions, met Dina's eyes across the room. She was sitting in the back of the room with a smile on her face, hanging on every word. To David her smile seemed mocking. It was both tender and provocative. Was she expecting something from him? He would have dearly loved to be able to ask her. Her smile made him think that she was watching his every move. Was the fever pounding in his temples nothing more than his great fatigue? Was the little dimple at the corner of the young woman's mouth a sign of more inner turmoil to come? Suddenly, he felt like surprising her, attracting her attention to him. The guttural sounds of his voice became melodious and spellbinding, like those of a desert storyteller. His voice was really directed toward Dina as he answered the old rabbi.

"A day without a night, a night without a day, neither deserves being called One," he began. "It is the same with the Eternal and the people of Israel. As long as the children of Israel suffer in exile, the One who Is cannot be truly called One. He will only be able to called One when His people are back on the land that He has given them!"

The Messenger's eyes were fixed on the old rabbi, but then they looked out across the people in the room and came to rest on Dina. After a short pause, he continued.

"How could returning to our homeland offend the Creator?"

A long silence followed, punctuated by the sound of the wicks sputtering in the oil lamps. David, his eyes burning with fever, turned and spoke directly to the Fattori.

"Who," he asked, "can redeem the sins of men if not men themselves? Who can re-establish Unity if not men? Who will save the world and God Himself, if not men?"

In spite of the throbbing pain in his neck, he smiled.

"And what I am saying is neither unseemly pretension nor sacrilegious pride. As it is written in the Kabbalah, the will of man is powerless against the will of God. But when it is acting according to the wishes of the Eternal, it has power over Everything!"

The Fattori were impressed but remained silent. Once again, however, old Obadiah da Sforno, his hand sparkling with the magnificent ruby that seemed to be calling on heaven to be his witness, had something to say.

"Your words blossom like an echo of the Talmud, my son! You are the Messenger we need to convert the pusillanimous. You must realize that I was only presenting the doubts that are shared by some in order to test your resolve, to determine the strength of your convictions. Allow me to express all my gratitude and that of my friends."

On the other side of the room, Dina still retained a little smile on her face. David's head was buzzing, but he thought he could read admiration in her smile. The lamp flames were dancing along with her smile, and the young woman's eyes seemed to be the source of each light. The man from the desert staggered. Joseph, his attentive servant, hurried over to help him. Doctor Zarfatti also went over to lend a hand.

"Thank you," David murmured weakly, his words directed to Obadiah da Sforno, whose unexpected fatherly familiarity had moved him almost beyond words. And then, his voice breaking, he added:

"Please excuse me, honorable representatives of the Jewish community in Rome, but it has been a long day and I must..."

He had to pause, wracked with spasms.

"I must take leave of you," he managed to whisper.

To climb the stairs leading to his room, he needed help from Joseph and the doctor, and they were pleased to provide it. Exhausted, he collapsed onto his bed and drifted off into sleep.

Chapter sixteen

Fortune and a Fall

During the night, the Envoy knew that he had dreamed, but no memory of his dream remained. All that he could recall was a laugh, a long laugh echoing through an endless corridor in which David Reubeni himself was walking, and the corridor had no exit. The more he searched, the more impossible it became to find a way out through the incessant crystalline laugh. In the darkness of his room, he tried several times to get up. In vain. An incomprehensible force prevented him from moving the slightest muscle. Was he also dreaming that he was awake? Finally, he managed to lift one hand to his forehead, and it was burning. He touched his neck. It was dripping with sweat, and with the tips of his fingers he could feel strange little painful swellings. He decided to light a lamp and leaned over toward the bed stand. But he was so weak that nausea washed over him, and he lost consciousness. His body rolled off the bed and fell to the carpet.

When morning came, a servant appeared with a tray and knocked at the door. But the Messenger didn't open the door as he usually did. In surprise, the servant went to tell Joseph Zarfatti. It was also a surprise to Zarfatti that David was still in bed, for he knew how little David normally slept. But he didn't want to break down his guest's door, thinking that he was perhaps in prayer. As for Joseph Halevy and the other servants of the man from the desert, Raphael, Tobias, and Joab, they were in the kitchen, waiting for the master to give them information regarding his plans for the next few days. They were beginning to feel impatient when the news came: His Holiness Pope Clement VII was inviting David Reubeni, prince of the Jewish Kingdom of Chabor, to come to see him that very afternoon in the Vatican! Cardinal di Viterbo had just sent a special envoy to bring the message personally to Doctor Zarfatti! An event like that needed to be brought to David's attention immediately, and the doctor, carrying the important missive, hurried to David's room, followed by Joseph and the other servants. He knocked at the door, but it didn't open. He knocked more loudly and called out. Nothing but silence. Anxiously, Joseph tried the doorknob. When he walked into the room's cold shadows, the smell of vomit almost gagged him. He drew back the heavy velvet drapes and threw the windows open wide. Then he saw his master's body. With the help of the other servants, he lifted David up and put him back in his bed. With concern on his face, he turned to the doctor. The doctor came to the bed and took the Messenger's pulse. David's breathing was shallow. The doctor raised the sick man's eyelid and then carefully examined his hands and his neck. That's when he discovered the small dark abscesses behind David's right ear. Doctor Zarfatti's expression grew serious. The immense weight of responsibility overwhelmed him. His voice was sharp as he spoke quickly:

"Bring some spirits, lots of spirits, and be quick about it!"

One of the servants standing at the door ran off. The doctor called to one of the others.

"Is the best fireplace we have the one in my sister's bedroom?" he asked.

"The best...fireplace, Master? Yes, it's the one in Miss Dina's bedroom."

"Well then, go ask my sister to move her things out and find a different room. Change the sheets and light a hot fire in the fireplace. Quickly!"

But Dina had already appeared, alarmed by the noise and people running back and forth through the house.

"What is happening?" she asked worriedly when she saw the consternation on everyone's faces.

Her brother chased away a fly that was crawling on David's forehead, and then he got to his feet with a sigh.

"The Eternal alone knows."

When he saw Dina walking over to the sick man's bed, he grabbed her arm.

"Don't come in. Don't touch anything! And may God protect us!"

"What is it exactly?" asked Dina in fear.

"We shall take our guest to your bedroom. I have already given orders. David needs to be kept warm, very warm. I have asked to have a fire lit in the big fireplace. Can you go see that things are taken care of as quickly as possible?"

"But, tell me. Do you know what he is suffering from?

"The worst thing possible."

The alcohol he had requested appeared. A full demijohn. Joseph Zarfatti ordered everyone to splash it on their hands. Then he poured some into a basin and lit it. He put his hands in the dancing blue flames. Then he extinguished the fire and asked everyone who had touched David to cleanse their hands in the same manner.

David was carried to the young woman's bedroom. At the doctor's orders, they removed his clothes and burned them in the fireplace, and then they rubbed his body for a long time. Finally, they covered him with thick blankets.

After some time, and for the first time since that morning, David began to move. His eyelids flickered. His breathing grew less labored. But he still remained unconscious.

"Let us pray," said Doctor Zarfatti.

Prayer shawls were brought in, one for each person. Now protected as if by spiritual shields against the assaults of evil, they gravely began to pray.

Look, O My God, and answer me, O Eternal!
Give light to my eyes
So that I do not drift into the sleep of death...

Chapter seventeen

At the Trou Tavern

O f her own accord, Dina offered to replace her brother at the sick man's bedside. The doctor was then able to carry the news of David's condition to Cardinal di Viterbo, requesting that he be so kind as to take David's excuses to His Holiness the pope. It was clear, alas, that David Reubeni would not meet Clement VII that afternoon. And no one knew, not even the good Doctor Zarfatti, if he would make it through the terrible test that had smitten him.

The rumor quickly spread through the city and beyond its ramparts. The immense majority of the Jews in Italy were in great consternation. They had all been hoping and longing for that unbelievable meeting between the Messenger from a Jewish kingdom and the head of Christendom. For them, such a meeting would have been an unprecedented sign, as if the world, through the audience that Clement VII granted to David Reubeni, would restore their dignity to the Jewish people who had been persecuted for centuries. Alas! Now that sign was disappearing into the realm of the improbable, and the Messiah was perhaps on his death bed. Cruel was fate, and cruel was hope. In the eyes of most people, the Envoy's illness appeared to be the final test before they could be liberated from exile, a painful foreshadowing of victory, like the dawn of their return to Israel. For others, on the other hand, it was more like punishment for overweening pride. And the ways of the Eternal—blessed be His name!—remained impenetrable.

When Moses de Castellazzo heard the bad news, he decided to leave Venice that very day. He wanted to be by the side of his friend David Reubeni, and he lost no time reaching Rome. The old banker Mechulam del Banco would have liked to go along with him, but the state of his health made it impossible. After traveling three days and three nights and taking two different coaches, the first to Ravenna, where the artist spent the Sabbath, and then to Perugia, finally he arrived in Rome. He took lodging at the Trou Tavern. They readily rented rooms to artists, and he had stayed there several times in the past. It was located just across from one of Michelangelo's studios, and Moses never failed to pay Michelangelo a visit whenever he was in Rome.

Three days before, also in Rome, Giacobo Mantino had held a secret meeting with an old friend, Dom Miguel da Silva, the Portuguese ambassador to the Holy See. The famous doctor, president of the *Va'ad Hakatan* in Venice and the prestigious translator of Averroes, was completely preoccupied with the David Reubeni business. When he agreed to meet David in Venice, he had never expected that the "imposter," as he liked to call the Envoy of Chabor, would ever be able to reach the Vatican. And now the adventurer had received the unconditional support of Cardinal di Viterbo, advisor to His Holiness. And he also enjoyed the support of Cardinal Pucci, the spokesman for the pope, who in Mantino's mind was too greatly influenced by the Kabbalah. And now, in addition, he was going to be received by the sovereign pontiff himself! For Clement VII to meet the imposter, that was just too much! In the eyes of Giacobo Mantino, such a meeting was simply beyond belief. A wind of irresponsible dreaming must be blowing over the Vatican! Was it possible, was it even conceivable to allow the imposter's worrisome act of charm to produce its effect and fail to stand in the way of the madness? Should not a Jew try to prevent another Jew from dragging their people into calamity by inducing them to follow a mirage? Should he not take into account the inevitable repression that would surely strike the community once the mists dissipated from around an adventure condemned to failure? In such a situation, was it not the duty of any clear-thinking man to put a stop to the dubious rise of this man David? To halt the trajectory of this swindler, this false prophet?

Giacobo Mantino sincerely believed that it would be impossible to retake the land of Israel by a military victory over one of the world's greatest powers, the Ottoman Empire. Nor did he believe that European sovereigns would necessarily agree to support an enterprise of that kind, because he knew they were too preoccupied with their own internecine quarrels on European soil. On the other hand, the effervescence rising out of the imposter's plans appeared to be an early sign of great peril to come. He could already imagine how kings and bishops would begin to lose trust in their Jewish subjects, and they might even begin to doubt their loyalty. They could suspect that Jews wanted to leave the country just when they were finally being accepted by the majority of citizens. In sum, Jewish subjects would be considered capable of betrayal. As for Giacobo Mantino, he felt his mission was to save the Jews from the temptation, even if they did not want to be saved. Yes, he would be able to put a quick stop to the folly of this imposter from Chabor before it was too late! Although many Jews and even some Christians (and not the least among them!) had already lost their heads, his own head was still resting solidly on his shoulders and firm in its logic.

When he met up with his old friend Da Silva in a corner of the Trou Tavern, he explained all that to him, tearing apart the imposter's plans. His voice was quiet but resolute as the two friends talked in the shadows, emptying a decanter of dark Chianti.

Dom Miguel da Silva was a tall balding man with graying hair. He appeared to be older than his fifty-five years. Da Silva's aristocratic bearing, his cunning manner, and the proud way he held his head did not keep the diplomat from being accepted in many different levels of society, in which he seemed as much at ease as if he had always lived there. For the moment, his sharp-featured face emerged out of a white lace jabot, which itself extended above a navy blue coat that hung down to his ankles. He was considering the problem Giacobo Mantino laid out for him almost from an aesthetic point of view. As he spoke, he kept tapping a long ivory-handled knife against the edge of the decanter of Chianti, and his eyes seemed to rove from the wooden designs on the table to the carvings on the ceiling beams. When on rare occasions his green eyes bore directly into those of his interlocutor, Mantino would nearly give a start. Everything in those strange irises and tiny pupils seemed to express pure innocence. The diplomatic corps in the Vatican and in Rome recognized Dom Miguel's many qualities, and though apparent innocence may have been among them, no one considered him naïve.

"Please understand me, my dear Giacobo," said the ambassador. "I have my own reasons to worry. Imposter or not, from my point of view there is little difference. What I fear comes from elsewhere. I know my master, the King of Portugal. Joao III would like to please the man he admires above all others, the pope. So, if the pope succumbs to the charm of this schemer from nowhere, the odds are good that he will ask Portugal to develop the navy that would be necessary for the conquest of Israel. And Joao III will accept! That is what bothers me, for I love and support my king. I support him as best I can, in particular against the growing power of the queen and her friends who are close to the Spanish Inquisition. They are fervently plotting to establish an Inquisition in Portugal as well. They all, and especially the queen, are waiting for the king to make a false step so they can usurp more of his power. Any support Joao III offers to this reckless adventurer would certainly provide them with a new weapon against him, perhaps even the possibility of removing him from power completely. Such an outcome would sorrow me greatly. To say nothing of the fact, indeed much less important, that I myself would lose my position as ambassador to the Holy See. Of course, we may still find a way to influence the king. I am thinking specifically of Diego Pires, his friend and advisor. He is a brilliant young man, and well-educated. He is the same age as Joao III, twenty-four years old. Aside from his friendship with the king, he is also the secretary of the Royal Council. If I manage to convince the young man, as I hope I can, it will advance our cause. In short, my dear Giacobo, I cannot fully understand what your grievances are against this David, and my reasons to oppose him are not the same as yours. But I am pleased to find in you not only the same friend as always, but also a Jew who can assure me that other Jews like you do not intend to let themselves be fooled by this troublemaker from the desert who is trying to lead the world astray! We shall unite our efforts and finally silence him, my good man! We'll clip the wings of that bird of discord, or as you say, that prophet of doom!"

"Miguel!" said Giacobo Mantino, with a bigger smile than usual and a knowing look, "I expected nothing less from you!"

And he raised his glass:

"To our success!" he said. "And to the imposter's defeat!"

"To our success!" Dom Miguel da Silva replied.

They clinked their glasses together.

They would have celebrated with more assurance if they had known the situation their enemy was in. They had no idea that the Messenger, at that very moment, was wrestling with death.

Chapter eighteen

The Unspeakable Word

For several days, first thing in the morning, a huge crowd had been gathering in the street just outside Joseph Zarfatti's house. The news of David Reubeni's condition attracted sad throngs, pondering fate's cruelty and dressed in a variety of colors. The Messenger's illness was of concern to not only the Jewish community, but also to many Christians. Many of the people who gathered daily wept and prayed as if they were at a funeral. It seemed to them that they were watching their hopes die. Others were lamenting their future. Some of them were truly in despair. Two asthmatics with shrill voices were chanting the interminable lists of their mistakes and sins that morning, beseeching the Eternal to absolve them since His Envoy himself was going to perish. One crazy young woman had torn her clothes off and danced naked on the frozen puddles, monotonously chanting words no one could understand. Another poor fellow in the depths of despair was beating his head rhythmically against one of the corner houses. An old one-eyed man had cut off his hand there in the street and was walking about dripping blood on the paving stones. Among the motley crowd there were also worrisome people lurking. With sardonic expressions on their faces, they seemed to be enjoying the situation. They would take the risk from time to time to explain things to the others, to the ignorant ones. They kept saying that the man in Doctor Zarfatti's house could clearly not be considered the Messiah any longer because he was dying from some ordinary disease like any other man. Does a Messiah get sick? Can a Messiah succumb to a fever?

When Moses de Castellazzo arrived from the Trou Tavern, he immediately ran into those venomous smiles and those birds of ill omen. He had come as quickly as he could. His stockings were splattered with mud, and he was sweaty and panting. Seeing such unsavory individuals, he was reminded that a tower can be measured according to its shadow and that a man of worth can be measured by the number of people who envy him. He had to fight to make his way through the fray. The closer he got to the doctor's house, the denser the crowd became. Soon, still several steps from the threshold, he could go no further. In spite of the big redhead's size, the Venetian artist was helpless against that last barrier composed of fervor, aberration, and perfidy that stood between him and David Reubeni. Neither force nor persuasion could open a breech.

"The Messiah is dying!" someone shouted.

"What from? What is his illness?" a small husky voice asked.

The old woman asking was trying desperately to hide her rags under a garish scarf.

"Don't you know, my good woman?"

A man with a red beard and white hair, dressed in the long red and black robe of the Knights of Saint-John, answered using a series of troubling riddles:

"*It* comes from the Orient on Genovese ships. *It* casts moribund crews, putrid cargoes, and realms of loathsome rats onto our shores. Wherever *It* stops, life also ceases. We can stop the French; we can stop the Spanish or the Turks. But *It* is something else. *It*, nothing can stop. Do you know what it is, my good woman?"

The little old woman did not reply. The man in red and black went on:

"*It* fears neither militias, nor hunting parties, nor ambushes, nor prayers, nor exorcisms. We can, my good woman, barricade ourselves behind our doors, fill our moats, pull up the drawbridges, drop the portcullis, pull the shutters, and close the windows. All for naught. When *It* has come, there is nothing but horror. Do you understand me?"

Little by little, the people around the knight had stopped speaking to hear what he was saying. Fear began to take hold of them. Their eyes opened wide, expressing anguish and horror. Moses de Castellazzo went into a rage. He abruptly stepped forward and grabbed the man dressed in red and black, lifting him off the ground kicking and screaming, as if he were nothing more than an ordinary bundle of laundry.

"Enough!" the artist roared. "Enough spreading terror!"

"Let me down," yelped the knight. "We're not talking about fear. *It is the plague! The Black Death!*"

The unspeakable word, the fatal word had been spoken. The crowd scattered in all directions.

As if he were getting rid of garbage, the artist, his face twisted in anger, gave the knight a violent shake and then tossed him aside. As he fell, the knight also knocked aside several of those people who were massed near the door. When Moses saw the opportunity, he hurried to the front door. But there, guards were waiting. He was about to challenge them when Joseph Halevy, who had come to the window when he heard the altercation, recognized him. He told the guards to let the giant in. Moses's red hair was disheveled from his brief struggle. When finally he walked into the house, the doctor himself came to welcome him. Neither was smiling as they greeted each other.

"How is he?" the artist asked, his voice low.

"He is still in real danger," Joseph Zarfatti whispered.

Chapter nineteen

The Shadow Ritual

The Messenger remained in delirium for eight days and eight nights without regaining consciousness. Dina never left his side. Doctor Zarfatti and Joseph Halevy came daily, the doctor to examine the patient and his servant to check on his condition and bring clean clothing. Dina had been transformed into a vigilant nurse. She never left the room, and she spared no effort by the bedside of a man whose life was hanging by a thread. According to the doctor's instructions, the servants kept a fire going in the fireplace, and the room had become as warm as a Turkish bath.

David sweated profusely, and Dina, her lips and throat dry from the heat, kept wiping the sweat from his face. She also took on the responsibility of David's care whenever her brother was not there. And she, too, was the one who would watch to see if he was breathing normally, listen to his heart beating, and try to make out what he was saying when bits of sentences escaped confusedly from his lips. She had decided to give herself body and soul to the task, though the outcome was uncertain. To that end, she devoted all her time, and all the devotion, vigilance, and tenderness of which she was capable.

One day, the Messenger began to speak about his mother, about the ocher-colored scarf she covered her head with. He talked about her sparkling jade-black eyes and about an ocher-colored village clinging to the slope of a mountain, but he never was clear about the exact location of the village. And then he mentioned, through allusions often interrupted by fever and delirium, a girl, his sister, decapitated by an Arab horseman. Several times he pronounced the word 'Jerusalem'. Dina would have loved to know if and when he had lived there. She leaned over and gently asked him. But strangely, though the sick man's lips could form sounds, his ears seemed unable to hear anything.

Whenever her brother was gone, Dina had to rub the Messenger's body. Sometimes she almost wore herself out, because she knew friction was the only remedy against the disease. They had to maintain the heat of life and prevent the coldness of death from taking over the body.

During those eight days of constant care, Dina must have only been able to sleep a few hours. Her physical resistance was sorely tested, and from time to time she felt an almost irresistible desire to stretch out at the Messenger's side, just to rest, to unwind without having to leave him alone. She would not have yielded her place near him to anyone for any price. Deep within her she felt a sense of duty, that *gemilut hasadim*, "deeds of loving kindness." It was true charity, totally selfless since it was directed toward a sick man who could not reciprocate. And along with modesty, she also displayed a kind of pride that allowed her own worth to shine through. For she was trying to save a man who was destined to save an entire people. Surely that thought spurred on her pride. But in the heat of the relationship she had established with David, there was also that tension, physical and intimate, that arises between two individuals when they both, abandoned in the hold of a ship in the grips of an ever-strengthening current, are irresistibly carried along toward the depths of *Sheol*, the "Kingdom of Death."

Little does it matter in that case if one is in good health and the other near death. The urgency of escaping from the peril is the same for both. Each movement counts when one's minutes are numbered. Thus, an involuntary touch feels like a caress, and the slightest glance can awaken desire. Dina tried to chase away such thoughts and drew closer to the bed.

"Cold," murmured the Messenger.

She did not understand what he was saying. She was about to lean over to ask him when suddenly there was a flash of lightning. Thunder rolled. A whirling gust of rain began to hammer at the windows.

The room was so hot that the wax candles were beginning to soften. One of them went out, and the smell of wax filled the room. Dina finally realized that David was trying to say he was cold. She had to intervene. She picked up the basin of alcohol and pulled back the blankets. The Messenger's dark, muscular body began to shiver. She rinsed her hands in the alcohol, but then suddenly she was overcome with lassitude. She stood still, waiting, as if her mind were elsewhere. Her finely sculpted face and aquiline nose were framed by two black braids, and her eyes kept staring vacantly ahead. It was as if she had already fulfilled her duty, laid down her burden, and now was ready to face eternity. For days, fatigue had squeezed her forehead in a vise. She knew that getting some rest was absolutely the most important thing for her to do. She had to lie down, if only for a minute. If only for a few moments. She looked at the sick man. He lay there naked and trembling, like a shortcut leading to the tragic, somber heart of the faith. A passage from the Book of Kings came to mind: *King David was old. They covered him with blankets but could not keep him warm. His servants said: "We must go look for a young virgin for our King, so that she can care for him and lie against him! Then the Lord our King will be warm."*

She touched the Messenger's dark body lightly with her fingers. He opened his eyes. Could he see her? He looked at her as if he were seeing a shadow. But the burning hand he placed on Dina's own hand showed not only that he was feverish, but also that he was conscious. The sick man's hand grasping her own suggested that desire was not far away. She squeezed his hand for a moment, and then she pulled away and went to the door to turn the key in the lock. Back beside the bed, she slowly undressed. When she lay down naked beside the Messenger, his body moved slightly.

Faith, it is said, can move mountains. For Dina, what she did was an act of faith. An act of that absolute faith that can hold disease at bay and sometimes even raise the dead. Outside, the rain ceased. A star appeared, and it seemed to be hanging just above the window-sill, almost within reach. But Dina gave no thought to touching it. David had raised himself to his elbows and she felt his hot, dry lips on her eyelids. He was shivering. The young woman guessed what he was thinking just as she could smell his scent. Her body nestled against the Messenger's body. She felt sharp pain and was surprised and aroused. For several long minutes their union electrified them, until finally David gave a gasp. For a moment he seemed to rise above his fever, and then he dropped back into the semi-consciousness in which he had lain for more than a week.

Dina opened her eyes. Did that sudden obscurity followed by intense brightness announce a miracle? As if miracles were indeed possible! But who was she to doubt? She hesitated a moment, then leaned over the Messenger. He was sleeping. He was breathing normally and his face was calm. With a tender gesture, she brushed back the lava-colored hair from his forehead and touched her lips to his. If it should please the Eternal to give a man back his life, might He not also generate a little love in the same man?

Chapter twenty

Milchemet Mitzvah

It seems that the imposter is improving."

"I, too, have heard the same thing. And that is quite surprising. The plague doesn't give up its prey so easily."

"Are we sure it is the plague?"

"Yes. All the doctors that Joseph Zarfatti called to examine the sick man agree."

"Don't you find it strange that he is the only person affected? Normally, the plague washes over a community like a wave."

"Unless he carried it with him from the Orient."

"What do you plan to do now?"

"First of all, to check out the rumor. Is the imposter really better? Or is it just another manifestation of his delirium?"

"And then?"

"Then? To try to prevent the plague he is carrying from contaminating the whole Jewish community, for which I feel responsible."

"How do you plan to proceed, Giacobo, my good man?"

"Don't forget, Miguel, my friend, that I too am a doctor. Furthermore, I'm the president of a large Jewish community."

Leaning against the guardrail in the loggia just above the table where the two conspirators were speaking, Moses de Castellazzo caught every word of this new conversation in the Trou Tavern. The Portuguese ambassador to the Holy See and the president of the *Va'ad Hakatan* in Venice were meeting for the second time in ten days. The news concerning David's improving health was upsetting their plans, but not their intentions. A third man whom Moses did not recognize was seated at the same table with Dom Miguel da Silva and Giacobo Mantino. He said not a word, pouring glass after glass of Chianti while his two companions conversed. Although his little beard was grey, he appeared to be a young man. With his black garment and slumped shoulders, he reminded Moses of a burial casket. He had a surprisingly sharp-featured face, and the reddish reflection in his large eyes suggested something disquieting, something worrisome. Moses continued to listen to the conspirators, and soon he learned the man's name. He was none other than the brother of Balthazar Castiglione, the author of *Il Corteggiano*, and his name was Bernardo. He was an organizer of festivals and carnivals, and in Rome he was known as a man who could find a solution for any problem, even the most extreme one. Finding money for a noble traveler in search of pleasure, helping a lord in disgrace change identity, making a cumbersome competitor or an overly-pugnacious adversary disappear, whether he belonged to the Borgia or the Colonna clan. He was a master of all kinds of shady operations. By inviting him to join their conversation, Dom Miguel da Silva wanted to be sure that when they decided on a course of action it would be carried out. The news of the Messenger's arrival in Rome and the warm welcome extended to him in the Vatican had reached Lisbon, and Joao III, King of Portugal and Dom Miguel's master, was beginning to show interest in the plans of the man from the desert. In the eyes of the ambassador, there was little time, and they needed to act quickly.

Dom Miguel's green eyes, full of that provocative candor that caused so much comment in the Vatican's hallways, looked deeply into the eyes of his accomplice.

"So," he said to Giacobo Mantino, "what is the radical medicine my friend, the doctor, will prescribe for the sick man from Chabor?"

Giacobo grew pale. In his wide, clean-shaven face, his pale eyes were still for a moment. A few strands of brown hair streaked with white extended out from under the Venetian beret he always wore. He answered Dom Miguel's question with another question:

"Under what circumstances," he asked, "under what particular situations is it legitimate to begin a war? Do you know? Do you know when it is our duty, and therefore our right, to remove a danger by eliminating an adversary?"

Then, raising his fleshy hand to his wide forehead, he continued:

"It is not an easy question, I know. On that subject, our Torah mentions two kinds of situations in which Israel has the right to begin a conflict: required war, *milchemet mitzvah*, and permissible war, *milchemet reshut*. According to the Jewish philosopher Maimonides, a prescribed war is above all a war undertaken to defend a collective good. It is an action taken for the survival of a people, and beyond that, for the protection of all humanity."

"If I follow you correctly," Dom Miguel cut in, "you believe that we are in a situation such that the Law authorizes you to begin a 'prescribed war,' a *milchemet mitzvah*?"

"Yes," Giacobo Mantino said with a sigh.

"I can only approve such an analysis! But then we must turn to our good and faithful Bernardo Castiglione. You and I have good reasons to begin a war. But he has the means to win it."

The man in black blinked and then put down his glass. In a thin voice, almost like a woman's, surprising from someone with such sharp features, he gave his assurance:

"I am at your complete disposal, Milords."

A tall, thin girl, whose surprisingly large bosom seemed to be pulling her forward, brought them another pitcher of Chianti. Bernardo Castiglione waited until she left and then continued:

"Tomorrow, carnival begins. And during carnival, anything is possible. Firecrackers and fireworks cover up the noise of firearms as well as any calls for help…"

Up by the railing just above the conspirators' table, Moses de Castellazzo had thus far not lost a word of the conversation. But just as Bernardo Castiglione was about to reveal his plan, the artist's attention was distracted. The innkeeper, a fat Roman dressed Spanish-style in a short sagum over a doublet with polka-dotted sleeves, came up the stairs to the loggia. Moses greeted him, pretending to pull up his stockings. The big man seemed to want to start a conversation, so Moses claimed to have an urgent meeting and ran down the stairs and out the door into the street, hoping that Giacobo Mantino had not recognized him.

Carnival was to begin the following day, but already there were groups of young people joyously trying out their firecrackers, laughing and joking with each other. The artist walked faster. He met some masked men riding on donkeys, and then a group of pilgrims. In the Campo dei Fiori, workmen were setting up arches. On Via dei Negozi Oscuri, as well as on Via dei Banchi, the crowd got denser. As night was falling, people began lighting torches here and there. Moses de Castellazzo was worried. With his unruly hair flaying, he hurried toward Doctor Zarfatti's house, pushing his way through the crowds. He was considering the conversation he had been able to overhear, although he didn't hear the end. One image of Giacobo Mantino stood out in his mind: a satanic figure; the incarnation of the devil. The artist knew that by resisting the devil, assuming that one could recognize him, Man always put the devil to flight. Fate had decided that Moses would uncover both Giacobo Mantino and his foul plans. He wanted to inform his friends about Mantino as quickly as possible. He ran so fast that he was soon gasping for air, and his heart was beating as if it would burst. Moses kept praying to the Eternal—blessed be His name!—begging that he wouldn't arrive too late.

Once there, he was led to David's room. The entire household was gathered for evening prayer, and the prayer was just beginning when Moses walked in. *And God, always merciful, forgives us our sins. He does not bring about destruction, and often He holds back His anger. He does not unleash His wrath. Lord, come to our aid! May the Lord our King answer our prayer when we invoke His name.*

Suddenly Moses was filled with fear. Was the Messenger's condition worse? He was reassured a moment later when he saw that David was sitting upright in his bed, his back against the headboard, reciting the prayer along with the others. In great relief, the artist had barely enough time to join the assembly and say "Amen" with the rest of them.

Shortly thereafter, away from David's hearing, Moses de Castellazzo told Joseph Zarfatti about the plot. The doctor was dismayed by what he heard and wanted to go right away to the *borgello*, the chief of police. But Moses talked him out of it.

"That man will do nothing to interfere, because Bernardo Castiglione is too useful to him. They might even be accomplices. If we speak to the *borgello*, we risk alerting the conspirators."

Joseph Zarfatti nodded. Then, raising his arms heavenward, he said:

"I'm sending right away for Joseph Halevy, David's servant, as well as for Obadiah da Sforno and the Fattori!"

One hour later, Moses de Castellazzo repeated to them what he had heard in the tavern. Old Obadiah da Sforno, his goatee trembling with surprise and indignation, expressed the general opinion.

"But that is impossible!" he exclaimed. "That is horrible! How can men like you and me decide in cold blood to kill a fellowman? How can a Jew wish for the death of another Jew? How can civilized men even have such ideas?"

"It's too late to be indignant," the artist noted. "On the other hand, it is urgent to come up with an answer!"

"You aren't considering starting a civil war here in Rome, are you?" a thin voice asked. It was one of the other Fattori, Rabbi Abraham Moscato.

"Certainly not. Because we would probably lose it…"

"Would you stoop to resorting to the same methods they do?" the rabbi wondered worriedly.

Moses was about to answer when he noticed Joseph Halevy tiptoeing quietly out of the room. Doctor Zarfatti then stepped in:

"I shall lay out the situation to Cardinal di Viterbo," he said. "But it will be hard for me to explain why Giacobo Mantino hates

David so. And it will not be easy to explain that a man responsible for one Jewish community wants to kill the man who has come to free the Jews…"

After two hours of impassioned discussion, they agreed that David needed additional protection. They needed to be extra vigilant. Especially during carnival, they could not allow any stranger to loiter around the house.

"This house," said Obadiah in conclusion, "must become a sanctuary, a shelter in which the Eternal will watch over David!"

The famous ruby on his finger sparkled as he raised his arms, calling on heaven to be his witness:

"Let us remember the prayer of the persecuted just man: *Eternal, O my God, in You I find my shelter. Deliver me, save me from those who pursue me…*"

Chapter twenty-one

"A Snare under My Feet"

As you see," Doctor Zarfatti explained to Joseph Halevy, "the Romans are passionate about their carnival. They pour all their energy into it and spend their money freely. There is something beneath all the amusement and forced laughter. As if they fear, each year, that the spectacle they throw themselves into will be the last. This carnival is no exception to the rule. It even seems wilder and more frenetic than ever. Look! The exploding firecrackers make the windows shake! And just listen to all those shouts, all that noise! I hope that all this racket won't keep David awake!"

Joseph nodded. He appreciated the doctor's concern for his master. Then he said:

"You have a great deal of admiration for him, don't you?"

"Yes. His courage is impressive. And his resistance as well. As a doctor, this is the first time that I have seen the plague retreat before a sick man's will."

"In the city, the Jews believe that he has been miraculously healed, and that it was because the One Who gives and takes away life intervened. What do you think?"

"As I said, the art of medicine finds itself confronting a very rare case, perhaps even one of a kind. My science is unable to explain what has happened. But reason forbids me to grant credit to any hasty, superstitious conclusions."

About twenty sturdy men were guarding the house, and they had all proven their worth protecting the community on several occasions. As for Moses de Castellazzo, he was no longer staying at the inn. He came and took up lodging in a room at the end of the corridor leading to David's room. He insisted on tasting any food or drink before it was taken to the Messenger.

"A man who sells poison advertises with an attractive floral sign," he said. "We must remain prudent, even here inside this dwelling."

In the large living room on the ground floor, friends came by regularly. Of course there were the Fattori, and also emissaries from Cardinal di Viterbo and Cardinal Pucci. Jewish bankers, like old Shimon ben Asher Mechulam del Banco back in Venice, were beginning to take interest in David's plan for military and economic conquest of the land of Israel. Among them, Daniel di Pisa—the eldest son of an influential family, for he was one of the pope's financial officers—along with Benvenida Abravanel, whom people called the Signora di Napoli. She was the widow of a banker from Spain, Samuel Abravanel, and sister-in-law of one of the greatest kabbalists of the time. She was ready, and she had declared so publicly, to place her fortune at the Messenger's disposal.

As for David, he was still too feeble to see all these visitors. Aside from the doctor and his sister, he saw no one. He did speak for a long time with the faithful Joseph Halevy. Joseph, accompanied by Raphael and Joab, soon disappeared. His other servant, Tobias, needed to remain behind, and he wandered around through the corridors of the house like a lost soul.

From Dina, David accepted everything: care, medicines, and food. Beyond such obvious trust, by observing them no one could have guessed that they were lovers. Each evening, however, as the day's activities began to calm down and as night fell under a brilliant sky, he would take her hand in his own and explain some of the enigmas of the Torah in his deep desert voice.

He talked to her about King Solomon, who went down into a *grove of nut trees*, according to the *Song of Solomon*:

"When the king picked up a nutshell and looked at it closely," the Messenger said, "he discovered an analogy between the woody layers of the shell and those spirits that awaken sensual desire in human beings, as it is written in the Zohar: *And the pleasures of the sons of men come from male and female demons.*"

On another occasion he commented, for Dina, on this sentence from *Genesis: And God said: Let there be light! And there was light.*

"That was the original light that God created," he explained. "The light of the eye. It is the light God showed to Adam, through which he was able to embrace the world from one horizon to the other. It is the light God showed to David, who, once he saw it and was able to see because of it, began immediately to sing His praises, saying: *How great is Your goodness. May You hold it in reserve for those who worship You!* It is the light through which God revealed to Moses the whole land of Israel, from Dan to Gilead. And that land will soon be ours once again."

And Dina listened. She loved to listen to him. It seemed as if long blue waves were lifting her up, transforming her body into a light boat. A subtle but powerful impression of space and freedom appeared to make the room larger. Dina was happy, though she couldn't put her finger on exactly why. She knew nothing about the saying attributed to Angelus Silesius, the mystic: "The rose exists without a why," but she seemed to quiver in harmony with the throaty, guttural voice that characterized this Messenger from the desert, this David who had come from the far reaches of the world to liberate a people. And she was the one who had saved him, or at least she had nursed him with a zeal she had never experienced before.

On the third and final day of carnival, alone for a moment in his room, the Messenger finally got out of bed. Standing upright for the first time in weeks, he suddenly felt empty and totally alone. He began to pray. And then he noticed his pale reflection in a mirror lying on the dresser near the window. His first thought was to walk over to the window and look outside, but felt wobbly and thought it would be best to sit down carefully in a rocking chair beside his bed.

He began to rock slowly, and the rocking stirred up a little breeze in the heavy heat of his bedroom. Looking down, he noticed a small column of ants crossing the room to reach the spot on the floor where Dina must have spilled a few drops of soup. The ants circled around and then headed in perfect order toward the opposite wall, under which they disappeared as they had appeared. With this vision of an army on the move, and pleased that he himself had finally been able to take a few steps, David fell asleep.

An hour later he was awakened by his host. The doctor was accompanied by Moses de Castellazzo and the old rabbi, Obadiah da Sforno, who waited by the door. Joseph Zarfatti was terribly upset. Arms raised heavenward, he came into the room just as the church bells were ringing.

"What is happening?" David asked in a whisper.

"Bernardo Castiglione...," the doctor began. His face was contorted with feeling, and he kept clasping his hands and then crossing them over his breast, or lifting them above his head.

The Messenger raised his eyebrows.

"Well, what is it?" he asked more forcefully.

"Bernardo Castiglione, the organizer of festivals and carnivals, that damned soul who is behind all sorts of conspiracies...," Joseph Zarfatti murmured.

David gestured impatiently.

"What I mean is," the doctor finally went on, "the man who intended to make an attempt on your life...well, he is dead!"

The man from the desert showed no reaction. His emaciated face was finally beginning to take on the undecipherable expression it had before his illness. Once again, the doctor raised his long arms heavenward:

"The Eternal must have wanted this to happen," he said, falsely fatalistic.

"The scoundrel drowned and was found dead along the banks of the Tiber," added Moses de Castellazzo.

"According to the doctors who examined him," said Obadiah de Sforno, "Bernardo Castiglione was probably drunk. The chief of police found a witness who saw him leave a tavern in a sorry state. He could scarcely walk and had to reach out to find support from the walls to stay upright."

The Messenger looked up and his dark, bright eyes met those of his friends. His eyes were glistening like mica. In a clear voice, he began to recite:

They have prepared a snare for my steps;
My soul is bowed down.
They have dug a pit before me,
Into the midst whereof they are fallen themselves.

"That is Psalms 57, verse 7!" cried Obadiah da Sforno, pleased to have recognized the passage.

David Reubeni closed his eyes. He motioned for them to leave, for he wanted to be alone.

The following morning, when Dina came to bring the Messenger a basket of fruit and a pitcher of water, she found him standing up fully dressed. He had regained his princely bearing and was walking back and forth in his bedroom, dressed, as he had been when he arrived, in a fine white woolen tunic with a Star of David sewn on it. All of his clothing had been burned, but Dina had lovingly made new garments just like those he wore before. He thanked her for the clothing, and then, just as if she were not there, he went over to his ebony chest and pulled out a bundle of sheets. His back was turned and he seemed to be unaware that she was moving around in the room, and a tear rolled down her cheek as she set the tray down on a little table. And then other tears followed, silent and scalding. Something had clearly changed between David and her. She could not hold back a sob.

"Try not to hate me," the Messenger said quietly without turning around. "Instead, please pray for me."

The young woman left without a word. A few moments later the door opened again. A familiar voice called out:

"The Eternal—blessed be His name!—has not forsaken us…"

"If the Eternal does not build the house," David replied, "those who build it are working in vain…"

And then, holding a few sheets filled with his script, he walked over to his visitor.

"And now, my good and faithful Joseph, go tell our host that I am ready to see the pope!"

Chapter twenty-two

The Pope

Three days later, David was on his way to the Vatican. In spite of the cool morning air, he was wearing only his fine white tunic. He looked very impressive on horseback, and as he rode, his white turban gave him the aura of a prestigious Oriental prince.

His retinue, with Joseph at its head carrying the white banner embroidered with Hebrew symbols, was composed of his armed servants, Doctor Joseph Zarfatti, and the Fattori, all on horseback, even old Obadiah da Sforno, sprier than ever. The little troop made its way across the city with huge crowds shouting their hurrahs and acclamation. As for Moses de Castellazzo and Daniel di Pisa, they had left earlier, and were on foot. They wanted to mingle with the people in the crowds so they could judge how they were feeling. Regarding David Reubeni, there was no mistaking what they felt. Their enthusiasm was obvious, and by the thousands they kept shouting, "Messiah!" "Messiah!" What they expected was clear, but for him it was painful to hear. After his meeting with Clement VII, how could he respond to their call for a Messiah? Low clouds rolled in, darkening the horizon and bringing a diversion. Rain began to fall in torrents over Rome, dampening the crowd's enthusiasm. The downpour continued, a liquid wall between David Reubeni and the Vatican. And then it was as if the light disappeared. Off in the distance, the Vatican was veiled in darkness. Now and then, lightning bolts illuminated what seemed to be a night sky in the middle of the day.

At the head of the procession, Joseph felt a chill. He turned back to consult his master. With one glance the Messenger signaled for him to continue on. He seemed impervious to the rain and the cold, indifferent to the rolling thunder and lightning bolts. As Joseph reined in his horse, David, his face full of energy, took advantage of a flash of lightning to say to him:

"When the moon is full, it can only wane. Keep moving!"

The rain stopped when they reached the Sant'Angelo Bridge. As they were crossing the bridge, dripping wet, a ray of sun broke through the clouds and a patch of blue appeared. And then, as quickly as the heavy storm had struck, the clouds were swept away, and soon there was nothing above them but the immense blue canopy of heaven. A cannon salvo boomed out, a salvo of welcome like those the Vatican reserves for its important guests. Then, to the music of trumpets and drums, David Reubeni was led by the pope's archers to Clement vii's palace.

Under the arcades, at the foot of a massive marble staircase, Cardinal Egidio di Viterbo was waiting. His imposing figure and ceremonial purple robe added solemnity to this important occasion. But his friendly smile and the mischievous look in his eyes reassured the Messenger. The delegation he was leading dismounted, and then, guided by the cardinal, they crossed an esplanade and walked past some unfinished structures, the gigantic vaults of Bramante, an enclosed area reserved for tournaments. Some of the buildings in the complex were still under construction. The pope's advisor, the subtle Di Viterbo, wanted perhaps to impress his visitor by showing the magnitude of the monumental projects the Vatican was undertaking, as if to display their symbolic value. For the pope's strength, audacity, and power were undoubtedly affirmed there.

The man from the desert was deeply aware that all palaces are nothing but piles of sand. He admired everything in silence but remained deep in thought. Following the cardinal, he crossed large galleries that were richly decorated and lined with sculptures from antiquity. Finally, they came out into a large square courtyard surrounded by arcades. Beneath one of the arcades, a guard of honor made up of Swiss lancers was waiting for them.

"This is the Saint Damase courtyard," Egidio di Viterbo said.

With a broad smile on his face, he turned toward the Messenger, whose tunic was barely beginning to dry, and continued in Hebrew.

God, in His infinite wisdom, dropped a downpour on you to bring you back to reality and remind you that…

David Reubeni finished the sentence himself:

…that when you see marble sparkling, you must not take it for water!

"That is from *Hagigah 14b* and the corresponding *Tossefta* in the Talmud!" cried Obadiah da Sforno, delighted to be able to display both his prodigious memory and his subtle knowledge.

The cardinal looked with amusement at the old rabbi, let his gaze wander over the entire group, and then burst out laughing.

"*Cum errate eruditus, errat errore erudito,*" he said in Latin before translating into Hebrew: "*When the scholar is mistaken, even his mistakes are scholarly.*"

And then, speaking to the Messenger, he added more ceremoniously:

"His Holiness in person will be here in a few moments, right here in the Saint Damase courtyard, to meet the Envoy from Chabor for a private conversation. As for his friends—as well as for his enemies—," he added with a wink, "they will not be a part of the conversation and will see him only after the meeting, and are kindly requested to wait. Such is the will of the sovereign pontiff."

The cardinal raised a finger to his lips. Beneath the arcades, a secret door had just opened. Pope Clement VII appeared, wearing a red hat, a white robe, and a garnet-colored velvet hood. His august white beard, in which his mustache with some chestnut-colored streaks was almost lost, framed his dignified face. His smooth pink skin and the dreamy look in his eyes showed that he was not an old man. As he drew closer, simple and majestic, the members of the delegation prepared to kneel. But he stopped them with a gesture, spreading wide his arms as he approached.

"My dear sons," he said.

Immediately, he took the Messenger from Chabor by the hand and pulled him into a small alley which led to a gallery decorated by Raphael. They entered a round room, and the semi-circle of windows opened onto a terrace where sunshine and shadows danced.

Meanwhile, Cardinal di Viterbo was leading the delegation to the meeting room where they were to wait, according to the pope's wishes, until the meeting between the head of Christendom and the Jewish prince of Chabor was over. Then he left, and he alone, to join the two men. The pope had asked that the private conversation include the cardinal. When he arrived, Clement vii and David Reubeni were already deep in conversation.

"A Jew who is also a warrior!" the sovereign pontiff exclaimed in his halting Hebrew. "That is something new for me!"

By using the language of the Kabbalah, the pope proved that he was keeping up with the times. For did not the times expect that most scholars would read the Kabbalah and the Bible in the original languages?

"I don't know what I think," he continued affably. "Up until now, I've always considered that one of the greatest qualities Jews have is that they know how to live in peace and refrain from using weapons. As they wait for the day announced by the Prophets, when the lamb will lie down with the lion!"

He smiled, and his large, drooping mustache bobbed momentarily.

"That is only a dream, of course, but a dream that I too share. The kings of France and Spain for too long have turned Italy into a bloody battlefield. They are constructing, if we can say so, only ruins and rubble. Should we wish for either one of them to triumph?"

Clement vii gave a sigh and moved toward the window. Outside, a few birds were hopping about in search of food. Clement continued:

"However, the whole world is seeking peace! People are asking for nothing else but peace!"

Cardinal di Viterbo, standing respectfully a short distance away, cleared his throat loudly to remind the pope of his presence.

"Ah," the pope exclaimed. "I go on speaking, and I'm forgetting to ask you, my dear Prince of Chabor, for the letter that your brother, King Joseph, has sent to me."

From his wide belt David pulled out an envelope sealed with wax and gave it to Clement VII, bowing his turbaned head three times. The pontiff studied the envelope, judged its weight, and passed it from his right hand to his left, inviting David to sit down in an armchair upholstered with black velvet and red fringes. Then, he himself sat on a sofa, facing his guest.

"I thank the Prince of Chabor for bringing me this missive," he said. "I shall take the time to read it later, but now I am ready to respond to any proposals it might contain."

And with that, he asked:

"And you, Prince, you who are passing through. Might you have some personal request to make?"

David Reubeni studied his interlocutor.

"Will Your Holiness permit me to answer with a question?"

The Messenger stood up. To express his deepest feelings, he always felt more comfortable on his feet.

"May I speak freely?" he asked.

The pope nodded. David glanced over at the cardinal standing behind the sofa. The cardinal made a little gesture of encouragement.

"Your Holiness," the man from the desert began, "was kind enough to quote Isaiah a few moments ago. I, too, share Isaiah's dream of universal peace. At the end of that sublime text, it is said that his prophecy will come true *Akharat Hayamim*, 'after some days.' We are all hoping for that day after some days, are we not? But *now*, before the days that we have ourselves slip away, what can we do, what must we do?"

David paused for a moment. The pope was fascinated. The Messenger's voice, tone, and bearing were compelling. A strange force emanated from this prince who had come from the depths of the desert. He had a rare presence, an undeniable power of conviction. Clement VII motioned for David to continue.

"In order for peace to reign," he went on, "we must find a way to impose it. Does Your Holiness have the means to force these make-shift armies to accept peace? These armies are made up of mercenaries who are constantly changing sides, and thus enemies and allies keep changing. Such changes are more favorable to hate than to love. Does Your Holiness have a political plan that can bring them all together? The exciting project that I am proposing now might guarantee Christendom's indispensable unity as well as give our persecuted people back their freedom and dignity…"

"Painful paradox!" the pope said, interrupting him. "We hope for peace in this world and yet we keep talking about war…"

"Because war is already present! Coming to Rome, on my way to meet Your Holiness, I rode through areas that have been completely devastated."

Up until then the pope's thoughts were clear, and he had been able to speak eloquently and with authority. Now he hesitated a moment before continuing.

"People are saying…We have heard the rumor…People say that you might be the Messiah that Jews are expecting."

David Reubeni took two steps toward the pontiff. Looking the pope straight in the eyes, he said:

"Those who spread such rumors are guilty of blasphemy!" he said with conviction. "But we must understand them. They are lost, penniless, and in exile, so naturally they dream. We, however, know that hope deferred brings sickness to the heart of men."

And then, with a half-smile, he went on:

"No, Holy Father, I am not the Messiah. Nor am I a prophet. I am simply a general who would like to offer his skills in the service of his people. And I do have a plan…"

"I know your plan. Cardinal di Viterbo has been enchanted with your words, and he has explained your plan in great detail."

Clement VII also got to his feet. His expression was still friendly, but now there was a touch of shrewdness as well.

"I find your vision of things interesting," he said. "Whereas Frances I is waging war on the Emperor Charles V for control of Northern Italy, Ottoman Islam continues to advance on every front. After conquering the land east of the Mediterranean, Soleiman the Magnificent has destroyed the Venetian navy in the Aegean Sea, occupied Serbia, then Rhodes and Sicily, and he is now moving on Central Europe, with his goal to be Budapest and Vienna. So it matters little whether or not your information is exaggerated. In any case, there is nothing that could reconcile the French and the Empire better than your project. An army of fifty thousand men that would serve the old plan of the papacy: to complete a successful crusade in the Holy Land, to turn the eyes of all Christendom and all Europe toward a common enemy, the Turk. Against the Turk, up to now we have been only able to send a few mediocre Venetian ships and pronounce a few useless sermons. The proposal I made to Charles V and Frances I to conclude an alliance and combine their forces against Soleiman would then cease to be simply a wish. It could turn into the creation of a real army. In all this, Prince, your perspicacity is perfectly well-founded. You are right: for the moment, all that counts are armies."

The pope, after his long speech, paused for a moment. Then, suddenly, he pointed his finger at the Messenger.

"The suggestion made by the Prince of Chabor to arm European Jews and send them to fight in the Holy Land seems like an honest proposal," he said. "But how about your brother, the king? How does he plan to participate?"

"I would prefer not boring Your Holiness with military details...," said David.

Clement VII opened his arms as if he were about to embrace the Messenger and smiled.

"My son," he said. "While I was still young, I learned from my uncle Lorenzo de Medici that it is important to think about war plans during peacetime, more so even than in the heat of the battle!"

David was startled out of his thoughts by the pope's comments, and what he managed to say was not at all optimistic.

"Much time will pass before men learn how to keep themselves out of war!"

But the pope did not appear eager to bring their conversation to a close. He motioned David back to his seat, and he returned to the sofa. He leaned forward and grabbed David by the arm.

"Since we cannot avoid war," he said, "what must we do to win?"

"I have carefully studied the different battles that have taken place on the Peninsula, and I can draw three conclusions. The French cavalry is held in check by the Swiss infantry's pike men formed in squares. But the Swiss squares are slow and hard to maneuver and inferior to the quick-moving Spanish infantry armed with round shields and short lances and swords. Such weapons can slip between the long pikes which are not useful in hand-to-hand battle. And finally, the agility which gives the Spanish the advantage over the Swiss becomes an impossible handicap when they must face the repeated assaults of the powerful French cavalry. So the question becomes one of inventing a third type of infantry that would combine the strengths of the Spanish and the Swiss but not their points of weakness."

David was speaking so excitedly that he had to stand up.

"If the Christian kings give me authorization to mobilize the young Jews of Europe," he exclaimed in his deep, guttural voice, "such an infantry will be ready in eighteen months! The cavalry is already prepared. No cavalry can stand up against my brother's cavalry. But future wars, we must admit, will be won by bombards. So therefore we need heavy cannons, perhaps twenty, to lay siege to cities. We will also need a few pieces of light artillery to help the advance posts of our army as it moves."

Then Clement VII also rose.

"All that shall be!" he said forcefully, reaching out with both hands to take David's right hand. "I will back your plans, and I will also send word to the court of Portugal that I support the idea. Since Portugal is less involved in European conflicts than other countries, it might be able to place a camp, men, ships, and weapons at the disposal of the Prince of Chabor. The Portuguese ambassador, Miguel da Silva, has just come recently to renew his Sovereign's cordial, faithful, and obedient homage."

His eyes shining, visibly moved by the discussion, the pope continued:

"In sum, what you are suggesting, by uniting our sovereigns against the Muslim invader, is to give Europe meaning that is currently lacking?"

"Yes," David replied, keeping his eyes on his famous interlocutor. "And you would be doing even more, since you would be able to reconcile Europe with its past by allowing it to participate in the creation of a Jewish kingdom in the land of Israel."

"Christendom would be coming to the aid of its origins," the pope sighed.

David finished the sentence the pope had left unsaid.

"...and fulfilling its ancient dream: controlling the Holy Sites in Jerusalem."

And then David added in his deep voice:

"Your Holiness knows full well: A plan of that kind is enough to justify a life."

Staring at each other, the two men remained silent for a long time. Then Clement VII led the Envoy from the desert out of the room. As they walked beneath the colonnades under the watchful eyes of the Swiss guards, they continued their conversation. Cardinal Egidio di Viterbo followed them, now and again supplying a Hebrew word that Clement VII was not able to come up with. As they were still conversing, they reached the meeting room where political and religious dignitaries, as well as diplomats, were waiting impatiently for them with many questions. The *cameriere*, looking like a priest in his dark, rigid corset and a gold choker, solemnly announced that the pope and the Messenger were arriving. All heads turned toward them.

Chapter twenty-three

Happiness with a Shadow

In the Vatican meeting room, the hubbub ceased. Clement VII walked in, holding David Reubeni by the arm.

The Messenger from Chabor, for a moment, was dazzled, and the moment seemed almost an eternity. His heart was pounding. "There are two categories of men," he thought, "those who could be happy and are not, and those who seek happiness without ever finding it." In which category did he himself belong? Within him, great happiness was at odds with a shadow. Yes, the pontiff had promised his help and would not stint with his personal support. Yes, Clement VII was also proposing Joao III's commitment to the cause of the European Jews. But alas! His commitment had to go through the Portuguese ambassador, Dom Miguel da Silva. David's expression was unreadable. His thin features seemed chiseled in black marble. His thoughts, turned inward, remained inaccessible. Life, once again, was forcing him to be devious, and being devious was not part of his nature. He made an effort to gain control of his feelings. There, before him, was a roomful of important people in a sparkling contrast of colors, shiny jewelry, greedy looks, silks, satins, and velvet. They all seemed to be wavering between respect and curiosity. Truly, there was the inevitable mix of friends and enemies, and the man from the desert knew it. The thought gave him new energy. Using deviousness? Why not, if his mission required it? The sovereign pontiff touched his forearm, reminding him of the ceremonial presentations that were to take place.

The front row of dignitaries parted to let the pope pass, as protocol demanded. Clement VII and David Reubeni walked from one end of the room to the other, stopping before each group so the pope could officially introduce the Prince of Chabor. When they came to the Jewish delegation, clearly proud to be there, Joseph's face relaxed and he was able to smile at Joseph Zarfatti, Moses de Castellazzo, and the Fattori. Apparently Giacobo Mantino had made himself scarce, and David was not surprised he was absent. Then, after warm greetings exchanged with different ambassadors, including the ambassadors from Denmark and Holland, the pontiff motioned two rows of guests aside and signaled one man to come closer. He was a tall man, and he bowed elegantly to kiss the pope's ring. His sharp-featured face extended above a white lace jabot. Instinctively, although he was seeing him for the first time, David knew who the man must be. Clement VII confirmed his intuition.

"His Excellence the Ambassador from Portugal!" he announced.

And then, turning to Dom Miguel da Silva:

"I have just spoken about you, my son, to our honorable guest, the Prince of Chabor. I have promised him the aid of our beloved Joao III, King of Portugal, whom you represent, to help carry out a plan concerning world peace and the glory of Christendom—a plan that I would not hesitate to call grandiose."

Dom Miguel, like a skilled diplomat, welcomed the pope's words with a subtle movement of his head and by placing his hand on his heart. As if he approved of them. As if he could taste their sweetness. Clement VII touched him on the shoulder.

"The Prince of Chabor," he added, "will soon be coming to your country. I am counting on you, my son, to obtain the necessary introductions for him and to guide him in his undertaking."

Then, including David in his words, he added:

"You need to meet again, and the sooner, the better."

The ambassador bowed a second time to kiss the pope's ring, murmuring in a tone that sounded like pure submission:

"His Holiness can depend on His humble slave…"

When he straightened up, his eyes met the eyes of the Messenger. David realized that, beneath an exterior like a frail antelope, this man was still dreaming of murder. Hate, apparently, was nothing but the defeat of imagination. That impossibility of seeing any other relationship with an adversary than one based on violence is what always ended in war. The Messenger from Chabor, on the battlefield, knew how to conduct a war. Here, they were imposing a war conducted in the drawing rooms and antechambers of power, more serpentine, more villainous than any other kind when measured by how much hypocrisy was required. To be victorious, one had to maneuver, change direction, use cunning, and lie. So he greeted the ambassador and then turned back toward Clement VII.

"In order to serve Your Highness," he said, "I shall go to Lisbon as quickly as possible!"

And then, to Dom Miguel, he declared:

"If I am not mistaken, Portugal would have a great deal to lose and to fear if it were to support a victorious Spain. For would not your country then become the vassal of another power and at the same time weaken the position of the Holy See, which your sovereign, the very valorous Joao III, venerates? In order to avoid that double danger, in order not to leave such a glorious nation outside of the events which are shaking and shaping Europe, we shall, with the authorization of His Holiness the pope, propose to Portugal a task and a mission. That mission and that task will inscribe in gold letters the name of Portugal in the great book of the history of mankind."

Once again the ambassador, though he really disapproved, nodded solemnly as David spoke. To see him, an ordinary person would never have doubted his complete devotion to David's cause. But the man from the desert was not taken in by such professional acting. The gazelle does not bleat for nothing.

The pope spoke once more.

"Tomorrow we shall compose a message for the King of Portugal, and our friend, His Excellence the Ambassador, will be so kind as to provide to the Prince of Chabor and his men the necessary passports and safe-conducts for their trip to Lisbon."

Then, after taking David's hands in his own, Clement VII bid goodbye to those gathered and gave them a cheerful blessing as he left the room.

Chapter twenty-four

Souls and Their Roots

Back in Joseph Zarfatti's house, David was not alone. In addition to his friends, the Fattori and other important people from the Jewish community in Rome were there as well. The doctor had quickly planned a celebration in honor of the great event. A Jew had just been received by the pope with all the honors due a representative of a nation. A nation, which *ipso facto* meant that the Jews were recognized as such. An event like that had not been seen since the year 538 before the Christian era, when Cyrus II, King of Persia, proclaimed an edict authorizing the Jews exiled in Babylon to return to Israel!

Joseph Zarfatti had brought up a dozen bottles of that good grey Veneto kosher wine, and his guests, excited by the day's fruitful events, drank to the Messenger's health after the wine was blessed:

We give You praise, our Eternal God, king of the earth and creator of the fruit of the vine!

Moses de Castellazzo raised his glass to Jerusalem, and Rabbi Obadiah da Sforno raised his to their deliverance:

"Rome destroyed the Temple in Jerusalem!" he exclaimed. "And now Rome will help rebuild it."

They talked about various things, but the old rabbi kept coming back to the same subject and finally it became the center of the conversation.

"Yes," he repeated, "we must now begin preparing to rebuild the Temple! After the Temple of Solomon! After Ezra! After Herod! Yes, today's Jews can and must begin thinking about the *third Temple*! About the Temple that David will erect, our own David Reubeni! Because the Temple is immortal. Because though it is now in ruins, the Temple still has life. Because the Temple is the sanctuary of the Imperishable. Because as it is written in the Kabbalah, *it is the stone that God destined to serve as the foundation of the world, and because the first circle around that stone, around the Supreme Point, is the Temple and the City of Jerusalem!* Let us rebuild the Temple from its ruins! Let us raise it from its rubble! Let us raise up the third Temple for all to see as soon as, thanks to David, we have finally returned to Jerusalem!"

The rabbi's ruby was sparkling, and so were his eyes. His little black goatee quivered with lyricism, and as he was finishing his speech, he kept rocking back and forth as if he were in a trance. Some of the guests applauded. People began to speak in laudatory terms. When Doctor Zarfatti raised his glass in homage to Obadiah da Sforno, everyone eagerly raised his own glass "to Jerusalem, to the return to Jerusalem, and to the *third Temple* of Jerusalem."

David Reubeni watched all this joy and good humor, all this agitation of hearts and minds with benevolent interest. And indeed, there was no one there who was malevolent. The Messenger could understand the feverish excitement that was seizing his friends. How could things be otherwise? Was it not because of him that all these Jews were acting so differently? For hope had dispelled resignation, and new-found dignity had swept away all fear. The bent spine of habit was being replaced by a spark of rebellion that he could see in their eyes. They were willing to reach beyond themselves, to march in conquest of the future. The Land that Moses had promised and was then lost, existing only in dreams, was again promised by him, David, "our own David," as Obadiah da Sforno had affectionately called him. So it was not surprising that all these people were both happy and deeply moved.

In the midst of the celebration, David did not forget Miguel da Silva's dangerous shadow nor Giacobo Mantino's suspicious absence. What interested him most, and what was at the same time the most disconcerting, was something else entirely. Dina was serving refreshments to the guests, moving around the room gracefully in an exquisite robe of fine velvet touched off with a scarf made of Damascus silk. She kept watching him out of the corner of her eyes, supplicating him with tender, quiet glances that gave an intense gleam to her pupils. She was in danger of betraying the nature of their relationship that David, but clearly not the young woman, now wanted to limit to something like that of a brother and sister.

He was truly embarrassed by the love Dina was expressing for him, and his own feelings were mixed. In his uncertainty, he pulled his dearest servant Joseph aside and consulted him about the situation. Joseph replied affably, asking him to be flexible, kind, and humane. In the sagacious, familiar style that he used only when he felt especially close to his master, Joseph spoke straightforwardly:

"You are obsessed by your mission, it is true. But you believe that something may be developing between you and Dina. Or may have already developed, but of course, that is none of my business. But I can see your disarray, trying to choose between your mission and love! Why does it have to be one or the other?"

"Because I must fulfill my mission!" the Messenger protested. "I can't stray from my path for love of a woman."

"You would be straying if you avoided it!" replied Joseph. "And perhaps your mission could suffer because you refuse to love. You pray and you fast. All that is well and good. However, you are not a monk, and you do not have the vocation of becoming a saint."

"I cannot waste any time with affairs of the heart!"

"Go ahead and enjoy life on earth! Even if you can't eat and drink like other men, at least you can learn to love and accept human love! A leader, if only from time to time in complete humility, must know how to share simple pleasures—eating, drinking, dreaming of freedom, and loving!"

Joseph paused for a moment. And then, scratching the top of his head, pretending to be embarrassed, he added slyly:

"Believe the experience of wise men. When an inspired man gives himself over to a woman's love, God's care never fails him."

David Reubeni burst out laughing.

"My dear Joseph! Your knowledge and realism are amusing even if they are irritating! That woman does move me deeply, that is true. But what would I do with her love?"

"Just trust. Your own love will provide an answer!"

They grew silent as Tobias walked by. With a smile on his face and a glass in his hand, he was in no hurry and kept his ears open. Tobias should not hear anything except what David thought might also be good for Giacobo Mantino to hear. But who, except for the Eternal who has the right to be present, can know the meanders of the human heart? David Reubeni's own heart was uncertain about choosing love, but his mind, on the other hand, remained vigilant about the dangers relating to his political struggle. There was no way that one of his servants could be spying on him without David at least trying to turn the situation against those who were plotting against him. Not daring to join their conversation, Tobias moved away toward an outside door, stumbling as if he were a little drunk. David nodded to Joseph, who got up to follow him. Where was the fellow going after midnight, out into Rome's infamous streets and back alleys?

The Messenger was again alone among those who considered him a hero. He was drawn out of his thoughts by the rustle of cloth behind him. A woman's voice, deep and melodious, murmured a few words that could be heard only by the two of them:

The Holy One—blessed be His name—plants souls here on earth. If they take root, so much the better! If not, He pulls them out. He pulls them out several times if necessary and keeps transplanting them until they do take root…

He had often meditated on that passage from the *Zohar*, but never had it been revealed to him in such a sweet, musical way. He turned around. The charming face he discovered was in complete harmony with the voice's power of enchantment. On him rested two large oval eyes, and they lit up the woman's oval face like two dark light shafts. With a sensual mouth, an aquiline nose, a high forehead, jade-black hair tied back and streaked with a few grey strands, she was a woman about forty years old whom he was seeing for the first time though she had been in Rome for several days and often came to Doctor Zarfatti's house. She was smiling at him in silence, as if to test the strength of his intuition. They stood close together, looking at each other. The Messenger could make out the little network of wrinkles that spread out from her intelligent, vertiginous eyes. She could be none other than Dona Benvenida Abravanel, the rich widow who had given him the superb steed he had ridden that morning to the Vatican. From far away, before he could make the slightest comment about the sentence from the *Zohar* that she had whispered to him, an unknown bird called out in the night. At the same moment, an oil lamp burning near them began to smoke. The woman turned to adjust the wick. It was as if the entire light in the room was concentrated in her movements. David's eyes were drawn to her strong body, her full breasts, her narrow waist, and her delicate wrists. The way women presented themselves here surprised him, for it was worlds away from what he knew in his own country. He could sense that this woman had grown up in cities and had been educated and shaped in active, cultured European towns. She was perfectly at ease with society's expectations and was fully aware of political and financial conflicts. It seemed to David that deep within her lay mysterious resources that were unknown to his experiences in the sandy desert and arid mountains. Where he came from, civilities were harsher, more direct, and less allusive. Back there, subtleties were often hidden. Here in Italy, transparency appeared to throw its veil over every situation, as if it were trying to steal any secret motivations and stress their shadowy nature. The man from the desert was disconcerted by that kind of *civilization*. When Dona Benvenida turned back once more to face him, he tried to speak, but all he could do was stare deeply into her eyes with such intensity that it was almost shameless, though that was not

"The Messenger from Chabor must surely have noticed and appreciated," she said in a tense, high-pitched voice, "that Dona Benvenida is devoting body and soul to his cause."

"*A jealous ear can hear everything, and even the slightest murmur does not escape it,*" he replied, gently scolding her.

Chapter twenty-five

Astra Regunt Homines...

That memorable day was followed by an unrewarding period marked by the uncertainty of waiting. It turned out that plans to leave for Portugal were difficult to arrange.

Two days after the meeting in the Vatican, however, Doctor Zarfatti, accompanied by Daniel di Pisa the banker, had been to see the ambassador. According to the pope's wishes, they had gone to request the documents that David and his men would need to go to Lisbon. Of course, Dom Miguel da Silva had politely received his visitors, with all the consideration due to representatives of a community recognized by the Vatican. But the meeting had ended with only vague references to how much time it would take to make arrangements. When they left after a short visit, the man with the innocent green eyes promised them, from the depths of his deviousness, to forward the matter immediately to His Majesty Joao III. A promise such as that, from a man like the ambassador, held out little hope, and indeed more fear than hope. Clearly Da Silva would do everything he could to delay David's departure. Joseph Zarfatti returned home in discouragement.

One week later, after a second meeting with Dom Miguel, he came home in a rage and slammed the door behind him.

"It will take months!" he shouted, arms raised heavenward in disgust when Moses de Castellazzo asked him about his visit. "Months and months!" he repeated indignantly.

The red-haired giant was so surprised that he dropped the "doctor's bag" (his portfolio) that he was carrying under his arm.

"But that is impossible!" he cried. "We must let the pope know! Or, better yet…"

He bent down, folding his huge body in two to pick up some sketches that had fallen out of the portfolio.

"Or better yet," he went on, looking up at the doctor, "let's go see Cardinal di Viterbo."

Joseph Zarfatti smiled sadly.

"For now, we have nothing to complain about. Miguel da Silva has done his job. We have nothing but suspicions, because we are so certain he is hostile to David and because he continues to conspire with Giacobo Mantino. The cardinal would not understand why we have come to see him nor why we are so impatient."

"But after all," the artist protested, getting back to his feet and running his fingers through his tousled hair, "shouldn't we tell the cardinal, and the pope as well, about the conspiracies those two men are planning in an attempt on David's life?"

"The cardinal is aware of all that…"

Moses stood there with his mouth hanging open.

"And the pope?" he asked.

"The pope is not unaware of what different people are capable of. He plays his cards knowing full well that he is putting Da Silva to the test."

Moses brushed back some hair that was falling down over his eyes, gave a sigh, and shook his head incredulously. Then he asked,

"Well then, what should we do?"

"Just wait."

"Wait? How long?"

"A month, perhaps two, perhaps even more. The time it takes for an emissary to ride rapidly to Lisbon and return to Rome. Or even, alas, the time it takes for an emissary with bad intentions to drag out the trip as long as he can..."

The doctor's body seemed to wilt, and he leaned forward dejectedly. His cape, decorated with a red hood and a fringed clasp, suddenly seemed much too large for him. His voice sounded discouraged when he finally picked up where he had left off.

"Yes, we are condemned to waiting. Only after a month has gone by, or two, can we legitimately claim to the papal authorities that an unreasonable amount of time has passed. Then, perhaps, we will be able to call Da Silva into question and accuse him of trying to thwart the plans of His Majesty the pope."

"Is the Messenger aware of all this?" asked the artist.

"Not yet."

"I'm afraid to have to deliver such news. Surely it will affect him. Perhaps it would be best to wait until tomorrow so we have time to prepare him."

"You are just trying to avoid the task, my dear Moses. I can see that. Let me do it."

The two men turned around. They had suddenly sensed the presence of Dina, who was standing in the doorway listening to them. She was smiling, but her smile was strange, and the expression on her face was one of spite, even of haughtiness.

"It seems to me that the Messenger will not be displeased to hear about the delay," she said, looking up at the ceiling.

And then, in a sarcastic tone, she added unkindly:

"He will then have ample time to discuss the holy Kabbalah with Her Holiness Dona Benvenida Abravanel!"

And with that she slipped away into the corridor, hiding the tears that were beginning to stream down her cheeks. The doctor and the artist, caught by surprise, looked at each questioningly. They didn't understand what Dina meant, and she had left before they could see her tears.

"A joke should be neither unpleasant nor boring," Dina's brother remarked before deciding to join David in his room, accompanied by Moses.

From his room, David had heard the doctor returning from his second meeting with the Portuguese ambassador. When the doctor had not immediately come to his room, he had concluded that the news was not good. And he wasn't particularly surprised. In the Vatican, he had met Miguel da Silva and realized that the man would do whatever he could to counteract his plans, delay his trip to Lisbon, and place numerous obstacles in his path. Furthermore, his faithful Joseph, returning from following Tobias the other night, had confirmed his suspicions. Acting like a drunken man wandering about aimlessly through the streets, chubby, jovial Tobias had gone directly to the Trou Tavern to give account of his observations to Giacobo Mantino. He told him about everything, the ambiance at Doctor Zarfatti's house, and what his guests were doing and saying. So apparently, the traitor had no qualms about the path he had chosen.

In spite of everything, David had not lost hope. The wait would be long, longer than had been the case at the earlier stages of his mission. Was that not because he was approaching his goal? He thought about all those people for whom waiting would be a difficult test. Yes, he knew from simple experience: With a pebble in your shoes, it is difficult to walk looking up at the stars. But whose fault was it? And was not the pebble also the work of the Eternal?

He dug deep into his memory to determine the precise moment when his strategy had deviated from its path. Soon he gave up. Like the sun, it was not a moment that one could look at directly. And what was happening in Rome was similar to what was happening everywhere else: The same people would take advantage of the same situations to harm their neighbors. It gave them pleasure to do so, and they did it proudly. Here in Rome, like everywhere else, there was never enough time to accomplish anything worthwhile. And as everywhere, people dreamed of escape.

Time passes, and it is painful to feel it pass. This keen sense of completed life, of life that is drawing to its end, where and how did it all begin? In a gust of wind? In the creaking of the staircase? In the flickering of a bitter candle? There is a knock at the door. It interrupts his reverie.

"Come in!" he called out in a strong voice.

Joseph Zarfatti appeared in the doorway, ready to speak, his arms raised heavenward.

"You don't need to say anything," David said. "I already know. We should have seen it coming. If you like, I can sum things up for you: Before we can apply the slightest pressure on Da Silva, we have to wait. That's right, isn't it? Wait for as long as it takes for a messenger to reach Lisbon and return to Rome. The time of an illusion. By the way, how long does such a trip normally take?"

"Ten days, or two weeks at the most if one hurries," Moses de Castellazzo answered from behind the doctor.

"Come on in, both of you!" David said when he realized Moses, too, was there.

The artist walked into the room.

"The time it takes to complete the journey," he explained, "depends on the itinerary. Da Silva's envoy goes to Lisbon either by sea, around Gibraltar, or he takes a ship only as far as Valencia and then crosses Spain and Portugal on horseback."

"The second itinerary is shorter, but it takes more time," the Messenger cut in. "It must surely take at least a month. Thirty days of waiting uselessly! Thirty days and thirty nights!"

He was almost shouting.

"Evidently," he continued, "we cannot go to Portugal without Joao III's protection. Imagine Jews crossing Spain on horseback or sailing along Spanish coasts scarcely thirty-two years after they were expelled! Unthinkable! Without royal safe-conducts, we would not get far."

His sharp features hardened, as if a sudden revelation had come to him. And then, to his friends' surprise, his features relaxed and he spoke this astonishing sentence:

"*Astra regunt homines, sed regit astra Deus,*" David said. And then he went on to explain: "That is the favorite proverb of our friend from Fossombrone, the scholar Vincentius Castellani, the man who gave us that indispensable letter for Cardinal di Viterbo."

He grew thoughtful.

"*Astra regunt homines*...the stars govern men; *sed regit astra Deus*...but God governs the stars," he murmured as if to himself.

And then, as if he had said too much, he closed his eyes. He gestured with his left hand, letting his friends know that he wanted to be alone.

"To pray," he whispered, "to pray."

For more than two weeks, in almost total solitude, David Reubeni never left his room, devoting himself to constant meditation along with prayer and fasting. Every day, however, he would briefly see the two Josephs, one after the other. Joseph Halevy, his servant and confidant, would bring him news from the outside, and Joseph Zarfatti, his host the doctor, would come to see what David thought about the news.

. During that time, only one person had the privilege of spending an entire day with the Messenger, and that was Dona Benvenida Abravanel. In the Zarfatti household, rumor had it that the day had been spent "talking about the Kabbalah."

For indeed, Dona Benvenida knew the Kabbalah well, and her commentaries on portions of the Kabbalah were keen and profound.

"The Torah," she said to David that day, "compares the Covenant between the Eternal—blessed be His name!—and the children of Israel to a marriage."

"That point did not escape me," David noted. "But what do you make of that comparison?"

"Me? Nothing, or almost nothing," she replied in her velvety voice. "But I note that the marriage metaphor allowed Moses, the prophets, and the cantors who provided the basis for the Song of Solomon and the Psalms, to describe the history of the Covenant like the history of a Love relationship. Between Israel and God, every phase, every situation that can be found in a relationship of love is always mentioned: from the awakening of feeling with the first encounters all the way up to betrothal, and then, too, the wedding, the birth of children, and even quarrels, jealousy, separation and divorce, widowhood, and finally passionate reunification and reconciliation…"

His eyes half-closed, David enjoyed listening to Benvenida's commentaries. In the scenario she had sketched, his role was one of mediation and reconciliation, and that was a role he would be pleased to play.

In addition to the conversations about the Kabbalah, Dona Benvenida was totally committed to the Messenger's cause. Thanks to her financial support, David had been able to hire two additional servants: Touviah the Lame and David Haromani, men whom Joseph had found in the city. Furthermore, all his servants received new tunics on which a star was embroidered with gold thread, thanks to the lovely, rich, and highly cultured Dona Abravanel.

A situation of that kind did nothing to calm Dina's jealousy. She could neither understand nor accept how David could devote a whole day to Benvenida when he scarcely looked at Dina. She missed the days she had spent alone with him during his illness, when they shared such strange, burning intimacy. They had been so close when David, at first delirious with fever and then inspired as he convalesced, shared his secret longings! Dina was unable to master the pangs of jealousy that were eating at her heart. As for David, he was not unaware of her painful struggles, but thus far he had been careful to stay closed up in his room, avoiding any confrontation with her.

The days were beginning to lengthen. Dawn came ever earlier, chasing away the night. The sun's first rays danced on the Messenger's half-closed eyelids as he said his morning prayers: *Eternal, O my God, in the morning You hear my voice, in the morning I pour out my prayer to You, and I wait...*

On that morning, May 20, 1524 of the Christian calendar, Moses de Castellazzo, still going about his mission of protecting the Messenger from Chabor, hurried in excitedly with a smile on his face.

"Well?" David wondered. "What is happening? I haven't seen you in such a good mood for a long time!"

"We've arranged a meeting."

"Miguel da Silva?"

"No! Michelangelo!"

"The artist?"

"Michelangelo Buonarroti in person. The greatest!"

Moses could hardly breathe, so great was his excitement. His heavy, unruly shock of red hair, tousled as usual, conveyed his enthusiasm.

"I showed him your portrait, the one I had sketched," he added. "And just now he is getting ready to sculpt Moses, our Moses. And your face, master, your face. He is ready to come here. He is eager to meet you."

Moses de Castellazzo's great excitement was a source of amusement for the Messenger. He smiled.

"Why Moses?" he asked.

"For the tomb of Pope Julius II."

"I still wonder why he's chosen to make a sculpture of Moses," David replied.

"But…"

The artist was disconcerted.

"Why not Moses?" he finally said. "Besides, Master, you can ask him yourself."

David raised his right hand and waved it before his eyes.

"He who sees the sky in the water can see fish in the trees," he said as if in a dream.

And then, changing the tone of his voice, he started toward the door.

"Let's go then. Let's go see this Michelangelo!"

Chapter twenty-six

Michelangelo and the Women of Israel

avid Reubeni and Moses de Castellazzo were about to step out into the street when Joseph rushed up out of breath.

"Master," he shouted, "it is unwise to use the front main entrance."

The Messenger turned and looked at his servant. As was his habit, he laughed aloud at Joseph's fears. It is true that Joseph, at moments like that, fell into his customary tick of blinking his eyes, and that gave a comic look to his face, even when he was doing his best to be serious and show the urgency of the situation.

"The man who flees from fear will soon fall into the ditch," said David before he, too, grew serious. "What should I be afraid of?" he asked. "Have not things changed? Those people waiting outside this house are our friends, are they not?"

"Yes," Joseph admitted, "but among those people some hostile spirits are hiding. And enemies. Have not wise men taught us that both love and hate can go beyond normal limits?"

Moses joined in:

"Perhaps Joseph is right," he said to David. "Is there another way out?"

"Yes," replied Joseph triumphantly. His relief was apparent. "At the back of the house, through the door in the small courtyard. In fact, I asked Touviah to have the horses waiting there."

The Messenger placed his hand affectionately on his servant's shoulder and invited him to lead the way. In the courtyard, he checked the saddle before mounting. The horse reared up and whinnied, its ears pricked up. David was about to ride off when Joseph grabbed the horse's bridle.

"Master," he said, his eyes blinking again and brow creased, "may I not know where you are going?"

When he saw the Messenger's surprise, he added:

"The city is not safe. It is crawling with conspiracies. In Rome, famous people can simply disappear. The science of poisons is widespread. People say that one of the most flourishing professions these days is that of a liquidator. The latest recipe for death, almost as dangerous as treacherous steel, a dagger in the back, or a cutlass from the shadows, is to use a grey powder. A mixture of necrotized donkey milk, spider venom, and cockroach ashes. The method is most popular; it is efficient, discreet, and affordable."

When David and Moses heard that, they could not help but smile. But Joseph was insistent, and his eyelids kept blinking.

"Master, I'm not joking. At this very moment there are at least five plots against the pope, and by that I mean five *known* plots! And though no one would suspect it, as for Machiavelli…"

Moses de Castellazzo, already on his horse, held up his hand to stop him.

"People lend only to the rich," he said with a smile.

But then his smile disappeared.

"But Joseph is right about the situation in Rome."

David began to speak:

"We are going to see Michelangelo Buonarroti, on Via Mozza, in the Florentine section of the city," he said quietly to his servant. And Joseph's eyes stopped blinking.

Like the Jews and other foreigners, the Florentine colony in

Rome was clustered in one part of the city. They had chosen an area near the Sant'Angelo Bridge that leads to the Trastevere. A large bend in the river circumscribed a number of streets that made up the neighborhood called the Ponte. In its center, on the market square, reigned the Camera Apostolica, the Holy See's chamber of commerce. On the outskirts, by the Tiber, and not far from the tomb of Augustus, goats wandered about, eating what little food they could find among the ruins of ancient walls and columns. In that grandiose yet desolate décor, David and Moses noticed some men were working to loosen big marble blocks that were then loaded on a cart, whose wheels sunk dangerously into the mud.

"What are you doing?" Moses de Castellazzo asked them.

"They are for Milord Buonarroti," one of the workmen answered. He raised his head, and then looked mistrustfully at the two horsemen.

"Are you friends of his?"

"Yes," Moses answered with a smile. "We are coming to pay him a visit."

The man made a welcoming gesture. They continued on their way.

"Those men love their master," David commented.

"Oh, many do love him," Moses replied, "and they have for a long time! He is famous, too, and has long been famous. Since the day when, as a protégé of Lorenzo de Medici, he began to work on an awkwardly-shaped block of marble, and out of it drew the famous *David before the Combat*, a naked young colossus who is concentrating all his forces on victory. The sculpture was powerful, brimming with life and intelligence, and that is what first attracted the pope's attention to Michelangelo, who was then only twenty-eight years old. And Pope Julius II immediately made the young man the rival of the great but aging Leonardo da Vinci. He summoned Michelangelo to Rome, and two years later gave him the task of completing a number of frescoes, the entire ceiling of the Sistine Chapel. Michelangelo himself told me that that is when he truly discovered the Bible."

"But tell me," the Messenger cut in, "why does he have this obsession with the face of Moses?"

"I know that Julius II, before he died, asked Michelangelo to decorate his tomb, and that once again the sculptor thought of Moses. I believe I can guess why. To symbolize the life of a supreme pontiff, who better is there than Moses, after all? Was Moses not the man who brought the Law to other men? But for five years now Michelangelo has been unable to begin because he has not found the right model! He has yet to meet a face which seems worthy of the prophet from Mount Sinai. Always before, he has chosen his Biblical models among the lower classes of Florence or Rome, but there is not a Moses among them, if I can put it that way. As we talked, he mentioned that Cardinal di Viterbo had told him about you, and the description he gave of your face set him to dreaming. So I showed him the sketches I had made, and then he said he had to see you, as I said. He thinks that only you, Master, can lend your face to Moses."

"The Eternal alone can lend a face to men," David murmured. "Let us see what kind of face He gave to Michelangelo."

When they entered the courtyard filled with blocks of stone and marble of all sizes, a long, thin figure came out of the Palazzo as they arrived, looked at them, and then moved away.

"Strange," said the painter. "What is Messire Orazio Florido doing at Michelangelo's?"

"Who is he?" David asked.

"The best friend of Balthazar Castiglione, the brother of Bernardo who died. He is also the right-hand man of the prefect of Rome, Francisco Maria della Rovere, and the prefect is a very powerful man. Several popes have come from the Rovere family. Orazio Florido here? Strange. What's expected never happens; it's the unexpected that shows up."

Michelangelo greeted them without turning around. He was alone, on his knees on the ground, bending over a drawing. Back from Florence, he had been in Rome for a month at Pope Clement VII's invitation. His normal retinue of young men and minions had not yet joined him, and neither had the cohort of his admirers nor the gall of his detractors.

In fact, the artist was so absorbed in his work that at first he had only noticed his friend Moses.

"So, De Castellazzo," he asked hoarsely, "where is that Prince of Chabor hiding?"

The first thing David Reubeni noticed was a large curly head set on a thick neck and powerful shoulders. When Michelangelo looked up, the Messenger was surprised by how far his eyes were set apart—"a desert lizard," he thought. The rest of his face included a pensive look, a flat, uneven nose, thin lips, a greying mustache, and curly beard. It all made David think of another picture, that of a melancholy lion wandering around outside a palm grove and forcing its way in from time to time.

And then, when he saw David, Michelangelo stood up straight.

"*Ecce homo!* This is the man!" he cried out enthusiastically. "The man in the sketch! For days, I've been trying vainly to reproduce his features!"

And he walked quickly over to the Messenger.

"*Barukh haba!* Welcome! Welcome to the prophet of the Jews!"

He opened his arms and introduced himself:

"The man who walks alone in uncharted territory..."

Moses de Castellazzo offered to translate, but David waved him off. Michelangelo burst out laughing, and his sonorous laugh made the oil lamps hanging above his drawings flicker.

"Men who dialogue with God," he said, "need no interpreter."

He adjusted his grey painter's smock that was smeared with paint and charcoal, and then walked up so close to David that they were almost touching. For a moment, Moses thought that he was going to throw his arms around David and embrace him. The Messenger didn't move a muscle. Then the artist laid his big calloused hands on the shoulders of the man from the desert and murmured in admiration:

"What a face! What an expression! A face that carries within itself dreams of liberation! That is surely how Moses looked! But do not all dreams mark the dreamer forever?"

He took a step backward, without taking his eyes off the Messenger. As if he were afraid David might disappear. He kept moving backward until he reached a stack of portfolios. He picked up one, the largest, and pulled out a sheet of paper and some charcoal.

"The coming of the Prince of Chabor, or God's desire!" he said hoarsely, sighing as he sketched the first lines on the paper.

Moses de Castellazzo was watching David intently. He didn't move a muscle. Immobile, he stood facing Michelangelo. But on his face there was an expression of curiosity, and perhaps of sympathy.

Time went by. Night had already fallen, and Michelangelo was still drawing. About ten sketches of David Reubeni already lay on the tile floor in the studio. Frozen in his role as a model, the Messenger had not moved for hours. Enveloped as he was in his white tunic, his body was now only a form that could almost be mistaken for one of the rough-hewn statues standing there in the semi-darkness.

Finally, Michelangelo looked up, got to his feet, and studied his work. He broke into a smile.

"I've made the decision!" he said. "My Moses will have the features of the Prince of Chabor! And he will stand between two women: Leah and Rachel."

The Messenger's eyes sparkled, but he remained silent. Moses de Castellazzo was the one who reacted.

"Why Leah and Rachel?"

"Because they were Jacob's wives."

"And why Jacob?"

"Because Jacob, after wrestling with the angel, took the name Israel."

"But why put Israel on Julius II's tomb?"

"Forget about the pope!" Michelangelo exclaimed. "Let us think about the man who liberated the children of Israel and then guided them to the Promised Land. Let us think about Moses."

Michelangelo was like a man possessed by some unknown force. His lizard-like eyes were bright. His massive body was trembling with excitement.

"Moses and the women of Israel," he mumbled several times.

The Messenger had spent all those hours in unwavering meditation, and now finally he needed to move. He noticed two statues under a vaulted ceiling in the corner of the room. They were both set on movable pedestals. They seemed foreign and even hostile to each other, and both were still waiting for the master's chisel and its finishing touches. David took several steps, breaking the charm that linked him with the two rough shapes. He then walked over to where Michelangelo was standing in a halo of light and looked at the sketches. He was shocked. It was indeed his portrait. But although he could recognize his eyes, nose, mouth and beard, all quite lifelike, he had the strange impression that he was in the presence of a different man altogether. Another man who had taken on his own appearance. Or perhaps the artist's genius, with his charcoal, had brought out some hidden portion of the Messiah that is part of every man.

Even Michelangelo himself seemed surprised by the result of his long hours of work. He studied his sketches. It was almost as if he were breathing in their scent, circling them like a lion around its prey, as he muttered in delight:

"This will make some people grind their teeth, you'll see. Some will say it's scandalous. In my Moses, others will see reflections of the cold wisdom of Rosselli's Perugino, the ethereal grace of Botticelli, or the strength of Ghirlandaio, my old master. I'm telling you, people will be grinding their teeth and many tongues will be clacking."

"Without a good model there can be no good copy," Moses de Castellazzo remarked with pride as he took the Messenger by the arm. Night would soon be finished. They took leave of the artist just before dawn.

David Reubeni and his friend rode through the Florentine neighborhood as it was barely awakening. When they reached the old paleochristian basilica and its broken, fallen columns, not all of which had been carried off, Moses de Castellazzo pulled his horse to a stop. He felt the need to pour out his feelings, to talk about some of his memories.

"When I came to Rome for the first time," he said in a half-whisper, "I went to the top of the Quirinal Hill, where there are official palaces. From the promontory I looked for hours out over the brown roofs of the city, its smoke, and as evening came, the mists rising from the bend in the Tiber. I had the feeling that I was discovering life…"

And then, as the man from the desert remained silent, he asked:

"What did the Messenger think of Michelangelo? You didn't say one word the whole night, Master!"

"Words are action's shadow," David murmured.

And then, after a few moments, he added:

"Vincentius Castellani, the scholar from Fossombrone, told me that in his opinion Dante had been God's penholder. So I would say that Michelangelo is His brush."

He prodded his horse forward, and the two set off once more, leaving the old basilica to its ruins. Moses de Castellazzo rode behind David in silence. The more he observed David Reubeni, the more fascinating he found him. Both in the way he held himself in the saddle and in his comportment with men, there was such natural nobility in him! It seemed to Moses that he was looking at a being from nowhere and yet from everywhere, a man who still carried the Arabian Desert under his feet, Israel's hope and memory in his heart, and the history and customs of Europe in his head. Although he seemed like a foreigner everywhere, on the other hand, nothing was truly foreign to him. Had prophets always been composed of the same stern elements?

"Does the Messenger have any regrets about being Michelangelo's model for Moses?" Moses asked.

David did not respond immediately. Twenty or thirty meters further along, to the rhythm of his trotting horse, he began to explain.

"If I were to fail, if once again my people could not return to the land of their ancestors, if such were the will of the One—blessed be His name—who controls our destinies, then Michelangelo's Moses would bear witness. It will be there to remind people that Israel does exist, that its memory remains, that its hope is alive. And perhaps some day it will reawaken our ancient dream."

He smiled as if to himself:

"Moses and the women of Israel," he repeated quietly several times.

In the ensuing silence, Moses de Castellazzo, over the sound of the horses' hooves on the pavement, caught the Messenger chanting a prayer: *I cry toward God, and the Lord delivers me. Morning, noon, and evening, I will groan and sigh so that He might hear my voice.*

Little by little, dawn was breaking. Above the Tiber the sky was getting lighter, licking the facades of the palaces on the Quirinal Hill with rose and mauve. Throughout the city birds were beginning to chirp. The last bits of the night's calm were disappearing under the pressure of gates screeching and shutters banging. Someone shouted out. Once. Twice.

"I think somebody is calling for help," Moses said.

At the next moment, just as they were riding out into Piazza Navona, near the palace of the Mellini family who were close to the Sforzas, they saw three men beating some poor fellow. As the three ruffians were about to leave their victim, one of them changed his mind and said: "We forgot to leave our signature!" And the three brigands turned back to the man who was trying to get to his feet and fell on him once more.

David Reubeni gave a terrible cry and galloped toward the men, surprising the bandits. Two of them were thrown to the ground by the powerful horse. The Messenger leaped from his mount and caught the third ruffian as he tried to flee. As he had done on the ship near Pesaro, he picked up the man as if he were a sack of dirty laundry, lifted him in the air, and tossed him onto the two others who were trying to get back to their feet. All three went sprawling, but then other bandits brandishing swords appeared from out of nowhere. They charged at the Messenger. Moses de Castellazzo had dismounted as well. He hurried to David's support. At the same time horsemen burst out of the Navona Palace. The swordsmen paused, unsure of themselves. With blood streaming over his face from cuts above both eyes, the man David had handled so roughly was able to get up.

"Let's get out of here!" the man said.

All three fled. A few moments later the horsemen arrived. They were the Messenger's servants. At their head was Joseph, a long dagger in his hand.

The area began to come to life. Windows and shutters opened on all sides of the piazza, and the faces that appeared showed fear and questioning. The door of the Mellini Palace was flung open, and a dozen guards dressed in purple and armed with lances appeared, responding much too late to the disturbance. The artist and the Messenger turned to check on the victim. Although his face was swollen and his tunic covered with blood, he was a mature man and not without style. White, unkempt hair escaped from under his black hood, but he made an effort to stand up straight and regain his dignity. He was taller than it first appeared when he was curled up on the ground being beaten by his aggressors. In a strong voice, though he was covered with blood, he said:

"Thank you, Milords, thank you! They did a good job, didn't they?

"Yes, indeed," Moses replied. "And they even came back to put the final touches on their work."

"Well, then, we have nothing more to fear for the time being," said the old man with a touch of humor. "It is those things that are only halfway done that have consequences. If they had really wanted to kill me, I'd be long dead."

"Come and let us take care of you," Joseph broke in. "There's an inn across the square."

The wounded man leaned on the artist for support and was led toward the inn, while Joseph took it upon himself to take care of the horses.

"Do you have any idea," Moses asked, "who could have it in for you like this and why?"

The old man, with much difficulty, smiled before answering:

"Everyone, young man, everyone!"

"Excuse me, Milord, but who are you?"

The man raised his head and looked his interlocutor straight in the eyes, and then, as if he were presenting his excuses, he smiled once more with false modesty before introducing himself.

"Usually people call me Niccolò Machiavelli."

Chapter twenty-seven

A Dove in the Conspiracy

Giacobo Mantino was still raging. The suspicious drowning of Bernardo Castiglione, the man who was to make an attempt on the Messenger's life; the favorable reception given David Reubeni by the pope; the constant popular support the exiled Jews were offering to the man from Chabor—all those things obsessed and infuriated the president of the *Va'ad* of Venice. Because he did not want to lose contact with the man he called an imposter, he had made the Trou Tavern in Rome the headquarters of his permanent conspiracy against the man from the desert. Of course, his friend, the Portuguese ambassador Dom Miguel da Silva, had indeed been able to delay the imposter's trip to Portugal, but for how long? Mantino knew that neither he nor Dom Miguel, nor any of those people who believed as they did in the real danger that David Reubeni represented for Jews in Europe, as well as for those in the Ottoman Empire, could do anything against a decision made by the pope and by any kings who would support him.

The street outside Doctor Zarfatti's house was never empty, and Giacobo Mantino knew that the day David Reubeni finally set off toward Portugal, tens of thousands of fervent Jews would accompany him.

As the translator of Averroes and a disciple and commentator of Aristotle, Mantino was an established scholar, and he admired Maimonides for the intellectual effort he had made to attempt to rationally explain the necessity of God. How could he, with his logical mind and careful rigor, how could he remain passive before this uncontrollable movement of messianic faith that had developed around this imposter from the desert? How could he, responsible for a large Jewish community, pretend to ignore that the Inquisition that had already ravaged the condition of Jews in Spain was only waiting for a pretext to set upon the Jews in Italy? It was his clear duty to do something! In such an emergency, there was no room for tolerance. Against supernatural hope, no sermon, no speech, no arguments would have any effect. The *milchemet mitzvah*, the required war, was clearly necessary. In a situation like this, what stood out was the necessity of a preventive war. And the preventive war would have one objective—eliminating the troublemaker. The more he examined his conscience and principles, the more Giacobo Mantino was led to this irreversible decision: It would be necessary to kill. To kill the Jew who was leading other Jews astray. To kill the Jew who was leading not only the Jews astray, but others as well. To kill him because he was jeopardizing the equilibrium of the entire world!

As he was thinking such thoughts, he reached the Piazza Colonna, where Dom Miguel da Silva lived. The plan he had thought up was diabolical, but in a war, must not one subordinate the means to the expected end? The Portuguese ambassador would be his accomplice once again. For this new conspiracy, he had also obtained the services of the elegant Orazio Florido, the man in charge of dirty tricks for the Prefect of Rome. He was happy to avenge the death of Bernardo, the brother of his best friend, Balthazar Castiglione. Orazio Florido was already waiting with Dom Miguel when Mantino joined them in a room decorated with rich velvet tapestries from Alexandria.

The ambassador's sharp features bore a smile, and his apparent openness spoke volumes about how perverse the man must be.

He loved nothing more than complicated, sophisticated conspiracies, and the conspiracy they were planning was just that.

"The young woman was contacted by your man," he said to Mantino. "She reacted as you suspected. She will be here momentarily."

And indeed, a few moments later, a valet announced a visitor. Giacobo Mantino slipped away to hide in the adjoining room from where he would not lose a word of the conversation. The valet ushered in their guest.

"Come in! Come in!" the elegant ambassador greeted her gallantly. "Welcome, Signorina Dina Zarfatti, and thank you for agreeing to meet with us."

The young woman blushed, both surprised and intimidated by the luxurious furniture and décor. She bowed, and then sat down in a heavy, blue velvet armchair that Dom Miguel da Silva very obligingly pushed toward her.

"Yes, Milord," she said, and her voice sounded like a little girl's. "I've come at the request of Tobias, one of the Prince of Chabor's servants. He brought me your message."

"We are agreed are we not, Signorina?" the ambassador asked. "No one must know anything about your visit here. The slightest indiscretion could foil our plans, and worse, might even harm the life of the Prince of Chabor."

"No one knows, Milord. No one."

"I am relieved to hear that, Signorina."

Waving his long aristocratic hands with false compunction, Miguel da Silva walked around the armchair and stopped, facing Dina:

"Signorina Zarfatti," he began with his unctuous voice, "I allowed myself to contact you because I know how fond you are of the Envoy from Chabor. You love him a great deal, do you not?"

Dina made no comment, but she blushed and lowered her eyes. A sardonic glimmer appeared in Da Silva's eyes, though normally they displayed nothing but innocence. He continued:

"The Messenger mistrusts me. Quite mistakenly, I assure you. But that's the way things are. He thinks that I wish him ill. He is wrong, alas! He believes that I am intentionally delaying his trip to Portugal."

The ambassador paused for a few moments. He sat down, a contrite expression on his face, in an armchair opposite from where the young woman was sitting. Orazio Florido had been standing silently a little behind Da Silva ever since Dina had arrived. Da Silva went on:

"So the Messenger is wrong about me. But it is true, nonetheless, that Rome is crawling with people who are not all admirers, who are even mortal enemies of his cause and his person. Some, I know, wish his death—and may God preserve us from their intrigues! David Reubeni is right about that, and he owes it to himself to remain vigilant. And indeed that is why I can't blame him for mistrusting me. On the contrary, I am seeking a way to help him and protect him from the dangers that threaten him. I, too, am upset by how long it is taking to arrange his trip to Portugal. I am worried, Signorina, I am worried."

He suddenly got to his feet, rubbing his alabaster hands together, and once again started to walk slowly around Dina's armchair, as if to hypnotize her:

"You see, Signorina Zarfatti, more than three weeks ago now, upon His Holiness the pope's demand, I sent a request to Lisbon to have documents and official authorizations sent back for the trip planned by the Prince of Chabor and his retinue. However, I have lost all trace of the messenger I sent for that purpose. It appears that he has never reached Lisbon. It is even to be feared that he will never reach Lisbon. I wonder…Yes, I wonder if perhaps he has been waylaid by evildoers in the pay of one or another of David's enemies."

"Excuse me, Milord," Dina interrupted him.

"Yes, Signorina?"

"I am grateful for this information, but I do not understand why Your Excellence expressed the wish to see me."

"I can understand your impatience, Signorina. So this is what I would like: In order to respond to the pope's request, I would like to see my message arrive in Lisbon, and even, to be more precise, directly in the hands of my beloved sovereign, King Joao III. For I wish to see the Prince of Chabor leave for Portugal as soon as possible."

"That is also my wish, Milord. But I still fail to see how someone like me can be of any use."

"Well, Signorina, the noble gentleman here before you, good Orazio Florido, an advisor to the Prefect of Rome, is leaving tomorrow for Lisbon, where he will be received immediately by the king himself. He, himself, spontaneously offered to give the king a letter addressed to him by the Prince of Chabor. Such a procedure would accelerate things considerably and would allow the question of David Reubeni's trip to be settled quickly. It is an opportunity that the Prince of Chabor owes to himself to seize."

Orazio Florido moved his long figure and leaned over Dina's armchair, forcing her to look up at him. His face was as thin and long as his carcass. He had protruding eyes with brown irises, a thin nose, lips as thin as knife-blades, and graying flaxen hair pulled back in a ponytail. He was about forty years old, and he often managed to get the better of his interlocutors by his strange appearance alone. He stood nearly two meters tall, and when he looked down toward those he was speaking to he displayed obvious condescension almost in spite of himself for everyone, male or female. The condescension was stronger than the deference and respect he had learned to show through his words and gestures. A person could endure only a few moments of his penetrating stare before agreeing with him. The serpent in the Bible appears humbly, but in total superiority, for it knows ahead of time that it will entice Eve. Thus it was with Orazio Florido and Dina. His soft, velvety voice stood in stark contrast with his sharp features and angular body, and he planted his enormous eyes directly into hers as he whispered:

"Yes, lovely Signorina, His Excellency the Ambassador Da Silva is right. I am leaving shortly for Ostia where I can get a ship that is sailing tomorrow evening for Lisbon. I suggested to His Excellency that he entrust me with a personal letter from the Prince of Chabor for King Joao III. And I say this in all sincerity, Signorina, it would be a great honor, in this circumstance, to be the prince's emissary."

Dina was not sure what to think. She looked back and forth at the two men. They seemed sincere, and she was beginning to guess what they were coming to. She twisted her hands nervously. Then she unfolded them and laid them flat on her dress. She started to speak and then hesitated.

She is beginning to bite, Miguel da Silva thought before speaking again, and Orazio Florido, with one hand on the back of the young woman's armchair, kept gazing at her like a boa preparing to swallow its prey after squeezing all life out of it.

"That is why I asked you to come here, Signorina Zarfatti," the ambassador continued. "I would like you to speak with the Prince of Chabor about this. I would like you to explain this new opportunity. He, himself, must write to Joao III! But I could never say all this to him. He would never trust me. But you, he will trust! You, he will believe, will he not? This is a unique opportunity. He must seize it!"

He paused, lifting a finger in warning:

"But be sure, Signorina, not one word about me! Do not speak to David Reubeni about me!"

And then, with a good-natured smile, he added:

"Tell him, for example, that you met our fine friend Orazio Florido in the flower market. He happened to speak to you, asking if you were indeed Doctor Zarfatti's sister and saying how much he admired the Messenger from Chabor. You can also say he told you that when he was at Cardinal Pucci's, he heard how the Jewish prince and his retinue were waiting so impatiently for Portuguese passports. And finally, you can say that he offered to carry a missive from David Reubeni directly to Joao III himself. In the letter the prince could explain to the king his desire to visit him in Lisbon, according to the instructions of His Holiness Clement VII. Believe me, Signorina, this is an unhoped-for opportunity. Of course I can always send another official courier to Lisbon as early as tomorrow, but I fear he, too, might be intercepted. Whereas I am sure that Orazio Florido will be able to reach Portugal and see the king! Nobody could suspect him of carrying a letter of that kind!"

Dina got to her feet. The room's atmosphere, too rich, too heavy with velvet and gold trim, was oppressive. The two gaunt men's persistance in trying to persuade her made her head spin. Should she trust them? Or should she let herself be guided by the hidden fear that had gripped her ever since she had set foot in that room? She took a few steps away from the armchairs and stopped near a table on which marble and gold vied for light. She immediately felt more sure of herself. Yes, she would play a part in their game. After all, would she not be helping David? Why, on what pretext, because of what vague fear should she refuse to contribute to the advancement of the man she venerated, even though she also felt spite and jealousy eating at her heart? Furthermore, she felt a wave of happiness sweep over her when she made her decision. Helping David, how better to get close to him so that he might look more favorably upon her? Her voice was calm when she gave her answer.

"Very well. I'll deliver the message. I promise."

She turned toward Orazio Florido.

"Where should the Messenger from Chabor bring his letter for King Joao III?"

But the reply came from Miguel da Silva.

"Milord Florido will be leaving for Ostia today, and he will be there until tomorrow evening..."

He pretended to be thinking aloud:

"Let's see. It might be best if Orazio Florido met the Messenger..."

Orazio Florido agreed.

"His Excellency is right," he said. "Tomorrow I shall expect the Prince of Chabor in Ostia, between five and six in the afternoon. Just opposite the quay is an inn, The Thermopolium. That's where I'll be."

"But how will he recognize you?" the ambassador asked.

"I'll be able to recognize him. I happened to catch sight of him not long ago in Michelangelo Buonarroti's studio, Michelangelo the sculptor."

He seemed to bend his long body almost in half as he bowed in perfect deference to the young woman, and then he stood back up straight before speaking again.

177

"You can be proud of yourself, Signorina! Together, we shall move the cause of the Prince of Chabor forward. But don't forget. After six o'clock tomorrow evening in Ostia, it will be too late. I'll be on my way to Lisbon."

When Dom Miguel da Silva led Dina back to the front door, he whispered in her ear, as if he were afraid that someone might hear.

"The future of the Prince of Chabor's mission is in your hands, my dear Signorina Zarfatti. But you must be sure not to tell anyone about our meeting!"

A moment later he rejoined his two fellow conspirators in the living room.

"What do you think, my dear Giacobo?" he asked.

"I could hear everything from behind the door," the doctor answered. "Very interesting, and quite skillful indeed! You demonstrated great powers of persuasion, my dear Dom Miguel. And you too, Orazio. My congratulations! But I was unable to observe the young woman. I wonder what her attitude and her reactions were."

"Just as you had predicted, my dear Giacobo! First she was mistrustful, then confused, then flattered, and then finally she was proud to be able to prove to her beloved that she can do more for him than Benvenida Abravanel."

The ambassador rubbed his hands together in satisfaction. There was no longer anything of the false prelate's unctuousness that he displayed when he stood before Dina, rubbing his hands together with his eyes half-closed. Now those strange green eyes sparkled as he exclaimed:

"What shall we drink, Milords? We must surely raise our glasses and drink to the success of our enterprise, must we not?"

David Reubeni, along with Moses de Castellazzo and Joseph, was about to leave Doctor Zarfatti's house when Dina came back with armloads of flowers. When she saw the three, she hurried up to the Messenger.

"Master!" she cried.

David turned to her.

"I have an urgent message for you," she said.

And lowering her voice, she added for him alone:

"Very urgent and very important."

The man from the desert gestured to his companions to wait for him. With Dina, he went into the dining room on the ground floor. Through a window, he could see Touviah and Tobias out in the courtyard saddling the horses. He listened quietly to the young woman's story, asking a few questions for clarification, but made no comments. When she had finished answering his questions, he studied her intensely for a moment, as if he would have liked to bare her soul so he could read it as an open book, and that is perhaps what he was doing. Dina was disconcerted by his gaze, and she could feel her heart beat faster. Her cheeks grew warm. David brushed her cheek with the tips of his fingers and murmured:

"Your secret is your slave, but if you allow it to escape it becomes your master."

At the moment, Dina gave no thought to the wisdom of that old saying from Hebrew wisdom. She assumed he had guessed her deepest thoughts, and shame made her tremble. She had the reflex to ask a question that seemed perfectly appropriate.

"But…how about the letter and the rendezvous? What are you going to do, Master?"

"Think," the Messenger said as he left the room, "think."

When he pushed open the door, he looked up and saw a flock of black cormorants squawking as they flew by.

Chapter twenty-eight

Machiavelli's Advice

David Reubeni rode off at a trot, followed by Joseph and Moses de Castellazzo, who made sure they stayed close behind him. At a reasonable distance, the other servants followed. Joseph was wary and did not want to take the risk of being caught in some ambush. Back in Naples, didn't his family always say that a man who's been bitten by a serpent is afraid of a rope?

The weather was good. They had plenty of time before the Messenger's meeting. So he suggested to his companions that they make a detour through the Pineto, a pine forest a few leagues from the Vatican that covered a valley carved out by water, and that people called Hell Valley. He loved those trees with their reddish bark and their majestic parasol shapes. He felt protected by their branches, and he found their shade reassuring. And he needed reassurance, for Dina's story and demeanor were disconcerting. He didn't question her sincerity or loyalty, but he knew from experience that sometimes sincerity was itself the cause of errors, that loyalty sometimes caused pain, and that love could be the source of calamity.

From Dina's words he had learned two lessons. The first reminded him that the temptations he had been resisting for years were beginning to get the better of him now that he was in Rome. The pleasure he experienced when meeting famous people for example, or the satisfaction of being loved had caused his sense of action to atrophy. His vigilance and his strategic intuition had been altered. For, there was no denying it, the idea of sending a missive to the King of Portugal by another channel than through Ambassador da Silva should have at least crossed his mind much earlier! David examined his motives carefully and unsparingly. The second lesson had come from Niccolò Machiavelli, but at the time he hadn't thought it important. After he had been soundly beaten in the Piazza Navona, had not that counselor of kings declared that "it is those things that are only half done that have consequences?" The man from the desert should therefore expect some unpleasant surprise. Is that what he should be seeing, veiled insidiously, in the message Dina had brought to him?

Beyond those two lessons there were still two questions he needed to clear up. Why was Orazio Florido, a hired hand of the Prefect of Rome, taking such interest in him? And why had he chosen the young woman to be his messenger? David knew how much Dina loved him, and her love was flattering. He also knew how naïve she was, and her naiveté was touching. But he had not failed to notice that she was jealous, and that worried him. For jealousy, like tears, often blurs one's vision. And it is sometimes the cause of aberrant, dangerous actions. But the whole story might also be plausible, and a chance encounter in the flower market between Orazio Florido and Dina was perfectly possible. The kind of fortunate opportunity that allows a blind man to catch a hare. However, the desert man's experiences had taught him that if the hare ended up being eaten by the blind man, chance didn't really have much to do with it.

A flock of scolding magpies, more and more numerous in Rome, brought him back to reality. He called out to Joseph as his servant rode up to get his orders.

"Let's go! It is now time to honor our meeting."

Joseph agreed, but he couldn't refrain from asking his master a question before they rode off. The question had been burning his lips, as it had Moses de Castellazzo's, ever since they had left Doctor Zarfatti's house.

"What did she tell you?"

"Dina?"

"Yes."

"She gave me a good idea and suggested a poor way of carrying it out."

The three men were ten minutes late when they reached a modest dwelling at the corner of Via dei Coronari and Vicolo Domizio. Beside the open gate, a niche in the wall held a Coronation of the Virgin. At the far end of the courtyard, in an attractive little two-story building overgrown with ivy, Niccolò Machiavelli was waiting for them.

He got up quickly as they approached and held out his hand to David Reubeni.

"Welcome to my benefactor!" he exclaimed.

The Messenger was astonished at the man's metamorphosis. He even wondered if he would have recognized him in the street. Machiavelli seemed younger and larger than when David had helped him to his feet, dripping blood, from the pavement in the Piazza Navona where he was lying. His long grey hair, now carefully combed back, displayed a wide forehead. Beneath a long, aquiline nose, his mouth was nicely shaped and his chin showed determination. Furthermore, instead of the dark rags he had been wearing when he was attacked, he now was dressed in an expensive green velvet doublet that curiously hung down over his stockings as a dress might have done. A fine linen garment extended out from under a high collar. Machiavelli must have sensed his visitor's surprise. He smiled.

"When I come back home to work in my study," he said, "I cast off the rags I've been wearing during the day, covered as they are with filth and dirty looks, for then I prefer wearing clothing fit for royal courts."

His entire being seemed to be concentrated in his smile.

"I owe as much to these men: Antiquity knew how to live, and they knew how to think."

And as he spoke he gestured toward the hundreds of volumes that covered the walls of the room. He continued:

"Here, welcomed by these men, I can revel in the only food that suits me and for which I was born. I have no qualms or shame conversing with them, questioning them about the reasons for their actions. And they, with all of their humanity, are always able to answer me."

He caressed a few of the bindings.

"This is my garden," he said. "The garden of knowledge."

"I understand," said the Messenger. But his companions weren't sure if he was talking about the language—the Italian Machiavelli was using—or the deep meaning of the man's words.

"I understand," he repeated, reaching out with his left hand to touch a few of the books. "Few men escape unharmed from passion of that kind."

Machiavelli raised his eyebrows. David Reubeni began to speak once more, as if he were a storyteller, as he did when he had decided to charm his audience, to put forward a grand vision using the winding detours and fascination of legends.

"Our wise men," he said, "tell about the adventure of four scholars in the garden of knowledge. All four were rabbis, and their names were Ben Azaï, Ben Zoma, Ben Abouya, and Ben Yossef. Only one man, Rabbi Akabi Ben Yossef, was able to leave that famous garden, the Pardess, unscathed. The three others suffered horrible fates. Ben Azaï died. Ben Zoma went mad. Ben Abouya abjured his faith. One sentence, perhaps, can help us understand the reason for their failure: *When you reach the sparkling marble,* it is said, *don't misunderstand, and don't say 'Water, water!'*"

Niccolò Machiavelli seemed to appreciate those words, and he slowly clapped his hands with obvious enthusiasm.

"Superb metaphor!" he exclaimed. "It is true for knowledge, for all approaches to learning, but also for power."

And then shaking his head, as if he suddenly realized how thoughtless he was, he said:

"But I am forgetting all my duties! Please do sit down, Prince." And he pulled a chair over, placing it near his work table, where he himself sat down after pointing out another chair near the window for Moses de Castellazzo and a sofa a little further away for Joseph. As he sat at the table, he made no move to pick up the pen that occupied center stage, but instead, he leaned forward on his elbows to address the Messenger.

"Where can one find the story you told us?" he asked.

"In the Talmud," David replied. "It is written in the Talmud."

"That's a book I have heard much about. And it seems fascinating!"

And then he changed the subject.

"I owe it to you, Prince, that I am still alive today."

And he brushed aside the expression of modesty that he could read on the face of the man from the desert.

"Don't be modest, I beg of you! What you did was exemplary, and nothing makes people esteem a prince more than when he himself sets the example."

David Reubeni looked embarrassed.

"Our wise men," he said, "claim the following: He who saves one human life saves all humanity."

"That is hardly modest!" Machiavelli said mockingly.

"They claim as well that he who destroys one life also destroys all humanity."

"Nor is that very modest..."

"Yes it is, since the man who kills boasts of it, whereas the man who saves never even speaks about it."

"That is wisdom, Prince. But my role is above all to show interest in what you are interested in."

A little irritation showing in his voice, Machiavelli continued:

"When we have the opportunity to meet someone who, in civilian life, has accomplished something extraordinary, *we must speak about it.* Especially when it is a prince who, in addition, is the bearer of an ambitious political project! He himself must find ways of making his actions known. People will esteem him more when they learn how, intuitively and out of the goodness of his heart, he spontaneously came to the aid of an unfortunate stranger who was being beaten black and blue. In this particular case, the "unfortunate stranger" happened to be Niccolò Machiavelli. Even if I am not universally loved, at least people are not indifferent to me, and your help to me, Prince, will enhance your stature in everyone's eyes. When I say *everyone*, I'm including even your enemies."

"I follow what you are saying, and I accept your reasoning," the Messenger responded. "However, I was not trying to gain any benefit by what I did."

"Of course not," Machiavelli acquiesced, "of course not. But the Prince of Chabor, in addition to his moral qualifications, is a political man. So it is his responsibility, even required of him, to consider that his conduct in every situation, and, for example, during the attack in Piazza Navona, *can and must serve his plans*."

He turned to Moses de Castellazzo, who was nodding as he listened.

"It is your job to spread the information! People will esteem the prince all the more if they believe him capable of selfless friendship. Many will then aspire to join his close circle."

David Reubeni smiled. His eyes narrowed, but they were sparkling.

"You are just as I was told," he sighed.

"By whom?"

"Vincentius Castellani."

"Ah, my old friend from Fossombrone!"

A servant brought refreshments and then disappeared. Machiavelli leaned over toward the Messenger once again.

"They say you posed for Michelangelo's Moses."

"How do you know that?"

"For a public man, knowledge is the greatest power."

Machiavelli radiated good humor, though in the tiny wrinkles at both corners of his mouth there were nuances of irony.

"The Messenger of Chabor, descendant of the lost tribe of Reuben, to incarnate Moses! Disturbing, is it not?"

"Pure chance," said David, trying to set the record straight.

"I am not unaware that chance governs half of our actions. However, the other half is left to our free will. The first half may be inherent in any political action, but it is the means we choose, and only those means, that determine whether our enterprise will succeed or fail. And we are free to choose our means."

He watched as the Messenger's expression grew more intense and his eyes brighter. Then he went on:

"Take Moses, for example. When we examine his life and actions carefully, there is only one small trace of chance—he happened to be the man who was needed at that moment, the man for a particular situation. The children of Israel, held in slavery by the Egyptians, were ready to follow him in order to escape their servitude. For everything else, it was because Moses had talents as a leader that he was able to restore hope and the taste of freedom to his people."

His demonstration seemed to amuse him.

"What a lesson for you, Prince!"

"Perhaps," David replied. "But I would point out to you that, according to tradition, Moses was really called and chosen by the Eternal—blessed be His name!—to accomplish that task."

"But we must also admire Moses the man, if for nothing else than the grace that made him worthy to speak with God," Machiavelli countered skillfully. "Nor do I forget the courage he had to have to confront Pharaoh."

A cloud hid the sun, and the room grew dark. Nobody spoke for a few moments. Machiavelli remained in thought, stroking his chin. But as a ray of sunlight reappeared and slid like a blank sheet of paper over the table on which his elbows rested, the old man once again leaned toward his guest.

"Some people are claiming that you are the Messiah, the One the Jews have been expecting for centuries…"

David gestured impatiently, interrupting him.

"Those people have not understood a thing. Our wise men tell us that one day a man asked the prophet Elijah:

"When will the Messiah finally come?"
"Go ask him directly," Elijah responded.
"Where may I find him?"
"At the entrance to the city."
"How will I recognize him?"
"He is recognizable among the poor," Elijah added.

So the man went outside the city. Among the poor, he identified the Messiah and asked him:

"When you will come to walk among men, O Master?"

"Today," the Messiah replied.

Then the man went back to the prophet Elijah and said to him:

"The man who claims to be the Messiah lied to me. He told me he would come today and he did not."

The prophet Elijah answered:

"The words he said to you are written in a psalm: 'O, if only today you could hear His voice!'"

"Magnificent!" Machiavelli cried. "And where is that written?"

"In the Talmud."

The old man raised his arms, as if to give thanks for a book with such strength.

"I absolutely must read that book," he added, his face radiant.

Moses de Castellazzo, who had followed with great interest the exchange between the two men, intervened. He was fascinated by the confrontation of these two cultures, both of which were also his own, and he was delighted to note that they could coexist and reinforce each other. But one question kept haunting him, and he could not wait to ask it.

"Milord," he said, "you who know everything that happens in the city…"

Niccolò Machiavelli stood up, interrupting the artist.

"Young man, I know what you are going to ask. I am indeed aware of many things. I was going to talk about them with the Prince of Chabor, and I had planned to do so today, during this meeting…"

He walked over to a cabinet where there was a large bowl of grapes. He took a bunch and held it in the palm of his left hand, while with his right hand he held out the bowl to the Messenger. David nodded his thanks. Then, as if in a dream, the old conselor of princes went back to his seat behind the reading table. Looking up at the ceiling beams, he began to speak once more, as if he were discussing philosophy aloud or drawing the first rough lines of a sketch.

"A prince must fear two things. The first, inside his own country, concerns his subjects. The second, outside, concerns foreigners. From worries of that kind, he will defend himself with good weapons and good friends, and there is no question but that he can find good friends if he has good weapons. He knows that domestic affairs will remain calm if foreign affairs remain calm, unless some conspiracy comes to perturb them. But if his people believe in him and if he has good friends, a prince has nothing to fear from conspiracies, and indeed he need not pay much attention to them."

Machiavelli looked amused, and his gaze settled on each of his guests in turn as he took the time to eat a few grapes. Moses de Castellazzo was deep in thought, pushing his hand through his huge shock of red hair. Joseph Halevy, trying to restrain his obvious excitement, eyes wide and stomach round, was almost beside himself with contentment there on the sofa. As for the Messenger, he was perplexedly stroking his little beard. His only response was to murmur:

The evil perish
And the enemies of the Eternal,
Like the loveliest pastures
Vanish in smoke.

"Is that too in the Talmud?" Machiavelli wondered.

"No, it is in the Bible. It's a psalm of David."

Moses de Castellazzo took advantage of the ensuing silence. He brushed back those rebellious red locks, stood up, and finally asked the question that was on his mind.

"Milord Machiavelli is therefore aware of the new conspiracy being fomented against the Prince of Chabor? Does he know who is behind it and what is involved? Perhaps he already knows all the details about how it is to be carried out?"

Machiavelli looked questioningly at the Messenger with laughter in his eyes. As David did not say a word, he turned back to the artist and answered.

"The initiative for this new conspiracy comes from that damned soul, the honorable Doctor Giacobo Mantino, the man responsible for the Jewish community in Venice. The idea was refined by the

Portuguese ambassador Dom Miguel da Silva, and it is to be carried out by Orazio Florido, the man in charge of secret missions for Francesco Maria Della Rovere, the Prefect of Rome. Everything is to happen tomorrow in Ostia, because the conspirators believe, and they are right, that the Prince of Chabor has too many friends and allies in Rome."

"What would Milord Machiavelli advise the prince to do?" asked the artist.

"The prince must not believe everything he hears and act too hastily. He must avoid being too fearful and proceed in a manner that is tempered by wisdom and humanity. Thus he can avoid two pitfalls. One is to be overly self-confident, for too much self-confidence can lead to imprudence; the other is to be overly mistrustful of others, for mistrust can lead to intolerance."

Once more he got to his feet, walked around the table, and stood near David Reubeni, who was sitting upright in his chair. He appeared to be meditating. Machiavelli leaned down and, taking pains to pronounce each syllable clearly, he whispered the following sibylline sentence:

"I, Niccolò Machiavelli, have an idea. But you too, Prince of Chabor, you too must have an idea."

The Messenger looked up at the old man. Their faces were nearly touching. Both seemed to be looking intensely into the same brilliant darkness.

"I do indeed have an idea," said David. "I do not know Ostia. So first I must get a detailed map of the port. Must we not set a trap for those who are trying to entrap us? Well then, I will act in my manner, or rather in the manner of my ancestors when they would say: *Evil men draw their swords and bend their bows…But their swords will enter their own hearts and their bows will break.*"

"That is what I thought. Does that too come from the Talmud?" asked Machiavelli, raising his eyebrows before going back to his seat at the table.

"No, that is from David again. Psalm xxxvii."

"Do you have enough men?"

David glanced over at Joseph. He was enthralled with the discussion and was still smiling broadly. Since they had arrived, Joseph had not uttered a word. But now he reacted immediately:

"We have good, strong men," he affirmed.

"Good," Machiavelli said. And turning to the Messenger, he asked: "But afterward, what do you plan to do?"

"Afterward," David replied, "I will indeed be sending a message to the King of Portugal, but through another channel than through his ambassador in Rome."

"Would the prince allow me to make a comment?"

"Please do."

Niccolò Machiavelli placed his hand on the Messenger's shoulder.

"The prince should not worry about being considered cruel. The prince has been able to inspire love. Now he must learn to inspire fear. But he must not let himself be carried away by his courage, which is natural and spontaneous, as he has already demonstrated. For my part, if I were the prince, I myself would not go to Ostia."

He grew quiet, and then he licked his lips greedily, as if he were savoring in advance the trick he would be playing on the adversaries of the Prince of Chabor.

"If I were the prince, I would send someone else in my place. Orazio Florido has seen you briefly only once, in Michelangelo's dark courtyard. He can be duped, at least up until the last minute, and that will make the difference, by a man your size dressed as you are. On the other hand, I do approve of the rest of your plan, although…I can offer the prince a group of my friends in Ostia to reinforce his troops. I know that Orazio Florido will not skimp on preparations, and he will be waiting with a large number of men he has dug up from among the riffraff in the port. He must suspect you will not come alone. As far as my friends are concerned, they know their own city inside and out, along with the port, its quays, its tiny streets, and its courtyards. The best map in the world is not as good as firsthand knowledge of the area."

He took a few steps away from the table, stopped for a moment beside the bowl of grapes, then turned back and burst into laughter.

"When I think of it! The greatest evildoers sometimes make the stupidest mistakes! Does the prince realize that ships for Portugal leave from Livorno and not from Ostia?"

Leaving the grapes untouched, he came back to the Messenger.

"On the other hand," he continued, "the idea of sending someone with a letter for Joao III without going through Miguel da Silva is excellent. But I must point out that it is indispensable to entrust the letter to a gentleman who is close to the Church, close to Clement VII. In addition, the missive must emanate not from your own hand but from the hand of His Holiness."

He paused, thought for a moment, and then continued, his voice both calm and inflexible.

"The prince must assemble all his trump cards so that they can work for him. For all the reasons we have already mentioned, the man who depends totally on good fortune will come to nothing if his fortune changes."

Moses de Castellazzo also got to his feet. Keeping in mind the practical side of things, he asked:

"Might Milord Machiavelli know, for this important mission, a man who fits the description he has just given?"

"To carry the letter, yes. But it is up to you to be sure that the letter is written. Do you not know Cardinal Egidio di Viterbo quite well?"

And then, turning to the Messenger, he added:

"As for the person in the prince's retinue who has let himself be manipulated and taken advantage of..."

David interrupted him with a smile and quoted the following lines:

"Do I wish the evil man to perish?" saith the Lord, "or rather for him to change his behavior and live?"

"Is that one of David's psalms?"

"No. The words come from Ezekiel."

Chapter twenty-nine

The Woman Who Wanted to Die

T

he fight in Ostia was bloody. Even the settling of old accounts between the Colonna and the Borgia families had never had so many victims. The news swept into the city of Rome and spread throughout all of Italy.

Orazio Florido, the Prefect of Rome's right-hand man, was very seriously wounded. The prefect, the powerful Francesco Della Rovere, provided to anyone willing to listen an "honorable" version of the events. According to him, his protégé had happened by chance to be in the inn and was stabbed with a dagger when he tried to separate the adversaries. Such specious explanations fooled no one. Two weeks later, Francesco Della Rovere found himself forced to accept the nomination to become Duke of Urbino and leave Rome.

David Reubeni meditated on the ambush. He had to admit that Niccolò Machiavelli understood men better than he did. David knew the human heart as it should be. But Machiavelli knew it the way it really was. Since the latest conspiracy had been crushed, people, both celebrities and ordinary folk, including those from the Jewish community, showed the Messenger more respect. When he passed by in the streets, an additional nuance of deference was added to the fervor and curiosity that normally surrounded him. People grew respectfully quiet as they greeted him. The Prince of Chabor was indeed a warrior, a leader to be both feared and respected. Cardinal Egidio di Viterbo himself, to whom David paid a visit along with Joseph Zarfatti and Obadiah da Sforno, gave him more attention than usual. He composed a letter on the spot for the King of Portugal and expressed his wish to see the Messenger once more before he left for Portugal, perhaps for an audience with the pope.

Machiavelli had recommended and vouched for a man who could carry the missive. Count Ludovico Canossa accepted the mission. A native of Verona, he had been an ambassador for Pope Leo X. Later he was named Bishop of Bayeux, and served as the ambassador from the King of France to Venice. A great lover of reading, he would travel all over Europe looking for rare manuscripts and books. Chance had it that he needed to go to Lisbon. An early work by his friend Erasmus had just been discovered in Lisbon, and he was eager to acquire it. So he embarked for Portugal, carrying the precious letter for Joao III, along with a sum of one hundred ducats given to him by Benvenida Abravanel.

During this time, the Messenger had made a point of not seeing Dina. He feared having to face the young woman's regrets and tears, for she knew she had been manipulated by David's enemies and that she had betrayed him out of jealousy. He had already forgiven her and had no desire to humiliate her. Did not the wise men say that even if nine hundred and ninety-nine people out of a thousand condemn the sinner, one voice in the sinner's favor is enough to declare him innocent?

But fate leads the man who consents and draws along the man who resists. That evening, David had closed himself up in his room to work on his journal and prepare for his trip to Lisbon. As was his custom, he was meditating before beginning to write. The door was flung open. The Messenger gave a start. It was Joseph Zarfatti, looking horribly distraught. His arms were raised heavenward and he could barely get any words out.

"Quick! Quick! A disaster!"

The man from Chabor took him by the shoulders and shook him. But the doctor staggered and almost collapsed. David had to hold him up.

"What's happening? Tell me!"

"Dina! Dina! Quick!" Joseph Zarfatti said haltingly, dragging David out into the corridor. They were almost running when they reached a large bare bedroom with a tile floor. The unmade bed seemed almost to have been left there by mistake. A candle's heavy flame was making shadows dance on the walls and on the ceiling's painted laths.

"Dina," the doctor moaned.

A few moments later, once his eyes had adapted to the half-light, David saw the young woman. She was lying motionless on her stomach. Beside the bed, a pail filled with vomit, a jug of milk, and a goblet with its sides streaked with a sinister-looking grey powder. He shivered. A hand tugged at his sleeve. It was Joseph Zarfatti, and he was weeping. The Messenger took him by the shoulders and asked:

"What happened exactly?"

"She closed herself up in here after the business in Ostia. She had all the furniture removed and stopped eating. And then, just a moment ago…"

"What can we do?"

"I've already tried everything. I managed to make her vomit so she could purge herself. And I got her to swallow some milk as an antidote."

"And now?"

"We can only pray…"

David walked around to the other side of the bed and looked at Dina. It seemed to him that the young woman's eyes were open and that she could follow his every movement. Was life really slipping away from this supple, firm body? In his mouth the bitter taste of nostalgia rose up. He was going to do the impossible. He had to save her from the jaws of death. Had she not risked her own life to save his?

He looked over at Joseph Zarfatti. The doctor was over-whelmed with anxiety, staring vacantly. David realized immediately why a doctor should never take care of his own family. Feelings are too strong, clouding judgment and stifling initiative.

He touched the young woman's forehead. It was cold. He laid his hand on her chest. Her heart was still beating. But the brief contact with the young woman's naked body and its persistent pulsations of life stirred him deeply. He took a step backward as if he had been too close to a blazing inferno, shouting to the doctor to send for hot water, towels, and clean clothing. But the doctor didn't move, and David had to raise his voice and scold him:

"Come on! Don't just stand there!"

Finally, Joseph Zarfatti stirred. He went out to call the servants. Suddenly the house was filled with footsteps and whispers. While some were cleaning the bedroom, and others washed the young woman and changed her clothing, the Messenger, standing motionless, prayed.

> *My soul blesses the Eternal!*
> *May all that is within me bless His Holy Name!*
> *And forget not all His benefits.*
> *It is He who pardons all iniquities,*
> *Who heals every sickness…*

By the time he finished his prayer, the room was clean again. The young woman, washed and combed, was now wearing a long white cotton gown. The doctor, on his knees by her bedside, got back to his feet. The Messenger took him by the arm.

"Go get some rest," he said. "And have some hot wine sent up. I'll watch over her."

Joseph Zarfatti looked up, his eyes overflowing with tears, nodded like a child, and left the room. A short time later a servant appeared with a large bowl of steaming wine. The Messenger remained alone with the young woman. She was still unconscious. Little by little, the house grew silent.

David, although trying to remain optimistic, still expected the worst. He must stay at the ready, be on the alert. If the Eternal decided to preserve this young life, then he, David, could save her from hordes of assassins, and he was counting on that divine mercy, praying for it with all his might. But if the Eternal—blessed be His name!—refused His grace, then David knew that his own safety was in jeopardy as well. He gently raised Dina's head. Her eyes remained closed. He pried open her lips to force her to swallow a few sips of hot wine. She almost choked and then coughed. Long red streaks ran down the white sheets. He made her drink some more. This time, she did swallow some of the hot liquid. When she had finished the whole bowl, her cheeks slowly began to regain a little color.

The situation was quite complex. The Messenger dreaded death. And he knew that death would frighten him still more the following morning. And yet he felt strangely attracted to it. Would death not make things much simpler? He went to latch the door and then undressed.

When he penetrated the young woman, she did not react. No movement. No moaning. He was anchored to a living body, but a body that remained inert. He had hoped that pain, surprise, or even desire might disrupt her death-like sleep and bring her back to life. And he still had hope. He pressed his entire body against her in a kind of rage. He caressed her, crushing her breasts and thighs, covering her body with kisses. "Wake up! Come back to life!" His whispers in Dina's ear became more desperate, and he squeezed her more urgently. Finally he noticed a slight gasping for breath, and she began to breathe normally again. The young woman's eyes were still closed, but her body was beginning to rock. He looked at her. "Whoever said that fallen angels are ugly?" he thought. He could bear witness that the opposite was true, that they were beautiful, light, and radiant.

Suddenly there was a cry, a cry of unbearable pleasure. David wasn't sure if he or Dina had cried out. He raised himself up onto one of his elbows. The young woman's eyes were open, and she was looking at him tenderly. He smiled. She whispered something he could not understand. He leaned down. She repeated:

"Has my master forgiven me?"

He kissed her.

"I have come to thank you," he said. "Thanks to you, my mission to Portugal will soon get under way."

Dina was now alert and out of danger. She snuggled against him and listened as he told her in detail what had happened over the past several days. Little by little, comforted by the music and vibrations of his voice, she fell asleep, but now her sleep was refreshing. He spent the rest of the night watching her sleep. Just before dawn, the candle sputtered and went out. In the half-darkness, in that period of hesitation between night and day, he could no longer see Dina's face clearly. But in his memory he could see other faces filing by. In his great fatigue, he was troubled to realize that the other faces all looked like Benvenida Abravanel.

At the break of dawn, he got dressed and went to awaken Joseph Zarfatti, who was dozing in an armchair on the ground floor. He told him that the crisis was over and that he could go up to see his sister.

Four weeks later, Count Ludovico Canossa was back in Rome. He had traveled quickly, and he was pleased to have found and been able to purchase the Erasmus manuscript. Furthermore, he had met the king's young, influential confidant, his counselor Diego Pires, who had arranged a personal meeting with Joao III. In answer to Cardinal Egidio di Viterbo's letter, he was also bearing an official invitation from the King of Portugal. Prince David Reubeni, Messenger of the King of Chabor, was invited, along with his retinue, to come to Lisbon. In a separate missive that Cardinal di Viterbo agreed to give to Miguel da Silva, the Portuguese king requested that the ambassador provide all the documents that would be necessary, according to the king, "for this mission that is so important for the interests of Portugal."

It would soon be time to celebrate Rosh Hashanah, the Jewish New Year, at the dawn of the year 5285 after the creation of the earth by the Eternal—blessed be His name!

Chapter thirty

The Year of All Hopes

In his bedroom, David Reubeni was reading aloud the beginning of the second part of his journal. He was reading what he had just written, and the ink was not yet dry. He was careful, as he held the sheet, not to smear it. He loved clean pages.

"Finally, now that I have the official documents and the support of both the powerful and the humble, I am preparing to leave for Portugal at the head of an important mission. My faithful Joseph, the attentive Benvenida Abravanel, Doctor Zarfatti, and all my friends are doing their best to help me. Soon, tens of thousands of young men will be able to join a Jewish army. How great has been the road I have traveled since leaving Egypt! May the Eternal—blessed be His name!—protect me in my mission!"

He put his writing material—pen, inkwell, blotters—and his journal back in the ebony chest. Then the Messenger went down to the large room on the ground floor. There he found his friends, who had been talking since nightfall.

They were discussing the coming Jewish celebrations. David, as he listened to them, was reminded that although up until now he had been able to control his destiny more or less, there was little he could do about time or the calendar. Indeed, there were only ten days until the month of Tishrei. During that month, which corresponds to September and early October in the Christian calendar, four of the most important Jewish holidays are celebrated: Rosh Hashanah, the New Year; Yom Kippur, the Day of Atonement; Succoth, the Feast of Booths; and finally Simchat Torah, celebrating the gift of the Law. Obadiah da Sforno, the ruby on his finger sparkling, turned to David.

"The Month of Tishrei is both sanctifying and sanctified," he said. "Moses designates it as the *Accomplishment* and as *Total Perfection*. It is the transition between the past year and the year to come. It is the passage between the old and the new, between the knowledge of servitude and the work of liberation. Will the Messenger of the Jewish Kingdom of Chabor leave for Portugal without consideration for these ceremonies? Would our prince not participate in these solemn rituals?"

David Reubeni smiled. He liked the rabbi's enthusiasm and childish provocations. He laid his hand on the old man's shoulder.

"Of course not!" he replied. "Even though it is difficult for me not to set out today!"

"I knew it!" said the rabbi in jubilation. "For a man from the desert like the prince, used to wide open spaces without borders or obstacles, with no checkpoints or protocol, it must indeed be hard not to gallop off as soon as his horse is saddled!"

He gloated mischievously:

"Is that not what I had predicted?" he added, triumphantly. "Even if no one remembers today, had I not reminded us of what the Eternal reserved for Moses? Had I not foreseen that before allowing the Messenger to set out on his long journey to Israel, the Eternal, as He did for Moses in the past, would reserve one final, subtle test for him?"

Moses de Castellazzo cut in:

"Our master will still be in Rome for a long time before starting out for Lisbon. As for me, I admit I'm of two minds. I am proud to be counted among the Messenger's friends, and I, too, will stay in Rome as he long as he does, although I am beginning to miss Venice and my studio."

David smiled once more. The rabbi was right. It would be impossible for him to leave before the feast days of the month of Tishrei. Joseph Zarfatti displayed his delight, happy, he said, to be able to keep the Envoy of Chabor nearby for another few weeks. As for his sister Dina, although thinner because she had refused to eat and because of her attempted suicide, she had regained her color and beauty from before the events in Ostia. Her love was no less strong. Even though now she was better able to control its manifestations, it was clear that the delay suited her fine.

During this time, only Joseph Halevy did not allow himself to be governed by feelings alone. He continued to make active preparations for departure, though he did not yet know on what day exactly they would be leaving. With money provided by Benvenida Abravanel, he had hired another twenty servants to step up David's security, providing them with clothing, weapons, and horses. He had even reserved space on a French ship that was to sail from Livorno at the end of the month of Tishrei for Portugal via Gibraltar. In the Sant'Angelo, Rigola, and Ripa neighborhoods, all predominantly Jewish, preparations were moving ahead at a feverish pace for that year's feast days.

And how could it have been otherwise? Did not the year 5285 after the creation of the world appear to be starting out as the year during which all promises would be fulfilled? The return to the land of Israel that people had been dreaming about for centuries, in the eyes of the Jews living on the Italian Peninsula, seemed finally within their grasp. Also within grasp was the guarantee of certain rights for those who would not be leaving, along with compensation for those people who had been exiled from Spain and Portugal. The recent events surrounding the activities of the Messenger of Chabor, events that seemed to many unthinkable and even impossible, raised their ancient hopes to the level of the thinkable, made them appear as something possible. Up until that time they were really more like nostalgia and dreams. Even the most skeptical began to wonder: Had not David Reubeni, brother of the Jewish King of Chabor, just received an official invitation from Joao III to come to Portugal, a country from which scarcely thirty years before the Jews had been driven out? Had not Pope Clement vii, head of all Christendom, during a reception in honor of the Messenger, publicly pronounced his support for the Jews' reconquest of the land of Israel? Were they not seeing the enemies of Chabor perish one after the other? And recently, had not numerous artists and scholars, for the first time in living memory, proclaimed their solidarity with the persecuted Jews and their support for the Jews' claim for a country of their own? The artists and men of letters were among the most famous. Protégés of princes, admired by society, they bore names such as Ariosto, Pico della Mirandola, Guicciardini, Michelangelo, Machiavelli, Signorelli, Berbo…so many talented people gathered together as members of one family! Yes, this semi-lunar year that included parts of the Christian calendar's 1524 and 1525 was starting out as the year of liberation for one of the oldest peoples on earth…

As the first evening of Rosh Hashanah drew near, Obadiah da Sforno was happy to explain the importance of the first day of the Jewish New Year to anyone who would listen, and especially to his Christian friends, some of whom were hearing about the feast day for the first time.

"On this day, the Eternal—blessed be His name!—appears in all His power as King and Judge Supreme, and all His creatures pass before Him so that He can inscribe their names in the Book of Life or the Book of Death. During Rosh Hashanah, says the Talmud, the names of the just are inscribed so that they might live another year; the names of the ungodly are also written, but to announce their deaths. As for the fate of the undecided, it will not be set until Yom Kippur. They will have the right to live only if they repent. So, after the first evening's service, everyone exchanges the same wish: "May you be inscribed and sealed for a good year!"

Raising the suspense, he would add:

"On the second evening of the festival comes the solemn moment of sounding the *shofar*. The *shofar* is a kind of trumpet carved from a ram's horn. Its hoarse, plaintive sounds are designed to awaken the consciences of those who sleep. According to tradition, we also hear other echoes: the echo of Creation, the sacrifice of Isaac, and even the revelation on Mount Sinai, the Final Judgment, the deliverance of Israel and the liberation of all of humanity from the clutches of evil."

That year, on the second evening of Rosh Hashanah, a veritable crowd had invaded Doctor Zarfatti's home in spite of all the guards. For the occasion, the large dwelling was decorated entirely in white, the color of innocence. So he could point them out to the Messenger, Moses de Castellazzo sought out the many Roman dignitaries, the princes, the churchmen, the artists who had been eager to pay a visit, on this day of the Jewish New Year, to their "elder brothers," and to display their friendship.

Obadiah da Sforno, who had already drunk a great deal and spoken even more, was setting meetings for the following year with everyone he met: "Next year in Jerusalem!" When Moses de Castellazzo teasingly pointed out that it seemed a little premature to invite people to the Holy Land for the following year, the rabbi rebelled:

"What do you mean, *premature*?"

"But after all," Moses replied, "we first need to take the land back from the Turks! And then we will need to rebuild it. Has it not been left abandoned and given back to the desert?"

As his only response, the old rabbi raised his gnarled hands heavenward, and rocking back and forth almost ecstatically, he began to quote Isaiah:

The waters will gush forth from the desert,
And streams from the solitude.
The mirage will become a lake,
And the dry earth will yield its springs.
In the ancient jackals' den
Bullrushes and reeds will grow.
There will be a path opened up, a road
That we will call the holy way.

No one could keep from applauding, even those who had heard the same text from the time they were children and never found it particularly appealing. For now they discovered, at this exceptional moment, how strong the words were and how powerfully they attracted them.

After that memorable New Year's day came the third day of Tishrei, the fast of Gedaliah. That Jewish governor of Israel, appointed by the Babylonians in 586 after the taking of Jerusalem, was assassinated seven months later by another Jew named Ishmael. His murder was the prelude to the massive deportation of the Jews into Babylonia and the flight of the survivors toward Egypt.

Obadiah da Sforno had not failed to point out that by celebrating the memory of deportation, the fast of Gedaliah is dedicated to repentance, and therefore the following invocation was always read: *Return, O Israel, to the Lord thy God! Say to Him: 'pardon all our iniquities, and may Your goodness welcome us!'*

Such repentance is the necessary prelude to the solemn day of Yom Kippur, the Day of Atonement, which comes six days later.

David Reubeni participated in all the festivities, but kept his feelings to himself. He remained impassible when people, so many of them, congratulated him. The man from the desert knew that there was nothing easier to give than compliments. But on the evening of Yom Kippur, covered with the *tallith*, the prayer shawl, when like all Jews he enumerated his sins in a low voice before the Eternal—blessed be His name!—he wept. Later, after the prayer, he thought about the upcoming feast day, Succoth, the Feast of Booths, also called the Feast of Tabernacles. Did not that day remind the Jews of their long wandering in the wilderness just after they had left Egypt, and the huts they had to live in then? That the Tabernacle, that is the Temple, could have been a *succoth*, a simple cabin or hut, did not seem strange to these wanderers, these peasants from the desert. David remembered that the Psalms referred even to the Jerusalem Temple itself using the metaphor of the *succoth*: *For He shelters me in His hut on the day of misfortune...His hut is in Salem, His dwelling in Zion.*

After Succoth came Simchat Torah, the Day of the Gift of the Law. It brings to an end the cycle of the festivities of the month of Tishrei with songs, visits among friends, and the distribution of confectionaries. According to an old saying, the joy and jubilation manifested on that day come from the sincerity of the penitence and prayers offered up on the Day of Atonement.

Once the final evening of festivities was over, David Reubeni went to his room to meditate, still in the semi-darkness. Then he went to bed. But when he couldn't fall asleep, he went back downstairs. In the room on the ground floor, he was able to sense rather than actually see that many chairs and sofas, and even the floor, were occupied by sleeping forms. Even some people who were not fully asleep had remained. Dawn was not far away, but the house was still bathed in semi-darkness. The windows were closed. Not a breath of air was stirring. The flames from the candlesticks on the sideboard did not flicker. Joseph Halevy was the only man still fully awake, standing among those sleeping people and the absurd candles. He swayed as he walked, and he seemed to be speaking for his shadow that was dancing on the wall as well as for himself. What he said was practically inaudible, except for a few words that stood out and came back again and again: Chabor, Israel, and David Reubeni's sacred mission.

In the shadows, the Messenger listened to his servant. He kept expecting someone to laugh cruelly, but nothing happened. Nobody was making fun of him. Joseph's words were not considered absurd. And so these men must believe! Like thousands of others, they, too, had confidence in him! Could he keep from disappointing them? He withdrew and tiptoed back up to his bedroom. Never had he felt so alone.

The following day he was received by the pope. Clement VII had insisted on wishing him a good and fruitful journey in person. Thousands of Jews accompanied David to Viterbo, where the cardinal had him spend the night, and then all the way to Pisa and Livorno.

Joseph Zarfatti, the doctor, dreaded goodbyes. He preferred saying goodbye in Rome. His sister Dina also stayed in Rome. "May the master return to us safe and sound," she had murmured passionately to David. On the other hand, Moses de Castellazzo went with the Messenger to Livorno. Had he not done so before, when he accompanied him to the port in Venice? Obadiah da Sforno, in spite of his advanced years, would not have missed such events for anything. So the old rabbi, too, made the journey to Livorno, though he did go by carriage. Of David's original servants, only Tobias was not part of the expedition. The Messenger's retinue was impressive. It was made up of about thirty men, all of them armed, all of them on horseback, all of them dressed completely in white. And there were about twenty more on mules, bringing along presents for the King of Portugal.

In the port of Livorno, David Reubeni sought in vain for the sight of his benefactress Benvenida Abravanel, for it was she who had allowed him to recruit all these men. He was a bit surprised and disappointed not to see her there, but said nothing. From among the crowds, where there were many Jews, but also some Christians, either his supporters or those who were simply curious, he had the pleasant surprise to see Benvenida Abravanel finally emerge. In fact, she had come a day early so that she could be waiting near the ship. When he saw her figure enveloped in a long brown cloak and her large dark eyes looking out from between a velvet cape and a white fur hat, the man of Chabor was both moved and delighted. He went over to her. They gazed deeply into each other's eyes.

"Thank you," he said.

"May the Eternal grant you protection," Benvenida replied.

Then, suddenly lowering her eyes shyly like a girl, she added:

"Come back to me quickly!… Little Dina, I know, will be your nostalgia. But I will be your reward."

At the same instant, before David could react, she slipped away, disappearing into the crowd.

Shortly thereafter, to the sound of trumpets and cheers, along with prayers, the ship *La Victoire* put to sea. The white banner and its Hebrew letters embroidered with gold thread flew above the flags of the twelve tribes of Israel, they too provided by Benvenida's generous kindness.

Giacobo Mantino and his friends could only brood in anger. Among the crowds in Livorno, as had been the case all over the Peninsula, there was no one, not one single Jew who did not wish the ship a safe journey. As the ship sailed away from the Italian Coast, it carried with it all of Israel's hopes.

Part Two

Chapter thirty-one

On the Way to Portugal

The Tuscan coast was slowly dropping below the horizon. David Reubeni stood lost in thought on the ship's deck, pondering over the fact that men get so used to people, places, and things that when they must leave, they feel nostalgia. A gust of wind filled the sails. He shivered. And how about misfortune? Could one be nostalgic for the sufferings of the past? The crests of the waves were boiling, and heavy clouds were beginning to scurry across the sky. He had to admit that the past's misfortunes are no longer misfortunes, but only the past. He thought about Giacobo Mantino's plotting. Here, on the moving planks of *La Victoire*, Mantino's sinister treachery seemed to belong to olden days. Now a page had been turned, even if memory's tablets did still preserve some episodes. But who is not attached to his own memory? Can memories slip away like a bird from a snare? He fondly recalled his arrival in Venice, the painter Moses de Castellazzo and his spacious studio in the Ghetto Nuovo, as well as old Vincentius Castellani in Fossombrone and Rabbi Obadiah da Sforno in Rome. In gratitude, his mind went back to Joseph Zarfatti's welcome and Dina's sweet smile. To Cardinal di Viterbo's laughter, Niccolò Machiavelli and his bowl of grapes, or Michelangelo speaking so fondly of Moses. Benvenida's whispers also came back to him. In the port in Livorno, just before he left, she had said: "I will be your reward." Would he be worthy?

Now they were completely out of sight of land. Solid ground was only a memory, just like his Italian friends, like the canals of Venice, like the small streets of Rome or the Vatican's square courtyard. Only the sea remained. The Messenger held up his hand to protect himself from the sea spray that was burning his cheeks, and then he murmured the travelers' prayer:

May it be according to Your holy will, O Eternal, our God and the God of our fathers, that we travel in peace and that we arrive in peace...

La Victoire had been sailing for five hours against a strong headwind, tacking back and forth but not really making much forward progress.

"Perhaps these swells will be more favorable when night falls," said Joseph to his master.

David Reubeni appeared not to have heard. His eyes were closed, and now he was voluptuously letting the wind and spray strike his face.

"The sea reminds me of the desert," he said after a moment. "Do you remember the desert?"

"Yes," Joseph replied. "And I can still see its dunes, its waves."

"But you can't remember my father, galloping through a sand storm," the Messenger noted dreamily. "If you had seen him, you would understand what a real horseman is!"

The storm seemed to be growing in fury.

"Close your eyes and listen to the moaning," he said to his confidant. "Can you not hear swirling sand, a yellow, ocher whirlwind? The color of my mountain, the color of my mother's scarf..."

"She would be proud of you, Master."

"So far, there is nothing to be proud of!"

"But you have already obtained support from the pope!" Joseph exclaimed. "You, the Jew from Chabor! Are you not already on the way back home? Back home to Jerusalem?"

A heavy wave crashed over the deck, and the ship began to list. David grabbed a rope, and then, once he had regained his equilibrium, he asked, changing the subject:

"What did you do about Tobias?"

"Do you really want to know?"

"Yes, I do."

Joseph's laughter was lost in the wind. Night was falling, but the pitching and rolling went on unabated.

Finally, he answered. "I sent him to take a carefully sealed letter to Ambassador da Silva."

David nodded for him to continue.

"Inside the envelope, I slipped a letter in my own handwriting that appeared to be for Tobias himself."

"And what was in the letter?"

"I thanked Tobias for warning his master, David Reubeni, in time about the Ostia conspiracy."

"Your story is not credible," David objected with a half-smile on his face. "Do you think it could fool a man as clever as Da Silva?"

"You may be right," Joseph admitted. "But it is enough to cast doubt and may have some effect. From now on, Mantino and Da Silva will not be able to trust Tobias. Mistrust is like water: Drop by drop, it can wear away the hardest granite."

"The ambassador may try to get revenge…"

"True, but that would not be much different from his initial desire to cause harm. He is a close ally of Queen Catherine and the Dominicans who are urging Joao III to follow the Spanish model and set up a court of the Holy Office of the Inquisition. Refugees have told me that for more than thirty years while Joao II and Manuel I were kings, tens of thousands of Jews were dragged to the baptismal fonts. They were forced to became Christians in spite of themselves, and they are still closely watched and controlled. They don't even have the right to leave Portugal, but at least they are still alive. If the Inquisition is established in Lisbon, there is no doubt that they will perish one after the other at the stake!"

Far from weakening with nightfall, the swells were getting larger. The ship shuddered as the waves pounded against it, and the two men had to fight to maintain their balance. While the ship kept up its dance on the waves, David Reubeni remarked to Joseph that it was time to say *Ma'ariv*, the evening prayer. As the wind whistled through the rigging, he began:

And He, full of mercy, forgives our sins…

The next morning, the sky was perfectly blue. The wind had turned. Two days later, after favorable winds, *La Victoire* lay anchored in the port in Marseille. The captain was a big bald man with rippling muscles, answering to the name Fernao de Morais. He explained to the Prince of Chabor that he needed to replenish his stock of hay for the animals. The donkeys and horses belonging to David's retinue had been eating with great appetite, thanks to the sea air. Captain de Morais was the son of a Portuguese family that had settled in Fez two generations earlier. He worked for the French and was conversant in Arabic.

"I prefer stopping in Marseille rather than in some Spanish port," he explained. "Just imagine the look on the Inquisitors' faces if they could see your banners!" And he laughed uproariously at such a crazy idea.

"Back in Fez, I knew many Jews," he said. "They were good friends of mine. Among them was a rabbi, Yehuda ben Moshe Halewa, a kabbalist. He left for the Holy Land just before I went to sea. His son is still living in Fez."

Fernao de Morais was clearly pleased to be able to converse with a Jewish prince, especially with a prince who was a protégé of the pope and who had been invited to Portugal by the king.

"Is the prince aware that thanks to the Jews Martin Behaïm, Master Rodrigo, and Master Joseph we have been able to measure the height of the sun and navigate on the high seas?" he asked, proud to show off his knowledge for such an illustrious passenger.

Rumors were more rapid than a powerful ship, more rapid than history. Scarcely had *La Victoire* dropped anchor in Marseille than a delegation of Jews made a discreet appearance on board the ship. At the head of the delegation was a small friendly-looking man with a white beard, Rabbi Aba Mari.

"Here in Marseille, where Jews are barely tolerated, we, too, are awaiting the great Return. Here in Marseille, we have confidence in you!" he declared. His voice was shrill, but fire danced in his eyes.

David was touched to see the man standing before him. And then he noticed the man's yellow hat and realized what it was.

"Back in the old days," the rabbi explained in his halting Hebrew, inflected with Judeo-Provençal, "the Jews were expected to wear the mark of infamy, the yellow badge. But Pope Clement VII, in his great mansuetude..."

He didn't finish his sentence, looking at David conspiratorially:

"The pope, who is also the protector of the Prince of Chabor, has just replaced the yellow badge with this hat. And women are obliged to wear a cockade of the same color. It is variously called a *patarassoune* or a *guevillon*, depending on the region."

"And if you refuse to wear these hats?"

"Well then, we have to expect a fine of two hundred gold crowns!"

A wave of tenderness washed over David.

"How long, O Eternal? How long?" he murmured.

And then, in a loud voice, speaking to the other members of the delegation, he quoted a Psalm:

The eyes of the Eternal are on the Just
And His ear is attentive to their cries...

Then, now that he was so close, Rabbi Aba Mari summoned up his courage to question David Reubeni. He had one burning question, and he asked it without beating around the bush:

"May I ask the Messenger if he is a prophet, or as some say, the Messiah? People are also saying that..."

"People say a lot of things," David retorted. He frowned and creased his eyebrows, interrupting the rabbi. But then he realized that he had put the rabbi in an awkward position.

"I come from the little Jewish kingdom of Chabor, at the confines of Arabia, and I am the brother of the King of Chabor. That being said, I am just like everyone, a poor sinner and a penitent. I know how to plan and win a battle. But, to go to war, one needs an army. And without weapons there can be no army..."

He gratified the rabbi with a smile.

"And that is the only reason for my trip to Portugal!"

The old man with the white beard and his companions relaxed. There followed a general discussion that lasted for hours. After the forage had been loaded, if Captain Fernao de Morais had not asked the Marseille Jews to leave the ship, no doubt they would have continued all night long by lantern light, telling David about their daily life and explaining all the hardships and hopes of the Jews in the Kingdom of France.

When *La Victoire* raised anchor and sailed out of the Marseille harbor toward Mallorca, they were still standing on the quay, waving their yellow hats and praying for the Messenger's success.

Three days of smooth sailing followed, during which the docile waves seemed to propel the ship along toward the southwest. It was Sunday, the day after the Sabbath. The day before, the Messenger and his men had solemnly celebrated the Sabbath rituals in the company of Captain de Morais, who had asked to join them. He had been so delighted to participate in the prayers and chants that marked the day of rest that Joseph suspected he must be a descendant of those *Conversos*, those only recent Christians who had been forced to convert. He mentioned the possibility to David, but his master listened to his conjecture without commenting.

So on that Sunday *La Victoire*, pushed by favorable winds, arrived in view of the Baleares. Through a slight haze, Mallorca's white coast sparkled in the distance, but behind it dark clouds were beginning to build up. Suddenly, the man on watch called out. He had spotted a galiot, flying no flag and heading straight for them.

Captain de Morais, who was conversing with David, adjusted his glass:

"Barbary pirates!" he shouted, spreading his arms. "I know them! I know them only too well!"

The galiot seemed determined. All its sails were unfurled, and the pirate vessel had the wind behind as it maneuvered toward *La Victoire* as if to come aboard on the windward side. And then, it fired a fourteen-gun salvo. But Captain de Morais was not caught unawares.

He positioned his sailors, each with a harquebus, at their defense posts. The stern, prow, and upper deck were bristling with firearms. Seeing that the situation was taking a dangerous turn, David asked Joseph to summon his own men, but Joseph didn't have time to do so. There was a volley of violent explosions, for the cannons on *La Victoire* had just answered the pirates' salvo, and they were relieved to see the galiot suddenly change course and sail away.

"What is happening?" the Messenger asked the captain.

The captain pointed out to sea. A large fleet flying Spanish flags was moving toward the coast. The Barbary pirates had good reasons to flee. An enthusiastic shout rose from the crew of *La Victoire*, and they began to maneuver toward the port of Mao Mah, not far from the point of Mallorca. But just then a gale struck from the northwest. In just a few moments the sky had turned black. Heavy clouds from the east had covered the sky, and the gale followed hard on the heels of the galiot's attack. Most of David's men, unused to such rough waters, got seasick. Standing on the deck alone with the captain in the midst of the crashing waves, the Messenger listened with interest as the captain ordered different maneuvers.

"I am going to bypass the port. With this weather, we could never get to shore!" he shouted as he hurried past the man from Chabor who was having trouble maintaining his footing.

The tempest was growing stronger, and the captain, fearing a disaster, reduced the sails to five or six spans to keep them from tearing. As he rushed back past the Messenger, through the whistling wind, crashing waves, and creaking masts, he shouted loudly enough to be heard.

"We need to move away from the coast. In a storm like this, the reefs are too dangerous."

But once night fell, as the waves pounded the ship and washed over the deck, it was impossible to see the shoals near the island and the reef extending out of the water. The shock was so great that David Reubeni lost his balance and fell, washed forward with the breaking waves. He managed to grasp the rail and get to his feet. He was about to go join the captain when he heard someone praying near him in the semi-darkness: *Return, O Eternal!* Through the screaming tempest he recognized Joseph's voice.

It was only with the arrival of dawn that the winds finally abated. *La Victoire* had withstood the storm well. Except for one crack they managed to caulk and the loss of a donkey that had been trampled by the other animals during the frightful night, there was little damage.

After three more days of sailing with clement winds, the ship was within sight of Gibraltar. David and his men celebrated a second Sabbath in the Gulf of Cadiz, and then they made land in Tavira, the first port in Portugal. Finally, the Messenger from Chabor was able to set foot on Portuguese soil. Two weeks had elapsed since they had left Livorno.

Tavira was a prosperous, well-protected port in which numerous ships were loading fruits and wines destined for Flanders, and a royal delegation was waiting for them. That was a surprise; David Reubeni had assumed that the first official contact would take place in Lisbon. The king's delegation was composed of four men. At their head was one of the court counselors, Diego Pires. He was a very young man with a pale complexion and violet-colored eyes. His smile was both timid and ironic. When he took off his hat, flat, velvet and decorated with a feather, David could see that he was blond. Captain de Morais did the honors on board his ship for the ambassador, welcoming him with great ceremony. When he saw the Messenger from Chabor, Diego Pires, the counselor, seemed disconcerted. He quickly pulled himself together and bowed gracefully. He spoke in Portuguese, and the Captain offered to be the interpreter, clearly delighted to be able to play such a role.

"Here is a welcome letter from my king, His Majesty Joao III," said Diego Pires softly. "The king asks me to inform the prince that the Court is staying at the moment in the Almeirim Castle, near Santarem, and not in Lisbon, which, alas, has been in the prey of the plague for the past ten days."

He bowed again:

"His Majesty suggests, therefore, that the prince and his suite come join him at Almeirim by land. A royal escort will be here soon in Tavira and will accompany the ambassador from Chabor. As for me, I must return without delay to the Court so the king will know you have arrived."

David Reubeni waited until the captain had finished translating Diego Pires's words, and then he smiled. His only response was a quotation in Hebrew:

Jacob went on his way; those sent by the Eternal met him. Jacob, when he saw them, said: "This is the camp of the Eternal." And he gave to that place the name Mahanayim: *two camps.*

Diego Pires's violet eyes grew bright. Even before anyone attempted to translate the text, he exclaimed: "That is from Genesis, isn't it?"

And abruptly, as if he was afraid he had said too much, he turned away. Followed by the three gentlemen who were accompanying him, he left the ship.

Chapter thirty-two

Court Clans

Almeirim was a little town with pink hues backed up against an imposing Moorish castle, and in it there were a convent of Clarissa nuns and a Gothic church. The town lived according to the rhythm of the king's whims. The town would awaken with the arrival of the Court that followed the sovereign for several days of vacation, taking advantage of the splendid view over the Tagus and the Ribatejo, and then it would fall asleep after its illustrious visitors left.

But the epidemic raging in Lisbon forced the Court to remain in Almeirim longer than usual. Rumors and exacerbated passions ran higher than in the capital because of the limited space and the lack of distractions. For that reason, the arrival of the Messenger from Chabor, whom they quickly nicknamed "the pope's Jewish envoy," set into motion all sorts of conjectures, including cutting remarks and endless disputes. Two clans formed. One gathered around King Joao III and his confessor Antonio de Ataide, and the other around the king's spouse, Queen Catherine of Austria and her ally Rodrigo de Azeveido, grand master of the order of Jesuits.

One month after the death of Vasco de Gama, who had opened the route to the Indies, the first of the two clans realized the value of involvement in a plan that would allow Portugal to establish trading posts on the routes to Asia, and especially in the Red Sea. With the king, they approved of the pope's initiative and the support he lent to David Reubeni. The queen's clan, on the other hand, was more focused on the situation inside the kingdom's borders, and they feared that those tens of thousands of Jews converted by force to Christianity might reconsider Judaism now that the Prince of Chabor had come. They were afraid that serious problems might break out all over Portugal. For them, it would be a fatal mistake to give any support to this David Reubeni and his plans.

It was in this tense situation that Dom Miguel da Silva intervened. The Portuguese ambassador to the Holy See had insisted on leaving Rome so he could encourage the king to reconsider his position. He knew that Joao III respected him and was kind enough to appreciate his analyses. Perhaps the king would heed his arguments. What's more, the sovereign had agreed to receive him the very day he arrived.

"Milord," the ambassador began, "you are jeopardizing the peace of the kingdom by receiving this questionable adventurer from who knows what Jewish desert! This man David Reubeni will reawaken dangerous passions among us. Your Majesty should consider the people's reaction! How can we, your loyal subjects, explain that after expelling all the Jews from Portugal the king has welcomed one of their princes with all honors? And that, what's more, he is agreeing to finance and organize the man's army?"

The ambassador's sharp features expressed deep worry. Beads of sweat pearled on his forehead.

"Even the nobles are grumbling," he added.

Joao III rubbed his short, curly beard and looked up impatiently at Miguel da Silva. The ambassador paused.

"My dear Dom Miguel…"

The king's voice was astonishing, for it sounded young and brittle at the same time. He paused for a moment, obliging the ambassador to pay closer attention, and then counterattacked:

"A man as sensible as you, as well informed as you are! How can you believe such nonsense? This very morning I granted an audience to a delegation of noblemen. Among them were the Braganças, the Continhos, and the Melos. And do you know why they came to see me? To offer their support and to encourage me to commit the kingdom still further. To commit to what? To help the Prince of Chabor achieve his goals!"

The blow struck home. The ambassador tried to regain his composure by adjusting his lace jabot before deciding to risk an objection:

"Would Your Majesty permit me to make an observation?"

"Go ahead…"

"According to my information, the Melos and the Continhos have friends and creditors among the Jewish confession…," he pointed out.

Joao III cut in sharply.

"There are no longer any Jews. There is no one belonging to the Jewish faith in Portugal!"

Miguel da Silva bowed, and then he looked up at the king with those falsely innocent eyes that amused the courtesans in Joao III's entourage as much as they did the members of the Curia in the corridors of the Vatican.

"Your Majesty quite rightly brings me back to order," he said. "But according to my information, a number of these *Conversos*, these converted Jews, have kept their old customs. They still refuse to eat pork, and they continue to pray to their God in caves they have made into synagogues. In fact, they have not really abandoned their religion. They still act as Jews in the shadows, and God only knows what will result from their shadowy secret meetings, their intrigues, and their plots!"

Then, standing up straight like a bullfighter before the kill, the ambassador came to his point:

"It is time, Milord, it is high time to follow the example of Castile, our elder sister, and undertake a massive campaign to purify the kingdom! Today the plague threatens our bodies, but the Jews are causing our souls to rot!"

The king got to his feet. Joao III was of medium height, and his youthful face looked almost infantine in spite of his black beard.

He did not appear as mature as people usually expected kings to be. But the expression in his eyes was profound, and he wore the crown gracefully. His purple cape spread open to display a doublet made of brocade and a large silver cross. He walked briskly to the French doors at one end of the room and stared for a long time at the bend in the river, especially wide at that spot. Then, suddenly, he turned back toward the ambassador.

"My dear Miguel da Silva," he said. His thin voice was firm, but it quavered as if he could scarcely contain his feeling. "Here in Portugal we will not set up a court for the Inquisition!"

And he moved closer still to the ambassador, saying:

"The Inquisition would destroy everything creative and productive in Portugal! It would impoverish our country."

Joao III continued speaking, his voice now almost a whisper, as if he were speaking to himself:

"After all, who has Jewish blood in his veins? And who does not? So many converted Jews have married members of Portuguese nobility! Would not attacking their grandchildren today imperil the equilibrium of the kingdom itself?"

At that moment a secret door opened. Diego Pires walked in. He was coming, as usual, to take his orders for planning the next meeting of the Royal Council. However, when he saw Miguel da Silva, he bowed and made a move to withdraw. The king stopped him.

"Please stay, my dear Counselor! Remain here with us."

The ambassador stepped to one side, placing himself between Joao III and Diego Pires.

"Will His Majesty permit me to make one further observation?"

"Go ahead."

"According to my information, the kingdom's coffers are empty. If we got rid of these *Conversos*, the king's treasurer would inherit a considerable fortune…"

This time, Joao III's voice showed his irritation as he interrupted Miguel da Silva:

"And what capital would be available for our country for producing any future wealth? Who will provide the means necessary for maintaining the Court? Who will continue to finance those expeditions toward far-off countries that have been the pride of Portugal and contribute to its grandeur? Who indeed, since, as you say, the coffers of the kingdom are empty?"

The ambassador bowed. He could scarcely hide his disappointment. He had additional arguments to make, but he found it difficult to express them in the presence of young Pires, whom the Court nicknamed "Angel Diego." He did not want the news of his failure to reach the important men of the kingdom. He preferred leaving the impression that it was simply the first of a long series of conversations that he, Dom Miguel da Silva, would be having with Joao III about David Reubeni's plans. He also wanted to meet in private with the young counselor, thinking he might be able to turn him into an ally. Seeing how firm the king was, he risked another question:

"Does the king permit me to...?"

"Go ahead and speak."

"May I count on another audience with Your Majesty before the Royal Council next meets?"

"Yes," Joao III agreed curtly.

The meeting was over. The Royal Council meeting devoted to David Reubeni's arrival was to be held two days later, and Da Silva knew that Queen Catherine would find herself quite alone facing the king and those opposing the Inquisition. However, the ambassador was not ready to admit defeat. He did not despair about not changing Joao III's mind, and he still had not given up on finding a way of finally getting rid of that pernicious guest that the Messenger from Chabor was turning out to be. To that end he considered how the powerful network of friends belonging to the "Spanish clan" could help him. They met regularly in the home of the Spanish ambassador, Luis Sarmiento de Mendoza. However, except for Dona Maria de Velasco, the queen's confidant, and Brother Bernardino de Arevalo, who belonged to the order of Saint Francis of the Observance, none of the members of the Spanish clan had a seat on the Royal Council. And neither the queen's confidant nor the Franciscan had enough authority to stand up to the king's will. "If a court for the Holy Inquisition were already in place in Portugal," he thought, "we would not be in such a situation!"

After the ambassador left, Diego Pires remained alone with Joao III. The king often asked him to keep the minutes of the council meetings. It was in that capacity that he attended, but he did not have the right of the floor. For the past few days, the young counselor had been carefully keeping his eye on the subtle play of influences and manipulations always active at the Court. In spite of Joao III's strong support of the Prince of Chabor's plan to raise an army to take back Israel, doubt was beginning to raise its head here and there, and especially among the hidalgos, the king's vassals. At times they spoke against David Reubeni with such violence and so much hostility that Diego Pires even feared for the life of that strange man who, on the deck of *La Victoire*, had so impressed him.

He was obsessed by the image of the Messenger of Chabor. The way he looked at you, his graceful demeanor, and his thin figure from which such strength emanated disturbed him greatly, and it was hard for him to understand why. Was it because the Prince of Chabor's plans were so exciting? Or was it the fact that he was Jewish?

"Angel Diego" had heard a great deal about the Jews, especially about those who, not so many years before, had lived in Evora, Lisbon, and Santerem. He knew that some had been expelled from the country and that others had been converted by force. But he had never met any of them. One day, at the University of Coimbra, a student had called one of his acquaintances a *Marrano*. Although he didn't really understand what the word meant, he still felt vaguely offended for his friend, and he had even slapped the offender. Curiously, it was only a year later, in the College Sainte-Barbe in Paris, where almost all the Portuguese students in Paris would gather, that a friend from Santarem explained that the word *marrano* meant "pig" in Spanish, and that it was a derogatory term used to refer to those converted Jews.

Back in Lisbon, Diego Pires had unsuccessfully tried to question his father—a partner in an international business venture with Rodrigo d'Evora, the nephew of the Jew Abraham Senior. Why indeed did his father, a fervent Catholic and cousin of the canon of San Salvador de Vilas, so obstinately refuse to talk about the Jews? Might he himself be a descendant of those people who had been converted by force during the days of Manuel I or even before?

Thus, Diego Pires had been interested in Judaism from his youth. At the home of a friend of the family, the writer Joao de Barros, he had discovered a copy of the Old Testament, which at the time was looked down on in Portugal, and he had learned the rudiments of Hebrew.

Joao III esteemed his counselor, whose tormented soul appeared to him to be a quality rare among men. They were approximately the same age and the same height. But one was blond and the other darkhaired. The king appreciated Diego's spontaneity, his aggressive innocence, and his love for books. Even for those that were forbidden.

One day, as he was passing through Seville, Diego Pires had been present at an autodafé. On the square in front of the cathedral, a screaming crowd was throwing sacred books from the Jewish tradition on a fire. When he described the scene to the king, tears came to his eyes.

"Milord, it was as if they were burning people."

Joao III was also moved to tears, and he promised that such autodafés would no longer take place in Portugal.

"How easy it is to name those things that are not in heaven!" Diego said to him after the ambassador had left. "Words are made to describe what our senses can perceive. When we say *light*, we can think only of the sun, of love…"

The king enjoyed hearing his friend and counselor ramble on. Did not Erasmus say that fortune loves the foolish?

It did him good to talk with Diego Pires for a few moments after the audience with Miguel da Silva, though he was still troubled by the ambassador's arguments. He was not unaware that they were shared by a large part of the nobility. Lovingly watching his counselor kneel down before him to take leave, the king leaned slightly forward and helped him to his feet, and to his counselor's surprise, he gave him a warm embrace.

Chapter thirty-three

Distance and Obstacles

Diego Pires did not trust Dom Miguel da Silva. He did not like him—for no particular reason. Or perhaps because of his eyes, because of their falsely innocent look. Or perhaps, on a deeper level, like many people at the Court, because he feared the ambassador. "Angel Diego" hated relationships based on fear and seduction. He recognized, however, that Dom Miguel was a skilled diplomat and unusually intelligent. He was dismayed to see him use his qualities in tortuous ways, and almost always in the service of evil. But Diego Pires, like the king, was also troubled by the ambassador's arguments.

How indeed could Joao III justify his support for the Jewish prince after expelling his fellow Jews? How would the prince ever be able to put together a Jewish army in a country from which all Jews had officially disappeared? Unless one accepted the idea put forward by the Spanish clan that Jews were still present in Portugal, but hiding behind a veneer of Catholicism. And if that were the case, Dom Miguel da Silva was within his rights to call for setting up a court for the Inquisition. Diego remembered the words of his friend Joao de Barros, the writer: "The Jews, by their very presence, pose a problem of conscience for non-Jews."

Suddenly he felt the need to see old Barros again. To ask him some questions. For there were too many questions jostling around in his head. Until he found some answers, it would be impossible for him to help the king's enigmatic guest, this Prince of Chabor, whose enterprise he knew was threatened, as was no doubt his life.

He sent a messenger to David Reubeni with orders to go to Santarem with his escort. There, a palace had been specially prepared to receive him. Diego himself saddled his horse and galloped off toward Lisbon. In Lisbon, Joao de Barros owned a house in the Belem neighborhood, at the foot of Rostelo Hill, on the banks of the Tagus.

Diego Pires followed the road along the river to Salvaterra de Magos. There he stopped for an hour to eat and rest his horse. He finally reached Barreiro as night fell. On the other side of the Tagus the city lights were sparkling. Fortune was with him, for a ferry was ready to depart for the other side just as he reached the dock. As they passed the Belem Tower that Manuel I had built in the middle of the river, he could see fires flickering in the hills. The wind brought with it the smell of burnt flesh. The plague. But the Belem neighborhood was not yet under quarantine.

The old writer was surprised and delighted at the unexpected visit.

"What is happening, my young friend?" Joao de Barros asked, his voice cracking. "You seem worried. Your clothing is covered with dust."

And then he laughed.

"You must have remembered the saying: '*Quem naõ tem visto Lisboa naõ tem visto coisa boa*'—'He who has not seen Lisbon has seen nothing beautiful.' So you got on your horse and here you are! But unfortunately Lisbon is no longer that beautiful city that used to inspire such desire…Have you seen its devastated streets, cluttered with refuse and strewn with dead bodies?"

"No," said Diego as he sat down. "I crossed the Tagus on the Barreiro ferry."

Joao de Barros sat down across from his visitor, his elbows resting on a massive table piled high with books. His large study opened out onto the river through French doors. The flames of twenty candles shimmered in a Venetian chandelier. And bookshelves extended out into the semi-darkness, stuffed with manuscripts and rare texts.

"Something to drink or eat?" the old man asked. "Maria has made some cod croquettes: *baccalau*, just as you like."

"No thank you," Diego replied. And then, when he noticed the disappointment on his friend's face, he added: "But I would love to have a glass of your excellent *carvacalos*..."

Savoring that famous topaz-colored Lisbon wine, they spent the night talking. Totally exhausted and half-drunk, at dawn Diego's head dropped, and he fell asleep right there at the table. The coming-and-going in the house and shouts from the port woke him up later that morning. Joao de Barros walked with him back down to the dock where they said goodbye, and Diego embraced him fervently.

As he started back to Almeirim, his heart felt miraculously lighter.

Chance willed it that David Reubeni reached Santarem just as Diego Pires reached Belem. A curious incident had slowed the advance of his large retinue. As they were crossing the Raia, a small river running through the village of Mora, the wooden bridge had collapsed beneath them. Luckily, only one cart filled with gifts for the King of Portugal had fallen into the water. The chests were fished out of the water two leagues downstream by the Portuguese guards who were accompanying the Messenger of Chabor and his escort.

"The Eternal—blessed be His name!—wanted to remind us that we are going through the country of Dom Miguel da Silva," Joseph noted in exasperation.

David Reubeni shrugged his shoulders.

"He who must break his neck will not fail to find a stairway in the shadows," he said.

"The Latins say that danger comes more rapidly when we scorn it."

"We are not Latins!"

The rest of the journey was completed in silence. But Joseph seemed suspicious. He remained on his guard, carefully examining each peasant they met on the road, and their shadows began to lengthen as the day drew toward its close.

The Messenger was up at dawn the next day. He took a short walk in the vast garden surrounding the Santarem castle, washing his hands and face in a fountain's cool water. And then he returned to his room, and standing by the narrow window, through which he could see, built against the mountainside, the old city dominated by the Alcazabar—the half-destroyed fortress—he recited the morning prayer:

My God, the soul You placed within me is pure. You created it. You shaped it. You gave it life. You preserve it within me. Some day You will take it and return it to me...

He paused for a moment. The sun reflected off the muddy waters of the Tagus. Grey-green smoke was rising above hillsides covered with olive trees. The land of Israel and the hills of Judea came to mind. He whispered:

Guardian of Israel, protect what is left of Israel. Do not let Israel perish, for it proclaims Your holiness—Holy! Holy! Holy!

His room, spacious but dark, was on the second floor of the former Templar palace the king had put at his disposal. The meeting with Joao III was scheduled for the next day, just after the meeting of the Royal Council. David Reubeni could already feel the early signs of impatience burning in his chest. "So near our goal," he thought, "so near!"

He was just about to pick up the journal in which he had been writing for months. When he looked at it, however, he had a strange reaction, pulling back as if to protect himself from some imminent danger. He began to pace up and down the room, and the only window cast a rectangle of light on the floor. He had just realized that if he wanted the king to listen to him, he needed to change the way he talked about his plans, giving them a different shape than what he had presented to the pope. In order for the Royal Council to agree to his plans, the conquest of Israel would need to become essentially a Portuguese project. David thought he could demonstrate to the king that Portugal's commitment to the Middle East would strengthen its position in the East Indies, in Goa, in Macao, and even in Brazil. But there was one reality, as David knew full well, that would be difficult to justify and impossible to control. And that was the reaction of the Portuguese *Conversos*, those Jews who had been forced to convert to Catholicism, and who, more numerous than expected, had publicly displayed their joy when the Messenger from Chabor had arrived.

For indeed, in Beja and Evora, first by the hundreds, and then by the thousands, they had appeared from out of the countryside and nearby towns to applaud, to acclaim him, or simply to come kiss his hands. And yet he had done everything he could to dissuade them, to keep them at a distance, even to push them away, by insulting them. But nothing could make them leave. When he reached Santarem, there were thousands there, too, waiting for him. With a heavy heart, he refused to receive a delegation of elders who had come to greet him in the name of the city's inhabitants. In spite of all his denials, he knew he would have to explain himself to the king regarding the crowd's behavior. The Spanish clan, whose power and intentions he knew, would surely not fail to lose such a great opportunity to accuse him, David Reubeni, of coming to Portugal to bring the *Conversos* and their children back to Judaism.

Contradicting oneself, he thought, is like knocking at one's own door to find out if there is anyone home. And here in Portugal, he was venturing into true contradictions. There seemed to be new ones sprouting daily from the soil he trod upon. The people's outpouring of joy demonstrated better than could any words that he was taking the right approach. But at the same time, that same outpouring probably jeopardized the process of liberating the Jews and helping them return to the land of Israel even more than plots by people like Mantino and Da Silva and other supporters of the Inquisition. From the land on which he now walked to the land to which he dreamed to lead the Jewish people, the distance was great and strewn with many obstacles. Yes, David Reubeni knew better than anyone that thorns can hide under the shimmering of roses.

Chapter thirty-four

"Portugal Is Great..."

The meeting of the Royal Council began a half-hour late due to a slight indisposition of the queen. She was three months pregnant and not feeling well. Catherine of Austria, pale beneath her little veil, finally appeared with Dona Maria de Velasco. She walked in proudly, her pregnancy already beginning to show, wearing an embroidered yellow dress. Over her dress she wore a *ropa*, a garment that originated in the Orient and was highly prized at the Spanish and Portuguese courts. It was a kind of coat that was open in the front, hung below the waist and had shoulder-puff sleeves. The queen's *ropa* was made of dark brown velvet with gold embroidery, and its very simplicity added to its elegance.

When Catherine of Austria came in, the king rose quickly from his throne. The other council members were already standing, and they waited until the queen was seated. Catherine arranged her hair and smiled at everyone, as if to be sure that she was excused for being late.

The council room was longer than it was wide. There were two rows of ten armchairs facing each other, reserved for the council members. The throne was at one end, on a platform dominated by a majestic cross. Off to its right, at a slightly lower level, was the queen's seat. At the far end, beyond the two rows of armchairs, were a table and a chair. That is where Diego Pires sat to take notes for the minutes of each session.

Upon the king's suggestion, the Council began by dealing with the problem of supplying wheat to Portuguese strongholds in Morocco. As Antonio Carneiro, the king's secretary, explained, Spain had set up a blockade "to force Portugal to pay its debt to the emperor." The debt, contracted a year earlier, came from the purchase of the Molucca Islands in the Indonesian archipelago. The seller was the Emperor Charles v. Dona Maria de Velasco stated that the queen had intervened with her brother Charles. In a letter that had just arrived the day before, the emperor had promised to reschedule the debt payments and to lift the blockade.

The king smiled, but it was more of a grimace than a smile. This was not the first time that Catherine was using her family ties to change the emperor's policies toward Portugal. Joao III did not enjoy this kind of situation. He felt humiliated. It was as if the word of the King of Portugal and his personal authority counted for nothing in his relationships with Charles v, Emperor of Germany and the King of Spain. He refrained from making any comment. But he could not hide his irritation when the queen herself then brought up the question that was on everyone's mind: David Reubeni's presence in Portugal.

"We have heard," she began, her voice deep and almost masculine, "that the arrival of the Jewish mission from Chabor—recommended to His Majesty, it is true, by His Holiness the pope—has already triggered serious disturbances in the kingdom."

Catherine's double chin quivered nervously. She was not comfortable speaking in public.

"Does not the Council find that such demonstrations of dual allegiance are shocking and disturbing?" she continued. "As Christians, Portuguese owe their allegiance and loyalty to the Church, and as subjects of the kingdom, to the king. But now we see that some are bowing down before a Jew and kissing the hands of a foreign prince!"

Joao III, sensitive to her second argument, was disconcerted for a moment by the queen's words. But Antonio Carneiro, his secretary, shook his white head.

"If the king allows me…," he said

"Please go ahead!"

"With all the respect I owe the queen…"

"Go on," the king ordered.

"I myself witnessed, Milord, the outpourings of welcome for the Prince of Chabor when he arrived in Santarem. I can attest to there being as many old Christians in the crowd as there were *Conversos*."

"What does that prove?" asked Joao III stubbornly.

"That proves, Milord, that the majority of your subjects approve and support the plan the Prince of Chabor proposes of taking back the Holy Land."

"If the king permits…," another voice spoke.

The man who asked for the floor was thin, somewhat stooped, and dressed entirely in black. He pulled himself out of his chair. He was the king's confessor, the famous Antonio de Ataide.

"Go ahead," said the sovereign.

"The facts also prove, Majesty, that there is no evil intention— neither against our holy Church nor against our beloved king—on the part of those people who throng around this David Reubeni. I even believe that these outpourings represent as much a support for the pope who has sent him as for His Majesty's policies. For let us not forget: The person who invited the Prince of Chabor is none other than the king himself."

Joao III smiled, and this time his smile did not disguise a grimace. Since Antonio de Ataide had begun speaking, the king had been busy wrapping curls from his thick beard around his index finger. That, as everyone knew, was an indication that he was in a good mood.

Diego Pires, at the opposite end of the room, also smiled. The clan opposed to the tenants of the Inquisition was winning out. But then the raspy, convincing voice of the formidable Brother Bernardino de Arevalo broke in. He was a chubby man dressed in purple. Brother Bernardino was an accomplished orator, as much because of his trickery as because of his eloquence.

"If the king permits…," he began.

"The floor is yours."

"Might the Council know our true interest in this adventure? As far as we know, our coffers are empty. We have just learned that we need to negotiate a delayed payment schedule for our debt to the emperor. However, arming thousands of soldiers and preparing a military expedition from the coasts of Africa to the Red Sea will cost the kingdom a fortune…"

Antonio de Ataide stretched out his thin body and held up his index finger:

"If the king permits…," he said.

"The floor is yours."

"I would like to respond to the honorable representative of the order of Saint Francis of the Observance."

"Go ahead."

"Portugal is great, not only because of its own territory, but because of its presence around the world. Our flag flies in Africa, in the Orient, in Asia, and in the Americas. Our navy sails on every ocean and controls the silk and spice routes. However, the kingdom is losing its forward progress. The Turks are supplanting us in the spice markets, and our expensive expedition to take Diu, on the Kathiawar Peninsula in the Indies, ended up a failure. We need, and quickly, both money and a new step forward."

Antonio de Ataide paused. His little grey eyes looked around at all the councilors before coming to rest once more on the king's face. The king smiled his encouragement and even gestured for him to continue.

"So what is our interest in supporting the Prince of Chabor?" asked Antonio de Ataide.

He raised his left index finger and grasped it with his right hand.

"First of all, it is our duty, in a world beset by great religious schisms, to support the policies of His Holiness the pope. Secondly…"

He held up two fingers and closed his right hand around them.

"It is also our duty as Christians to participate in taking back the Holy Land and liberating Christ's tomb. Thirdly…"

He held up three fingers and did the same thing.

"This expedition will allow us to set up trading posts along the Mediterranean and the Red Sea, in places where today the kingdom is absent. And fourthly…"

The queen had trouble sitting still, and she interrupted him:

"All that you say, Dom Antonio, is wise, as usual. But where will we find the money?"

"If the king permits…"

"Go ahead."

"We will get the money from the Jews, Your Majesty."

"From the Jews?" the queen asked.

"Yes. From the Jewish bankers who were expelled from our country and who have moved to Naples, Bordeaux, and Amsterdam. They are still homesick for Portugal, and they cannot refuse to answer our call to support the Jewish Prince of Chabor. We will also find money among the *Conversos*."

He was quiet for a moment. Everyone's eyes were hanging on his words, and it was clear he was enjoying his position.

"If the king permits…"

"Speak."

Antonio de Ataide turned toward the queen.

"I will speak frankly. Those who are advising Your Majesty to have the Inquisition set up in the kingdom are not totally wrong when they suggest that many of those we have converted continue to practice the Jewish religion in secret."

The silence that followed showed how tense the councilors were. Diego Pires instinctively held his breath. More than ever, the wise and wily Antonio de Ataide was able to hold everyone's attention.

"However," he went on, "after weighing the pros and the cons, right here in this very Council, we decided by majority vote not to do any harm to those people. Because they are loyal to the king, and because, thanks to their talent and their hard work, they produce wealth. That wealth, up until now, has filled the Court's coffers and financed our maritime expeditions. Was it not thanks to them that our regretted Vasco de Gama was able to discover the Indies? Getting rid of the *Conversos*, exterminating them, would be drying up the very source of our finances. And we must not forget that such killing would itself clearly be an anti-Christian action, a horrible sin. But…"

He raised his thin hand, as if he were calling on God to bear witness:

"Should not those wanting to get rid of these *Conversos* who have not really been converted be pleased at the idea that a large number of them would leave with the Prince of Chabor to take back the Holy Land? If this operation is handled properly, should it not satisfy everyone?"

The discussion continued for a long time, but Joao III was no longer listening. He was eager to finally meet that mysterious Jewish prince about whom so many calculations and political vortices whirled. After bringing the session to a close, he immediately went to talk with Diego Pires about his next royal audience—devoted specifically to David Reubeni.

Chapter thirty-five

The Prince and the King

Preceded by his white banners, David Reubeni arrived at the palace on horseback. He was accompanied by an honor guard sent by the king and followed by two carts filled with gifts for Joao III.

When such an imposing delegation rode through Almeirim, as had been the case in Santarem, there were acclamations of joy by the *Conversos* and crowds of curious people along the streets.

Antonio Carneiro, Joao III's secretary, greeted the Jewish prince, wishing him welcome and introducing an interpreter, a small affable man who knew only several words of Hebrew but handled Arabic reasonably well. The interpreter presented his excuses for his limited knowledge of Hebrew and let it be understood with a hint of regret that there was no longer anyone who spoke Hebrew in the entire kingdom. He continued speaking as he led David Reubeni and his retinue through the labyrinth of gardens, patios with colonnades, and corridors to the great hall where the King was waiting. The Messenger from Chabor noted with pleasure that standing near a magnificent canopied fountain was the blond gentleman who had welcomed him to Tavira, Diego Pires. He nodded to him and was ready to respond warmly to his greeting, though the intense look in the young man's eyes worried him. He was displaying such admiration that David Reubeni was troubled. He was too well aware that there are fanatics who expect nothing less than love and to whom proposing only friendship is like giving bread to a man dying of thirst in the desert.

They finally reached a rotunda. Its floor was unusual, covered with Arabic-style ceramic tiles arranged geometrically. The raised design of the *arestas* which separated the tiles was indispensable, explained Antonio Carneiro, so that the colors would not run when the tiles were fired. The king's secretary asked the man from Chabor to kindly wait a few moments while he announced to the king that he had arrived. Joseph Halevy took advantage of the opportunity to check on the gifts they had brought for Joao III.

In fact, the door to the adjoining room was slightly ajar, and the King of Portugal could observe his Jewish guest without being seen. He was impressed by the man's bearing and the way he was dressed. Joao III motioned to Antonio Carneiro to have David Reubeni and his interpreter come in. The Messenger from Chabor was surprised by how young the sovereign looked. He bowed respectfully and was about to express how grateful he was for the King's hospitality when the King took him simply by the arm and led him to a red velvet armchair placed facing the throne.

The King waited until his guest was seated, and then with his reedy voice went straight to the point:

"Please tell me, Prince, about your kingdom. Tell me about Chabor."

David Reubeni was not expecting such a question. For a moment he thought there must be some trap. But he read sincere curiosity in the king's eyes. So, his voice warm and gravelly, he began to describe his homeland.

"The Kingdom of Chabor, Milord, is composed of several oases which can be reached in a week by caravan from Jeddah. My father, the great Solomon, may memory of him as a just man be blessed, bequeathed his crown to my brother Joseph, who now reigns over the 300,000 Jews from the tribes of Gad and Reuben as well as the half-tribe of Manasseh…"

He described in great detail the particularity of his people. And then he explained how his brother and the Sanhedrin, the Council of the Seventy Elders, had charged him with a mission to the head of Christendom, Pope Clement vii. And finally he explained why the sovereign pontiff had recommended him to His Majesty the King of Portugal.

Joao iii was enthralled, and he asked David about his plans for retaking the Holy Land. As if he had been waiting for precisely that question since the meeting had begun, the Messenger got to his feet.

"I need, Milord, ten ships and twelve thousand men..."

To punctuate his words he nodded energetically. Strands of curly hair slipped out of his turban and hung down over his forehead.

"Seven vessels will sail along the African coast to the Red Sea. In Ethiopia, the armada will receive logistical support from the Christian King John. His Holiness Clement vii has already sent him a letter so that he can be ready. And then we'll start for Jeddah. By taking the port of Jeddah, we will open the path to the interior of Arabia and the Kingdom of Chabor."

He took a step toward the king. Joao iii, his chin resting in his right hand, was listening with obvious interest. Antonio Carneiro, his secretary, standing behind the throne, appeared fascinated. The interpreter was also fascinated, but he conscientiously tried to render in Portuguese the subtlest nuances of David's words.

"Three other ships," David continued, "will go through the Straits of Gibraltar and make for the port of Joppa, for there the Turkish military presence is almost nonexistent..."

The King raised his hand. David paused. But he stepped forward once again as if his body, carried along by his thoughts, continued to accompany his words. Joao iii smiled.

"Who will lead the expedition?" he asked.

"The troops, Milord, will be made up of Jews. There are many Jews throughout Europe who would like to enroll in my army. The commandment will be entrusted to an admiral, a Portuguese admiral chosen by Your Majesty. I will stand by his side. Furthermore, the sovereign pontiff has assured me and my brother Joseph that we will also be able to count on Your Majesty to provide officers, cannons, engineers, and gunsmiths."

The King turned around, trying to catch Antonio Carneiro's eye. His secretary nodded. Joao III turned back to David and asked:

"And what about the Turks?"

"Today, Milord, the Turks are in full expansion. Their navy controls the great merchant routes of the Occident. Only a surprise operation like ours can force them to loosen their grip. Our troops will need to form three columns to take back the Holy Land. One will leave from Arabia; the second, made up of elite cavalry belonging to my brother Joseph, will come from Chabor; and the third will leave from the Mediterranean coast."

"And how will Portugal benefit from this adventure?"

"Your Majesty's kingdom will draw considerable advantages from this expedition! Currently, Moorish merchants follow the route from the East Indies through Constantinople and then on to Europe, providing strong competition to Portuguese trade. That route will be cut. New establishments and trading posts in Barbera, Jeddah, Chabor, and Joppa will constitute solid bases from which the Portuguese navy, strengthened and enlarged, will be able to sail on to conquer the Malabar coast: toward cloves, cinnamon, pepper, and ginger, as well as camphor from Borneo and musk from Tibet. Thus Portugal will reach the treasures of Calicut, whose sales and profits have for the most part remained in the hands of the Moors thus far."

Joao III was observing the Prince of Chabor with great curiosity. He had never met a Jew like this. The prince was taller and thinner than any *Converso* he had had the occasion to meet. His complexion was darker and so were his eyes. And that strange white tunic with the Star of David embroidered with gold thread on his chest! And his sword, shorter than usual, enclosed in a scabbard made of richly carved metal hanging from a black velvet belt lined with purple and also sewn with golden thread! The King was torn between his desire to keep listening to the strange prince speak or to hear the opinion of his secretary, the wise old Antonio Carneiro. He wanted to know what his secretary thought before beginning a new discussion with David. And that is the course of action he took, the most reasonable one. He thanked his guest for his excellent presentation.

"We find the Prince of Chabor's words quite interesting. We would be delighted to discuss them further, tomorrow at the same time," he said, rising from his throne.

"May the Eternal, Master of the Universe, bless Your Majesty," David replied, his eyes bright.

He bowed before the king and then went back to join his men, still waiting in the rotunda.

"What a plan!" exclaimed Joao III. He was alone with Antonio Carneiro and his face, looking younger than usual, was glowing. "What a plan!" he repeated. "And what a strange man!"

"Yes," said the secretary, his white hair flying as he nodded. "A strange man, but he does make sense."

"Indeed he does."

The King returned to his throne and invited his secretary to take the seat David Reubeni had occupied.

"What you think, my dear Dom Antonio?"

"Like Your Majesty, I was impressed by the man and by how much he knew about our interests in the world. Of course, such an expedition would serve above all his own interests, but…"

Antonio Carneiro shrugged and gestured with his hands.

"Does the king allow me…?"

"Go on."

"It could also serve Portugal and contribute to the glory of its king."

The king stroked his beard and looked up at the ceiling as if he were seeking inspiration.

"Never once did the Prince of Chabor mention how much the operation might cost," he noted gently.

"If the king permits…"

"Go on, my dear Dom Antonio, go on."

"I am convinced that he has already found a way of financing the expedition."

"The way Antonio de Ataide imagined?"

"Yes, Milord."

"In that case, we must immediately plan to open a training camp for the Prince of Chabor's army."

"We already have one not far from here, between Almeirim and Alpiarça, Milord."

"Excellent," said the King. "That will allow us, as we are giving this David Reubeni our help, to keep an eye on what he is doing. But what will be our stance concerning those *Conversos* who might express the desire to join his army?"

"Does the king allow…?"

"Speak."

"I agree with Antonio de Ataide. Let those men who would like to enroll in his army do so, and let them leave the country. Good riddance! The most sincere of those who have truly converted will remain in Portugal and continue to serve its King. But first we must consult our military advisers and wait for tomorrow's meeting."

Chapter thirty-six

A Meeting
and a Celebration

W ell then?" Joseph asked anxiously as he rode up beside the Messenger.

David Reubeni looked affably at his companion.

"Everything will be decided tomorrow," he said.

"But what was the king's attitude?"

"Friendly, kindly."

"And?"

"We find out definitively tomorrow. 'What the eyes see,' said the Ecclesiast, 'is preferable to desire's rambling.'"

As they left Almeirim, the Messenger reined in his horse and turned toward Joseph.

"For tomorrow's meeting, we must give some thought to how we would like to organize a training camp for our future soldiers. One never knows."

And then, before spurring his horse to a gallop, he added:

"Even when setting out on a rabbit hunt, it is wise to choose a weapon that could kill a tiger…"

247

The two men were unable to finish their conversation about how to organize the military camp. In Santarem, a large delegation of Jews from Morocco was waiting for them. At the delegation's head was Rabbi Haïm Ben Yehuda Halewa from Fez, together with Rabbi Abraham Ben Zemmur from Safi. David Reubeni remembered the stories told by the captain of *La Victoire*, Fernao de Morais.

"You are the son of Yehuda Ben Moshe Halewa the kabbalist," he said to the first man. "Your father went to live in Jerusalem, right?"

The rabbi was flattered and turned toward his companions to be sure they had noticed. So the Prince of Chabor knew his name and his father's reputation!

After reading the letters of support that the rabbi carried from the Jewish communities of Safi, Fez, Tlemcen, Mascar, and Oran, along with a warm message from the King of Morocco, David Reubeni then astonished the members of the delegation even more when he declared:

"And you, the rabbi from Safi, are you not Abraham ben Zemmur, the celebrated sage of Moroccan Judaism?"

Contrary to his custom and to Joseph's great surprise, the Envoy from Chabor invited the entire delegation to join him for dinner. They were not *Marranos*, Portuguese converts, but true Jews who knew the scriptures and shared the faith of Abraham, Isaac, and Jacob.

During the meal he learned that the news of his arrival in Portugal had already reached the Arab Orient. Rabbi Halewa reported that he had heard about a Muslim prince from Hormuz on the Indian Ocean not far from the Chabor desert who had paid a visit to the King of Morocco. He had been questioned at great length by the king about David Reubeni while he was still in Rome

"Do you know this desert kingdom?" the King had asked.

"Yes," replied the Arab prince. "Many prosperous Jews live in Chabor, and they have large herds. At their head there is a king named Joseph and their government is made up of seventy elders..."

David Reubeni glanced knowingly at his faithful Joseph, who was standing at the other end of the table where people were seated for the meal, keeping an eye on the servers.

"To what do I owe the honor of receiving such a prestigious delegation from the Jewish communities in Morocco?" David asked.

Rabbi Halewa looked over at Rabbi Ben Zemmur, but the rabbi from Safi motioned to the rabbi from Fez to answer. He hesitated, then replied.

"Our communities are wondering…And so too are our Muslim friends. As the Prince of Chabor knows, the longing to return to the land of their ancestors is shared by every Jew. But there remain many questions…"

"Which questions?" David asked with an engaging smile.

Rabbi Halewa sat up straighter.

"Why did you come from the Orient? What do you really want?"

David smiled:

"In Chabor we have been waging war for a long time with swords, lances, bows, and the valor of our warriors. We would like, with the help of the Eternal—blessed be His name!—to set out for Jerusalem and take back our homeland. I have come to Europe to seek skilled craftsmen who can help us make modern weapons, harquebuses, and cannons…"

"Do you believe that the day will come when independence will be granted to Israel?" Rabbi Ben Zemmur risked asking.

David pounded the table with his fist.

"No!" he exclaimed. "Independence will never be granted to Israel! We must win it ourselves!"

Then, lowering his voice, he added firmly:

"It is for that war that I have come."

There was a moment of silence. The energy displayed by the man from the desert impressed his audience. Finally, Rabbi Halewa took it upon himself to ask another burning question.

"The Jews in and around Fez, as well as the Muslims, are wondering about you. Who are you? A prophet? A messiah?"

David shook his head and burst out laughing. As he laughed, his eyes half-closed, and his dark hair fell in disorder over his forehead.

"The Jews in Marseille asked me the same question! I shall give the same answer..."

He paused. A bee began buzzing around Rabbi Ben Zemmur's head and they all turned to look. He waved his hand to chase it off. Then every eye turned back toward the Messenger, and everyone was hanging on his words.

"Far from me such blasphemy!" he finally said. "I am only a sinner as other men, and I have even been forced to kill. I am neither a scholar nor a mystic, neither a prophet nor the son of a prophet. I come from Chabor, where I am a military leader, the son of King Solomon. The *Conversos* of Portugal, the Jews in Italy as everywhere else, in every country I have traveled through, have imagined, believed that I was a great kabbalist, a prophet or the son of a prophet, a messiah—and who knows what else? I have always told people that I am only an ordinary sinner and that I have been devoted to the art of war since I was a child."

The Moroccan delegates were deeply touched by his frankness and the unusual bearing of a Jewish prince, who spoke excellent Arabic and was proposing the reconquest of Israel as if such an enterprise were possible. The atmosphere at the dinner grew more relaxed, and people freely exchanged comments and promises. When the delegation took their leave, they assured David of their full support, and many of the young Moroccan Jews volunteered to join his army.

The Messenger from Chabor thanked them, bade them to carry his homage to the King of Morocco, and added:

"It is time to say *Minha*, the afternoon prayer."

And then he left them, leaving Joseph to see them out.

He spent the time between *Minha* and *Ma'ariv*, the evening prayer, jotting down notes. Sometimes he would stand up and pace nervously about in his room. Through the narrow window, he could still see the half-destroyed Alcazabar fortress silhouetted against the deep purple sky that remained after the sun had set. As he contemplated the fortress, he began to murmur:

"Powerful one day, dead forever."

He repeated the phrase in a low voice, and then he turned back to the sheets of paper that were spread out on the table and on which, in his compact hand, he was describing the manner in which they would enroll any young Jews appearing in the training camp and the list of weapons that would be needed for the expedition. He had even made sketches of the coasts of the Mediterranean and the African continent to show more clearly the route to be followed by the ships the Portuguese king was to provide. After reciting the words: *And He, full of mercy, forgives all sins. He does not consummate destruction. Often, He holds back His anger,* he summoned Joseph. They closed themselves up together for a long consultation that lasted well into the night.

The next morning at noon, followed by his large retinue, the Messenger arrived in Almeirim as planned. To his great astonishment, the area around the palace was jammed with carts filled with all kinds of merchandise. There were lines of servants carrying trays of fruit, sides of meat, and garlands of flowers. The commander of the Portuguese guards escorting David and his men had to shout several times before the King's guests could make their way through. In the square courtyard, grooms wearing their dress uniforms—green doublets and white gloves—were busy with the horses. It was clear that preparations were under way for some great event. David noticed groups of noblemen in festive attire conversing in the gardens.

Antonio Carneiro, the Royal Secretary, was waiting for him with the interpreter. Tossing back his white hair, he explained to David that the King had decided on the spur of the moment to organize a celebration, and that he was inviting the Prince of Chabor and his men to join in.

David Reubeni was aggravated. He had been prepared for a true discussion with Joao III and his people. He was hoping, thanks to the quality and the serious nature of his proposals, to finally get the support he so badly needed. This unexpected celebration would set everything back. But he managed to hide his disappointment and calmly asked:

"What is the purpose of the festivities?"

"Pavia, Prince! Pavia!… Oh, I see that you have not heard the news! Nobody has talked about anything else all morning long."

David Reubeni stared at the king's secretary curiously.

"Well, what is the great news?"

"Pavia, as I told you. The battle of Pavia! Emperor Charles v has just defeated Frances I, King of France."

"And?"

"And the King of France has been taken prisoner!"

When he saw that the man from Chabor remained impassible, as if he didn't realize how important such an event was, Antonio Carneiro went on:

"This victory changes the balance of power in Europe. The prince knows that the emperor is the brother of our beloved Queen Catherine. The French were intending to establish settlements on the coasts of Brazil, and that would have been detrimental to our own presence on the American continent. The defeat of the French cannot fail to please our king. And so he has decided to mark the occasion by organizing a grand celebration in the palace."

David Reubeni did not share the secretary's enthusiasm. He himself was in favor of peace between the Christian kings and had even encouraged the pope to work to that end. He was convinced that only good relationships among the European powers would allow them to support his plans. If they were caught up in their own fratricidal wars, they would not be able to confront the real danger that the Muslim Turkish Empire posed. In order to counterbalance the Ottoman Empire in the world, it was urgent to carry out the old Carolingian dream, the dream of a united Europe. Far from failing to understand how important the Battle of Pavia was, he was on the contrary, measuring its possible negative consequences and the delay it meant for his own enterprise. But after all, he said to himself, why leap into the water before the ship sinks? So he kept silent and followed the king's secretary through the gardens and covered patios he had seen the day before. But today they were lined with magnificently set tables around which people in festive colors were crowding.

When the Jewish delegation arrived, a hush came over the crowd. Everyone in Portugal had been talking about the Prince of Chabor, and now the noble guests were finally able to see him. And they studied him with great curiosity and little fear. The prince's noble bearing, his tunic, his sword, and his banners were the objects of much whispering. But as soon as the Messenger moved away, they went right back to their conversations. The buzz that followed him everywhere was a little amusing, and he had a smile on his face when he presented himself to the king.

"I am pleased that the prince has accepted my invitation," Joao III said.

His eyes were sparkling, and he looked more like a child than he had the day before. The Court grandees had removed their hats and were standing waiting to greet the king, accompanied by their spouses and children. There was a long table covered with a white cloth, and from it delicious aromas were arising from a variety of dishes. Beside Joao III, four judges were seated, each holding a long cane. They used their canes, according to David's interpreter, to chase away undesirables. Every judge in the kingdom received one of these canes from the hand of their sovereign, and the cane was the symbol of their authority as judges.

An orchestra began to play. A large silver basin topped with a golden ewer was carried in. Before pouring water on the royal hands, a servant drank a few swallows to be sure, as was the custom, that it was not poisoned. The archbishop, the king's brother, blessed the assembly, and then Joao III invited his guests to come to the table.

Antonio Carneiro placed David opposite the king, but during the meal no serious discussion was possible. At the end of the banquet, all sorts of gifts, including those David had brought the day before, were given to Joao III, eliciting great admiration from the guests. The guests all congratulated His Majesty and bowed before Him. Then the king rose, saying that he was going to join the queen. As he passed near the man from Chabor, he invited him to come along.

The queen was in the company of her ladies in waiting. When she saw David, she turned up her nose in annoyance. Her eyes narrowed and she opened her fan nervously. She was able to master her feelings, however, and forced herself to smile.

"So," she exclaimed in her low voice, "this is the famous Prince of Chabor! Ambassador Dom Miguel da Silva has told me a great deal about you, Prince."

"Only good things, I hope!" David replied, bowing before Catherine of Austria.

The queen pretended not to hear his comment.

"I shall be frank with you, Prince," she continued. "Neither the ambassador nor I are among your admirers, but I am delighted to be finally able to meet you."

"If Your Majesty allows me…"

"Well, go ahead," said Catherine of Austria.

"The Ancients say that it is wise to hate one's enemy as if he might one day be your friend, and that is wiser still to love your friend as if he might one day become your enemy…"

"Nicely put!" said the king, clapping his hands.

The ministers who had accompanied him applauded in turn. The queen did not take umbrage. She turned casually to her husband:

"It appears, Milord, that there is a captain who has been in a dungeon for more than a month waiting to be judged. Would it not be appropriate, for a Very Christian King, to take advantage of this day of celebration and announce the captain's sentence?"

The king went over and sat down beside his spouse. Carefully watching her face and the faces of his ministers, as if asking them to bear witness, he asked:

"And please tell me why this captain is in prison."

"On the way back from the Indies, he claims to have been attacked by Barbary pirates who stole his cargo. Our royal customs officials, however, accuse him of selling our merchandise to the Spanish…"

"Oh," said the king.

The queen's pale cheeks reddened, and her double chin quivered indignantly.

"Dom Miguel da Silva vouches for him," she said, her voice resonant with emotion.

Joao III realized that his "oh" had shocked the queen. He laid his hand on hers to ask forgiveness.

"Have the captain brought in," he ordered.

A few moments later, a large bald man was ushered in before the king. He was so intimidated that he could only stammer as he tried to answer the king's questions. But, to David Reubeni's great surprise (the interpreter was translating for him), the king spent very little time on what had happened to the cargo, but rather began to question the captain about an entirely different subject.

"Are there Jews in the Indies and in Calcutta?"

"In great number, Milord," the seaman answered. "Many live in Ceylon, ten days sailing distance from Calcutta."

The ministers and counselors grew more attentive. The captain told them extraordinary things about those Jews in Ceylon. And the king kept asking questions about their numbers, wealth, and power...

When David Reubeni took leave of the sovereigns, Joao III whispered into his ear, as if he didn't want his spouse to hear:

"Be here tomorrow at the same time. I shall sign the decree."

Chapter thirty-seven

From All Over Europe

A great deal of improvisation went on constantly at the court of Joao III. On the day after the celebration, the meeting to which the king had convoked David was cancelled. The interpreter brought a message from Antonio Carneiro: The secretary announced to the Prince of Chabor that His Majesty the King of Portugal had decided to go to Morocco to visit the fortified areas that belonged to his kingdom. The Envoy from the desert was dismayed. The royal decree that was to establish the training camp for the Jewish army would have to wait for the king to come back before it could be signed.

The interpreter explained to the Messenger that Joao III had ordered the impromptu trip in response to pressure from the Council, for the Council wanted the king to relinquish his trading posts in North Africa because they were costing the Treasury dearly. But Joao III felt it was important for Portugal to keep its presence in the world, and by traveling to Morocco, he wanted to display his determination to reinforce his kingdom's influence.

"When it seems no hope is left, one should not despair," thought David Reubeni. But that could not help him shake his despondency.

He felt like a man lost in the desert who thinks he has caught sight of a well, but as he draws near it disappears. As a true desert man, he was well acquainted with the kind of hope that encourages mirages, and he had also experienced the disappointments that follow.

This latest complication reminded him once again that Jews, as long as they remained dispersed around the world, were always at the mercy of the will and mood swings of kings, emperors, and Church dignitaries. Only if his people were freed and returned to their ancestral lands would they have true political choices. Given that perspective, was it not worth waiting a few extra months and even undergoing additional humiliations?

During the period that followed, David Reubeni rarely went out in public. He slept very little and spent his time in prayer. Only his faithful friend Joseph was allowed to share some of his thoughts in the strange atmosphere during those rain-filled days and nights in Santarem. The city seemed to bathe in lament, as if life were made up of sad guitar music. Counselor Diego Pires had not gone to Morocco with the king, and twice a day he came asking to speak to the man of the desert. In vain—David refused to see him. Though he wasn't sure exactly why, he didn't completely trust the young man. Perhaps because the man was too intense, so intense he seemed almost mad. The man from the desert feared events and people that seemed to escape the control of reason. He spoke to Joseph about the counselor. In reference to the young man, Joseph quoted a Turkish proverb that made David laugh until tears came to his eyes.

"We must not forget, Master, that a madman is capable of turning himself into a eunuch just so he might accuse his wife of adultery in case she becomes pregnant. And I don't know what more Diego Pires could do to try to get close to you."

"What could he have to say to me that is so important?" David asked.

Joseph shrugged his shoulders.

"You'll know soon enough," he sighed, and then he left the room, leaving the Messenger to his meditations and his journal writing.

The first signs of spring were appearing. The clouds that had been hanging over the mountains for the past several months were now beginning to dissipate. Once again the sun shone. The man from Chabor was always surprised by the tiny miracle of light that chases away the shadows. His smile returned, and he suddenly felt the urge to visit the Santarem market, the largest market in Ribatejo Province. Along with his men, he spent several hours walking through the market, taking time to speak with rope makers, coopers, blacksmiths, and pewter smiths using the few words of Portuguese he had learned. He even accepted the invitation of two men on horseback to try some of the regional wine. One of the men, Captain de Sousa, had served in Morocco and could speak Arabic.

Finally, the king came home. He immediately sent Antonio Carneiro to Santarem to inquire about the Jewish prince's health and convey royal greetings. However, urgent business awaited His Majesty, and he could not receive the man from Chabor right away. In the days that followed, Queen Catherine gave birth to a son, her firstborn. The Court talked about nothing else. Unfortunately, the child, named Alfonço, died when he was only one month old. His death caused great disappointment in the kingdom. David Reubeni's plans once more had to be put on hold until the king could again be available. The king finally signed the decree that would set up a training camp for the Jewish army, under the Prince of Chabor's direction. That was on the seventeenth day of the month of Iyar of the year 5286 after the creation of the world by the Eternal—blessed be His name!, or April 30, 1526 according to the Christian calendar, a few weeks after the Jewish Passover which commemorated the liberation of the Hebrews from slavery in the land of Egypt and their departure for the Promised Land. A sign? Predestination? When he thought about it, David Reubeni realized that the people in their zeal would inevitably see it as a sign.

And the news did hit like an earthquake. In Portugal, the *Conversos* organized public festivities. Everywhere else, all over Europe, Jews in their synagogues gave thanks to the Eternal—blessed be His name!—for finally answering their prayers.

The military camp in Alpiarça, more or less abandoned for years, began to take on new life. The enormous quadrilateral was surrounded by two-story buildings and crenellated walls. Bathed by the Tagus River, the camp lay backed up against an ocher-colored village huddled around a Gothic church. To the west, in the direction of Almeirim, there was a little cluster of about ten houses with mud and wattle walls that had been used during the reign of Manuel I to house conscripts. To the east, along the river, there was a shooting range reserved for harquebusiers. Four leagues away, a large deserted area had been set aside for cannon practice.

The camp buildings were used as offices, mess halls, and infirmaries. In the central group of pink stuccoed buildings were officers' apartments. The man from Chabor and his retinue moved in there. By a fortunate circumstance, the energetic Captain Martin Alfonço de Sousa, who would one day be viceroy of the Indies, and whom David had already met in the Santarem market, had been charged by the king with helping David. He preferred living a few leagues away and making the daily ride back and forth between Santarem and Alpiarça.

On the day after that unprecedented decree was promulgated, young men already began to flood into the Alpiarça camp. They were eager to join the first Jewish army since the Bar Kokhba army dared face Rome and Emperor Hadrian in the year 132 of the Christian era. Among the enthusiastic volunteers who became more numerous daily, the Portuguese were the first to come. They were sons and grandsons of *Conversos*. Later, there appeared young Moroccan Jews, from Fez, Safi, and Mascara. And then, in secret, "new Christians" came from Spain. About a month later cohorts of young men began to arrive from Italy, France, Germany, Holland, and even Poland. Sometimes they came in groups, sometimes alone, and they typically were exhausted when they arrived. Starving, penniless, mistreated, they had sometimes been robbed as they crossed borders. They spoke a variety of different languages and were dressed in an array of rags. But they all shared the same dream: taking back the land of Israel.

Some, their feet bleeding, had to drag themselves in. But when they spotted the princely banner covered with Hebrew letters, and flags representing the tribes of Israel that Joseph had put up on twelve poles near the camp's entrance, they would drop to the ground to pray and thank the God of Israel for allowing them to live until that day. Forgetting their suffering, they would then throw themselves whole-heartedly into dances and songs of joy.

The man from Chabor, standing on a second-floor balcony, watched all this with great emotion. He, too, felt like thanking the Eternal for having preserved, through so many persecutions, young men capable of such enthusiasm. When Joseph showed him the hundreds of letters of support that had arrived from all over Europe—and among those letters, congratulatory notes from his friends Moses de Castellazzo from Venice, and Doctor Joseph Zarfatti from Rome—he began to recite the following words:

O God! You are my King:
Order Jacob's deliverance!
With You we can overthrow our enemies!
With Your Name, we can crush our adversaries...

Blond or dark-haired, with complexions that were pale, tanned, or dark, on horseback, on donkey back, or on foot, more and more men continued to come to Alpiarça. In a few weeks, the little Portuguese village near which the military camp was based looked more like a suburb of Jerusalem. It was beginning to resemble an antechamber where meetings that had been so yearned for and delayed so long could finally take place—meetings between a people and their land. Alpiarça, or the gates of Israel—such was the vision attracting young Jewish men from all over Europe.

Soon they numbered six thousand. Then eight, then twelve, and every man professed unlimited devotion for David Reubeni. They were all determined, conscious of their transient nature there in Portugal for military training, and they all were waiting for one grand event: the day they would set sail to go liberate the land of Israel. Very quickly it was clear that the initial plans for housing were inadequate. Tents had to be erected. And the first thing to do was to be sure that all those young men regained their health. They were obviously courageous, but all the same, many of them were in bad shape after such long, difficult journeys. Some of them were not even able to walk from where they slept to the camp—scarcely two leagues! The nurses were overwhelmed. They turned two stables into hospitals, and the doctors recruited from among the *Converso* communities in Beja, Evora, and Faro were unsparing in their time and efforts.

The Portuguese officers in charge of the training, carefully chosen by Captain de Sousa, quickly began to express their admiration for so many young men who would voluntarily appear for training exercises even though they could still barely walk. It was now the month of September in 1526, according to the Christian calendar. It was almost time for the Jewish New Year, Rosh Hashanah, in the year 5287 after the creation of the world by the Eternal—blessed be His name!—and the training had advanced sufficiently so that a part of the Jewish army was ready for combat. David Reubeni could already count on thirty-five *lances*. Each *lance* was made of ten horsemen and three hundred foot soldiers. With one hundred *lances*, he would then have a thousand horsemen and an army of thirty-thousand infantrymen. The army would be divided among lancers, men with knives, pages who served the armed men, and archers. Some of the archers could also fight from horseback, and it would be the job of the men with knives to slit the throats of any enemy horsemen who were thrown from their horses.

The Messenger from Chabor, who could still remember the ambush Giacobo Mantino had set for him on the Camerino road in Italy, also felt he should include some harquebusiers. Captain de Sousa pointed out to him that the Portuguese army had one harquebusier for every foot soldier. David Reubeni decided to quadruple the number. As for cannons, he thought it best to reduce the calibers. Smaller cannons would be more maneuverable, and furthermore, they would need to be loaded on ships and then unloaded. In just a few months, to the Portuguese officers' great surprise, David was able to introduce Hebrew as the common language among these men of different languages, since all of the men had learned the rudiments of Hebrew. The young men were so motivated that the military training was able to progress much more rapidly than they had expected. Martin Alfonço de Sousa was carefully monitoring their progress, and he thought they could leave for the Orient by the beginning of October. David Reubeni suggested that they leave a month later, due to the upcoming long procession of Jewish religious celebrations, beginning with Yom Kippur and ending with the Gift of the Torah. Two years earlier, the same celebrations had delayed his departure from Italy. But he could not ignore those holy days. Besides, he had no wish to avoid them.

He used the extra time to prepare his army even more meticulously. With the help of Captain de Sousa and his officers, he pored over every detail of the expedition: stopovers, relay stations, and farms where they might stay on the way to the port in Faro, where the ships lent by the king were waiting. Everything, the sailing orders, the way to divide up the weapons among the different ships, and even the weight and contents of each soldier's rations were considered, reconsidered, and planned with the utmost care.

In the Alpiarça camp, Yom Kippur was a day of fasting, and the text of the *Haftara* was read to everyone gathered in the immense central courtyard. The voices of those thousands of young men echoed like a declaration of principles, like a commitment, a promise:

This is the fasting I love: breaking the chains of injustice, breaking every yoke, freeing the oppressed...Sharing your bread with the hungry, taking in the homeless; when you see a man naked, give him clothing...

At such moments, David Reubeni could feel his heart bursting with irresistible pride. Thirteen days later, for the Feast of the Gift of the Law, Simchat Torah, it was not only the Jewish army in Alpiarça that was celebrating the traditional feast day, but all of Portugal, as if it were a national holiday. In all those cities and towns where there were large numbers of *Conversos*, both Jews and Christians gathered to organize popular celebrations on squares decorated with garlands. They danced and drank to victory over the infidels, to the liberating of Christ's tomb, to the Kingdom of Israel as well as to the health of King Joao III and the Prince of Chabor.

Chapter thirty-eight

A Meeting with Diego Pires

The date for departure was set for the end of October, and final preparations were under way. Captain de Sousa went in person to the port in Faro to inspect the ships. David Reubeni was nearing his goal. After so many struggles and so much effort, it now appeared that nothing could stand in the way of his plans. The age-old dream of returning to Israel was finally taking concrete shape. For the first time in centuries, Jerusalem seemed within reach of the Jewish people.

Soon there were only ten days left before the fateful moment. Ten more days to wait—the most difficult. Ten days, and the army of the man from Chabor would set sail. The grand adventure of reconquest would begin. The Messenger, as time went by, could not stop worrying. He could no longer sleep. He could not control the nervousness he felt. When the sun came up, he would be standing on his balcony, struggling with insomnia that kept him counting dawns.

"Nine more!" he murmured softly that morning.

The barracks were devoid of life, the sky transparent, the world quiet. Everyone was still sleeping. Then a sound like that of rustling pages broke the silence. David Reubeni looked up. A flock of wild geese was crossing above him. Little by little, the camp came back to life. Horses whinnying over by the stables began to wake up the soldiers. In a few minutes there would be patrols, trumpets would be sounding, some would begin their daily training exercises, and all would be carefully rehearsing, today as yesterday, actions devoted to liberating Jerusalem. Only nine more days until they sailed.

"Master…"

The Messenger turned around. It was Joseph.

"Nine more days, Master!"

"Yes," David sighed, coming back into the room from the balcony. It was a large, bright room, sparsely furnished. Besides a bed, a chair, and a table, there was also a sofa covered with a rough beige and white goatskin. That's where the Messenger's confidant sat down, facing David who was seated at the table.

"According to the Koran, God is with those who are patient," Joseph sighed.

"Of course, but is the Koran with us?"

They got up to leave. Someone knocked. Martin Alfonço de Sousa's large frame filled the doorway.

"What's new this morning, Captain?" David asked in Arabic.

The captain had worked in Morocco and could get along reasonably well in Arabic. The Messenger thanked his good fortune daily for a partner who had such a lively intelligence and true military talents. He was of medium height, wore his hair long, and always looked cheerful. He took his work very seriously. The mutual respect and admiration the two men had felt immediately when they had met in the Santarem market were even stronger now. They had worked together productively and faithfully over the past few months. Since the king had charged the captain with helping the Envoy from Chabor, Alfonço de Sousa had literally made the Jewish cause his own.

"The king's counselor would like to see the prince," said the captain.

"The king's counselor?"

"Yes. Milord Diego Pires."

"Does he come on behalf of Joao III?"

"That is what he says…"

It was difficult in such conditions for David not to receive the persistent young man. He agreed, though he kept his guard up. When Diego Pires came in, Joseph and the captain discreetly withdrew, leaving the prince and the counselor alone.

Diego Pires removed his large velvet hat with a feather and bowed. When he looked up, David Reubeni realized that his premonition had been correct. The intense eyes, their strange brightness, their unfathomable appeal, all that, David thought, was like vertigo. A vertigo of evil, just as there are politics of evil.

"His Majesty the King sends the Prince of Chabor the expression of his admiration for the work the prince has accomplished in such a short time," the counselor said in muted voice.

And then, as if in confidence, he moved closer to the prince, adding a few words in his Portuguese-accented bastard Hebrew.

"All of the military advisors who have visited this camp share the king's opinion…"

"I thank the king's counselor for this message that brings precious encouragement," the Messenger replied.

"The king," Diego Pires went on, "asked me to say that he would be pleased to receive the prince in the Almeirim Palace before the Jewish army sets sail for the Orient."

This time, it was David Reubeni's turn to bow slightly, signifying his pleasure to see Joao III once more and to be able to express gratitude for his help and generosity. Diego Pires's face muscles grew tense, as if he were asking for something with the strength of his eyes alone. In a barely audible voice, finally he asked:

"Has the prince noticed?"

"Noticed what?"

"My Hebrew…"

"Yes, I have," the Messenger conceded. "The counselor's Hebrew has improved greatly since we first met."

In a stronger voice, the young blond man explained proudly:

"Since we met, Prince, I have been studying every day. First the written Law. Then the oral Law. And now, the secrets of the Law…"

He began speaking faster. Now he was speaking with animated gestures:

"A Jew who doesn't know the Torah is worth little more than a jackal!"

David Reubeni was beginning to lose patience. This Diego Pires was clearly beginning to worry him.

"The king's counselor is not a Jew!" he noted sharply.

"But...yes he is!" the other exclaimed. Now he was even more excited, and he began to tell the Messenger how he had always been intrigued by the Jews, and how in order to come to grips with his doubts and questions he had gone to see the old writer Joao de Barros, a longtime friend of the family.

"Do you understand what I am saying, Prince?" he asked. "The shock I felt when I saw you for the first time on the bridge of *La Victoire* moved me deeply. It was as if you were opening up a path within me. So, when Joao de Barros realized how sincerely I was asking, he could not hide from me any longer the truth that my parents had done all they could to keep from me. My family is indeed of Jewish origin. They come from Spain, where they were linked with the great kabbalist Moïse de Leon. They took refuge in Portugal after the Spanish Inquisition's first persecutions, and the Pires family was converted by force during the reign of Manuel I."

The man from Chabor listened without a word to the counselor's revelations. As the man laid out his story, David's anxiety kept growing. Far from being enthusiastic about the young man's Jewishness, he felt burdened by it.

"I have always felt, beneath my identity, that there was something missing, something incomplete," added Diego Pires, twisting his hands together feverishly. "The same feeling that a man has who has never known a female."

He smiled, as if to ask to be excused for that comment.

"And yet, women do not interest me in the slightest."

He looked up at the ceiling.

"The answer came to me from the *Zohar*," he said. "Does not the Book of Lights say that the word *Ehad*, 'one,' when it is pronounced appropriately, can help Israel become one with God as a female becomes one with a male?"

David Reubeni did not want to get caught up in a theological debate. He took a step backward and looked at his interlocutor. Since the counselor had arrived, they had remained standing.

"That doesn't change anything. The king's counselor, being the son of *Conversos*, is therefore Christian and not Jewish," the man from Chabor objected coldly.

And then, unexpectedly, Diego Pires threw himself at the Messenger's feet. As he knelt before him, his voice broke with emotion as he stammered:

"Prince! Prince! When I saw you in Almeirim Palace standing so nobly, so proudly, and so handsomely before the king and the grandees, when I saw the *Shekhina*'s great wing hovering over your head, then, then I realized that my duty was to return to the faith of my ancestors and finally become one forever with the Eternal, the God of Israel, blessed be His name...!"

David Reubeni stepped back once again in horror. The man's inappropriate, mystic, uncontrollable faith seemed like a mountain stream rising to its flood stage and about to wash everything away before it. Neither reason nor wisdom would be able to contain it. This "new Jew" jeopardized the critical balance David's plans to retake the Holy Land had been able to establish. If he were allowed to continue, Diego Pires would endanger the entire enterprise and perhaps even all their lives. Would not people accuse the Messenger from Chabor, under the guise of returning to Jerusalem, of trying to bring Portugal's *Conversos* back to Judaism? David was almost brutal as he jerked the young man back to his feet, and he shoved him toward the door.

"I am sorry," said the Envoy in a neutral voice, "but I have not come to convert Christians to the religion of Moses! If the king's counselor wishes to embrace the Jewish faith, he should not be speaking to a general..."

"Prince," the man protested, "do you not know...?"

"Not know what?"

"Do you not know that the person speaking to you *knows who you are?*"

He reached out his hands once more toward David as if in supplication to a divinity, saying:

God sends the Man of the Good News...
The nations will fight,
Heroes will push,
The enemies will be crushed,
And we shall enjoy peace...

His voice grew stronger.

"The Man of the Good News, Prince. That is Who you are. And I, Diego Pires, I know it as no other knows it, as no other can know it!"

He broke into a laugh, and then he began to make his case once more, sounding both plaintive and reproachful:

"And how about all the others? All those *Conversos* who have joined your army, that magnificent Jewish army?"

"They have remained Christians," David objected. "You are certainly aware that your king's decree allows everyone, even Christians, to join the army leaving for Jerusalem."

As he spoke, David Reubeni walked over and grabbed the young man by the shoulders to shake him, to convince him, to force him if possible to abandon the dream in which he was losing his faith. When he grabbed him, he could feel the young man trembling violently. He let go immediately and gave him a push, as if the brief contact had burned him. Diego Pires stumbled and nearly fell, and his velvet hat with its feather slipped off his head. He groped around on the floor for it, as if he couldn't see. He looked like a sleepwalker who had just been startled awake. He finally picked up his hat, looked up furiously at the Messenger, and his violet irises proudly threw darts of resentment:

"You! You!" he shouted.

"Me?"

"Yes, you! How could you do that? You dared to put your hands on me. You have hurt me!"

"I am sorry. But it is time for you to leave."

"Leave? But I have come to…I love you! I want to follow you! Like all the Jews!"

The young's man's anger had been replaced by a cajoling smile. Suddenly he was like a choir boy, an abandoned child asking for help. David Reubeni grew even more irritated. The visitor's excitement and cunning innocence were frightening. Is not some innocence truly perverse? David took a step back toward him.

"Don't touch me!" Diego Pires screamed shrilly.

In order to stand up to such delirium, the Messenger offered a silent prayer: *Eternal, O my God! Do not punish me in Your anger; do not chastise me in Your wrath!* He was a man on whom one could count to free other men, but he was not prepared to save souls. The king's counselor was a real danger to his cause, but nonetheless, he remained an enigma. The sharp realization that David would not be able to do anything about the situation came to him. In spite of Diego Pires's shouts, he reached out and placed his right hand on the young man's shoulder. In a calmer voice, as if he were speaking to a sick man, he murmured:

"Please calm down!"

And then he repeated:

"But as I have told you, it is time to go. Other duties await me."

"Go? No, Prince! I want to…I have to follow you. For *I know.* Don't forget. I know *who* you really are!"

And therein perhaps lay the difference between David Reubeni's own faith and the faith of Diego Pires and of all those others who had followed David since he undertook his mission. Did they really believe in God? They kept expecting Him to provide proofs, and they kept looking for His chosen one. Whereas he, the man who had come out of the desert, was trusting. Trusting in God's justice. Trusting in His love. And even trusting in the man God had made in His own image. Truly, David trusted in God's promise. Was that the difference between the faith of the leader and the faith of those who followed? Between a guide's faith and the faith of those who are guided?

He watched Diego Pires. The young man still wasn't moving. He kept folding his velvet hat with his pale fingers and stood with his back to the door. Someone knocked sharply three times. The Messenger gave a start as if the three knocks were announcing some threat. He glared at his visitor.

"Get out of here!" he said to Diego Pires.

He grabbed his arm and pushed him toward the exit.

"And please convey my homage to His Majesty the King!"

Chapter thirty-nine

In Which Diego Pires Becomes Shlomo Molkho

After Diego Pires left, Joseph Halevy came to see his master. David was seated at the table, his face in his hands.

"What happened? Is there bad news?" Joseph wondered.

David Reubeni looked up. Joseph was surprised by the look in his eyes. It was as if the Envoy from Chabor had just met the devil.

"Bad news?" he repeated.

The Messenger got to his feet without an answer. Abruptly, he asked:

"What did your famous Turkish prophet say? That the foolish man becomes a eunuch so he can accuse his wife of adultery in case she should become pregnant?"

"That's right," said Joseph in surprise.

"Well, Diego Pires wants to convert to Judaism!"

"That's the last straw! What did you tell him?"

"I sent him away. It's not my job to hang a bell around the necks of crazy men!"

"But he will probably come back…"

"Alas!"

Their prediction was not baseless. Forty-eight hours later, at about four in the morning, just as the sky was beginning to pale in the east, the Messenger from Chabor was drawn from his meditation by the sound of a galloping horse. Soon, the horseman was right beneath his balcony. When David leaned over, he saw three watchmen with their torches helping the visitor dismount. Even before anyone came to alert the man from the desert, he knew it must be Diego Pires. The rider had scarcely dismounted when he fainted away. The guards carried the king's counselor immediately to the Messenger's room. David sent for Joseph and asked everyone else to leave.

The young man was pale and unconscious. He appeared to be totally exhausted. His stockings were splattered with blood, and even his shoes had blood on them. Joseph appeared, his eyes still heavy with sleep. David sent him to get a basin of water, clean clothes, and some spirits. The dried blood had caused the stockings to stick to his skin, and Joseph had no choice but to cut them off. The young man moaned and briefly opened his eyes.

"God be praised," he sighed, grabbing David's hand. "Here you are, Prince! Now I am completely Jewish!"

His eyes rolled and he drifted off once more into unconsciousness.

"Give him some spirits," the Messenger told Joseph.

Joseph lifted the counselor's head and forced him to drink. Diego Pires swallowed some of the spirits, coughed, and spit. He shivered, but did not awaken.

"Circumcision has never killed anyone," David Reubeni said coldly. "But the circumcision this crazy man has just performed upon himself may well cause many victims."

He laughed bitterly. He had never been able to take seriously the obstacles that fate placed in his way. Might there not be the slim possibility that this incident, if unnoticed, could save a man's soul, even a man who was so deluded? He paced back and forth in the room and finally went to sit down at the table, at some distance from the bed on which Diego Pires was lying. He turned to Joseph:

"We must find him other stockings. Once he is cleaned up and dressed, he will be able to leave before dawn. And the sooner, the better!"

Joseph hurried out, almost at a run. A strange silence had fallen over the camp, and it seemed to rise back up from the ground along with the mist. After the excitement of Diego Pires's arrival, everything had become quiet, like at the beginning of an armistice when the cannons cease. The Messenger from Chabor stood there, watching the young man. He realized that even in his foolishness the man was not without charm or courage. For rare indeed are those men who are capable of signing a covenant with the Eternal in their own flesh!

From outside, a voice called out:

"Prince, do you need any help?"

It was one of the guards.

"No, thank you," David replied.

They needed to act rapidly, and there was no room for mistakes. *He that hasteneth with his feet will surely fall.* David was well aware of that Biblical warning, and he tried to analyze the situation as carefully as possible. The guards had seen a bloodied Diego Pires appear and he had fainted away when he got off his horse. Later, they would see him leave. David owed them an explanation. He might say, for example, that the king's counselor had been hurt during the night when he fell off his horse. Such a version of the facts would be plausible and would not seem strange. At least at first. For the young man would not return to Almeirim, and his absence would not fail to worry those around the king and even the king himself. They would learn that he had disappeared just after paying a visit to the Prince of Chabor. From there it would be an easy step to think that the strange Jew with the dark complexion who had come from so far and about whom people knew little had whisked away or kidnapped the pure, blond Christian. And David knew that those hostile to his plans would quickly take that step. But he saw no other solution. It was less dangerous to be thought to have done away with a man than to be accused of having performed circumcision on that same man in order to force him to become a Jew. It was only seven days until the day when the Jewish army was to leave for its reconquest of Jerusalem, and suddenly the future seemed dark.

Diego Pires moaned softly. David walked over to him. The young man smiled weakly and once again seized the hand of the man from the desert.

"I've changed my name," he whispered. "From now on my name is Shlomo Molkho, *Angel Solomon*..."

He closed his eyes and let go of David's hand. The Messenger leaned down to study the "Angel's" face. But the young man was breathing evenly. Just then, Joseph arrived with some shoes and stockings. Together, they managed to bring the counselor back to consciousness and to slip his new clothes on.

"The stockings are a little large," Joseph grumbled, "but nobody will notice."

Daylight was streaming into the room. Still wobbly, the former Diego Pires was finally on his feet, though he had to lean on David's shoulder.

"Does the prince know why I have chosen the name Shlomo Molkho?" he asked, his voice getting a little stronger.

"No."

"Because up until now my nickname has been 'Angel Diego.' 'Angel' is Molkho, and 'Shlomo' is Solomon, the son of David!"

"So it is," said the Messenger, placing his hands on the young man's shoulders and holding him at a distance. "And now," he continued. "Listen carefully, my dear Shlomo Molkho. If someone should denounce you, if someone notices or already knows that you have converted to Judaism, even though you are the king's counselor, you will be burned at the stake, and thousands of innocents along with you! As for retaking Israel, that will surely be compromised or perhaps put off definitively..."

Shlomo Molkho stood there motionless looking up at David, listening rapturously. One would have thought it was a father scolding his son.

"I will give you two fresh horses and one hundred ducats," the man from the desert went on. "That is more than you need to leave Portugal immediately."

The other man stood up straighter, his eyes suddenly sparkling.

"Prince, O Prince of Israel, I will do whatever you say, whatever you ask, on one condition…"

"What is that?"

"That you allow me to announce your coming. From Rome to Avignon, from Salonika to Jerusalem, wherever I go to announce the good news, I will always find the words to say *who* you really are, to exalt your presence among us, to glorify your mission!"

They could now hear voices in the barracks courtyard. The soldiers were beginning to wake up. Horses snorting in the stables called men back to their daily duties. The "Angel" could not stay there any longer. David Reubeni began to show his impatience.

"Of course, of course!" he conceded, in order to avoid further discussion. "But you must promise, in the name of the Eternal, the God of Israel, All-Powerful God, to leave Portugal this very day, without speaking to anyone or stopping anywhere."

Shlomo Molkho smiled, and as if some invisible being were dictating words to him, he began to recite:

With hidden words
I shall say to men
Words chosen
Like perfumed powder
From Mount Carmel…

The Messenger broke in:

"Do you feel strong enough to ride?"

"Yes. Will not the Eternal, blessed be His name, give me the strength to announce to the world the coming of his Envoy as well as the end of the world? Apart from your own mission, Prince, do you know of any mission more sacred?"

His voice was now more confident. He was no longer wobbly. Raising his arms heavenward, he shouted:

"Diego Pires is dead. Long live Shlomo Molkho!"

David Reubeni shrugged his shoulders and turned toward Joseph.

"Have two horses saddled, the best you can find, and hurry! In that way, our friend will always have a spare. Give him one hundred ducats for the journey as well."

Then, once that had been done, he accompanied Shlomo Molkho to the door. In the courtyard, near the gate, the young man bent down to kiss the hand of the man from the desert. But David quickly pulled his hand back. When he had said goodbye, he returned to his room. Shlomo Molkho climbed into the saddle and waited for a few moments until David reappeared on his balcony. So, the Messenger was watching him leave! Then he sat up straight on his horse and proudly rode off with a shout:

"It is up to us, Prince. We shall free the people of Israel!"

He pulled on the reins, and as his horse reared up in impatience, he added:

"We shall meet in Rome, Prince! Rome destroyed, Rome subjugated, Rome conquered!"

Tired of listening to the young man's ravings, the Messenger pulled back from the balcony. He had little time to reflect on the event or on his own responsibility, even involuntary, in the young counselor's crazy conversion. Now he would be considered a renegade *Converso*, and could be sent to the stake. Nor did David have time to consider all the consequences and perils that would result. He had always known that an argument about danger is effective only with those people who live in safety. Finally, exhausted by the sleepless night, a night when so much had happened, he drifted off into refreshing sleep.

An hour later he was awakened by Captain de Sousa. As soon as he had reached the camp that morning, the captain had been informed of the royal counselor's strange visit. David Reubeni did not wish to lie to his Portuguese friend, but neither could he tell him the entire truth. So he retold the events without mentioning either the circumcision or the young man's disappearance. And then he shut himself up to pray.

He had just finished *Minha*, the afternoon prayer, when Captain de Sousa announced a messenger from Almeirim. He was asking for both of them to come immediately to the palace. The king wished to speak to them. Urgently.

"The sun has shone too long for clouds not to appear now," thought the man from Chabor. His instinct told him, however, that those clouds would not be simply bringing rain, but perhaps a squall, or even a violent storm.

The little group composed of David Reubeni's retinue and the captain's escort entered the courtyard in the royal palace late that afternoon. As they handed their horses over to the groomsmen, Antonio Carneiro, the king's secretary, came to greet them. He was friendly, but he had a serious look on his face.

"The king's counselor has disappeared," he said. "His disappearance has greatly affected His Majesty and the entire Court."

The interpreter joined them as they reached the arcades. Joao III had made a point of sending for him, as well as for Ambassador Miguel da Silva, who greeted them with a honeyed smile.

"When Da Silva smiles, Jews will weep," Joseph muttered under his breath.

The delegation found the king in spirited conversation with his confessor, Antonio de Ataide. Joao III gestured for them to wait. After several additional exchanges with his confessor, he finally turned toward the Prince of Chabor.

"So, some sad events are taking place in the Alpiarça camp? Is it to thank me for my welcome, for my help, and my friendship that you are turning my kingdom upside down?"

Joao III's expression was somber. Even his curly little beard seemed aggressive. David Reubeni grew pale, and he tried to control his anger. He stepped forward and looked straight into the king's eyes.

"Milord, I came as a friend and as an ally. Today, more than ever, I am in your debt. How could Your Majesty believe that I could have betrayed his trust in any way?"

He took another step toward the king. They were almost touching.

"But perhaps Your Majesty can explain to me what is troubling him?"

There was a long silence. A cloud passed, and the shadows deepened. Joao III was staring at his guest as if he were seeing him for the first time, and he found the man as impressive as always. David's proud stature radiated extraordinary strength. His dark skin and his features that seemed to have been carved out of rock compelled trust. And yet, at that moment when darkness was invading the reception room, the man's white tunic with the Star of David that stood out in the fading light worried the king, as if he were a child facing the unknown. What sort of man was this David Reubeni? What was the essence of his charm?

But weather can change almost as rapidly as the mood of a king. The wind blew away the clouds, and once again the brilliance of the setting sun lit up the room. The king relaxed. He went over to the throne and sat down, motioning for Antonio Carneiro to speak. The secretary summed up the situation. The arrival of thousands of Jews in a country from which they had been expelled thirty years earlier was beginning to cause concern. The fact that these Jews were only passing through Portugal, since they were joining the Prince of Chabor's army and would be leaving soon for the Orient, had not satisfied those who were protesting. The protesters were being encouraged by the "Spanish clan," the camp of those who supported the Inquisition. Indeed, the protesters were backed by a good portion of the clergy, and they had begun a country-wide campaign. According to them, the kingdom was in danger of falling under the control of a foreign power. And their campaign was beginning to bear fruit. Already there had been demonstrations in several cities in which people were shouting *"Death to the Jews!"*

Antonio Carneiro tossed his head, and his white hair fell back into place.

"And what's more," he said, "for the first time we have been hearing people in Santarem shouting slogans against the Prince of Chabor. People accuse him of trying to convert Portuguese Christians to Judaism."

"But that is absurd!" David Reubeni protested.

"Perhaps," Antonio de Ataide broke in, "but as of this morning, since Diego Pires, the king's counselor, has disappeared, since people have been claiming that he has been circumcised by the Prince of Chabor, yesterday's rumors have become dangerous reality in the eyes of most Portuguese."

The man of the desert could not ignore information of that kind. He paced up and down for a moment, brow knitted, hands clasped behind his back. And then he turned toward Joao III.

"If the king permits…"

"Speak."

"I had foreseen, Milord, yes, I had foreseen that our enemies might accuse us of trying to bring *Conversos* back to the Jewish faith. That kind of perfidious accusation was the only accusation that could harm us. For that reason, ever since I arrived in Portugal, I have done everything possible to prevent the slightest incident, to clear up the slightest misunderstanding which might endanger our plans to take back the Holy Land or damage the reputation of our benefactor, the very Catholic Joao III, may the Eternal grant him protection…"

He gestured toward Captain de Sousa, who was standing a little behind him.

"Captain Martin Alfonço de Sousa will be my witness. I have always considered the *Conversos* as true Christians. And I can swear on my honor that *not one* conversion has taken place in the Alpiarça camp."

"And how about Diego Pires?" the king asked.

"If the king allows me…"

"Speak."

"The young counselor did indeed come to see me unexpectedly three days ago. He was carrying a message from Your Majesty, kind words of encouragement which meant a great deal to me. And then…"

Tension filled the room.

"And then?" Joao III asked impatiently.

"Well, he began to rave."

"To rave?"

"Yes. About his Jewish origins. About wanting to join our army and leave for the Orient along with us."

"What did you do?"

"With all due respect to His Majesty…"

"Speak!"

"I told him that I had not come to Portugal to convert Christians. That it was neither my goal nor my job. And…"

"And?"

"I ordered him to leave immediately."

"Did he leave?"

"Yes. He left."

"But he returned?"

"Indeed, he did. Forty-eight hours later, during the night. He was wounded and was bleeding profusely. He told me he had had an accident. His horse had thrown him. With the help of my servant Joseph, who is here with us now, I gave him the care he needed."

"And then?"

"Then he asked me once again to let him join the Jewish army. And then, if His Majesty can forgive me…"

"You are forgiven. Go on."

"I sent him away."

David Reubeni reached up to adjust his turban.

"It is something I deeply regret," he added. "Diego Pires is an extraordinary young man with obvious qualities. Furthermore, he is close to the King of Portugal, whereas I am only a foreigner, someone passing through. But I could in no way allow any doubt to persist."

He paused, and then continued.

"Your Majesty can trust me," he said in his deep voice.

As soon as he had spoken those words, he began to expect the worst. "What a stupid thing to say," he thought. "What does that mean? Why can I not come up with any good arguments to convince the king?" He looked carefully at his surroundings: the meeting room, the dais with the throne, the enormous cross hanging on the white wall. It was just like in the outside world. Everyone was always watching for the opportunity to spy on one another, to accuse one another, to kill one another, and what was more serious, to annihilate any dreams, to ravage all hope. Yes, rather than a privilege, the power to speak to others was often a peril. Without really knowing why, he repeated the sentence:

"The king can trust me."

Joao III and Antonio Carneiro glanced at each other.

"Exactly, Prince," said Carneiro. "That is the problem. The king no longer has confidence in you."

"The strongest door is the door that can be left open," David Reubeni murmured.

The interpreter didn't hear him, and asked him to repeat what he said. After the interpreter had translated the Messenger's words, Joao III smiled for the first time since the meeting had begun. For a moment he toyed with the heavy cross hanging around his neck, and then he replied:

"I would very much like to leave the door open, Prince. But unfortunately many trustworthy witnesses claim to have heard Diego Pires say before he went to see you in Alpiarça that he was going to be circumcised…"

Chapter forty

A Difficult Test

Alas! No protest, even in good faith, no argument, and no beautiful speeches could now save the situation. In spite of the good opinion the king and his counselors had had of him, David Reubeni knew that his plans were compromised, if not doomed to failure. The evil had been done, and it was substantial. The simmering discontent among a part of the clergy and nobles was one thing. But the terrible accusation of circumcising a Christian, and what's more, a Christian close to the throne, could neither be rationalized away nor forgiven. Especially since those who had witnessed Diego Pires's dangerous confessions had already been heard by the Royal Council. It made little difference whether the Prince of Chabor had been the instigator of that reprehensible act or if Pires had done everything himself. No one could really believe that David Reubeni had had no part in the counselor's aberrant act. For too many years, circumcision had been the object of the wildest fantasies among the throngs. Such an event could not slip by unnoticed nor be easily forgotten.

To get out of the situation without too much damage, in order to keep the plan to retake Israel operative, the king suggested to David Reubeni an honorable way out. It would be necessary to delay the

Jewish army's departure until the Prince of Chabor could meet Charles
v. The emperor, after a perfidious suggestion from his sister Queen
Catherine, had written to Joao III, asking him to send the man from
the desert to see him before he left for the Holy Land. He wanted to
hear about his plans, and he invited David Reubeni to come discuss
them with him in Ratisbon. The King of Portugal thought that would
allow things time to cool down in his own kingdom.

"Jerusalem has been waiting so many centuries to be free!" he
said lightly. "It can surely wait another year…"

David Reubeni had no choice but to accept. Nonetheless, he
was deeply shocked. What the king didn't understand, or pretended
not to understand, was that it was not simply a question of freeing a
city, even a holy city, but rather the liberation of an entire persecuted
people. And they could not keep hopelessly waiting in vain.

There was still one thankless task he would need to undertake. He would have to explain to the soldiers in the Jewish army,
those young recruits who had come from far-off countries with their
enthusiasm and faith, that the departure they had been waiting for so
ardently for so many months would need to be put off for another year.
L'Shana haba B'Yerushalayim: "Next year in Jerusalem." That sentence
that their ancestors had been repeating unsuccessfully for more than
fifteen hundred years would need to be recited for another year, as if
they were trying to reawaken a pious but impossible dream…

Captain de Sousa's friendship and devotion turned out to be
essential for the task of informing the soldiers. The captain understood
David Reubeni's delicate situation, and he offered to tell the young
soldiers in the Jewish army about the king's decision. He justified the
delay by saying how important it was for the Prince of Chabor to
meet Emperor Charles v. He even managed to present the prospect
of their meeting as a trump card that would help move the Jewish
people toward their goal of returning to the land of their fathers.

However, the disappointment was great. Some of the young
men expressed the desire to return home to see their families. Others
preferred waiting in the Alpiarça camp until the departure date was
set, even if they would have to wait for an entire year. A small group
came up with the idea of taking over one of the ships in the Faro

port and setting out to take back Jerusalem as best they could, even without the support of the Christian Kingdom of Portugal.

David Reubeni spoke with some of them and negotiated with others for hours. When spirits had calmed a little, he took advantage of some time alone in his room. He needed to think things through, as he always did when there was a threat to his life or to his plans. Why had the Eternal, blessed be His name, decided at the last moment to suspend the march of the people of Israel toward its liberation? Rabbi Yochanan taught that "the son of David would come only when there was a totally virtuous generation or a totally perverse one." But in this world, neither hypothesis was conceivable. In the eyes of the Envoy of Chabor, the choice remained in the hands of men, and the choice was not simple, because it brought about hatred and confrontations.

At the king's invitation, he had gone once more to see him in Santarem. They had talked for a long time without reaching the slightest solution, for Diego Pires was still nowhere to be found.

In order to combat his increasing lassitude, David Reubeni opened his ebony chest and pulled out his journal. "Paper accepts everything without blushing," he thought. He felt like telling his story and sharing it with others. Did not Rabbi Tarfon say: "It is not incumbent upon you to finish the task, but you do not have the right to refuse to try"? He took out his ink bottle, diluted the ink, and trimmed his quill:

"Answering a convocation from the palace, I went to see the king," he wrote. "Immediately, he asked me: 'What are your intentions? What are you planning to do? What destination have you chosen?' I told him that my decision was to return to Rome to see the pope. I asked His Majesty Joao III to kindly provide me with letters of recommendation, which would attest to the relationship between us and which would prove to my brother, King Joseph of Chabor, that I have indeed sojourned in the Kingdom of Portugal. I also asked him to provide me with a safe-conduct to guarantee my safety among Portuguese Christians. The king agreed to all my requests. He ordered his secretary, Antonio Carneiro, to prepare the various documents for me, and he promised to send me three hundred ducats for my journey to Tavira or to Faro where I could board a ship.

"After my meeting with the king, I talked with several *Conversos* who reported how here in Portugal some Christians were hanging me in effigy so that people could mock me publicly. They also told me about clashes that often followed, for the Marranos often came to my defense and attacked the mockers.

"Two days later, the king's brother, the archbishop, summoned me. I went to see him along with the Arabic interpreter. He showered me with honors and greeted me warmly. He wanted information about my banners and my itinerary. I told him that the banners were the emblems of the Jewish tribes and that Rome was my destination. Then the archbishop said to me:

"'If you agree to convert to Christianity, I will make you a royal minister!'

"I answered: 'Do you think I am like the raven that Noah turned loose from the ark and that never returned? That would displease the kings, my ancestors. I myself am the son of a king, and my fathers would never have acted as you suggest. Would I have traveled all through the Orient and Occident for the sole purpose of converting? Far from me is such an idea! I have come to serve God through the mission I have undertaken. How do you dare ask something like that? What would you think of me if I suggested that you convert to Judaism?'

"The archbishop said: 'I would say no, categorically.'

"'There is an Arabic proverb,' I noted, 'that says: *Let each man keep his religion and work things out alone with God.* Indeed, you maintain that "outside the Church there is no salvation," and I "that Judaism is the Truth." Therefore, it is preferable that we each keep our own religion.'

"The following day, it was the queen who summoned me. She, too, wanted to know about our banners and where I would be going. I replied to her as I had to the archbishop. Catherine of Austria said she was satisfied and wished me a safe journey to Rome. Before leaving me, she added: 'The king still esteems you highly. I know that he has written letters recommending you to the pope.' All that is well and good, but I know how to read the apparent kindness of the queen and her clan.

"The Marranos gather day and night before my house, sorry to grasp that I will be leaving. Many kiss my hand in the presence of Christians. I can see that these gatherings will probably continue until I leave. I give thanks to the Eternal. Nowhere in Portugal have there been any attacks against *Conversos*, and the king has never stopped showing his kindness to me, even after his counselor disappeared."

David Reubeni read aloud the pages he had just written. He left out many details, descriptions, analyses, and judgments. But why was he keeping a journal? To portray feelings? Or more simply, narrate the facts? Does not the Talmud correctly say: *Woe to the dough against which the baker bears witness?*

He began to write again. When he finally looked up from his writing, daylight filled the room. He blew out the candles, put his journal back into the chest, and devoted himself to the morning prayer. Then he summoned his men. There were thirty of them. Only five had known him for a long time and traveled with him from the Orient. The sixth, Tobias, had disappeared. As for the others, they had been hired by his Italian friends before he left for Portugal. When he announced his intention to return to Rome, two of his longtime companions, natives of Egypt, said they would like to go back to Alexandria. Since they would be leaving Portugal in any case, they preferred going straight home. Soon the rumor spread that the Prince of Chabor was looking for new servants. A number of the young Moroccan recruits offered their services. Joseph Halevy chose seven of them.

The following day, at the head of a large escort, David Reubeni was on his way to Tavira, where the king had arranged for a ship to be waiting. In the towns of Coruche and Mora, crowds of Marranos wept as they passed through. The Jewish prince's departure dashed their hopes. On the other hand, in Evora, there were hostile shouts, for the Spanish clan had established an important network there. In Beja, there was even a pitched battle between *Conversos* and "true

Christians." There as well, a few hotheads were trying to burn an effigy of David Reubeni in front of the church.

After three days of forced march, they reached Almodovar, where a messenger from the king was waiting. Joao III sent word to the prince that the ship that was to take him to Livorno was not in Tavira but rather in Faro. Finally, after spending the night at the home of a rich Marrano, the group reached Faro in a driving rain. When they got there, another message was waiting, this time from Miguel da Silva. His letter was particularly friendly, and the ambassador wished the Prince of Chabor a pleasant trip. He also asked, in the name of His Majesty the King of Portugal, for the prince to go to Lagoa, where an escort would be waiting to take him to his ship. Because in fact, the ship was anchored not in Faro but in Lagos, at the mouth of the Bensafrim River.

The unexpected message from Dom Miguel da Silva put David Reubeni on his guard. He questioned the governor of Algarve Province, a pleasant man who was a descendant of those famous *mouros foros*, free Moors, who had lived in the region during the thirteenth century. The governor confirmed the contents of Da Silva's letter. The ship that initially had been planned for the Prince of Chabor had raised anchor two days earlier for an unknown destination. On the other hand, the governor was aware of the fact that several carts full of supplies and food had left Loulé for Lagos, via Lagoa, where it was rumored that a ship was soon to set sail for Italy.

Instead of continuing directly toward Lagoa, the man from Chabor was mistrustful and decided to remain in Loulé for a day or two. Loulé held the largest agricultural and forestry market in the Algarve, and its *Converso* community was particularly powerful. In that former Muslim stronghold, David Reubeni was welcomed enthusiastically, and he was especially pleased to find his old friend Captain Martin Alfonço de Sousa.

A scholarly old aristocrat housed David and his men in his castle. The captain explained why he had come to Loulé:

"The demonstrations in the Prince of Chabor's favor, along with the incidents they have provoked—like, for example, in Evora, where several Christians were hurt—have turned the king against you. Ambassador Da Silva, with the queen's support, took advantage of the situation to have the king cancel the ship that was to take you and your men to Italy. And of course, the three hundred ducats Joao III had promised for your trip were also withdrawn. But, thanks to Antonio Carneiro, the king's secretary, he has reconfirmed the money, on the condition that you leave Portugal as discreetly as possible from a distant port. That is why Lagos was chosen. As for the three hundred ducats, Antonio Carneiro has asked me personally to give them to you once you and your retinue are onboard ship."

David Reubeni showed no emotion when he heard those decisions, one of which was close to pure provocation. Under pressure from the Spanish clan, the Royal Council had entrusted Miguel da Silva with the duty of verifying that the Messenger and his escort would leave in good conditions and that no *Converso* would be able to take advantage of the opportunity to leave Portugal.

"So, Prince, you will no doubt see your old friend Da Silva on the quay in Lagos!" he concluded.

But David knew that the ambassador had been hard at work since the day before. He smiled and changed the subject, asking how the captain had managed to find them.

"It was not difficult at all," he replied. "In every city you went through, Prince, your wake carved out a valley of tears."

David's expression darkened. He shook his head sadly, and his hair fell over his forehead.

"Not only tears, Captain. Not only tears…"

He was interrupted by a sudden clap of thunder. The wind picked up before the coming storm.

"I'll be back," murmured David.

All grew dark as the storm approached. Lightning bolts tore through the semi-darkness. The captain laid his hand on the Messenger's arm. In a scarcely audible voice, he began to recite:

"He lays two fingers on a man's eyes, two on his ears, and one on his lips, saying: 'Be still…' Do you know the answer to this riddle, Prince?"

"It is destiny!" the man from Chabor replied.

"Bravo!" said the captain. "It was indeed destiny. And you know as well as I do, Prince, that each man must follow his own destiny."

"I am not following my own destiny, Captain, I am provoking it!"

"For the moment, it is your destiny that is provoking you…"

"No, my dear De Sousa. It is not my destiny that compels me to leave Portugal, but rather the king."

"And Diego Pires?"

And without waiting for an answer, the Captain continued on: "Just between us, Prince, who are you really?"

"The Envoy of the King of Chabor."

"But in addition… People are saying…and even me, as I watch you, I have come to the conclusion that…that you are not just an ordinary man."

David Reubeni burst out laughing.

"Of course not, Captain! Of course not! Why would I be *extraordinary*?"

"Of all the men I have met, Prince, you are the only one who does not show fear."

David frowned. As if to himself, he whispered: "Perhaps it is when a man thinks of others that he can forget himself and no longer be afraid."

They remained in Loulé the following day. There was a constant coming and going in their host's castle. Hundreds of *Conversos*, both young and old, came to speak to the Jewish prince, to touch him, to be sure that he would not forget them. All those faces that passed before him and all those hands clinging to his tunic moved him deeply. He explained as best he could to one old woman who spoke little Hebrew and no Arabic at all that what she was expecting was for the moment impossible, but that she needed only to believe for it all to become possible again. She nodded and seized his hand.

"Messiah!" she exclaimed.

The meaning of the word changed according to the stress. Sometimes it sounded like an explanation, sometimes a warning, and sometimes a threat. Perhaps the woman wanted to show that she had hope for the future, that she was expecting the weather to clear, but that it was still raining…

David Reubeni felt some comfort, in spite of everything, to have Captain de Sousa at his side. His presence was reassuring. Indeed, if there were such a thing as one's destiny, then destiny had not completely abandoned him.

The escort Ambassador da Silva had told them about was waiting in Lagoa as announced. At its command was a young Portuguese with a thick black mustache. He seemed surprised that there were already two groups escorting David Reubeni. For, indeed, David's own escort had been supplemented by the captain's. He said nothing, but clearly he had not been expecting Martin Alfonço de Sousa to be there. And thus, accompanied by more than one hundred armed guards, the Prince of Chabor made his entrance into the port of Lagos.

Chapter forty-one

From a Trap Set by the Ambassador to an Encounter with Pirates

The commander of the port of Lagos, Alvares Nobrega, had placed his own house, large, gray, and weather-beaten, at the Jewish prince's disposal. In the outbuildings set aside for David's men, two old Portuguese servant women carried in a meal for everyone. Ambassador Miguel da Silva was expected later that afternoon. As for Captain de Sousa, he went to inspect the ship that was to take David to Italy.

Since leaving Loulé, the Envoy from Chabor had eaten only sugar—large brown chunks the size of a lizard's head—and had not exchanged a single word with anyone. What would be the point? Because the only words, or nearly the only words, he would have in common with other men would be words of disappointment or sadness. The departure of the Jewish army had been delayed, and the army itself, which had been formed so enthusiastically, now was being dismantled before it could set out. So now he needed to go back to see the pope with the hypothetical hope of getting plans back on track for retaking Jerusalem, although no one could imagine that would happen any time soon. Clearly, there was nothing positive to look forward to for a long time! David Reubeni preferred retiring to his room in Alvares Nobrega's house, where he could remain alone in prayer:

> *I believed when I said "I was greatly afflicted"*
> *In my anguish I would say*
> *Is not every man deceitful?*
> ....
> *I shall keep my vows to the Eternal*
> *In the presence of all His people...*

He didn't have time to finish his favorite psalm, Psalm CXVI. Someone was pounding at his door. It was Captain de Sousa. The captain was dripping wet from the rain, and he had an angry look on his face. He had found out that the ship Ambassador da Silva had chartered for the Prince of Chabor belonged to Dom Henrique da Silva, the ambassador's cousin, whose villainous reputation was well known. According to the information Captain de Sousa had been able to gather, Dom Henrique was intending to steal the three hundred ducats and everything that belonged to David Reubeni, and then get a handsome reward by handing him over to the Spanish Inquisition in Cadiz!

Martin Alfonço de Sousa was so offended by the plot that he wanted to take his soldiers and go arrest Dom Henrique and take him to Almeirim in irons. There, the Royal Council would interrogate and judge him. David Reubeni was able to talk the captain out of it. Because Miguel da Silva, as an ambassador, would immediately have his cousin set free, and he would not really have to answer for his treachery. Captain de Sousa, on the other hand, would be in danger of receiving a sanction or even banishment for exceeding his authority.

"But what then can we do?" he wondered.

"In Chabor, Captain, it is said the Arabian desert jackal can be tracked down only by Arabian dogs. And you, my good man, you are not like the Da Silvas."

"So then, what shall we do?" the Portuguese officer repeated, his voice showing his discouragement.

"Find another ship!"

"But neither the ambassador nor the port authority will allow you to do that! Are you going to fight?"

"No, no," said David with a smile. "I am simply going to make sure that another ship can be available once my men have made Dom Henrique's ship unseaworthy…"

The captain's eyes grew wide.

"A sailor friend of mine had to pay a fine of one hundred ducats for trying to sabotage a ship!" he said. "And since he was penniless, they sentenced him to a month in prison…But why are you smiling?"

"For no reason. Everything seems to be so peaceful here. Wouldn't prison be the ideal place to meditate? To let me recover from all that has happened?"

And they both laughed knowingly.

Dom Miguel da Silva arrived late. That evening, he came to pay a courtesy visit to the Jewish prince and agree on a time to inspect the ship together the next morning.

"The Royal Council requests that the prince leave Portuguese territory before Christmas," he said. "The king does not want to risk the slightest disorder in his kingdom on the anniversary of the Christ Child's birth."

The ambassador appeared to be somewhat less at ease here than he was in the corridors of the Vatican. His face, ordinarily pale, was now almost livid, similar to the color of his white lace jabot. His elegance, his smile, and even his solicitude should, however, have dispelled any mistrust toward him. The man from the desert had never been taken in by the man. He knew from experience that even when a serpent seems affectionate, it is unwise to use it for a necklace.

The following day, along with Captain de Sousa and their respective escorts, David Reubeni reached the port. On the quay, he ran into a crowd of onlookers, who were watching the sailors work and making comments. The sailors had formed a chain and were passing buckets back and forth from the ship to land.

Ambassador da Silva, with a pained look, came to meet the Prince of Chabor.

"The ship is taking on water," he announced. "And yet, it is almost new. The captain assures me that it will not take more than ten days or so to make the repairs."

And then his haughtiness returned, and he said:

"Of course, the royal treasury will cover the expenses of the prince and his people until they are able to leave Lagos."

"Except that in a few days it will be Christmas," David Reubeni replied. "As you said, Excellency, the king would not be pleased for me to still be in Portugal on that day."

Miguel da Silva's angular face grew tense, looking as sharp as a knife blade.

"And yet, Prince, that is the only solution."

"There is another."

"What do you mean?"

"It would suffice for my men and me to embark on a different ship."

"Indeed. That might be possible. But you would do well to be prudent, Prince. Some captains…"

"Are not trustworthy, is that what you mean? And even a trifle dishonest?"

"Yes, indeed. And furthermore, any other captain than Dom Henrique will demand a much greater sum for the journey from Lagos to Livorno, since it will be an unplanned journey."

"With the three hundred ducats that His Majesty has entrusted to me for the prince," Captain de Sousa broke in, "I think he will have enough to make up any difference in price."

"And I would like to remind His Majesty that we Jews will soon have our own celebration: Hanukkah, the Feast of Lights. Frankly, I would be sorry if celebrating Hanukkah on Portuguese soil could be considered a provocation…"

And then he turned to De Sousa.

"May I ask you, Captain, to negotiate passage for us on the galiot anchored at the end of the quay?"

Caught totally by surprise, Miguel da Silva turned even paler than usual, and he could come up with nothing to counteract the idea. So he watched from a distance, furious but powerless, as Martin Alfonço de Sousa negotiated rapidly with the captain of the galiot, a certain Garcia de Sá, who agreed to take them to Livorno. And though he did ask for fifty ducats more than his questionable competitor, it was so he would be able to prepare a cabin with new flooring for the Prince of Chabor.

The ship was called the *Baçaim*, and it sailed that very evening as the sun was setting in all its glory. To maintain a sense of decency, David Reubeni preferred avoiding effusive goodbyes. However, he couldn't keep from waving enthusiastically to Captain Martin Alfonço de Sousa. He felt that he was leaving a true friend. In the gathering dusk he could still discern the outline of the village. The white stucco houses huddled around the ocher-colored church. A few lamps were being lit, and people were carrying embers to the poorest of the houses.

As the coast slowly disappeared into the night, Joseph came over to David, gave him a tentative hug, and kissed his hand. The Messenger pulled his hand away and said sharply in Arabic:

"You too, Joseph?"

The new Christian year of 1527 came upon the *Baçaim* as it was near Cadiz. The man from the desert thought fondly of Captain de Sousa. Without him, without his vigilance, he would now be in the hands of the Spanish Inquisition. In spite of favorable winds, the ship was making little headway. A galiot is not a ship suitable for war. With its bulging sides and its slow response time, a ship of its kind designed for trade was not made for speed. At the moment, it was rolling and pitching through heavy seas and driving rain. Occasionally, bolts of lightning tore through the darkness, allowing glimpses of the coast stretched out like a curtain on the horizon.

"What will we be doing in Italy?" Joseph asked his master.

They were seated in the large cabin that had just been renovated, and they could smell the new planks.

"We will start over again!"

"How many times? How many times will we need to begin
again?"

"I don't know. But what I do know is that each time we are
closer to our goal."

They grew quiet. They could hear steps in the gangway. Someone climbed down the wooden staircase. The door opened onto the
darkness behind it. A voice cursed, then complained that it was too
dark to see anything. Someone brought a torch, and behind it they
could first see a wide dark chin and then their visitor's big reddish
face. David Reubeni and Joseph recognized short, chubby Captain
Garcia de Sá, a man who loved to talk.

"The rain has ceased," he announced. "We are near the
straight."

The three men climbed to the deck. The *Baçaim* was being
driven along near the African coast by a land breeze. Even though
the wind from the southwest was not perfect, they were able to continue their course during the first part of the night. Soon after the
first watch had been relieved, a sudden gale blew up. Several times
the *Baçaim* nearly foundered. When the storm was over, the crew
checked out the damage. The galiot had survived, but it was in a
sorry state. Masts and sails had been torn down, and the hold was
leaking in three places. The ship could not continue its journey as
before. Should they anchor in a Spanish port to get some help? They
couldn't think of it, for that would have meant falling into the hands
of one of the many courts of the Inquisition. Therefore, Captain
Garcia de Sá decided to break out the oars and row toward Melilla,
a port on the African coast. For two long hours, they rowed as best
they could toward Melilla. As they were nearing the Cape of Three
Forks, someone gave the alert: A fleet of unknown origin was heading
straight for them. Leading it was a long, sleek two-master that cut
easily and rapidly through the water, using both sails and oars. It was
a heavily-armed galleon that must surely be carrying the fleet's commander. The fleet included a number of other galleons and some rafts

made of logs tied together, they too using both sails and oars. Without any summation, the attackers opened fire from small cannons at their prows. The sea currents were in their favor, and the ships, well equipped, bore down on the *Baçaim* as the rowers shouted and the harquebuses thundered. Soon, Captain Garcia de Sá himself went to raise the white flag over what was left of their mast.

David Reubeni shouted out in anger. He strode quickly across the deck and grabbed the captain by his shoulders.

"What are you doing?" he roared.

Garcia de Sá pulled himself free.

"Please, Prince. Have you seen how many ships there are? Have you noticed how well they are armed?"

"Yes."

"And you would prefer going down with my ship?"

The Messenger from Chabor calmed down.

"You are being wise," he admitted. "But your wisdom is a bitter medicine."

"Perhaps you would prefer ending up in some shark's stomach?"

David Reubeni smiled. It was not the first time he had faced danger, but the situation seemed strange. He looked carefully at the captain. With his chubby face, he looked like a doll made of crumpled cloth. In any case, he was overcome with fear.

"To whom do those boats belong?" David asked. "Barbary pirates?"

"I don't believe so. This is not their strategy. The way they are attacking makes me think they are Italians, or more likely, French."

"French pirates?"

"Yes. And according to the flags on their masts, the fleet belongs to a certain Count of Clermont."

Chapter forty-two

Words and Prophecies from Shlomo Molkho

Shlomo Molkho believed in coincidences. He was convinced that individual destinies could be superimposed and complete each other. He probably would have been comforted in that view if he had realized that at the very moment he was arriving in Rome, in the seat of Christendom, to announce the arrival of the man from Chabor, David Reubeni had just been made prisoner by French pirates. *Unknown mystery, the object of every desire*, words mentioned by the Kabbalah, were the supreme reference governing his thoughts.

In the same vein, the pope would ask him when they met:

"Are you a clairvoyant?"

In his angelic voice that so fascinates Clement VII, improvising brilliantly, he would say as if the answer were obvious:

"No, but I know and I see. That is why I believe I can announce to you that the Messiah has come. You have met him, you have helped him, but you have not known him as he has known you. He will come again, I say unto you. He will come again when the time is ripe, and that time is near. Rome will be sacked. Rome will be destroyed.

Rome will groan beneath its ruins, and the entire city will implore David on its knees!"

Shlomo Molkho reached Rome on January 27, 1527, which is the twenty-fifth day of the month of Shevat of the year 5287 after the creation of the world by the Eternal, blessed be the Lord. His journey had not been easy. He traveled by horseback to Porto, where he met some Marrano merchants from Bayonne who agreed to take him by boat to Bordeaux. Then, once more on horseback, he crossed the South of France, went up to Switzerland and reached Italian soil through the Piemonte, where war was raging. Was it not written that he who wants to become a dragon must eat many vipers?

Indeed, during his journey, Diego Pires really did become Shlomo Molkho. He matured, and he felt more than ever that he had been entrusted with a divine mission. Quickly, and in spite of his youth, he would soon be considered a master. His erudition and his knowledge of the Kabbalah and the Talmud were reinforced by a gift he began to discover as he met ordinary people. He was developing the gift of inspiring people with his words, making them feel that they had access to all the secret domains of history and the mind. He had the talent of an orator, the ability to persuade, and an extraordinary aptitude for languages. These unusual qualities struck many of the people he met. The scribe in the grand synagogue of Avignon, after hearing him comment in French on Hebrew texts, wrote in his journal: "We all agree that Molkho, that pious man, may he be blessed, was suddenly inspired by the spirit, the wisdom, and the knowledge of the Kabbalah. He himself did not know where the words came from. It was as if Heaven's grace had opened his heart as one opens a book…"

In Rome, where he arrived penniless after having given away the money David had offered him when he forced him to leave Almeirim, he mixed in with the poor and the beggars, as he ordinarily had done since leaving Portugal. He realized that his words were indeed touching people. In the market, along with the barkers, the sword-swallowers, and the followers of the Reformation, his speeches were more popular than any others'. Crowds came to wait for him, and they respectfully made way for him when he passed. He spoke in his own way about David Reubeni. It sounded paradoxical, because he said that the Messiah would not simply come, but that he would *return*, because in fact he *had already come...*

But Shlomo Molkho was not overly impressed by Rome. The city was unlike any other. Inside the city walls there were grapevines, gardens, and even empty parcels of land and thickets that provided habitat for deer and boars. Old ruined villas covered with vines and wild roses gave shelter to hundreds of pigeons. On the wooded Palatinate, Caelian, and Aventine hills, farms and convents alternated with broken-down monuments that had been used as stone quarries by generations of Romans. Shlomo Molkho barely glanced at those parts of the ancient city. "You cannot announce the good news to ruins, but rather to men," he thought. But he felt quite at home in the tiny streets and alleys of the center, between the Corso and the Tiber. That's where the crowds gathered, cosmopolitan crowds speaking every language. A French baker on Piazza Navona explained to him where the different people lived. The Jews were numerous in the Regola, Ripa, and Sant'Angelo sections of town. The Spanish, about seven thousand of them, lived along the Tiber. The French, mostly pastry and candy makers, were concentrated in the streets around Piazza Navona. The German community was known for its hotels as well as for butcher shops and printing shops. The city was like a human anthill and captivated Shlomo Molkho. He spoke to people in their own language, asking about daily life, and he never failed to announce the good news to them: the Messiah would return.

Of course, Romans were used to preachers and street barkers who were always announcing all kinds of "good news." But this man was different. He was blond, armed, dressed like a Spanish gentleman, led two magnificent purebred horses, and spoke numerous languages. In his strangely melodious voice, he would tell about his own conversion and his reasons for traveling from Lisbon to Jerusalem, and his audiences were fascinated. Those hearing him speak realized that Rome was only a halt on his journey. Jerusalem remained his goal, first of all so that he could kiss the soil of the Holy Land, and later, along with the Messiah, so it could be freed. Jews and Christians alike, both men and women, found him likeable and eagerly listened to him with great respect.

On that particular day, after conversing with a number of people, he found himself near the Theater of Marcellus, a circular building whose base was made of large rough-hewn blocks of stone and whose walls were made of brick. The theater had rows of seats out in the open like the Coliseum and was located just at the entrance of a Jewish quarter. Perhaps that is why the gathering crowd seemed more attentive to his words than usual.

"Wake up, people!" he shouted.

Everyone stood still, surprised by the harangue coming from a stranger. With a strong yet graceful gesture, he caught their attention. He held his hands straight out toward the Jews, recognizable because their clothes were marked with the yellow circle:

"You Jews," he went on, "you are the poorest among the poorest, the most persecuted among those who are persecuted…"

There were people drinking in a nearby wine shop called The Wine Nectar according to its flowery sign. He turned toward them and continued: "And you, Christians, you are just as poor and just as penniless as your Jewish neighbors whom you hate so much. Look around you and what do you see? Everywhere there is war, misery, and exclusion! The Christian kings tear each other apart and the Turk is bringing his columns in behind them! The Cross is wobbling and the Crescent of Islam advances!"

He was quiet for a few moments while he waited for the bells to finish ringing, and then he continued:

"But who will redeem human sins if it is not Man? Who will bring justice, if not Man? Who will save the world and God himself, if not Man? Man without pride or pretension who knows he can do nothing outside the will of the Eternal, blessed be His name, but who also knows that if he acts in accordance with divine will, he has power over everything?"

Joseph Zarfatti, the pope's physician, and his sister Dina were coming back home to the Sant'Angelo quarter. As usual, they walked by the Theater of Marcellus and were intrigued to hear the unusual voice. When they joined the crowd, they could see the young orator with the distinctive blond hair, and they began to pay attention to what he was saying.

"I met a man," he said in his Hebrew-accented Italian. "Through that man I encountered the will of God. That man is the bearer of God's desire. He is dreaming of liberation, for the Jewish people and for all of humanity. And he is working to bring about that liberation! According to God's will, he has come and he will come again. That man showed me the path. He will lead us, some day soon. He will lead us to Jerusalem, and he will lead us toward freedom!"

He paused for a moment. The crowd waited with bated breath.

"Look at me," he said. "I was a man who had everything: wealth, honors, and power. I was the most trusted advisor to Joao iii, the Most Christian King of Portugal. I believed that the world was mine. But which world? I discovered the real world in the eyes of the man I am telling you about. That man came to Europe to show us the path, open the way, give our lives meaning. Now, at the head of an immense army, with the blessing of the pope and the help of the Eternal, blessed be His name, he will go liberate the Holy Land and give the Jewish people back their homeland and Christ's tomb to the Christians! Then you will understand that he was the Messiah! Then you will want to kiss even the trace of his shadow! Then humanity will be cleansed of its sins and lifted up to be with God…"

"But he is talking about David, about our David!" Dina exclaimed, and color came to her pale cheeks.

"Let's go talk to him!" said the doctor.

The crowd was still growing. People who had just stopped out of curiosity had stayed, surprised and even subjugated by that captivating voice that foretold such strange things. Here and there, some were commenting about particular words. There were even some carriages that were unable to get through the mass of people. In one there was a churchman, as could be seen by the coat of arms on the door. The important man leaned out his window. It was clear he was paying special attention to the stranger's words, for he was leaning forward, his large brow wrinkled, and he watched the speaker carefully.

"He will come!" said the stranger. "He will come again, and you will follow him. By the hundreds, by the thousands you will be at his feet!"

His voice began to chant, much like a cantor in the synagogue.

"When the Law was given to Moses," he continued, "myriads of celestial angels came to try to consume it with their fiery breath, but the Holy One, blessed be His name, protected It. In the same manner, He covers and protects all words of wisdom as well as those who speak them, so that the angels cannot envy or become jealous before the word can be transformed into a new heaven or a new earth..."

"That is from the Midrash," Joseph Zarfatti whispered to his sister Dina.

Together, they tried to push their way through the growing crowd, and people grumbled as they moved through.

"A strange man," said Dina. "He speaks as if someone were dictating words to him."

"You are right, Sister. It is as if...as if someone were using his mouth to speak to us."

A voice rose from the crowd:

"Who can guarantee that this Messiah you are talking about will ever come?"

"I can," the young blond man replied.

A murmur of doubt ran through the audience.

"I can, I, Shlomo Molkho!" he repeated. "Because I have seen him! Because I have touched him! Because I have given up everything to exalt his word!"

"A man is worth more than the guarantee," someone sitting in The Wine Nectar shouted.

"Even if he is following the word of the Eternal, blessed be His name?" replied Shlomo Molkho.

"It's been a long time since we've heard anything from your Eternal...!"

That brought a few laughs to the crowd. Angel Shlomo's face darkened. His violet eyes stared at the troublemaker who had just spoken. Quickly, he climbed up onto a barrel. Standing high above the crowd, he asked:

"Do you not believe me?"

There was complete silence. Finally the same voice from the wine shop called out:

"No!"

"You will be forced to believe me," Shlomo Molkho said, "when you *actually see* what I am saying. Listen: Rome, great Rome, the Eternal City, will be sullied! Rome will be ravaged! Rome will be destroyed! Listen: And after that catastrophe, another catastrophe will follow. There will be ruins, and the ruins will be submerged in floods. Flooding will follow on the heels of destruction! When you see those signs, you will realize that I am speaking the truth. But then, O divine mercy, the man from the desert will come. He will come back to deliver us!"

The young man pointed toward the man who had contradicted him.

"I say to you: He will be here, and all of you, Jews or not, will bow before him to implore his aid, his power, and his mercy!"

The crowd began to sway, and there were murmurs. People were clearly worried.

"I can see," he went on after a moment of silence, with his disarming smile that both charmed and intimidated, "I can see that you do not believe me. You don't like bad news, but what I'm bringing you is *good news*! I say unto you: After the destruction will come liberation."

"When?" a woman asked.

"What do you mean? The liberation?"

"No. The destruction."

"Soon. Very soon. In four or five months. I say unto you: Go and spread the word, warn your families, your friends, and your neighbors. And even those people you meet in the streets: *Roma delenda est*, Rome must be destroyed, and destruction is near!"

His voice began to tremble:

"And I, too, will come back, to contemplate the destruction. And you will recognize me. And then I will show you the One whom you should have seen but did not. The One whom you will see again. And at last you will see the One whom the Eternal has sent to free men, and once Rome has been destroyed, you will finally begin to hope for him with great eagerness!"

He climbed down off the barrel he had been using as his platform. The crowd surged back. Doctor Zarfatti and Dina took advantage of the movement to get closer. At that moment, the church dignitary, still in his carriage, called for the guards, an armed patrol whose job it was to maintain order near the theater. They must also have been fascinated by Shlomo Molkho's words, for they had hardly moved during his speeches. When the patrol commander saw the coat of arms on the carriage door, he bowed respectfully:

"What does Your Excellency desire?"

"Go bring me that preacher. Tell him that Cardinal Egidio di Viterbo would like to meet him and introduce him to the pope."

So, just as Joseph and Dina Zarfatti were about to speak to Shlomo Molkho, the guards pushed through the crowd. Joseph and Dina were shoved aside like the others, and the doctor could not hear what the patrol chief and Shlomo Molkho said to each other. But he did hear the final words:

"And how about my horses?"

"His Excellency will have them taken care of. They will be waiting for you in Sant'Angelo Castle."

The news spread rapidly through the Jewish community. The Prince of Chabor had sent a messenger to Rome, and Cardinal di Viterbo had invited him to stay in the Sant'Angelo Castle! Some even claimed that the pope was jealous of the cardinal and had demanded that Shlomo Molkho stay in his private apartments in the Vatican. When he heard the news, old Rabbi Obadiah da Sforno, still as thin and knotty as a grapevine, could hardly contain himself:

"We have to see this messenger!" he said, rocking back and forth from one foot to the other. Go find him quickly! We have to find out what's been happening to our David Reubeni!"

For indeed, since Joao III had signed the decree authorizing the Prince of Chabor to build a Jewish army to liberate Israel, no further news about the man from the desert had reached Rome. The entire Jewish community had been eagerly waiting. The arrival of this messenger

sent by David Reubeni was enough to start all sorts of rumors. Especially the name of the messenger, Shlomo Molkho, "the Angel Solomon." And then they had learned that Molkho had been a Marrano
named Diego Pires and that he had recently come back to Judaism.
And finally, word also spread that he had circumcised himself.

No one knew what this "new Jew" talked about when he met
the Head of All Christendom. But those who had contacts at the Vatican, including the pope's personal physician, Joseph Zarfatti, heard
that His Holiness Clement VII had Shlomo Molkho explain how to
read the future through the Scriptures.

"I hope that this Shlomo Molkho has given the pope the exact
date he is predicting for Rome to be destroyed," said Obadiah da
Sforno, winking at Dina.

"*I have put my words in your mouth…,*" said Joseph Zarfatti.

"Isaiah 51:16," cried the old rabbi. He was as delighted as usual
to show off his knowledge.

And then he raised his bony hands:

"Do you know what Rabbi Simeon said about that sentence?"
he asked. "The Holy One, blessed be His name, listens to the voice
of those who take care of the Law, and at the moment when a man
explains something new about the Law, his words rise to the Holy
One, blessed be His name, who takes it, embraces it, and crowns it
with seventy crowns, engraved and inscribed…"

Doctor Zarfatti also learned that the pope, enthralled by Shlomo
Molkho, had invited him to settle in Rome and enter the college of
Hebrew scholars at the Vatican. But "Angel Solomon" had refused the
invitation. He owed it to himself, he explained, to go first of all to the
Holy Land to meet the great Talmudists and deepen his spiritual journey. On the other hand, everyone had been able to witness that after
the young blond had been in the Vatican for a week, the sovereign
pontiff had assigned two hundred Swiss guards in full uniform, very
nearly an escort fit for a king, to accompany him to Naples. He had
also offered him passage on a ship leaving for the Holy Land.

Chapter forty-three

An Island
with Jasper Walls

A confirmed pirate, the Count of Clermont was nonetheless a man of consummate civility. He courteously explained that David and his followers were to be kept "under his safeguard." He welcomed David to his ship and even offered to show him around. With its two masts and their full complement of sails that could be supplemented by the arms of a hundred oarsmen, along with the many guns that garnished both sides, his galleon was surely one of the fastest and best armed in the Mediterranean. Deep down, the man from Chabor had to admit that by hoisting the white flag immediately, Captain Garcia de Sá had demonstrated prudent realism if not courage. And the victor in that battle without combat was more intriguing than he was worrisome.

For the Count of Clermont had neither the manners nor the bearing of a bandit of the high seas. He was tall, elegant, and dressed Spanish style with stockings and gargantuan padded breeches beneath a doublet with a high collar and a flat silk ruff. He was like Frances I with a teasing look in his eyes, and with his brilliant black hair, he looked more like some noble Castilian than a pirate. The only indication that he belonged to the fearsome brotherhood of pirates stood out on his oblong face: A scar ran from his right cheek up past his temple. But with a perpetual smile on his face, he was able to make people forget about his terrible scar. He was open and pleasant, and spoke Portuguese quite well. He also knew more than a smattering of Arabic.

"What have you done with my men?" David Reubeni asked.

"They are in the hold, but well taken care of, you may be assured," the count replied.

The captain's lips were thick, and the rasping voice that came from beneath his mustache had a strange timber.

"They will be treated well," he went on, "as long as you yourself will be, Prince."

"And how long do you think you will continue to grant me that favor?"

The count cleared his throat, and the effect made his voice sound even hoarser and set off two coughing spells.

"As long," he croaked as best he could, smiling obligingly, "as I have any hope of getting some good, shiny ducats in exchange for your freedom!"

He burst out laughing. In contrast to his weathered skin, the scar turned brick-red. Then he invited David into his cabin. It contained flags and banners from many countries—his hunting trophies. On the table, the man from Chabor recognized his own white banner, on which a psalm was embroidered in Hebrew characters.

"This will be proof," the count continued, "that you are indeed in my power, and that I am the man who should receive the fifteen hundred ducats for your freedom."

Unlike his servants, David was consigned to a comfortable cabin and was served a meal. But on that day he was unable to communicate with either Joseph or Captain Garcia de Sá.

At dusk, on a calm sea, the flotilla was making good headway south. David spent the night in prayer, dozing a little just as dawn broke. He climbed to the deck later that morning, and the sun was already warm in spite of the season. When the Count of Clermont saw the man he called his "guest," he walked over to greet him.

"This is the famous calm that follows the storm, is it not, Prince?"

"Where are my men?" David asked, paying no attention to the count's words.

"You will see them again in two days, Prince, once we have moored at the island where I am taking you."

"What do you plan to do with them?"

"Sell them in Algiers in the slave market. Unless…"

"Unless what?"

"Unless your friends, Prince, your fellow Jews, should accept your request to pay a few more ducats per servant."

The Count of Clermont literally practiced the commerce of men, and he talked about it so naturally and with such ease that one might have thought he was negotiating ordinary merchandise. His cynicism, however, did not impress the man from Chabor. But at least it allowed him to see clearly what the captain's plans were.

"Why do you think I am worth so much money?" he asked.

The captain made no effort to hide his calculations:

"I know who you are," he replied. "I have heard of you from Italy to Portugal and even in Spain. Just three weeks ago in Marseille, I heard a young man talking about you. He was giving his speech to some beggars before getting on a ship, for Rome apparently. He told them that you were the new King, the Messiah of Israel. I believe that your friends will be able to gather the necessary funds to pay me for my good care of you and for giving you your freedom."

And the pirate chief explained to David that he had good connections among Jews in the Comtat Venaissin, and that he knew a certain Samuel, a rich banker in Arles, whose brother David, a well-respected Jewish scholar in Avignon, had a good enough reputation that the Avignon community would surely follow his advice if he recommended paying the ransom. While they waited for the necessary negotiations to get under way, the Prince of Chabor would have to be content, for both himself and his men, with the generous hospitality the Count of Clermont would be offering on an island covered with gull guano…

The next day, however, the pirate made a goodwill gesture toward his prisoner. He allowed Joseph to join his master. David quickly told him what fate held in store for them. Joseph's first reaction was to think about planning an escape, but the Messenger talked him out of it.

"The trick of a man with no tricks is patience," he said. "We have a mission to complete, and for that, my dear Joseph, we must first remain alive."

Sailing under favorable winds, two days later the flotilla was within sight of the island. At about three in the morning, the Count of Clermont anchored a few cable lengths from shore. When dawn came, Joseph pointed out to the man from the desert that there seemed to be no guards on the island. There were no patrols and no armed men to be seen. But after he had studied the island carefully, David realized that it needed no surveillance.

It was entirely surrounded by a wall about twenty-five spans high. The wall was built with jasper stone, and the stones were so perfectly cut and so well assembled that it seemed as if the wall were made of one piece. The top of the wall was slightly rounded and set with solid grills. Along the metal fence, about every thirty feet stood monster gargoyle-like figures, holding hands as if for a strange dance around the island. David Reubeni was surprised at the sight, for he had never seen anything like it, in Arabia or elsewhere.

From the ships one could see some of the area inside the walls, including a grove made up of only dwarf orange trees. A quarter of a league further away, on a small hill, stood a few ramshackle buildings. It was clear that it would be very difficult, if not impossible, to escape from the island without outside help.

The Count of Clermont came up to David and said:

"Come, Prince, I would like to introduce you to your new companion, or if you prefer, your jailer…"

He had a skiff put into the water. Eleven armed pirates, their leader, Joseph, and David got in. Soon they reached shore. Once they were on land, the count drew a heavy sword and started toward the wall. Twice he struck a narrow, rusty iron gate that stood out against the jasper wall. They heard a voice:

"Praised be the Creator who painted the beauty of the heavens! Finally, you old rascal, you've made it back!"

The man who opened the gate with words such as those rushed into the arms of the pirate captain, pummeling him to show how pleased he was to see him. He was an old wrinkled man who must have been more than a hundred years old. He was dressed in a long robe of red damask and he had laid down his over-sized harquebus before greeting his visitor. When he saw David Reubeni and Joseph, he asked the count:

"Some more merchandise?"

"There are thirty-two others on board."

"To be sold?"

"No. For an exchange…"

David Reubeni's men and Captain Garcia de Sá were brought on shore at about noon and parceled out among the different buildings on the island. As for the crew of the *Baçaim*, they were kept under guard on board their own ship.

The count pointed to the old man and explained to David:

"Master François Xavier will show you where the kitchens and the storerooms are. Then it will be up to you to get things organized. Of course, you will think about escaping, and perhaps you will even try. That is all part of the game. But I must warn you that no one has ever escaped from here. Unless you think you are able to swim across the sea, you would have no chance."

The man from Chabor kept watching the pirate chief out of the corner of his eye. The man seemed very sure of himself.

"Old François Xavier will not be able to help you, Prince. He is too old and there is no way to threaten him. He is not clinging to life!"

Then the pirates sailed away from the island, adding the *Baçaim* as part of their flotilla. When they had gone, the little group of prisoners did an inspection tour of their meager domain. They had to admit that the Count of Clermont had not lied: There was no way to escape. As for the old gentleman who served as their jailer, they discovered that he was charming and perfectly harmless, as well as indispensable. For he was the only one who knew where springs could be found and the places where food had been cached here and there around the island. He was also the only one with a weapon. It would have been easy to take the harquebus from him, but to what purpose? The true enemy was the sea that rolled its foam up to the foot of the jasper wall. Who had built the wall? In what era? For what purpose? The old gentleman, living voluntarily in semi-reclusion, could not answer.

In that outdoor prison, they quickly organized their lives. Some who were bored with having nothing to do turned to gardening and expanded the vegetable garden. Although the pirates had stolen all of their hostages' weapons and belongings, the count had been kind enough to leave the man of Chabor the ebony chest in which he kept his journal. Since there were no candles on the island and the hut they lived in had no windows, David wrote during the day. He would sit facing the doorway through which he could look out over the orange grove, and beyond it, all the way to the horizon. But although occasionally one of his servants would walk past, the deserted countryside made it difficult for him to concentrate. He kept sharpening his quill unnecessarily, thinking back nostalgically over the past. He thought about Dina Zarfatti, about Benvenida Abravanel. He was beginning to forget how they looked. He could remember Dona Benvenida's last words: "I will be your reward." How surprised she would be to learn that there could be no reward because he, David Reubeni, still had not earned it.

To enter Jerusalem at the head of a Jewish army! All it had taken was one man's foolish act for the dream to be put into question once again, when it had been so close to fulfillment. Because now he had to start his quest all over again, begin once more his march toward Israel from Rome where he had support. And now he found himself kept hostage, a prisoner on some unknown island in the Mediterranean, at the mercy of a French pirate and perhaps of the generous good will of his Jewish brothers. Fifteen hundred ducats for his ransom, perhaps two thousand, were not so easy to gather! In an era that seemed to be losing its mind, all he could do was wait. How had things come to that point? He had probably underestimated the folly of hope. He had believed, or had wanted to believe, that men always naturally desired freedom. He had repeated again and again that the Messianic era would not be ushered in by some divine intervention, but rather by the work of determined men, and that it would depend upon their ability to fight. However, David Reubeni was sure that the interests of men and of God, blessed be His name, were one and the same when the Law needed to be defended and established. He had even demonstrated that the word *Messiah* could not be found in the Torah nor in any apocryphal writings, and that it had not been used by the prophets, for whom the only Lord was the Redeemer. But just let there be the slightest hope of a providential being! Then men, because they are afraid of their own responsibility, quickly give themselves over to some pale imitation of God! Was that not what had just happened? And was that not when the Angel passed by, the Angel Diego Pires?

A light breeze wafted perfume from the orange trees up to David. The slanting light of the setting sun pushed the shadows of the trees up to his door. The man from Chabor remembered the words that had been spoken to him in Hebron by an old Talmudic scholar: "Bar Kokhba, he who rebelled against Emperor Hadrian in the year 132 of the Christian era, reigned two and a half years. Then he said to the rabbis: 'I am the Messiah.' They answered: 'It is written of the Messiah that he is able to smell and then judge. Let us see if Bar Kokhba can do that.' When they saw that he could not *judge by smell*, they declared him an imposter."

Chapter forty-four

"What the Messiah Wants…"

Master François Xavier was fascinated by David Reubeni. Though the old man had often had occasion to guard prisoners on the island, it was the first time he was dealing with Jews, much less a Jewish prince. He was able to find among David's servants a young man from Fez, Yohanen, who spoke French and Hebrew and agreed to be his interpreter. Accompanied by Yohanen, the old man frequently came to see the Envoy of Chabor and discuss world affairs.

Six weeks later, in March of 1527 according to the Christian calendar, Master François Xavier brought a letter from the Count of Clermont. How had the message reached him? Had it been carried by a homing pigeon? Had someone landed secretly on the island and given it to him? The enigmatic old man refused to explain.

In the letter, the pirate captain was pleased to inform the Prince of Chabor that the negotiations to free him were moving forward as expected. The prince's Italian friends, including some from Venice and Rome, and in particular the bankers Mechulam del Banco, Daniel di Pisa, and Dona Benvenida Abravanel, had come up with nine hundred ducats, and the Jewish community in Avignon, six hundred more. In addition, communities in Arles, Carpentras, and Marseille had committed to redeeming the men in David Reubeni's service at ten ducats per person. If the prince had not yet been freed, it was because the Count of Clermont had not yet received all the necessary guarantees. He was insisting that the exchange of the prisoners under his control take place under the patronage of Francis I. Who better than the King of France to guarantee a proper transaction?

"You understand, do you not?" said Master François Xavier. "A transaction is a transaction. The count knows that the King of France himself was in the same situation when he was made prisoner by the Spanish in Pavia. The count could never expect to find anyone more appropriate or more understanding than the king!"

"And how about Captain de Sá?"

The old man was taken up short by David Reubeni's question.

"But he is not part of this deal. He is not one of your men, and he is not a Jew!"

"But he is nonetheless a man! I don't know what the count has done with his crew. On the other hand, I feel responsible for the life of the man who risked his own life for me."

Master François Xavier scratched his head in embarrassment.

"I will let the count know. I can make no promises for him. But I believe that with another twenty ducats…"

"Since you are able somehow to maintain contact with the count, tell him that I will not leave this island without Captain Garcia de Sá!"

The inner burden of responsibility suddenly overwhelmed David Reubeni, along with his love that was composed of tenderness, understanding, and solidarity. His love of all mankind, expressed through his love for his own people, exalted him and weighed him down at the same time. Among the Jews, some had no doubt already forgotten him. Others surely mistrusted him, and still others hated him. Does not every individual at one time or another feel a love that demands no reciprocity, as if he is struck by unnecessary gratitude? A feeling that lifts an individual above other men, even if only for a moment? Normally human beings spent their lives frozen in fear, demanding proofs, praying to be delivered from their suffering. Only a few were able to escape from such living hell. And though one could indeed place one's trust in divine mercy, there was no way to trust sickness, poverty, and evil.

Two weeks later, David Reubeni was taken by boat to Palma along with his men and Captain Garcia de Sá. In Palma, they boarded a ship for Marseille. Only then did they realize where they had been. The island on which they had been kept prisoner was none other than Santa Clara, one of the thirteen Canary Islands, a few leagues from Lanzarote. The exchange of the men for the ransom money took place on the ship taking them to Marseille. The brothers David and Samuel d'Arles had brought the money. Following Francis I's specific recommendation, the amount had been verified and guaranteed by Madeleine Lartessuti, a banker who financed ships for the King of France. Pope Clement VII was represented by a legate, François de Clermont-Lodève, who had his seat in the palace of the popes in Avignon, and he had insisted on coming for the express purpose of finding out if the Prince of Chabor was freed.

Before giving up his prisoners, the pirate captain had politely returned their personal effects and weapons, though he was careful to keep the three hundred ducats that the King of Portugal had given to David.

Waiting for David Reubeni on the quay in the old port was an imposing delegation of Marseille Jews. At their head was Rabbi Aba Mari, a small, pleasant-looking man with a white beard, whom the man from the desert recognized immediately because he had met him on the way from Italy to Portugal. Seeing him wearing a yellow hat, the distinctive sign imposed upon the Jews, he felt ashamed. Once, two years earlier, they had spoken and dreamed together. The rabbi did not even introduce the other members of the delegation to David. For him, David's failure was just another incident, an unfortunate disappointment, a slight wound that would soon heal. He was even proud to have discussed with the Jewish prince his magnificent plans, even if those plans now seemed blocked. On the other hand, David Reubeni felt deep pain. In his eyes, the failure was the end of the world.

How would the Jews from Provence react to his coming, to a man who had promised everything but produced nothing? And who was free only because each family had dug deeply into its own resources? He wondered if they would curse him and demand accounts.

"Blessed be the Jewish Prince!" Aba Mari said gently.

David Reubeni almost gave a start. The rabbi's solicitude was so different from what he had expected.

"All along the way from Marseille to Avignon," the rabbi continued calmly, "thousands and thousands of Christians, and also secret Jews, are awaiting the Messenger."

The Envoy of Chabor studied the rabbi's face as if to be sure of what he was saying.

"Why would they do that?"

"Shlomo Molkho," the rabbi replied.

"What do you mean, Shlomo Molkho!"

"Yes," said Aba Mari rubbing his beard. "Shlomo Molkho, the man who has come back to the Eternal, the God of our fathers, and who has been circumcised. That Shlomo Molkho to whom the Lord has given the wisdom of Solomon and who has become the wisest of men. Well, he came and announced your coming, Prince! He prophesied right here in Marseille, then later in Carpentras and in Avignon! He announced that famine was going to ravage the region and that then you would come, Prince, that you would come to liberate us…"

"And then?" David broke in.

"Then, Prince, last year there was a terrible famine throughout Provence. There was nothing left to eat, not even bread. The price of wheat climbed to ten florins. If the Languedoc and Arles had not taken the precaution of stocking wheat, many more people would have died. Even today, people come down from the mountains and from Nice with their animals to find food in Marseille, where wheat is sold for less than eight florins. And now, Prince, as Shlomo Molkho predicted, here you are!"

The four papal communities of Avignon, Carpentras, Cavaillon, and L'Isle-sur-la-Sorgue, at the behest of the legate who had received instructions from the church hierarchy, had gone together to purchase horses for David Reubeni and his men. Joseph unfurled the banners. The procession, including the papal legate and the King of France's banker in prominent places in their carriages, set out for Avignon.

The brothers David and Samuel d'Arles were also part of the procession. As they rode beside the man from the desert, the rabbi continued his story. Shlomo Molkho had, in his own way, managed to mold the minds that heard him speak. He had, they stressed, connections in the Vatican, and had he not embarked for the Holy Land thanks to the pope's support? He prophesied, and his prophecies were fulfilled. Crowds swarmed around him to hear him speak about the Messiah's coming, that is, to hear him speak about David Reubeni. As he listened to them, the Messenger from Chabor showed no expression. But his brow was wrinkled, and Joseph realized that his master was concerned. When they reached Avignon that evening, they would need to discuss the situation. Was not this Shlomo Molkho, with his desire to provoke fate, putting into question the very foundation of David's strategy?

As the rabbi had predicted, the crowds grew denser as they rode toward Avignon, and the people were obviously eager to catch a glimpse of the Jewish prince David Reubeni, the man sent by God, the liberator announced by the prophet Shlomo Molkho. People had come from all over the South of France, all different kinds of people dressed in a variety of styles, some in rags. Many of them had been waiting for hours, and then fell in behind the procession as it passed. When the Messenger reached Avignon just before nightfall, he was riding at the head of thousands of people. Throughout the day, he had the same feeling he had had in Italy of leading a weaponless army, an army of beggars who had no other weapons but the magnetic combination of their misery and their hope. In military terms, such an army could not compare with the one he had gathered together in Portugal and then had to abandon. But it perhaps surpassed all others in its naïve, pathetic faith and in its desire to seek not its salvation but its Savior! And if such faith had sufficed, there is no doubt that the return to Jerusalem would have been accomplished long before! But David was able to recognize, through the crowd's respectful undulations, in its cries of affection, and through its supplications, the voice of dreams, of folly, and of yielding to the supernatural. From all sides people kept shouting the words "Messiah! Messiah," whereas David knew that there were only false messiahs, because the true Messiah was not what they thought he was. David would have preferred that instead of waiting for and venerating a providential envoy, each member of the crowd would come to realize that within himself he contained a part of the Messiah and that therein lay his freedom, his original freedom, freedom which had formed him in the image of God. By making use of such freedom, it would be possible to liberate Jerusalem and take back the land of Israel. It would not be a miracle but rather the fruit of deliberate action. So that the people of Israel could finally return to Israel. So that, according to divine will, mankind could liberate mankind.

In the former papal city, François de Clermont-Lodève, the papal legate, had arranged for David and his men to stay in the Rascas Hotel. The hotel was situated at the corner of Rue des Marchands and Rue des Fourbisseurs, not far from the synagogue. In fact, it stood at the entrance of the "quarry," as the Jewish quarter was called.

The Rascas Hotel was a large corbelled building, lit up with dozens of torches, and it appeared more imposing than it really was. After the long, rustic stay on Santa Clara Island, David's men were delighted. But David himself didn't feel much like rejoicing, nor was his mind at peace. He asked the two D'Arles brothers to take him later to the Grand Synagogue that was referred to in the Jewish section of Avignon as *L'Ecole*. But before that, he wanted to spend some time alone with Joseph Halevy.

"Well then," he asked his confidant point-blank, "where is the Messiah?"

Joseph did not respond immediately, his eyebrows raised questioningly.

"What does this all mean? You are asking what all this means, right?" David asked.

"Yes, that's right. Did today's crowds impress you?"

"Not you?"

"I didn't expect them," replied Joseph.

"Nor did I," David sighed. "Even though Rabbi Aba Mari predicted that all these people might show up."

"I was surprised at how many there were. And the word 'Messiah' was on every lip."

"Yes. And I had expected them to hurl insults!"

"Shlomo Molkho excited them and made them see mirages."

"He attracted them with an image that resembles what they have been hoping for. Instead of freely exercising their freedom, men prefer leaders, idols, or some miraculous intercession," the Messenger noted in reply.

And then, after a moment of silence:

"In fact, they are not even waiting for the Messiah they imagine. If the word has any meaning at all, it is surely not to designate a simple leader of men, some acrobat, or some rainmaker! Any old charlatan could fool them. And sometimes they move so quickly. When times are hard, when exiles follow massacres, when all hope of dignity seems lost, then they rush to recognize the Messiah!"

"What is the Messiah, exactly?" Joseph asked quietly. "I remember you saying that the word messiah cannot be found in the Torah…"

"To be more exact, my dear Joseph, the word does not appear with the meaning it has taken on since. It refers to kings and prophets. But the idea of a man 'sent from God,' who must come to bring about redemption and the liberation of all mankind appears much later. There is perhaps a germ of the idea in some of the apocalyptic texts, such as in the texts of Baruch. But since Christians have decided to identify Jesus as the famous Messiah, rabbis have looked more seriously at the question, and particularly to discredit it. But the people do believe in the Messiah. The people dream of a Messiah. They need a Messiah!"

"Men do not realize what freedom they have within themselves. They are afraid of being free," Joseph said.

"Yes, Joseph. Of course. But what if they *need* a Messiah to help them take that first step toward freedom? Would it not then be charitable, even necessary to give them what they are asking for? In short, should I not, in spite of what it may cost me in terms of my own integrity, incarnate their dream?"

"But that would be giving substance to Shlomo Molkho's ravings!" Joseph protested. "After struggling for so many years, wandering in the desert, meeting all the obstacles in your path without losing sight of your mission, would you now abandon your strategic political principles? Would you now begin playing the role of a magician?"

"Nobody is playing, my dear Joseph. And my strategy must always take into account new situations and new facts. These crowds are moved by feelings, by irrational motivations. My strategy, my rationale, must be to incorporate the crowds into my plans. For I am fighting for such people, am I not? It is partly thanks to their support that I have been able to meet with the powerful men in this world and explain my goals. So it would only be right for me to meet the expectations of these crowds. Not by 'playing the role of a magician,' as you say, but by *explaining what the Messiah wants...*"

Joseph's brow wrinkled. His face took on a complex expression, composed of incredulity, astonishment, and gratitude.

"But in that case, you are..."

He muttered something incomprehensible, cleared his throat, and began again:

"In Italy one day someone said to me: 'And what if your master were indeed the Messiah, even if he didn't realize it?'"

"And?"

"The question upset me. And then later I couldn't get it out of my mind. Does that make any sense?"

"Must the arm know that it is an arm?" the man from the desert asked quietly, looking deep into his servant's eyes. "Can the Lord's Envoy know the Lord's Envoy? As you know, we have not seen the last of our problems, but sometimes riddles can be the bearers of the breath of the Eternal."

Someone knocked at the door. The D'Arles brothers were there to take David to the synagogue. His mind still spinning, Joseph greeted them and then withdrew. The Messenger left with the two men. It was a very dark night. There was still no sign of approaching dawn. A servant held a torch before them to light the path.

How had the Jews in Avignon found out that the prince would be going to the synagogue during the night? Had Samuel and David d'Arles told them? In any case, there must have been more than ten *min-yanim* waiting there for him. He could hardly see them in the darkness, but he could sense their presence in the long shadows cast by flickering torches. An old man, no doubt the rabbi, gave a short welcome speech in a Hebrew mixed with Languedocian. Then everything grew quiet. The Jews were expecting the Envoy from Chabor to speak. He was the man whom Shlomo Molkho, the brilliant young prophet—may God protect him!—had identified as the Man Sent by the Eternal, blessed be His name! But David Reubeni didn't say a word.

The door of the synagogue was furtively opened and closed. A man had slipped inside. Somewhere out in the darkness people began to whisper. Prolonging the silence would have added to the awkwardness. The man from Chabor remembered a psalm of David and began to recite it, his voice low and dignified.

In the Eternal I had placed my trust
And He turned His face to me and heard my cries.
He pulled me from the ditch of destruction,
From out of the mud,
And He set my feet upon the rock,
He helped me stand,
He placed in my mouth a new song,
Praises to our God!
Many have seen and have feared Him
And have turned to the Eternal…

He paused. His eyes tried to pierce the darkness. He could hear feet moving on the paving stones, people clearing their throats and holding their breath. He could sense the smell of bodies through the scent of melted wax. He began to speak more forcefully:

Happy is the man who puts his trust in the Eternal,
And who is not swayed by the proud and the lying!

The simple sentences were coming back to his memory, simpler than anything he could have invented. Once again the door opened. In the doorway he could see dawn's white veil as if it were spread over a baldaquin bed.

"*I proclaim justice in the great assembly,*" he went on. "*I publish abroad Your truth and Your salvation…*"

Chapter forty-five

David Reubeni in Paris

The next morning, the man from Chabor received a visit of the twelve members of the Council of the Jewish Community in Avignon. Once again, he had to face the messianic hope that Shlomo Molkho had inspired when he came through. The ravages of his lyric prophecies were having dangerous effects. As David stood before his interlocutors, he quickly realized that it would be difficult, if not impossible, to oppose head-on Molkho's pseudo-mystic perspective in which he himself saw only aberrations and lies.

Yesterday he had told them: "*I will lead you to Jerusalem.*" But here in Avignon, Jews were confined to their "quarry," tiny streets that guards sealed off at both ends every night. How could these persecuted and fettered people, always under suspicion, how could these people ever conceive of returning to their ancestral lands in any other way but by divine will? In their opinion, it would take a miracle.

But David Reubeni was betting on the will of men, perhaps in spite of themselves. He was willing to bet on full intelligence, on the people's ability to take charge of their own destiny and act for their own liberation. But was that still possible? Would he be able to give the people what they wanted, made up of mirages and an aura of mystery, without going back on what they had always felt or without risking a collective disaster? He was fully aware of the evil that self-proclaimed messiahs, by their irresponsibility, had already done to the Jewish people. Would he be capable of breaking the curse the prophets denounced?

He had lunch at the Rascas Hotel along with his servants, the brothers David and Samuel d'Arles, as well as Captain Garcia de Sá, who was to leave for Portugal the next day. Then, after publicly thanking the two brothers who had done so much to ransom him, David went to the palace of the popes. The legate from Rome wanted to deliver an invitation from Francis I personally. The King of France wished to see the famous Jewish prince. David Reubeni received the news with little enthusiasm. He was not keen on having to go to Paris. He was in a hurry to return to Rome to seek, along with the pope and his advisors, another way, another place where it might be possible to create a Jewish army. He knew he could expect no help from Francis I. After the King of France had been defeated in Pavia, France had needed to sign a treaty of friendship and mutual assistance with the Sublime Gate. So how, in such conditions, could France ever help him? But on the other hand, how could he refuse the kind invitation of a king? So the next morning, as soon as prayers were completed, the man of Chabor and his servants, escorted by guards sent by the French court, were already on the road to Paris.

It took them six sunny days to come to the gate in the Fort de la Tournelle, whose walls reached the Seine. It was in May of the year 1527 of the Christian calendar. The man from the desert was amazed at how many people there were. Carts, animals, and men vied for space in the dark streets, crowding through narrow passageways that smelled of garbage. Along with the perpetual activity, there were incessant shouts, cries, and screams, but also much singing and laughing. It is true—David was arriving right in the middle of the Saint Germain fair. On such occasions, all kinds of people from everywhere would swarm over the square in front of the church and in the adjacent streets and alleyways to buy trinkets, jewelry, and paintings. People also came to Saint Germain to enjoy spectacles of the most diverse kinds that were presented during the fair. They passionately watched acrobats and modern comedians who were now free from the clergy's control and no longer needed to present only mystery plays. Their theater spoke to everyone. They had become so popular and their plays so much enjoyed that the access alley leading to Rue du Four had to be widened.

When David Reubeni appeared along with his men, bearing his standards and dressed in their white tunics with the Star of David stitched chest-high into the fabric, people rushed to greet him, shouting and clapping their hands. When they saw the new troop arrive, in their jubilation they thought it was just another theater group coming to present some new spectacle. But it did not take people long to realize their mistake. The rumor quickly spread that the King of France had invited a real Jewish prince. Great excitement filled the city in which Jews had been forbidden to live since 1394, when King Charles v had expelled them. When David Reubeni and his retinue appeared at the hotel reserved for them, in Rue Saint-Gilles, just a few steps away from the royal Hotel des Tournelles, a large crowd had already gathered to welcome them.

For the Parisians, seeing a real flesh-and-bones Jew, and what's more, a prince, was unprecedented in living memory. One hundred thirty-three years had gone by since Charles v's decree, too many generations for anyone now alive even to remember if his grandparents had seen a Jew. From the vantage point of the man from Chabor, on the other hand, the fact that he was coming to a city where there were no Jews, the first since his feet had trod European soil, was the source of deep sadness.

"Have you noticed that strange vague feeling here in Paris?" he asked Joseph when his servant came to his room.

The French windows opened out onto a courtyard where carefully trimmed bushes formed three circular hedges. The hazy sun hesitantly cast its light over the garden like a halo. David looked out over the courtyard, his back to his trusty servant.

"You did not notice anything particular?" he asked again.

Joseph suggested worriedly that the city was densely populated and that the streets were very dirty.

"Is that all?" his master asked.

Joseph raised his eyebrows and shrugged his shoulders.

"How about the Jews?" the Messenger went on.

"The Jews? But of course," Joseph exclaimed, putting his hands to his head. "That's right! A city without any Jews! No one to whom we might say one word in Hebrew. Not a single synagogue..."

"Yes," David sighed. "And yet, back in the old days...Cardinal di Viterbo told me about a French bishop, a certain Grégoire de Tours, who lived here approximately one thousand years ago and who wrote about a large synagogue that existed here in his day, right in the middle of the Ile de la Cité."

"And how about Charlemagne?" Joseph added. "Did he not send his friend Isaac d'Arles as his ambassador to the Grand Caliph of Baghdad, Harun al-Rashid?"

That was the extent of their knowledge of Judaism in France. But in their eyes that confirmed a necessity. Only a country founded on the soil of Israel, on the land of their ancestors, would allow Jews to live in peace without constantly risking banishment or massacres. The conversation was interrupted by the arrival of a butler and a little bald man. The bald man, dressed in a brown soutane, introduced himself.

"Jacques Bédrot," he said cheerfully. "I am a Franciscan and professor of Hebrew in the Chéradame Academy."

The Messenger expressed how happy he was to meet him.

"Here's someone who speaks Hebrew," Joseph cried.

"Indeed," said the monk with a smile. "And I am here to serve as interpreter for the Prince of Chabor."

Thanks to the friendly Franciscan, David Reubeni learned that a number of Parisian academies taught three languages: Latin, Greek, and Hebrew. When he realized how sad David was that there were no Jews at all in Paris, Jacques Bédrot proposed visiting one of the two remaining Jewish cemeteries. It was in Rue Galande, very near Rue Saint-Jacques.

"The Rue Galande cemetery," he explained in perfect Hebrew that he had learned during a long stay in the Holy Land, "is included in the territory belonging to the Seigneurie de Galande, which now belongs to the Abbaye Sainte-Geneviève."

"Since we are unable to visit any living Jews…"

It was a small cemetery. The recent construction of Rue Galande, as well as two other streets, Rue des Trois Portes and Rue des Jacinthes, had changed the layout of the area and reduced the size of the cemetery. But the sight of even thirty tombstones over- whelmed the man from Chabor. As if weighted down by the years, some of them were leaning, ready to topple over. Others, their bases loose, seemed to be still standing only because ivy had wrapped its knotty branches around them in support. Of course, in the end, the ivy would bring them down. It was a vine related to thorns and couch grass, and it covered everything. Was it not in the slow process of obliterating the memory of an entire people, or a least the memory of a group that had disappeared, the Jews of Paris?

David Reubeni remained motionless, his brow creased and his right hand over his mouth, as if to prevent words from coming out. He didn't even hear Joseph pointing out a tomb on which, along with a Hebrew inscription, a five-branched candelabrum had been engraved. Looking up, he was surprised to see the figure of a man slipping through the gate in the low wall that surrounded the cem- etery. He was an unusual man, tall, heavy and imposing. His white beard was trimmed to a point, and he was dressed in a long linen robe buttoned in front. He was also wearing a strange, tall yellow hat that looked almost like an upside-down pail. His unexpected appear- ance made Jacques Bédrot give a start as well. The Messenger looked questioningly over at his interpreter. The man by the wall seemed as surprised as they were to see other visitors in the cemetery. He raised a large book he was holding as if to protect himself and started to leave. But the Franciscan was faster than he was.

"Don't leave!" he shouted in French. "Have no fear. I am with a Jewish prince…"

The man hesitated for a moment. He stopped, lowered the book, and walked toward them.

"A Jewish prince?" he asked. His voice was grave and nearly inaudible.

He turned his eyes, dark but veiled with blue, toward David Reubeni.

"So it's true…," he whispered.

He stepped even closer. This time he spoke directly to the Envoy from Chabor.

"You are indeed the…?"

David guessed what the stranger was about to say. He interrupted him in Hebrew.

"Yes, I am the envoy sent by the Jewish King of Chabor and invited by the King of France."

The man's face brightened.

And he, too, responded in Hebrew. "And I am the personal doctor of the Prevost of the Hotel de Paris. My name is Jacques Léon, and my home is in Senlis. The tomb the prince was studying just now is my grandfather's tomb."

He smiled, and went on.

"Each time I come to Paris at the request of the prevost or of some other member of the court, I come here…"

David Reubeni showed no emotion, but listened attentively. Jacques Léon paused for a moment, and then, clutching the heavy book against his chest, he continued:

"I am only a poor Jew. I don't have the right to live in the capital. I can only come here for the day from time to time to attend to my patients. But because tombs are books and so that our books do not become tombs, I devote my life to taking care of both. Here, I clean the tombstones, and sometimes I stand them back up. In Senlis, I spend my time studying…"

He took a step backward.

"But surely the prince has other, more important things to do than to listen to me, and my patients are expecting me."

The doctor moved toward the wall. After a brief nod, he stepped through the gate and disappeared.

David was so disconcerted by the man's strange appearance and the situation that he couldn't react. But he was sorry the man had left. There were so many questions he would have liked to ask him about Jews and about Paris!

He spoke about the man that very evening with the king. Francis I did not yet live in the Louvre, but that is where he liked to receive his guests. But before he could speak to the king, David had to participate in a tasty but interminable dinner. Platters, dishes, glasses, and trenchers with candied fruits and sweets were piled on the table along with baskets of bread and carafes of water and wine. An incredible number of servants came in and out, carrying dozens of the king's favorite dishes: pies stuffed with quenelles, calf's sweetbread, truffles, codfish, and bone marrow. The conversation was so lively, so loud, and so disconnected that poor Jacques Bédrot was unable to translate everything.

Finally Francis I stood up. He gestured graciously to the Prince of Chabor, inviting the prince to join him in a private room. The king was six feet tall and broad-shouldered. He had strong thighs and well-defined calf muscles, and his bearing was impressive. His face was framed by a short black beard, and his eyes sparkled with intelligence. He sat down in an armchair, beginning the conversation on a light note.

"Well, Prince, what do you think of Paris?"

The noisy conversation had ceased. Jacques Bédrot could finally play his role as interpreter.

"A splendid city, Majesty," David Reubeni replied after the Franciscan had translated for him. "But this is the first city I have visited where there are no Jews…"

"They are protected in other cities in our kingdom, as you know."

"Is Paris too beautiful for them?"

"Prince of Chabor, we would be pleased, I assure you, to have Jews among us, but their presence might cause problems…"

"I have seen many Jews around His Holiness the pope in the Vatican, Milord, and it does not appear that they have imperiled Christianity. I have seen the greatest of sculptors, Michelangelo Buonarroti, sculpting the face of a Jew—my own face—without concern that his art has been altered…"

"Of course, Prince, of course. But Paris is not Rome. However, France does have several advantages over Italy. If not, why would Leonardo da Vinci, the greatest of painters, have moved to Amboise?"

With a broad gesture, the king invited support from those around him. His doublet, with its wide sleeves raised over his shoulders, opened up to display his shirt, causing him to look like an eagle spreading its wings before diving to catch its prey.

"And Hebrew is taught in several Parisian academies," he added. "Is that not right, Budé?"

The man he spoke to stepped forward. He was tall and elegant, and with a smile on his face, he confirmed that the three languages essential for educated men were Greek, Latin, and Hebrew, and they could be studied in depth in the capital. But then he hesitated:

"However, Milord…"

"My dear Guillaume Budé, what is the detail that seems to be bothering you?"

"The Sorbonne, Milord…"

"The Sorbonne?"

"Yes. The Sorbonne has refused to include Greek and Hebrew in its curriculum."

"Oh," the king exclaimed. "But that must be a mistake!"

Guillaume Budé, the smile still on his face, bowed.

"Your Majesty guaranteed complete freedom to the Sorbonne. Therefore, we cannot intervene."

The king's eyes darkened. He turned toward David Reubeni.

"And you, Prince, what do you think?"

Thanks to the good work of his Franciscan interpreter, the man from Chabor had followed the entire conversation.

"Why not create a new academy, Milord?" he suggested. "A royal academy, for example, in which according to your will Hebrew would be taught?"

Francis I rubbed his beard, and his face brightened. He looked into the prince's eyes. The king's own eyes displayed what appeared to be admiration.

"What do you think, Budé?"

"By my faith, Milord, the idea seems excellent! Could we not call the new university the *Collège des Lecteurs Royaux*?"

David Reubeni was about to add that the king should invite several rabbis to the capital to teach the language of the Bible. That would be a way to bring Jews back to Paris. But an old man came in, interrupting the conversation. He was panting, and his sword was dragging along behind him on the floor. He went up to the king and whispered something in his ear.

"That is the Grand Marshal, Monsieur de Vendôme," Jacques Bédrot whispered to David.

The king leaped to his feet.

"Gentlemen! Gentlemen," he cried. "The armies of Emperor Charles v have just ravaged the Eternal City! Rome has been sacked!"

Chapter forty-six

"Angel Solomon" in Jerusalem

S hlomo Molkho learned the same news a few days later, in Jerusalem. Rabbi Moshe Barsola, a Neapolitan scholar who had just come from Italy intending to spend a year in the holy city and visit the country, was the first to tell him about the destruction inflicted by the imperial armies on Italian soil. He had not himself witnessed the sack of Rome, but before leaving for Galilee, he had heard the stories of several Jews who had fled the devastated city and taken refuge in Naples.

The destruction of Rome by the imperial troops did not surprise Angel Solomon. Had he not predicted such a disaster? However, the confirmation of his prophecy was not a source of pride nor did it bring him any satisfaction. For him, the events were evident: They had always been written in the sacred texts. Did not Rabbi Yohanen claim in the Talmud: *During the generation when the son of David will appear there will be few scholars, and as for the others their eyes will be worn out with sorrow and sadness?* The first part of his prophecy had come true. All that he needed to do now was to help fulfill the second: the Coming of the "Son of King David," or the Advent of David Reubeni. And he, Shlomo Molkho, knew where David was. The Eternal, His name be praised, had intentionally placed him on David's path.

"*Shout aloud, do not hold back!*" Isaiah said. And he went on: "*Lift up your voices like a trumpet!*" The young Portuguese was convinced more than ever to follow the prophet's command. He knew—or rather, he felt—that it was his job to announce to the world the Redeemer's coming. In his eyes, it was a divine necessity, an imperious moral obligation which was impossible to sidestep. The fact that the man from Chabor continued to deny his role as an envoy from God was at first disconcerting, but Angel Solomon did not let it discourage him. It reinforced his faith in the prince who, contrary to so many false messiahs, considered himself less important than his task. By his humility, was not David Reubeni revealing his true nature as a messenger from the Master of the Universe? As for David's oft-spoken wish to liberate the land of Israel by armed struggle, Shlomo Molkho saw it as simply an initiation rite, a way to test the Jews as well as the Eternal Himself, just as their ancestor Abraham had done when he agreed to sacrifice his son Isaac. In his view, even if he were to gather together a Jewish army, it would only be a parabola, like a mirror attracting larks, bringing in those lukewarm, hesitant, indecisive people who made him indignant because they would not accept God's will. In all good faith he assumed that the man from the desert, when he spoke of war, was simply using a metaphor to refer to the difficult, rigorous spiritual work that would be required of each and every Jew. Shlomo Molkho knew, along with Zechariah, that it would be *neither by force nor by power, but by the spirit of the Lord* that the Jewish people could be liberated and return to Zion. Although he had never broached the subject with the man from Chabor, he assumed that their thoughts were similar.

After learning through Rabbi Moshe Barsola that Rome had fallen to Charles v, Shlomo Molkho finally set aside some time to meditate. A heavy haze hung over Jerusalem. The sun was high in the sky, and it made everything look white—the houses, the hills, and even the sky itself—and it was so bright that men had to lower their gaze under God's light and keep their eyes half-closed. Everything moved slowly during those hours of blistering heat—bodies, carts, and merchandise. Sounds seemed to dissolve in air that was denser than molten lead. The young man from Portugal was filled with greater exaltation than usual as he climbed the slopes of the Mount of Olives almost effortlessly, almost as if on invisible wings. From the summit he looked out over the Valley of Josaphat, and could make out the Temple Mount on the far side. Further on, he could see King David's tomb and the grotto of the prophet Zechariah. On days of fasting, Jerusalem Jews would go there to pray. On the ninth day of the month of Av, for the anniversary of the destruction of the Temple, that is where they would gather to recite their lamentations.

All of Jewish memory was spread before him, watched over by God. Was there another city in the world where such a meeting could exist? The silence reigning over the city made it seem to Shlomo Molkho that heaven was giving its approval, and he hardly dared move for fear of breaking the spell. It must have been at a similar moment, when the silence was deafening, that the Eternal, the God of Israel, had spoken to Zechariah, the prophet whom Shlomo Molkho venerated above all others. And then Zechariah had proclaimed: *Cry aloud and proclaim: thus speaks the Eternal! My cities will once again live abundantly. The Eternal will once again console Zion. And again He will choose Jerusalem.*

Yes, the young man from Portugal loved that city where Jews, for the moment, were in the minority—three hundred out of twenty-five hundred families. Among those Jews, there were some whose families had never left Jerusalem. Their ancestors had seen the city destroyed and rebuilt several times. They were called the *Mustarabim* to distinguish them from those who came from North Africa, the *Moghrabim*, and those from Spain, by far the most numerous, called the *Sephardim*.

At first, the Jewish community had been mistrustful of Shlomo Molkho. His youth, his fragility, his blond hair, and his Christian background were at odds with their traditions, even though they did find him intriguing. But what worried them the most was his open declaration that the Messiah was coming. Over time, he had managed to win some of them over. For had not Jews been waiting for the Messiah for a long time? Even if they couldn't agree on when and how he would appear, if they quarreled about what roles they would have if he did appear, then they were indeed expecting the Messiah, and that is what the young prophet was announcing.

After his influence grew, Shlomo Molkho persuaded Rabbi Jacob Berab de Safed, in Galilee, to re-establish the *Semikha*, the ordination of rabbis as it had been done during the period of the second Temple. That would allow setting up decision-making courts as well as the *Sanhedrin*. And both would be decisive steps in preparing the Jews of the Holy Land for the Messiah's coming. But the project stalled because of opposition from Jerusalem rabbis who wanted to protect the holy city's privileges. The rabbis harbored a grudge against Angel Solomon because he had not included them in the initiative from the very beginning. The news of the sack of Rome, however, made them rethink their attitude, for it brilliantly confirmed the young man's prophecy. And they decided to forgive him publicly for his blunder. Shlomo Molkho was pleased, for the conflict with the Jerusalem rabbis had upset him greatly. He loved the city with its narrow streets through which dust swirled at the slightest breeze, blinding passersby and causing the donkeys with their wobbly packs to bray. He loved the tiny, dark shops where customers would come to buy some oil, soap, or spices, while pious Jews bowed over worn-out pages of the Talmud as candlelight flickered over heaps of the various products piled high on the shelves.

On the other hand, the ruins surrounding the city were painful for him to see. Throughout the centuries, he thought, fewer people had tried to build Jerusalem back up than to tear it down. Even the fact that Soleiman had ordered work to be undertaken to clear away the ruins along the old city wall was not enough to relieve his mind. Especially since Soleiman was also spending a fortune to cover the outside wall of the Dome of the Rock with marble and mosaic, and pouring more funds into gold-plating the Dome's cupola.

Rabbi Israel di Perugia, who was housing the young man, could not understand why he was so angry, and he tried in vain to calm him. On that particular evening, they began another conversation on the same topic, and Shlomo Molkho elaborated on his arguments.

"Was not that mosque built on Mount Moriah, where our father Abraham prepared to sacrifice Isaac? And Rabbi, was not that the very place where King Solomon's Temple stood? Only one wall is left, and it is piled high with debris and garbage all year long."

"Come now," Rabbi Israel protested. "The sultan himself has just ordered the debris to be removed from the west wall so that Jews can again pray there."

Shlomo Molkho's eyes sparkled violet.

"And *who* will give the order to destroy the mosque so that the Jews can reconstruct the Temple?" he cried, his voice unexpectedly loud.

Old Israel di Perugia started. To disguise his loss of composure, he got to his feet and hung up his large velvet hat that had been lying on the table. Then he came back to the young man, tugging at his thin beard. Calmly, he quoted Micah:

"*For all people will walk every one in the name of his god,*" he said.

"That is true," Shlomo Molkho replied. "But…"

Once again his eyes sparkled.

"That is true as long as the Messiah has not returned," he added. "For when he is here, *he shall judge among many people, and rebuke strong nations afar off.*"

He, too, was quoting Micah.

The next day, he obliged his host to accompany him to the *Haram el-Sharif* to visit the mosque. When they got there, they were attacked by a dozen young Muslims who were surprised to see two Jews there. The adolescents began to throw stones, shouting:

"Get lost, Jews! Get out of here! Your presence here is forbidden!"

Rabbi Israel was frightened. He did not need to be asked twice to return down the stairs toward the city. But Shlomo Molkho's face grew red and he refused to back down. He took out his sword and stepped toward their attackers.

"Your mosque will be destroyed by the hand of the Most High!" he shouted. "And the Temple of God will rise from its rubble!"

Some men came out of the mosque when they heard the shouts from the esplanade. When they were told of Shlomo Molkho's blasphemous words, they joined the adolescents and formed a hostile circle around him. At any moment, insults would turn to blows. As for the old rabbi, he had simply disappeared. Soon more people appeared, pressing in to see what was happening, and the threatening circle began to sway back and forth. Shlomo Molkho found that he was trapped up against the balustrade that looked out over the old city. If he fell, he would surely break some bones! A stone struck him on the shoulder, and he almost dropped his weapon. The situation would no doubt have become desperate if an Ottoman patrol had not happened by. When the soldiers saw the crowd, they charged into it. A huge man with a turban and a thick, black mustache was brandishing a scimitar with angry shouts. Another man, who seemed to be his superior, grabbed Shlomo Molkho by the shoulders, while the first man raised his hand as if to strike him. The crowd roared with delight. And thus was Angel Solomon saved from the angry mob and taken to see the governor of the region, the *Pachalik*, whose seat was the fortress-citadel that dated, it was said, from the time of Herod and stood beside the Tower of David.

The high dignitary was angered by the incident outside the mosque. If Moshe Hamon had not intervened when Rabbi Israel di Perugia alerted him, Shlomo Molkho would no doubt have ended up somewhere deep down in the sinister Lod prison. Moshe Hamon was the personal physician of the Sublime Gate, and that conferred upon him special influence over the sultan. He was a man of faith and hope who had come to the Holy Land to hasten the coming of the Messiah. He was able to convince the *Pachalik* to release the young man. However, Shlomo Molkho was released on the condition that he leave the city immediately. A Bedouin caravan was starting out that very evening for Gaza. He joined the caravan, leaving the city with no regrets. He loved Jerusalem and was certain he would return.

Two days later, he was in Gaza. During the journey his camel had fallen ill. A Bedouin had offered him another, a younger animal with a better, more comfortable saddle. Shlomo Molkho interpreted the man's help as a sign of encouragement from the Eternal. When he reached Gaza and realized that he had no money, he was anxious only briefly. He swept away his anxiety with prayer. Since his conversion, his trust in the Lord increased daily, it seemed. His destiny, he often said, was elsewhere. As for his word, it was formed in heaven.

He found a place to lodge near the sea, in a guest house. The building was not very attractive, and it looked more like a barracks than a manor house. But the room he shared with a Beirut merchant on the second floor was bright and sunny. The merchant, a man by the name of Yehia ben Abd'Allah, was a pious Muslim who prayed five times a day. Since he also spoke Hebrew, Shlomo Molkho took advantage of the opportunity to ask him about the Islamic Holy Book.

"In the beginning," the merchant explained kindly, "the Koran was a verbal message, not written. The word *Qurân* means 'to call.' So the Koran is an appeal, a cry. Its words were written on parchment only after the death of the Prophet. The Koran refers to the voice of a man who calls for the gathering of the living and the dead. The man who transmitted the call of Allah was first alerted by the Angel Djibril (whom the Jews and Christians call Gabriel), and he then devoted his life to the revelation that came to him from On High. That man was Mohammed."

The young man from Portugal was surprised by his interlocutor's knowledge and simplicity.

"I have never had the opportunity to converse with a Muslim," he admitted. "In Portugal, I did in fact have a few friends of Arab origin, but they were not nearly as wise and knowledgeable as you are!"

Yehia ben Abd'Allah's thin body changed position. His face, with its hollow cheeks and turban, broke into a smile. His white teeth contrasted with his dark skin.

"According to all accounts," he said, "soon you Jews will be celebrating a holiday. A joyous holiday that you call *Purim*."

"That is right. How do you know?"

"In my country live many Jewish scholars. My house is in the same neighborhood. Some of them are my friends, real friends. Some of them eat only at their own table, but others accept my invitation to come eat at mine—only fruit, of course, and no meat. We get along well, I believe, and we have high regard for one another."

"How does it happen then," asked Shlomo Molkho, "that here in the Holy Land we Jews cannot dialogue with the Arabs? They hate us. They say that they prefer dogs to Jews!"

Yehia ben Abd'Allah shrugged his thin shoulders.

"Only the All Powerful could answer you."

Then he raised his hand to his heart and to his forehead.

"May the hate found here between the two communities never reach Beirut!"

"Have no fear," the young visionary answered. "The Eternal brings low the ungodly and He raises up the just to the heavens. Soon, you will witness great things."

Shlomo Molkho's voice flowed more smoothly, more convincingly. His strange eyes with their violet reflections bore deeply into Yehia ben Abd'Allah's own eyes. His face was cloaked in mystery.

"There will be convulsions, upheavals, wars between great kings," he continued, his voice sounding like an oracle's. "And then, finally, Redemption will come!"

"Soon?"

"Yes. And I must go to Rome as soon as possible to make known the One whom we have been awaiting for centuries."

The merchant reached out his arm and placed his hand on the young man's hand. He seemed enthralled. And now it was with a tone of familiarity that he spoke to Angel Solomon:

"How do you plan to go? By what means? If I am not mistaken, my son, you are penniless..."

Shlomo Molkho did not answer. After a moment of reflection, he said, as if it were obvious:

"Tomorrow a ship will be leaving Joppa for Naples."

Yehia ben Abd'Allah brought his hand once more to his forehead and then placed it on his heart:

"May the All Powerful guide your footsteps! I myself will take care of the rest…"

Chapter forty-seven

The Envoy
from the Messiah

A fter an uneventful sea voyage funded by the kind Yehia ben Abd'Allah, Shlomo Molkho reached Rome on the 6th of June in the year 1527 of the Christian calendar, one month to the day after the sack of Rome and only a few hours after the pope had capitulated. Clement VII and the captain of the imperial army had just signed an agreement allowing the pontiff and the cardinals, including Egidio di Viterbo, to remain in Sant'Angelo Castle, where they had taken refuge when the Vatican was stormed. A German garrison was to keep them there until the Vatican State had surrendered all its strongholds and the entire amount due Charles V as war indemnity had been paid.

Shlomo Molkho entered the desolate, war-torn city along with a ragged band of peasants who were hoping to get their hands on some booty. The horde was following a group of lansquenets, a new kind of soldier from Germany who had defeated the pope's own soldiers. With their bouffant clothing, their lances, and their feathered hats similar to those worn by Swiss guards, these soldiers were more brutal than any other soldiers at the time. These Lutherans, as they were called, destroyed everything in their path, terrorizing people with their shouts of *Viva Lutherus Pontifex!*

In just a few days, thousands were killed, followed by systematic house-to-house looting. In terror, Shlomo Molkho watched horrible things take place, including a man who put out his own eyes so he wouldn't have to watch his wife and daughter being raped, lying naked on a cart stacked high with the family's belongings. Shlomo Molkho walked along with the pack of looters for what seemed like an eternity. Finally he reached the Theater of Marcellus and the Porticus Octaviae, where just a few months earlier, as he was haranguing the crowd, Cardinal di Viterbo had first seen him.

"We are near our goal," he thought. "This is what the Lord has wanted."

As he reached the wine shop bearing the sign The Wine Nectar, a stranger fell in step with him. The man was of indeterminate age. His tattered tunic barely covered his gaunt limbs. Shlomo Molkho tried to walk faster, but the man, too, increased his pace. Pointing one of his bluish fingers, he shouted out to the passersby:

"It's him! It's him! He's the man who prophesied the sack of Rome! He's the one who said that Rome would have the same fate as the bastard of Sodom, the prostitute of Babylon! He foretold all the destruction! Listen to him! Listen to him!"

People stopped, exchanging worried glances. Some of them did recognize Shlomo Molkho and tried to touch his clothing. A dozen lansquenets walked half-drunk out of the tavern. One of them, wild-eyed, stared at Shlomo Molkho for a long time, and then he reached into his bag, pulled out a ducat and threw it at him, as if he were a beggar, before catching up with his drunken companions.

The young man from Portugal was just about to give the gold piece to the man dressed in rags when a voice behind him rang out:

"Keep it! You'll need it..."

He whirled around. There standing in front of him was an old man bent over his white cane.

"The man you met here a few months ago would like to see you again," the old man said.

"Who are you? Where do you come from?"

"Let us say that I am a friend to the downtrodden, and that I come from Assisi where I prayed for a long time at the tomb of the good brother Saint Francis. I reached Rome a few days before you did and I have seen our poor pope…"

"Nobody stopped you?"

The old man burst out laughing, showing his yellow teeth.

"Why would they care about a poor fellow like me?"

And then he grew serious again.

"Do you smell that horrible odor? The pestilential smell of rotting bodies? The smell of gunpowder, of vomit, and of blood? There are false prophets everywhere in these difficult times. They proclaim that God's judgment has come down upon us. They are terrorizing the innocents. They are confusing God with Satan…"

He paused.

"Why don't you say something? Why don't you address the crowd?" he asked.

"I have already spoken," Shlomo Molkho replied.

"That is true. That is true. And are you pleased to see your predictions come to pass?"

Shlomo Molkho ignored the question.

"Who are you?" he asked again.

"I've told you. I'm a poor beggar, an old vagabond. I listen to some, and I listen to others. I listened to you as well, and I paid close attention. You also predicted a flood. When will the flood take place?"

"Soon."

"Very well," the man grunted.

He grabbed Shlomo Molkho by the arm.

"Go down to the cellar of the last shop under the arcades. Then, once night has fallen, follow the underground galleries. You will reach the banks of the Tiber. A boat will be waiting to take you secretly across to the foot of the fortress. There, you will be hoisted in a wicker basket…"

"Where do you get all this information?"

"I listen to some, and I listen to others. I have already told you—the man you met right here has taken care of everything."

He squeezed the young man's arm with surprising strength.

"Do not forget," he whispered. "The shop at the end of the arcades. It will be a moonless night. You can cross the river without being seen. But if a guard should happen to stop you, give him the gold coin…"

A broad smile spread across the old man's face.

"Money is not everything, but it can be useful!"

The strange beggar was right. That night, the gold coin did prove to be useful to gain the confidence of the sleepy Spanish guard who was urinating right at the place where Shlomo Molkho was supposed to get the boat. Chance did the rest, and he reached Sant'Angelo Castle without further difficulty. There, he was given a meal before being led to his bedroom. Early the next morning, two Swiss guards in dress uniform came to take him to see Cardinal Egidio di Viterbo. They walked through long dark corridors feebly lit by a few flickering torches. Heavy doors opened for them. After going through one of the doors, Shlomo Molkho suddenly found himself in one of the richest libraries in Rome.

On the marble mantel of a mammoth fireplace, he noticed a small bronze figure of Mercury. At the Portuguese court, the statue was considered one of the jewels of Augustan art.

"Welcome to the young prophet!"

In the candlelight, the cardinal's sharp features did not seem as pale as they had when they first met. And the large man's eyes had lost some of their intensity, seemingly veiled in grey. But they clearly expressed good will and intelligence.

When he realized how impressed the young man was to see books by Philo, Pico della Mirandola and Manunzio, Cardinal di Viterbo noted sadly:

"So many books in Rome have been burned! So many books! What barbarians! Burning entire libraries!"

"They have also burned men," Shlomo Molkho whispered.

"Is that not the same thing?" the cardinal replied.

And he added:

"You start with one, and you end up with the other."

Egidio di Viterbo sat down in a purple velvet armchair and motioned to his guest to sit on the sofa. Once Shlomo Molkho was seated, he asked:

"Why?"

The young man from Portugal frowned but made no answer.

"Why all this tragedy?" the prelate continued. "You prophesied the destruction of Rome, and Rome has indeed been brought low, sacked, and destroyed, just as you predicted! But people are wondering why. Why does the Eternal require so much killing in order to liberate the survivors? Especially when after the massacres the survivors themselves are beset by new calamities, by new trials. If this tragedy was essential for liberating some human beings, then Emperor Charles v should not be considered the assassin we believe he is, but rather someone who is carrying out God's will!"

The cardinal got to his feet and walked slowly toward the window. Outside, in the early morning fog, the imperial guard was warming itself around a campfire. Shlomo Molkho, not without sympathy, watched the prelate's imposing form cross the room. With enough questions, he thought, this man will end up Jewish…

Egidio di Viterbo turned back toward the young man.

"So then, why?"

Shlomo Molkho smiled:

"I don't have an answer, but I do have a story to tell."

"And what is your story?"

"A king forbade his son to go near a courtesan. But he also ordered her to seduce his son. If the son allowed himself to be seduced, he would be punished. The courtesan, on the other hand, risked no blame, whatever the son's course of action would be."

The churchman showed no reaction and simply waited for the rest of the story.

"Evil is the guarantee of human freedom," Angel Solomon went on softly. "It is freedom that man has chosen, for which he has accepted responsibility. Evil is the imbalance in the *Sephirot* between the forces of Rigor and the forces of Clemency…"

The cardinal could no longer keep quiet.

"Exactly, the *Sephirot*, the attributes of God!" he exclaimed. "His Holiness has charged me with reflecting on the causes of this horror, this misery, and this ravage that have devastated Rome. Why has the Holy League been so cowardly? And where have the French been? And especially, why has God seemed to remain absent?"

He strode quickly back to his armchair.

"No, that could not be natural. There are situations in which nothing seems just!"

He was quiet again, and then, in a confidential tone, he went on: "I have begun to write a treatise entitled *Shekhina*, from the name of the tenth *sephira* according to the Kabbalah."

Angel Solomon's violet eyes sparkled. He leaned toward the prelate. "And what is in your treatise?"

"It talks about what the prophets said when the Eternal, the God of Israel, allowed Jerusalem to be destroyed by the Egyptians, by the Babylonians, by the Assyrians, by the Romans. In my treatise, I even refer to you, my friend."

The cardinal closed his eyes to better recall his text, and then, almost in a whisper, gesturing with his right hand to stress certain words, he began to speak:

"Of Rome I had made my capital. Forgetting my kindness, Rome gave itself over to sin. I protected it as long as I could. I frightened it using prophetic voices, not long ago, threatening destruction and pillage. I exhorted its inhabitants to undertake moral reform…"

The door opened. Egidio di Viterbo stopped speaking and leaped to his feet.

"Your Holiness!" he exclaimed.

But Clement VII paid no attention to the cardinal. He walked straight toward Shlomo Molkho.

"Well then, the young prophet has come back among us and no one has let me know?"

The young man from Portugal was about to bow, but the pontiff stopped him.

"You predicted everything, my son. Everything! When I consider the perils and accidents to which weakness, chance, and violence expose human lives, there is nothing I admire more than a man who believes, who sees, and who predicts thing accurately!"

The pope had undergone great changes. His face was gaunt. His back was bent. Even his beard was different. Clement VII saw that Shlomo Molkho was studying him carefully.

"Does my beard intrigue you? I am letting it grow as a sign of mourning. Is that not what you Jews do in similar situations?"

He smiled sadly.

"And what about the Messiah," he asked, "the man from Chabor?"

"He is coming."

"Was he not taken hostage by French pirates?"

"All I know is that he is on his way to Rome."

"When will he arrive?"

"Shortly. Your Holiness will see him as He did two years ago and will recognize him. Afterwards, Your Holiness will be able to slip away from His guards, and from one of His strongholds, can negotiate an honorable peace, a more satisfactory peace than the one imposed upon you by the emperor."

"Is that a prophecy?"

"It is a certainty."

Chapter forty-eight

David Reubeni on the Way to Rome

When David Reubeni's meeting with Francis I took place, the King of France found himself in a fragile, uncertain situation. After his humiliating defeat at Pavia, he had been forced to sign a non-aggression pact with Soleiman the Magnificent. Under such conditions, receiving the man who was proposing to raise a Jewish army in Europe to fight the Turks seemed contradictory. When David noted the paradoxical character of the situation, Francis I stopped him.

"Would my support surprise you?"

"No, Milord," the Messenger replied. "It seems very diplomatic, and worthy of a great king. Furthermore, you are not threatening Soleiman. All you are doing is listening to a Jew who has come to ask for help in defeating the Magnificent. Your pact with him is therefore not at stake..."

Francis I loved those kinds of subtleties, and they put him in an excellent mood. He was eager to continue discussing all sorts of topics with David Reubeni and kept him for several weeks. The man from the desert charmed him. Looking priestly in his white tunic, during their conversations he proved to be the sharpest political mind the king had ever met. The king said that he would not necessarily refuse to help David later, even though at the moment he could not commit to supporting him openly.

As for David, he was dreaming of nothing else than reaching Rome to see his friends and make contact once more with Clement VII. Since hearing the news that Rome had been sacked, he couldn't wait to leave. Joseph, his wise counselor, encouraged him to do so quickly.

"You are wasting your time here," he would say. "Get back to your more promising options. This king is much too fickle."

But Francis I wanted to learn more about that mysterious country called Chabor.

Though he was unable to support the Jewish prince's plans, he still asked about how the pope was helping. He also wondered why David did not directly approach Soleiman the Magnificent, whose armies occupied the Holy Land, and ask for the right to establish a Jewish kingdom. It was difficult for the Messenger to help the king understand that a country cannot simply be a gift, but rather must be won by battle. Like freedom, a country has to be conquered and not simply received. In order to illustrate what he meant, he told the king the story about how the Jews in Egypt were set free.

The days went by. David Reubeni was given the promise that rabbis would be authorized to come teach Biblical Hebrew in Paris, in the new Royal College, as soon as it was opened. Then the king took him to Amboise where he visited Leonardo da Vinci's house. That is where, in the king's arms, the famous artist had passed away.

Finally, the king agreed to listen to the Messenger's wish to return to Rome and authorized his departure. To the small group made up of the Jewish prince's men, he added a large escort that was to accompany them all the way to the Italian border.

In spite of the war still being fought, David Reubeni and his suite rode through Northern Italy with few problems. His men's costumes, their weapons, and especially the banners they waved so proudly guaranteed them respect. No one dared ask which camp they belonged to. And many would have been surprised to learn that they were linked with neither side and that they were Jewish soldiers. Some people thought they were Spanish, and others took them for Germans. Some thought that they belonged to Charles de Bourbon who was supporting the emperor because he was an enemy of Francis 1, and still others confused them with one of the composite groups that made up the army of the Holy League. But no one caused them any problem. However, in that disorganized country with its roads cut and bridges burned, it took them more than two weeks to reach Rome. People were fearful. They feared strangers and were afraid to invite anyone in. In order to allay fears and find food and lodging, David's group resorted to using some lovely gold pieces that fortunately the King of France had given him.

As they were passing not far from Urbino, David Reubeni decided to stop and see the old scholar Vincentius Castellani, who four years ago had given him such a valuable letter of recommendation for Cardinal Egidio di Viterbo. It was partly a feeling of loyalty, but David also wanted to find out what the old man thought about current events and perhaps gain precise information about the military and political situation in Rome before he reached the city.

Vincentius Castellani had aged considerably since their previous meeting. "That is how things are," thought David. "A man can remain old for a long time, but then suddenly he ages definitively and dies." The old scholar had, however, kept his proud, dignified bearing, even though his back was now bent, even though his white hair was falling out, and even though his purple cloak had now become too large for his thinning body. He was touched by the prince's visit. Several times he had to wipe tears that rolled down over the deep wrinkles in his cheeks. During the meeting, he didn't seem eager to discuss theological subjects. On the other hand, he was able to give the Messenger all the information he was hoping for. David learned about the death of Niccolò Machiavelli in Tuscany barely a month earlier. That great mind had stayed away from Florence more and more, for he felt that Florence rejected his ideas. He remained off to himself, and yet, up until the end, the author of *The Prince* was still admired by many and feared by all. His death affected the Envoy from Chabor more than he would have thought. He also gleaned some good news from Vincentius Castellani. Cardinal Egidio di Viterbo, for example, was alive and in good health. He was staying with the pope in Sant'Angelo Castle. As for the Jewish community of Rome, it had been able to escape the destruction and find refuge on the other side of the Tiber. A part of the community was hiding among fishermen, and the others were living in the catacombs.

"You must talk to the pope," Vincentius Castellani told David. "Even though he is not as powerful as he once was, he can still provide your best support. Later, once he has reconciled with the emperor, he will regain most of his power. Rome will be Rome once more, and the pope will always be the pope!"

He turned his wrinkled face toward David.

"Do you know why? Because Charles v has no other spiritual authority to recommend in place of Clement vii!"

As he listened to his host, the man from Chabor let his thoughts stray toward those Roman Jews who had supported him for so long and given him shelter. He thought of the fragile Dina and of her brother, Doctor Joseph Zarfatti. He felt a twinge of regret. He quickly had to chase any sentimental feelings from his mind because they were too upsetting. Had not Machiavelli told him that one's feelings cannot define *virtue*?

The old man noticed that the Messenger's thoughts seemed to be elsewhere. Respectfully, he paused for a moment before continuing:

"Does the prince know that Shlomo Molkho, his young Portuguese friend who prophesied his coming all over Italy, is in Rome just now? Somehow, no one knows how, he managed to slip through the barriers set up by the imperial guard and join the pope in Sant'Angelo Fortress."

For David Reubeni, time stopped. He could sense the danger. He thought back to his first meeting in Portugal with the man who was then simply Diego Pires. He sensed that in his new identity as Shlomo Molkho, the young fanatic had become more dangerous still. He suddenly felt weighted down. How could he denounce such illusory promises of peace? How could he explain that outside of the freedom to believe, any belief is heresy? He knew that it would now be difficult, if not impossible, to reject Shlomo Molkho, to contradict his words in a ravaged city *whose destruction he had prophesied*! In the Almeirim military camp, with no witnesses, he had been able to get rid of him easily, but here? And finally, even if he did have to accept the fanatic's presence, would not Shlomo Molkho's word always win out over his own? Molkho seemed to be speaking with words from heaven, whereas he, David Reubeni, was only an *Am Ha'aretz*, a man of the earth. And in a debate between heaven and earth, heaven always has the final word.

He had the sudden temptation to give up. To stay away from Rome, to avoid Angel Diego, to escape from messianic mirage and disgrace. And yet the man from Chabor realized that like Jonah, he would be unable to escape his destiny. So he smiled weakly at old Castellani when he answered.

"Agreed," he said. "I will follow your advice and go to Rome to see the pope again. Even if I were to be swallowed up by a whale, like Jonah!"

The old man's eyes widened as he tried to understand. But David, keeping his thoughts to himself, did not explain. "The whale is one thing," he thought. "But history is the real danger!"

For the rest of their trip, the Prince of Chabor and his men often had to make detours to avoid battlefields and burning villages. On August 2, the last night before reaching Rome, they found themselves in Montefiascone, not far from Orvieto. The head of the League's armies, Francesco Maria della Rovere, Duke of Urbino, had pulled his army back to Orvieto. The suspicious innkeeper who agreed to give lodging to David and his men explained how the Duke, after sending scouts to the wall of Rome and learning that the imperial troops were getting reinforcements from Naples, had decided to retreat toward the north instead of fighting to retake the city.

Joseph reminded David that Francesco della Rovere, when he was prefect of Rome, had been the one who covered up the bloody ambush in Ostia, during which the Jewish prince was supposed to have been killed but which he had managed to foil with Machiavelli's help.

When night fell, clouds rolled in. Heavy drops of rain began to fall in the inn's courtyard. Then, after thunder had rumbled a few times, it turned into a downpour. Soon, brown stains began to form on the ceiling in David's room, and the saltpeter and mold on the walls proved that the place was often damp. After a quarter of an hour, water began to drip to the floor, forming a puddle right in the middle of the room. David placed a blanket over the ebony chest that held his journal. There was a knock at the door.

"What a storm!" Joseph sighed as he came in. "Might it be the flood that is to precede the Redemption?"

When he saw the growing puddle of water in the middle of his master's room, he burst out laughing.

"He who can recognize the blessings of nature is able to reap even more benefits," he said. "And what an inn! I hope that the water dripping through every fissure will also get rid of some of the vermin!"

"How are our men taking it?"

"Very well. Your servants are impatient to get to Rome, David. And they are afraid at the same time. For the moment, they are sleeping. There are four of them per room and two per bed. But these days young men seem to tire faster than old men!"

"Endurance comes only with age…"

Joseph smiled. Then, when he saw the chest, he changed the subject.

"If you want to write, take my room," he offered. "It is smaller than this one, but at least it is still dry."

The man from Chabor accepted his confidant's offer. It was indeed a tiny room, but there were no leaks. And what's more, it had the advantage of being lit by a resin torch. The torch, attached to the wall, was like the *lamparos* fishermen used at night. Joseph stayed in his master's room while his master wrote.

Three hours later, David was tired and laid down his pen. He began to think about Rome. For no apparent reason, a rarely-used text of Scripture came to mind: *Woe is me, for I have sojourned in Meshec, I have dwelt near the tents of Kedar! For too long my soul has remained with those who hate peace. I am for peace; but whenever I speak, they are for war...*

He spoke the passage aloud and then fell asleep.

The sound of a chair falling over awakened him. He leaped up, pulled his sword from its sheath, and quietly opened the door. There in the corridor, hidden in the shadows, were two strangers with daggers. He shivered. Was it because of the chilly, damp air or was it immense anger toward those two rascals who were forcing him to use violence and kill? He heard more noise from the room he had exchanged for Joseph's room the night before. His faithful lieutenant was in danger. The man from Chabor let out a horrible scream in which the Hebrew word for the Eternal was mixed with a flood of Arabic. Swinging his sword, he felled the two intruders. At the same moment, three other armed men came out of Joseph's room and rushed at David. He was able to parry their attack and took several steps backward. Joseph's heavy-set figure, his face covered with blood, appeared in the doorway. In his left hand he was brandishing a stool. His right hand held a dagger. When he saw the three men who had attacked him now attacking his master, he shouted at the top of his lungs for the Jewish army:

"Help! Come help us at once!"

And he threw the stool at one of the doors behind which some of the Messenger's men were sleeping. The noise was deafening. The whole inn came to life. David Reubeni's men rushed out, swords in hand. They could even hear the shots of harquebuses out in the courtyard. One of the assailants dropped, bloodied, to the floor. The others, surprised by the counterattack, turned and fled through a window at the end of the corridor. They crashed through the windowpanes, and glass flew everywhere. Then there were gruff shouts and horses whinnying as they galloped off.

"They've fled, the cowards!" said Joseph.

David Reubeni's servants found the innkeeper cowering in his room. Joseph's head wound was superficial. Once it was cleaned and bandaged, he immediately began to question the people who worked in the inn. It turned out that the attack was indeed the work of the former prefect of Rome.

"Those who hate you so much are certainly persistent," Joseph said jokingly to his master. "Their faithfulness to you is unshakable."

The man from Chabor mumbled some words.

"What are you saying?" Joseph asked.

"I am praying to the All-Powerful Eternal to give me sufficient strength to remain faithful to myself."

Chapter forty-nine

Becoming the Messiah

The next morning under a cloudless, transparent sky, David Reubeni and his men reached the gates of Rome under the warm early-August sun. Once inside the city that had been ravaged by the soldiers of Charles V, after a period of violence and pillaging, people were beginning to make the best of their misfortune. Part of the imperial army had ceased pillaging. Some soldiers were using churches and municipal buildings as if they were dumps. Others, on platforms set up in the streets, were brazenly gambling for treasures stolen from the Vatican. But many, particularly the German lansquenets, had left the city for fear of contagion. When David and his followers appeared, some Spanish guards tried to keep them from coming into the city.

"Halt! Who goes there?" shouted a short man with a strange helmet.

"It is the Prince of Chabor!" answered one of the young men with David.

The Spaniards glanced at each other in surprise, but asked no further questions. In those uncertain times, it was hard to know who was who, and the guards had no desire to keep fighting. Apart from that inconsequential incident, the Jewish Prince reached Doctor Joseph Zarfatti's house unhindered.

In the streets, there were rotting animal carcasses, excrement, and the smell of smoke. A strange odor from the ruins hung in the summer air, mixed with the stench rising from the sewers. The doctor's front door had been broken down, and now there were boards nailed across it. The little door in the courtyard behind the building was still on its hinges. Along with Joseph, David Reubeni went inside. Soon he was in the large room where two years before Doctor Zarfatti and Rabbi Obadiah da Sforno had organized his departure celebration. He could still almost hear Benvenida Abravanel's melodious voice chanting the Zohar. Wherever he looked, he saw destruction. The furniture had disappeared, and the walls were filthy. Here and there, columns of ants were feeding on mounds of garbage.

"Shall we go upstairs?" Joseph asked.

"No," David replied. "Instead of seeking out our memories, let us find the living."

"Prince! Prince!"

Two young men in his retinue came running up:

"The house down the street, near the river…"

"Yes?"

"We heard people talking inside, but when we knocked, everything got quiet."

"Is that the only house in the neighborhood where someone is still living?"

"Perhaps. We're still looking."

Suddenly, out in the deserted street, they heard an axle screeching. David's men drew their swords. But it was only a barefoot woman dressed in rags pushing a wheelbarrow. A child clung to her skirt. A man's body lay on the wheelbarrow. When the woman reached the little church at the edge of the Jewish quarter, she stopped and tipped over the wheelbarrow, dumping the body to the ground. Then, seemingly oblivious of her surroundings, she trudged past David and his men.

The men were greatly affected by such a sad scene. Lumps rose in their throats. No one dared speak, until finally Joseph broke the silence.

"Strange times. After massacring Jews, now Christians are killing each other."

"And all the while, Islam is making advances!" one of the young men from Fez added.

"Who then will help us take back the land of our ancestors?" another asked.

The Messenger made no answer. His face remained stony. He put his sword back in its sheath and then started walking briskly toward the house his two men had pointed out.

He knocked several times at the door. In vain. Then Joseph shouted in Hebrew:

"Open up! It is the Messenger from Chabor! Open up, and may the Eternal protect you!"

They could hear steps and the floor creaking. Then a woman's face appeared in a window on the second floor.

"Has David Reubeni come back?" she asked in Hebrew. "It's about time!"

A key turned in the lock. The door opened, and a man stood there. In a sing-song voice, he exclaimed:

"May the Eternal, the God of Israel, bless His son David!"

The man from the desert was delighted to recognize Obadiah da Sforno. He stepped inside and saw the old rabbi rocking back and forth, his head nodding as usual. He felt like hugging the man, but remembering his status as a prince, he was able to restrain himself. However, to show his friendship for the rabbi, he remembered a passage from *Pirkei Avoth* that he had quoted in a strong voice:

Accomplish the will of God as if it were your own, so that He may accomplish your will as if it were His own.

Erase your will before His so that He may erase the will of others before yours...

Obadiah da Sforno's face lit up. He raised his hand to speak. David Reubeni noticed that he no longer wore his famous ruby. The rabbi looked up, his face radiant. His goatee stuck straight out, and his index finger pointed toward the heavens.

"Those are the words of Rabban Gamliel, the son of Rabbi Yehuda HaNassi!"

But he was not taken in by David's stratagem, and he burst out laughing and took the Messenger's hands.

"The will of the Eternal, blessed be His name, has brought you back to us. Praised be the Lord, my son! Praised be the Lord," he sighed, his own hands clutching David's.

They stared silently at each other for a moment. Obadiah da Sforno finally let go of David's hands when his daughter Sarah, the woman who had called down from the upstairs window, appeared and briefly touched the Messenger's hands. She bowed, and said blushingly:

"I am going to spread the word among the Jews that the Messenger is back among us!"

And she slipped out, her skirts rustling.

"No one was willing to remain in the Jewish quarter," the rabbi said after she left. "Everyone was afraid. But at my age, what did I have to fear? Death? Come now! Sarah decided to stay here with me. Our street has not suffered greatly. All that the Christians had on their minds was to kill other Christians. As if the Eternal were trying to be sure that they, too, felt some of that fearful heat that emanates from the inferno into which they themselves were casting Jews not long ago."

Later that afternoon, hearing Sarah's news, the neighbors returned home, pulling carts and carrying bundles of clothing. The deserted street began to take on some life. People started cleaning up their houses and sharing what was left of their furniture. The Messenger sent Joseph and two others to purchase weapons to share with those who had returned. The young men in his escort finally felt that they were engaged in a true mission and acting according to the instructions they had received in Portugal at the Alpiarça training camp. As evening drew near, about fifty Jews convened for a meeting in Joseph Zarfatti's house; David Reubeni's men took charge of everything, caring for the visitors' horses and organizing the surveillance of the neighborhood, house by house, complete with passwords.

With tears in his eyes, the doctor reached out to grasp David's arms. Dina's face was pale, and she knelt down and kissed his hands. David shivered. The young woman's warm lips unsettled him. But in her eyes he saw no traces of her earlier passionate love, though that is what he would have perhaps liked to see. Now she was looking at him with religious respect, with the same adoration he had sensed back in Jerusalem in the eyes of Christians who entered the Holy Sepulcher or in the eyes of Muslims walking barefoot on the ground at Haram el-Sharif and in the Mosque of the Dome. To all appearances, Dina was still Dina. However, her mind and heart no longer reflected the woman she had been but rather the vision she was now living. Shlomo Molkho, alas, had also been in Rome!

As he was preparing for his meeting with his Jewish friends, the man from Chabor feared the questions they were sure to ask him about the uncertain future of the Jewish liberation army, about why he was expelled from Portugal. He thought that he would need to justify himself, to argue, and to demonstrate that his plan could still be carried out and that it was even more necessary now than before.

However, the Jewish community seemed content just to have him there. The Envoy, surrounded by his guards and preceded by the banners symbolizing the tribes of Israel, had been able to ride through the city without being stopped by soldiers. That was clear confirmation of Shlomo Molkho's predictions! David Reubeni was indeed the one they had been awaiting for so long! Now he was larger, stronger, and more mysterious than he had seemed two years earlier! During his earlier stay in Rome, why had they not realized who he was? Why had they failed to understand that a prince who had come from nowhere, capable of confronting the plague as well as men, could only be the Messenger chosen by the Master of the Universe, blessed be His name, to deliver his people and lead them back to Zion with shouts of triumph, to fill the earth with the knowledge of the Lord, as the old rabbi said, "like the bottom of the sea with the waters that cover it."

It did not take long for David Reubeni to sense what his friends were thinking. Through everything he said, through even the most straightforward description of the events he had experienced, they would now only be able to see allegories that Obadiah da Sforno could illustrate by convincing, poetic quotations from holy texts. Between them and him there was now an invisible, impassable wall—the very mystery of God. Should he attempt to get around the obstacle and find other Jews, other Jewish communities that had not been affected by this epidemic of messianic revelation? Or on the other hand, should he try to climb over the impassable wall and draw closer to the divine word? That is, should he abandon his own discourse, give up the *I* of his own will? Should he no longer speak to others except in the name of the Eternal, as before him so many true prophets as well as false had done?

He spent a wakeful night in the house. Dina had placed a mattress on the floor in the upstairs room he knew so well, and from which the German lansquenets had taken all the furnishings. He hoped vaguely, perhaps looking for a diversion, that the young woman would come join him. But when dawn came he realized that would never be possible. His status had changed. Has anyone ever seen a simple mortal woman make love with the Messiah?

He thought of Benvenida Abravanel, who was apparently in Naples. He also thought of Leah and Rachel, the wives of Jacob-Israel, whom Michelangelo, now in Florence, had sculpted to stand beside his famous Moses. David would have liked to see those masterpieces once more, but he did not know where they were.

"David!"

He gave a start. It was Joseph's voice.

"Come in."

"There is an old man downstairs. Our guards found him walking around outside the house. He is asking to speak to you and to you alone. He says he has an urgent message."

David Reubeni leaned out the window. Guarded by David's men, a bent old man, dressed in grey rags, was leaning on a white cane.

"Who are you?" David shouted in Hebrew.

One of the young guards translated into Italian.

"Who am I? A friend of the poor..." the old man replied.

"What do you do?"

"I walk around listening to people here and there...I have also heard our poor pope who is closed up in Sant'Angelo Castle. He asked me to bring you a message..."

David Reubeni motioned to the guards to let the strange fellow come in. He went downstairs to meet him. He nodded a greeting and immediately asked what the message was.

"His Holiness wishes to meet the Prince of Chabor as soon as possible."

"How did the pope know I was in Rome?"

"As I said, I listen to people here and there, and I find out things. And the things I find out I pass along."

"So you are the one who told him..."

The old man smiled, showing his yellow teeth.

"What do you expect?" he said. "In this city, where people have trouble distinguishing between God and Satan, someone has to keep a clear head."

"And you are not afraid to walk around in the midst of all these uncertainties?"

"Who would attack a beggar?" the man retorted, shrugging his shoulders.

"So," the man from the desert continued, "recently you took a young Portuguese man to see Clement VII."

"He too awaits you in Sant'Angelo Castle. Everyone awaits you, Prince..."

"And how does one get there?"

The old man leaned closer, lowering his voice.

"There is a tunnel leading to the Tiber. There, a boat will take you across secretly by night to the base of the fortress."

David Reubeni gestured impatiently.

"Impossible!" he said.

"But..."

"There is no reason to hide!"

"But, Prince, after all…"

"Tell the pontiff that the Prince of Chabor is delighted to accept his invitation, but that he will not go see him in secret like a thief or a spy. He will come in full daylight, leading his men!"

The old beggar lost his calm.

"That is crazy!"

He raised his cane heavenward.

"And it is dangerous…"

"*I trust in God, and I fear nothing. What can men do to me?*" replied the man from the desert.

Obadiah da Sforno, who had just arrived, could not keep from adding proudly:

"Psalms 56:11!"

But the mysterious beggar's face had grown rigid. His eyes, normally only half-open, were now open wide. His whole being displayed surprise, worry, and disapproval. He stammered one last objection:

"But, Prince, the imperial soldiers! They will never let you pass! On sight, Prince, they shoot on sight! Nobody, nobody can enter the fortress that way."

Then David Reubeni, half seriously and half in jest, said:

"Nobody, that is true. Nobody except the Messiah!"

Chapter fifty

"May Your Hand Sustain Me..."

Dav

avid Reubeni did as he said he would do. In full view, dressed in his white tunic with its Star of David, he rode across Rome at the head of his armed escort. The famous banners representing the tribes of Israel waved proudly in the morning breeze. People came out into the streets in surprise to see the cortege. Some applauded, and others, remembering Shlomo Molkho's prophecy that the Redeemer would appear after the desolation, fell to their knees as he passed. German and Spanish soldiers showed only astonishment, looking curiously at the white banners and their Hebrew characters. Some of them even saluted. The Prince of Chabor and his little escort crossed the city and the Sant'Angelo Bridge. By the fortress gates, however, a group of about a hundred lansquenets was waiting for him. With lances drawn, they were keeping everyone out. Joseph rode up to them and began to speak to the captain of the guard. No one knew what the servant of the man from the desert said to the German captain. People saw him show the officer a letter, and the man read it attentively. There followed a quiet conversation between the two men. A few yards back, the Jewish Prince waited impassively on his nervous horse.

Suddenly, the captain gave the missive back to Joseph and ordered his men to lower the drawbridge. Inside the fortress there was a solemn trumpet call. The bells in the nearby church began to peal.

Among the hundreds of curious people who had gathered in front of the fortress, several told the story later that the Jewish Prince had been received as the emissary of Emperor Charles v himself.

Once in the courtyard inside Sant'Angelo Castle, the imperial guard welcomed him solicitously, offering to take care of his men's horses. The pope's Swiss guards lined up as an honor guard on both sides of the steps and along the whole corridor. David's men took their places in the central hall on the ground floor, whereas the Messenger from Chabor, along with Joseph, was led by a chamberlain up to the first floor and into Cardinal Egidio di Viterbo's well-furnished library.

David Reubeni was filled with emotion as he entered the room where he had first met the prelate. Around the walls, there were still credenzas piled high with books. The same sumptuous carpets muffled the sound of footsteps. The cardinal seemed to have aged, but he had lost none of his good humor. He hurried to meet his visitor with a broad smile on his face.

"It is a strange situation," he said, his voice strong as he spoke partly in Hebrew and partly in Latin. "The pope cannot leave the castle, but a Jewish Prince is able to ride through a city that soldiers control, and not one dares to stop him! But our young Portuguese friend had warned us: The Messiah would not arrive in secret on some moonless night, but in full daylight, because he is protected by the *Shekhina*…"

All at once Egidio di Viterbo burst out laughing:

"Please excuse me, Prince. I have not properly greeted you!"

And he added, as he spread his arms:

"Barukh Haba! Welcome to the fortress-prison of Sant'Angelo…"

With the added years, the cardinal was now more bent, but kindness and intelligence still emanated from his large face with its wide, high forehead. As for his discourse, he was still just as skillful and as much at ease, and his words allowed for a variety of interpretations.

"I can imagine your disappointment, Prince, when our dear Joao III ordered you to abandon your army and leave Portugal. However, as our friend Shlomo was saying yesterday, quoting Zechariah: '*It is not by force or power but by the Spirit of the Lord* that the Holy Land will be freed and the Jewish people taken back to Zion.'"

The cardinal paused. Then he continued.

"We shouldn't stand here talking. His Holiness would never forgive us if we keep what we are saying between us. He is waiting impatiently to see you."

And then he led David through a door and down a long corridor, poorly lit by torches, leading to Clement VII's apartments. Joseph took advantage of the opportunity to whisper into his master's ear:

"It will be difficult for you to remain faithful to yourself…"

David turned in surprise to look at him.

"Even here," he added quietly, "everyone has been bewitched by that amazing Angel Solomon!"

The Messenger from Chabor did not answer, but he shared his lieutenant's feelings. The situation was indeed unusual. He would need to remain on his guard. When they entered the room with its high ceiling decorated with frescoes, in fact the first person he saw was Shlomo Molkho.

When he saw the man from Chabor, the young Portuguese prophet's eyes turned violet. Even before David Reubeni was able to respond to the greeting of the pontiff who was coming to meet him, Angel Solomon threw himself at his hero's feet.

"God be praised! My master has come!" he exclaimed. "Today on him alone depend our existences, and the only reason he has returned is to lead us to repentance. Our Redemption, Master, depends upon you! Our deliverance, Master, will be your handiwork! Speak, and we will follow!"

David Reubeni stepped back and raised his right hand to his face as if to protect himself, as if he had seen the devil in person. Paying no attention to the man kneeling before him, he turned to the pope.

"May Your Holiness permit me to quote the great Esdras who said: *'Don't be in a greater hurry than the Creator…'*"

Clement VII smiled in disillusionment.

"But what does the Creator desire?" he asked, his voice weak as he motioned to Shlomo Molkho to approach. And he added, without waiting for the Messenger's reply:

"Our young prophet is not totally mistaken to say that we are living through the *Hevle Mashiach*, the pains of bringing the Messiah into the world. How else can we explain the calamities that have befallen us during these times?

The pope's skin was now waxen, illustrating how tired he was. He collapsed into a brocade-covered armchair and sighed deeply.

"Everything started with Savonarola's madness," he added.

He gave another sigh.

"Decadence always begins with madness…"

In the respectful silence that surrounded him, he laughed nervously, shrugging his shoulders with a knowing look.

"Savonarola's madness, followed by the extermination of the Jews," he continued. "The Inquisition! I've always opposed its goals, but in vain. And then came these interminable wars, so cruel, between Christian kings, and the central role of the Church was brought into question. And when there was no longer any spiritual, moral, or political authority, then there was a bloodbath in Stockholm and the massacres in the Upper Rhine in Franconia and in Swabia. Later it was the plague's turn to ravage us. And now, Rome has been crushed! When men no longer have any recourse or reference points, they yield to despair, and despair is perhaps more fearsome than all of the other calamities put together."

Clement VII turned toward Shlomo Molkho as if to get his support. The pontiff's eyes were full of admiration and tenderness for the young man from Portugal, and David quickly realized how strong the spiritual and emotional link was between the two men. With his left hand, the pope gestured toward a high, narrow window through which the sun's rays poured. They formed an arrow of light on the floor, like the hand of a clock. He began to speak again, more profoundly:

"Did not the Lord say that despair resulting from such terrible ordeals is an early sign of the Redemption and that it foreshadows the end of time?"

He grew silent, as if burdened by his own words. He seemed to shrink down into his chair, overcome by total lassitude. The chair's brocade was hard to distinguish from the pontifical robe. The only thing that stood out was his white beard.

David Reubeni felt like telling Clement VII exactly what Nachmanides, the great kabbalistic scholar from Gerona, had said to the King of Aragon: *It is your task, O King, and the task of your knights, to put an end to all war as required by the advent of the Messianic era!*

But the pope had no more knights and truly thought of nothing else but avenging the affronts and humiliations that Charles V had just inflicted on him. The Messenger from Chabor, from the meeting's outset, had sensed that the sovereign pontiff would not listen to him, that only Shlomo Molkho's voice found favor in his ears, and especially in his mind. Joseph, standing beside his master, sensed the same thing.

"Talk to him about the Jewish army, about the liberation of Jerusalem," he whispered.

David Reubeni raised his arm. All eyes turned toward him, including the pope's.

"Oh, if only the King of Portugal had allowed me to leave with my army!" he sighed.

The pope was intrigued and leaned forward.

"The imperial army would have been chased out of Rome long ago!" David added.

"But what would the enemies of His Holiness have said?" Cardinal Egidio di Viterbo interjected. And he answered the question himself. "They would have accused the pope of being protected by those who killed Jesus!"

With a smile on his face, the cardinal added: "That would be the last straw!"

David Reubeni stepped forward:

"If Your Holiness would allow me..."

Clement VII nodded for him to speak.

"When I spoke the way I did, to my mind it would not have been waging war on Emperor Charles v. That would indeed have been a disservice to Your Holiness."

He moved still closer to the pope and continued speaking quietly, leaning down toward his interlocutor and looking at him intently, as if he was trying to catch his slightest reaction.

"Those loyal to Your Holiness are still in control of some regions. It would be an honor for my friends and me to help the pope link up with them. In Orvieto, for example. From there he would be able, as Urban II did five centuries earlier in Clermont, to launch an appeal for the liberation of the Holy Land. An appeal of that kind would be the best possible diversion and would become the rallying cry of all Christendom. For that very reason, the Church's centrality would be strongly reaffirmed. Except that the goal of this European army, made of people who had been each other's enemies, once it was en route to Jerusalem would not be to destroy the Jews, but rather to help them take back their ancestral land. We are free, Your Holiness, only inasmuch as others are also free."

Cardinal di Viterbo, standing back in the shadows of an old statue, stepped into the discussion circle, across the ray of light that was gleaming on the floor. He intervened with his customary sensitivity, with the air of someone who recognizes a good opportunity.

"The Prince of Chabor has just expressed an opinion that is worth taking seriously. Escaping to Orvieto could be a possible solution. Our pope has to be rescued from the claws of heretics. If we do not do so quickly, His Holiness will be discredited, and the whole Church along with him."

And then he turned directly to David Reubeni.

"I do not know, Prince, if everything you are proposing is feasible, but your ideas seem reasonable. In any case, they demand reflection. But I shall always prefer a dangerous truth to a useful error, for the truth can heal the evil it may have caused..."

The pope struggled out of his seat and began to pace back and forth, his hands clasped behind him. He walked past Shlomo Molkho several times, but the young man did not say a word. Finally the pope stopped and turned to the man from the desert.

"Alas, Prince," he said bitterly, "I am not Urban the Blessed, but rather Clement the Wretched! Neither the shouts of men nor the clash of weapons can dissipate the shadows. Only light can do that, even if it is only the flame of a candle. And if light comes from light, all light comes from God."

David Reubeni Was About To Respond To The Cardinal Who Spoke About Truth And The Pope Who Spoke About Light When He Realized That Shlomo Molkho Was About To Speak, And David Had No Idea What He Might Propose. He Sensed That If He Wanted The Conversation To Remain Anchored To Reality, He Had To Keep Angel Solomon From Speaking.

"*Eternal, God of hosts, hear my prayer,*" he said abruptly, quoting a psalm.

Without knowing exactly why, but intuiting *what needed to be said*, he went on and quoted another psalm. Was it provocation to remind them of war in a place that had just undergone war's ravages? To glorify force in a city plunged into mourning because of arms? In fact, with all the intelligence of the desert fox that he was, he had measured the inescapable necessity that weighed on his shoulders—did he not owe it to himself to take a step in the direction that everyone was expecting him to take? They all, even those crowds of Jews that venerated him as well as the pope, the cardinal, and the fanatic Molkho, were demanding a ray of hope, a reason to relieve their anxiety through some powerful dream. They were seeking a reason that could help them attain the impossible. They were thirsty for a solution that would justify folly. All he had to do was take one step in that direction, and, among other results, he would forever have the ear and the friendship of the sovereign pontiff, still the head of Christendom in spite of everything. And he still needed Clement VII's support, but the pope had eyes only for Angel Solomon's visionary prophecies. So to gain the pope's favor, he needed to neutralize the young Portuguese prophet, subjugating him without offending him. He had to keep him from speaking, from raving, from distorting the action needed to take Jerusalem. With a deep voice, almost solemnly, he continued to chant:

And you say: I have lent my help to a young hero,
I have raised up a young man among the people...

My hand will support him
My arm will give him strength...
I will crush his adversaries before him,
I will put his left hand on the sea
And his right hand on the rivers,
And he will call upon my name...

Shlomo Molkho did not let him finish. Overcome with emotion, he threw himself once again at the feet of the man from Chabor, seizing him by the wrist and shouting, an adoring look on his face:

"May your hand support me, may your arm give me strength. And more than ever I will call upon your name only, O Redeemer, O Messiah!"

David Reubeni shivered.

"Enough blasphemy!" he whispered between clenched teeth. "The Eternal alone is our Redeemer!"

But he did not pull away from the Angel's hand.

Chapter fifty-one

Toward a New Alliance

David Reubeni left the meeting with the pope deeply troubled. It is true that Clement VII had accepted the idea of fleeing to Orvieto, but he had rejected the proposal to call for freeing the Holy Land. He had conceded that he was in a weak political position relative to Charles V, and he had asked what the Messenger thought he should do. David, realizing that from now on the sovereign pontiff could give him little support, had answered sharply:

"Charles V has grown more powerful, has he not? Well, give him your papal unction—place a crown on his head! He is the only one who can give you back your miter…"

But more than the pope's powerlessness, what worried him was the net woven by Shlomo Molkho. The net was drawing tighter and tighter around him. He would now need to come to terms with the young fanatic. Perhaps, in order to carry out his plans, he would need to do what the young man expected and become the Messiah.

When late that afternoon David Reubeni went to Joseph Zarfatti's house, he was wracked with doubt and uncertainty. There must have been a hundred Roman Jews who had come. They had been waiting for him for a good hour, but when the man from the desert saw them through the ground-floor window, he knew that he didn't have the heart to meet them. So he slipped through a door in the courtyard at the back of the house and went straight upstairs to the room he knew so well. There, he lit a candle and placed it on the floor near the mattress that had been found and carried in. A few minutes later, the door opened to the sound of rustling silk. A feminine figure stood in the doorway.

"Are you sleeping, Master?"

He recognized Dina's voice.

"I am not sleepy."

"Blow out the candle, and then you might fall asleep."

"I hate the darkness."

"You remain silent. You have not even said a prayer, Messiah."

"Why do you call me that?" he asked curtly.

She entered the room.

"Oh, because that is what everyone is saying. For everyone here you are the Messiah."

"And for you, who am I?"

"Me? I guessed when I first saw you!"

She moved closer and was now no more than two steps away. For a moment he watched the silk dress moving in the semi-darkness and the reflections on the cloth from the flickering candle. Dina's dress shimmered, but he could barely see her face.

"For you, what is the Messiah?" he asked.

Dina's answer was straightforward, and there was no mistaking the sincerity in her voice. She was transparent and true to herself, and her words were calm and convincing:

"For me, the Messiah is the man who thinks first of others."

She paused briefly, and then continued.

"He is the man to whom the Master of the Universe has given the charge of liberating mankind."

"And yet, with that man, you have…"

Dina cut in, her voice supplicating:

"No. Don't say anything! Don't make me upset," she stammered. "It was…it was to save a life, the life of the Messiah…That is what the Eternal would have wished."

David Reubeni got up off the mattress where he was sitting cross-legged and stood in front of the young woman. Candlelight was dancing in Dina's dark eyes and seemed to multiply as in a set of mirrors. Now her face was turned up slightly toward his, and her lips parted. He could feel turmoil rising from his abdomen to the center of his chest, drying his throat and making his temples pound.

He placed his hands on Dina's shoulders. She did not back away. He pulled her to him, hugging her tightly and touching her forehead with his burning lips. The young woman's frail body made no effort to pull away. He could hear the sound of insects, and then a large moth fluttered around the candle, causing the flame to flicker. The couple's shadow danced on the walls.

"*Praise be to You, Eternal our God, who created man in Your image,*" he whispered, "*an image that resembles Your essence and who gave him another being so that…*"

He stopped. He was reciting the marriage blessing and had no right to do so. No, the man who had come to liberate a people had no right to personal happiness. The Messiah was not the spouse of only one being, but of all humanity.

"You are trembling, David," she murmured, using his first name as she had back in the old days when she had allowed herself a moment of supreme happiness.

"So are you…"

As if she hadn't heard, she asked:

"Do you have a fever?"

"Yes," he whispered.

His lips searched out Dina's. How long did they remain like that, standing with their arms around each other there in the semi-darkness? David would never have been able to say for sure. But he was aware that he was experiencing his last human kiss. Suddenly, an overwhelming feeling of how important he was washed over him. That very world of violence, hate, and lust in which his own desires were insignificant, in which he was only a tiny part, that was the world he needed to save. That world, but also Dina's world, in which frail poppies raised their petals from out of grass burned by the sun and the rain, and were always in danger of being trampled on by the soldiers' horses. His arms released their embrace.

"You will be leaving, won't you?" Dina asked.

"Yes."

"With the prophet from Portugal?"

"Perhaps."

The candle's flame flickered one last time in the molten wax and went out.

"Don't leave me," she said in desperation.

"Don't be foolish. You will forget me. You will forget what I once was…"

Suddenly her arms slid down over David's body. In the darkness, her hands clasped her lover's thighs. She could sense him slipping away from her forever.

"I'm afraid," she sighed. "I'm worried. There is a dark foreboding…"

Someone knocked at the door.

"One day," Dina continued, "a fortune-teller told me that…"

They knocked again, more loudly.

"Who is it?" the Messenger asked.

"Joseph," said the voice in the corridor.

David helped Dina back to her feet, kissed her tenderly, and led her by the hand to the door. Joseph Halevy watched without comment as she left the dark room. He waited until she had walked down the corridor and disappeared down the stairs before he spoke.

"Are you unable to sleep, Master?"

In response, the Messenger quoted a psalm:

"He who watches over Israel neither slumbers nor sleeps…"

"May the Eternal turn His face toward you and grant you peace!" said Joseph.

He came into the room while the man from Chabor was lighting another candle, and then he announced that Shlomo Molkho had arrived.

"Where is he?"

"He is downstairs speaking to the Jews."

"What is he telling them?"

"You can surely guess! He is transporting them to the end days… What do you plan to do?"

"Leave for Venice."

Joseph smiled.

"You can never stay long in one place, can you? Do you think that the Doge might be able to…?"

"Perhaps. We have to try. We know now that the pope can do nothing for us."

Someone was coming up the stairs. It was Doctor Zarfatti, and he joined them in the room. He was wearing his long cape with its red hood, and he had a worried look on his face.

"Master," he said, looking at David. "Why are you staying up here? Is there something serious? Some bad news?"

As the Messenger did not answer, he added that Shlomo Molkho was in the house.

"That is what Joseph has just told me. Apparently he wants to see me?"

"Indeed. He has come straight from Sant'Angelo Castle. He reports that the Chevalier de Fründsberg, the infamous leader of the Lutheran lansquenets, came from Germany armed with a golden cord. His horrible weapon was designed to strangle the pope, but God did not allow that to happen. Fründsberg had an attack of apoplexy in Ferrare and will never make it to Rome…"

"I imagine that bringing such news was not the only reason Shlomo Molkho has come…"

"No, of course not. He has come, he says, to follow you, to watch over…"

"Over the Messiah, right?"

"Yes."

"I understand why you find it hard to say the word…"

David Reubeni placed his hand gently on the doctor's shoulder.

"I find it difficult, too," he admitted.

As he started downstairs with the doctor, he motioned to his faithful servant Joseph, adding in a disillusioned voice:

"Since we can't confront history, let us go face destiny…"

The large room on the ground floor was as crowded as it had been two years earlier when the Messenger was leaving for Portugal. With the smoky oil lamps and the smell of perspiration from the people in the room, the air was stifling. However, perched on a stool, Shlomo Molkho, his eyes shining, was haranguing the crowd in his clear, persuasive voice:

"What will those people do who move from slavery to spiritual freedom, from the thickets of shadows into the pure light of the Torah that has given them back their sight? Ah, may the Redeemer and the Savior of the World be praised!"

His blond hair was hanging down over his forehead, and with a toss of his head he threw it back into place. His violet-colored eyes with their strange expression looked out over the crowd and noticed David Reubeni.

"Here he is!" he cried.

And the gathering, without cantor or rabbi, spontaneously began to recite *Ma'ariv*, the evening prayer:

And He, full of mercy, forgives our sins..., Eternal, our God, let us rest in peace and let our King rise up...

Shlomo Molkho spent the night in Doctor Zarfatti's house. Early the next morning, he went to see the man from Chabor. He had not spoken in private with him since their meeting in the pope's apartments.

"The time has come, the hour is near," he said. "The Eternal is with you as He was with Moses. Speak to the people and they will follow you!"

David Reubeni patiently explained to the young man that before inspiring the crowds, they needed to keep trying to convince the temporal powers and their sovereigns that one cannot build an army with lyricism alone.

"You have read, studied, and memorized the Scriptures," he said to Angel Solomon. "Remember Moses' combat with Amalek at Rephidim. Remember how the Eternal—may His name be blessed!—protected and helped Moses. But do not forget that it was Joshua's *army* that went into battle!"

Shlomo Molkho's eyes shone with excitement. The Messenger was talking to him; the Messiah agreed to discuss his plans with him! The Envoy was finally recognizing him as a privileged ally and assistant in his activities.

"Even if we did have an army, like Joshua did," he said tentatively, "we could not begin hostilities without putting the lives of our persecuted brothers in danger…"

"That is true," the man from Chabor replied. "But as you yourself said, do we not have with us the Lord and Master of the Universe, who is also the Lord of Hosts?"

Joseph, who was listening to their conversation, noticed that Shlomo Molkho seemed a little less sure of himself.

"O Master, O my King," he said, "then tell me what I must do."

"We are going to try to persuade the Doge of Venice to help us."

The word "we," including him in the adventure, touched Shlomo Molkho deeply. He immediately declared that he was ready to follow the Envoy wherever he might go.

But Venice was no longer the Venice it had been. Although during the Italian wars the City had been prudent and used its troops parsimoniously and skillfully enough to protect its own wealth and territory, it had however lost a great deal of its former influence. Its military dominance had given way to others who were more powerful, more determined, and more enterprising. The Spanish and Ottoman Empires had taken naval power to a new level in the Mediterranean. Indeed, the Turks had just captured Rhodes. After expelling the Hospitalers, the Knights of Saint John, now they were organizing a blockade and siege, hoping to take Algiers.

And the man from the desert was counting on the Venetians' frustration at their reduced splendor. He hoped to find, in the Senate of the City of Saint Mark as well as in the Council of Ten, serious support for his plans for a Jewish expedition against the Turks in the Holy Land. Anything that weakened the Sublime Gate could only be beneficial to the position of the merchants in Venice the Serenissime. But would he himself, David Reubeni, remain credible enough after the recent difficulties in Portugal for the Doge and the Senate to trust him? Would he not need to provide some guarantee of his power, of his ability to mobilize and conquer? Did he not first need to cause some event, create a memorable shock that would allow the Venetians to begin to dream once more?

He spent the rest of the day pondering such questions, his mind in turmoil. When he talked to Joseph about his concerns, Joseph agreed with him. For the City of the Doges to help them, they would need to impress Venice with some symbolic action.

"Just as we did when we first arrived back in February of 1524," he said. "Do you remember? Our clothing, our banner, and our weapons all were greeted with surprise and turned everyone's attention to us. If it had not been for the plots of that damned Giacobo Mantino, we would have been able to count on the City's support already back then…"

The Messenger listened attentively to what his lieutenant was saying. And then suddenly his face lit up.

"Joseph!" he shouted. "May God bless you!"

Joseph was taken by surprise and stared at his master. David's face was radiant. There was laughter in his eyes. He had not been so happy or so excited for a long time.

"With my masters," the Envoy continued cheerfully, "I certainly learned much. With my peers I learned more. But with my disciples, so much more!"

He embraced his right-hand man like a brother.

"And Shlomo Molkho?" Joseph wondered.

"We cannot allow him to remain alone in Rome. He has to come with us if we are to keep a check on his words and actions…"

Ironically, it was Shlomo Molkho, once he learned of the plans to go to Venice, who asked the practical question.

"And where is the money coming from for this trip?"

He remembered his feeling of helplessness back in Gaza when, without one ducat in his pocket, he had been able to embark for Italy thanks only to the generosity of an Arab merchant he had met by chance.

David Reubeni winked at Joseph, who smiled back at him.

"And what if we were able to plan to help the pope escape to Orvieto?" he suggested.

"Your vision be praised!" exclaimed Angel Solomon. "In exchange, Clement VII will certainly furnish us the means we now lack!"

Three months later, on December 6 of the year 1527 of the Christian calendar, the pope and his cardinals, who had remained locked up in the Sant'Angelo Castle, suddenly disappeared. A few days later they resurfaced in Orvieto. So it was from the new base of his papacy and under the solid protection of his Swiss guards—a much more favorable position, of course—that Clement VII was able to negotiate the conditions of his return to Rome with Charles V.

As for David Reubeni, along with his followers, including Joseph Halevy and Shlomo Molkho of course, they boarded a Venetian ship that raised anchor in the port of Naples on January 8, 1528, that is to say on the 17th day of the month of Shevat in the year 5288 after the creation of the world by the Eternal, blessed be His name. He was not intending to stay in Venice. He was on his way to a more distant destination—the Holy Land.

Chapter fifty-two

Back in Venice

The Prince of Chabor's sudden departure for the Holy Land was a surprise to the Jewish community in Rome, and people talked about it for a long time. Weeks and months passed. Then a year, two years. The total absence of news from the Messenger or from Shlomo Molkho, who had left with him, kept people wondering. As is often the case in such situations, the wildest rumors were circulating.

When the pope returned to Rome, the city's Jews began to assume that his protégés, David Reubeni and the young blond prophet, would also soon reappear. Some people claimed to have seen them in Venice. Others had seen the Messenger and his faithful lieutenant, Joseph Halevy, on a street in Naples. In Rome, old Obadiah da Sforno thought he was the victim of a hallucination. On the Sant'Angelo Bridge he had met a galloping horseman whose silhouette made him think immediately of the man from the desert.

On June 29 of the year 1529 of the Christian calendar, in Barcelona, Clement VII was finally able to come to a peace agreement with Charles V. On that occasion, Catholic dignitaries were the objects of a confusing vision: Among those invited to sign the peace agreements, people were saying, was the Prince of Chabor.

On October 8 of the year 1530, after several weeks of torrential downpours, the Tiber left its bed. The rising waters swept through the city, and the flood destroyed everything in its path. And then people remembered Shlomo Molkho's second prophecy. Messianic fever once more broke out among Jews all over Italy, soon reaching Portugal, the Comtat Venaissin and even Salonika and Constantinople. It seemed evident, even inevitable that the Messiah would soon be arriving, very shortly. But where? And from which port?

It was only two months after the Tiber had flooded, when on December 7, 1530, six years and two months to the day after David Reubeni had first appeared in Italy, the news arrived. Near the Customhouse, where the Dorsoduro begins, a bastard galleon with the name *Cornera* had just been tied up. It was one of those fast ships remodeled by the famous Vettore Fausto, the inventor of the quinquereme. The rumor spread faster than lightning, and the loudest thunder could not have made more noise: The Prince of Chabor was back from the Holy Land! Just as the Portuguese prophet had predicted, and he too had returned along with the Messenger. With them landed an impressive escort made up of more than a hundred men at arms.

Thousands of Venetians, Jews and non-Jews alike, hurried to the quay where the *Cornera* had been tied up and stared in wonder at the warship's masts. The twelve banners representing the twelve tribes of Israel were floating in the breeze.

"The Messiah has come!" For some, that cry was a password. For others, it was a call to assemble. The news took only a few days to spread all over Europe. How could people not believe in the Redeemer's coming when the prophecy predicting it had come true? First Rome was sacked, and then flooded, and finally the Messiah was here! There was dancing on the Piazza del Ghetto Nuovo in Venice, and in Rome, in the Jewish quarters Rigola, Ripa and Sant'Angelo. The event was celebrated as well in the "quarries" of Carpentras and Avignon. When the news was brought to the pope, who two weeks later was to crown Charles v in Bologna, he lit a candle to give thanks to God, for God in His mercy had spared His best children.

And then it was learned that the *Cornera*'s captain was none other than Campiello Pozzo, the same man who had captained the galleon *Alfama* on which David Reubeni had arrived in the City of the Doges six years earlier. For the two ships belonged to the same outfitter, Count Santo Contarini, a member of the Council of Ten, which, under the Doge's authority, governed the little Republic of Venice.

At that moment, Moses de Castellazzo was with the Marquis of Mantua, to whom he had just delivered the collection of illustrations he had drawn and engraved on wood as the noble art lover had requested. As soon as he heard the news, the large, red-haired man said goodbye to the marquis and got on his horse. He was eager to see the man from Chabor once more. He set off at a gallop for Venice.

The Doge of Venice, the Most Serene Andrea Gritti, sent word to Count Santo Contarini that he would like to see the mysterious Jewish prince whom he had not been able to meet during the prince's first stay in Venice. The count immediately invited the man from Chabor and his two advisors, Joseph Halevy and Shlomo Molkho, to move into his palace. The excitement surrounding their arrival had taken on such unexpected proportions that he could not decently let them stay in Captain Pozzo's house, as had been planned at first. The one hundred men who were part of David Reubeni's retinue were able to find food and lodging among those living in the Ghetto.

While the bells of the Campanile, at the entrance to the Grand Canal, were ringing wildly to spread the news, hundreds of boats and gondolas, cutting through the grey waters that smelled of mud and mold, converged near the Customhouse. For his part, in the Ghetto bubbling with excitement, Doctor Giacobo Mantino was quickly calling together the *Va'ad Hakatan*.

The Contarini Palace was absolutely splendid. And inside, it was even more impressive. Walking through the gate with its finely chiseled bronze hammer on Rio Terra San Patergnan, named for the nearby church, one entered an inside courtyard decorated with lovely plants. In the center was a well with its carved stone wall. Under the porticos, light reflected off the weapons and trophies hanging on the walls among a row of statues. To reach the apartment the count had reserved for him, the man from the desert climbed a large spiral staircase attached to the outside wall. The stairs spiraled up in a little tower with fine colonnades. The Contarini were very proud of its unusual construction. The large room David entered had a high ceiling with painted and gold-plated caissons. Through the stained glass windows, the light filtered through pleasantly, playing over the furniture and the floor. David Reubeni's personal effects, and particularly his ebony chest, had been placed in the adjacent room.

"Everything had to be hoisted up by ropes through the window," the count explained. "In fact, every house in Venice has ropes and a pulley attached to the roof."

A white-haired majordomo wearing a grey velvet doublet translated his words into Arabic. The Magnificent Contarini burst into laughter, showing his lovely teeth.

"Just try to imagine your chest being carried up a staircase like that one, Prince!"

And then he started toward the door.

"I'll leave you now. You surely would like to rest."

"No. Just say my prayers."

"I'll see you later, then."

And then suddenly the count turned back.

"Oh, I almost forgot. The Most Serene Andrea Gritti will join us at the dinner I am giving in your honor this evening, Prince. You will be able to speak to him about your plans."

He laughed once again.

"They have not changed, I hope?"

"No."

Santo Contarini's right hand paused for a moment on the hilt of his dagger, hanging from its shoulder-belt in its gilded sheath.

"I've put servants at your disposal, Prince," he added. "As for the prince's friends, Joseph Halevy and Shlomo Molkho, their rooms are on the lower story."

David Reubeni was not displeased. His arrival in Venice had already produced the expected effect. Perhaps even better than expected.

Events were gathering speed. He had not been expecting to meet the man whose support he was seeking on the first evening he was in town. But the Eternal, blessed be His name, had so decided, as if to point out clearly to the man from Chabor that he needed to act quickly so his adversaries would not have time to get organized. He went on with his ritual ablutions and recited the prayer:

Blessed are those who live in Your dwelling!
They can continue to praise You...

After he finished his prayer, Joseph appeared. He had heard that the Doge was coming to dinner.

"I hope the count has not also invited Giacobo Mantino," Joseph said. "I have heard that it was thanks to the Contarini clan that your sworn enemy received the dispensation from having to wear a yellow hat like other Jews."

"Giacobo Mantino—my sworn enemy? In any case, his intelligence makes him a dangerous enemy indeed."

"Do you think that he would dare react to your coming?"

"I believe he has already gone into action. In my opinion, at this very moment the *Va'ad Hakatan* must already be in session. We ought to have alerted our friends Mechulam del Banco and Moses de Castellazzo."

"I have written to them, but I didn't say exactly when we were arriving."

"In politics, our good friend Niccolò Machiavelli would say, it is better to plan for every contingency..."

Joseph smiled:

"But the Messiah has nothing to plan. The Lord can *see for him.*"

His master shrugged his shoulders and opened a window. There were low clouds, but here and there some narrow gaps in the clouds revealed a little blue sky. Suddenly, through one of those gaps, the Messenger saw a strange light with a bluish tint that blinded him for a moment. He squinted. "Could that be the *Shekhina*?" he wondered. "A burst of fire in the shadows? A light that allows one to see and blinds at the same time?" He heard someone speaking behind him. He turned around. Shlomo Molkho was in whispered conversation with Joseph. When the young man saw that David Reubeni was listening, he spoke more loudly:

"I have just been walking on the *documenta*. There are hundreds of people massed in front of the palace. They are waiting to see the Messiah!"

The man from Chabor responded with a quote: *If only they could hear His voice today.*

Shlomo Molkho had not changed. He still looked as young as before, and his blond hair still hung down over his pale forehead. Now, however, like all of the Messenger's servants, he wore the white linen tunic with the Star of David stitched in gold thread. He had kept only two of the attributes of a Portuguese nobleman, a velvet cap with a feather and a sword that hung from an oriental belt inlaid with precious stones. Excitedly, he jumped back into his story about the information he had gathered.

"I also found out that the famous rabbi Elisha Halfon is a strong admirer of the Prince of Chabor. Only a few days ago there was a public controversy, and he and the members of the *Va'ad Hakatan* were on opposite sides concerning the coming of the Messiah. He said very clearly what he thought. And he criticized the *Va'ad Hakatan* for the way it handled the prince's first visit. *The Messiah was in your midst and you did not recognize Him!* That is what he said to them."

"Who told you that?"

"An old bookseller by the name of Elhanan, Elhanan Obadiah Saragossi."

"What else did he tell you?"

"Nothing. He was interrupted by a strange man, a chubby, clean-shaven man who claimed to have been in the Prince of Chabor's service. Now he is working in the Ghetto, in an old Spanish synagogue. He even told me his name…"

"It must be Tobias," Joseph suggested. He had been silent up to then.

"How do you know?" Angel Solomon asked.

"It could only be him. I didn't realize he was still alive."

"He had an accident and lost an eye," Molkho added.

"The Eternal wished it so," David Reubeni concluded.

Then Joseph told the young man what Tobias and his new master, the worrisome Giacobo Mantino, had done.

Shlomo Molkho was obviously shocked by Joseph's story. He could not imagine, he said, that men could be so narrow-minded, so evil, and so spiteful, nor that an educated Jew could be capable of such villainy toward another Jew, going so far as to plot to kill him. But immediately, as if to ask pardon for taking on the right to judge, a right reserved for the Eternal, he quoted from Ezekiel:

"*'Is it my desire,*' said the Eternal, *'that the wicked should die? Would it not be rather that they change their behavior and live?'*"

"But the wicked still have to change," Joseph said. "And that man has already been involved in another plot. He is planning other evil deeds, actions that some say are the province of imbeciles. But they are also within reach of scholars!"

Angel Solomon looked thoughtful.

"And I always thought I knew something about men," he murmured.

"You know God," Joseph replied. "And you have an idea of what man should be if he is created in the image of the Eternal, blessed be His name. But many have departed from that likeness. And besides, if such were not the case, then there would be no need for the Messiah!"

"But here he is! He is right here!" Shlomo Molkho cried.

"Yes," said Joseph. "That is what I was saying. The Messiah is needed when most men have turned away from God..."

David Reubeni smiled. He knew all the twists and turns of the conversations between his two companions. During their journey to the Holy Land, from Jerusalem to Tiberias and from Safed to Joppa, the same discussion took place. And each time there were new arguments and new phrases to spice up their conversation. The various meetings with wise men and rabbis, both anonymous and famous, always set them off again. During the travels that had taken them all the way to the Nile following in the footsteps of Moses, the Messenger had finally become attached to the young Portuguese preacher. His natural spirit, his unbounded imagination, and his phenomenal memory of the holy texts had impressed David. And yet he knew that in politics such qualities can bring one down. But he had no choice. The known world was in turmoil. It was constantly growing and constantly changing. It was opening up to other continents, to America, to Asia. Communication between men and countries was becoming more rapid all the time. Galleons leaving Cadiz on October 21 had been able to round the Cape of Saint Vincent on the 22nd and Finisterre on the 24th, and reach Southampton on the 30th despite heavy seas and high winds. Those same galleons, leaving Southampton and setting sail for the New World, reached America only forty-two days later!

David Reubeni knew that events would leave him little respite. He couldn't waste a day's work if he expected to carry out his dream. He needed to establish a Jewish kingdom in the land of Israel as soon as possible, or his chances of doing so would be compromised for a long time. For the moment, people found his plan appealing. Along with the interests of the European powers, Europe's bad conscience after the massacres and anti-Jewish persecutions in Spain assured him of some support. But how long would that support last? Yes, he needed to move quickly. With Shlomo Molkho at his side, since that was the best way to keep a check on his exuberance. The man from the desert knew the perils of forced marches. By speeding things up, he would be in danger of catching up with calamity. But if he slowed down, it was clear that calamity would catch up with him. And if speed was important, he was fortunate to be able to meet the Doge of Venice that very evening.

The Most Serene Andrea Gritti was quite a powerful person. David Reubeni had been careful to gather as much information about him as he could. The Doge appeared to be a friend of the Jews, and he even spoke Hebrew. However, he was also close to the Turks. Once, during a long stay in Constantinople, he had been jailed for espionage. It was only thanks to his good friend the Vizier Ahmed that he was saved from the stake and then given his freedom. People claimed that he had an excellent reputation among the Ottomans. In such conditions, the man from Chabor realized that it would not be easy to defend a project designed to harm the interests of the Doge's Turkish friends.

Such an important meeting had to be prepared carefully. So David Reubeni left his friends to their customary arguments and retreated to his room alone to reflect. Did not the Venetians say that time spent in reflection always reduced the time needed for action?

Chapter fifty-three

A Dark Plot
on the Grand Canal

Dinner at the Contarini Palace had scarcely commenced when it began to rain. On the narrow *documenta*, passersby were buffeted by gusts of wind, and left Piazza San Marco like pigeons to take shelter under dark porticos. Only one gondola slipped noiselessly along the canal, lit by two lanterns. On board were five men wearing long cloaks, and their faces were hidden behind high collars and under black cocked hats.

Passing under the Rialto Bridge, the gondola turned up Rio San Marcuola, and then, moving toward the northeast, it stopped in Rio del Ghetto Nuovo, near the *Fondamenta* degli Ormesini. Its five occupants climbed out on the quay and started down a tiny street leading to a wooden bridge that resembled the drawbridge of a medieval castle. There they came to a large gate and were stopped by the ducal guard.

"Halt!" a voice called out. "Who goes there?"

One of the men stepped forward:

"His Excellency the Ambassador of His Majesty the King of England," he answered.

"Does he have written permission to enter the Ghetto at such a late hour?"

"Here it is."

The man held up a parchment scroll, and, trying to protect it from the rain with his cloak, he handed it to the captain of the guard. The captain examined it carefully by the light of his lantern.

"Very well," he said. "Do you know the way?"

"Someone should be waiting for us on the other side."

"Fine," the captain grunted, and then he ordered his men to open the gate.

"Do you expect to stay long?" he asked.

"No. Not more than an hour."

"When you come back, knock three times, and we will open up for you."

Beyond the covered passageway of the Sottoporteggio lay the Campo, the Ghetto's large public square. It was empty. Under the Banco Rosso arcades, a corpulent man appeared. He was wearing a large shawl to protect himself from the rain and had a band over his left eye.

"Gentlemen," he whispered, "I've been asked to take you to the honorable Giacobo Mantino."

He led the five men to one of the houses along the Campo. There, they were ushered into an impressive room with windows that looked out over Rio del Ghetto Nuovo. The mysterious delegation had come to see Mantino, the rabbi, rather than Mantino, the doctor. When he appeared, they greeted him, removing their cloaks and showing their faces. Three of them, Venetians, were young, and the president of the *Va'ad* wasn't sure if they were the advisors or the bodyguards of the two older men. Mantino was well acquainted with the English ambassador to Venice, the churchman Jean-Baptiste de Casal, for he had met him on various occasions at official receptions in the ducal palace. He was the man who had organized this meeting upon the request of Richard Croke, special envoy from King Henry VIII.

Giacobo Mantino could guess the motive behind the clandestine visit. Everyone knew that the venerable Richard Croke, instead of devoting himself to his holy ministry in Cambridge as usual, had been traveling all over Europe for weeks looking for scholars, Jews included, who as specialists of the Holy Book might perhaps find some biblical justification allowing the King of England to divorce. The affair was causing shock waves all over Europe and had already started serious quarrels in both the political and religious realms. King Henry VIII had married Catherine of Aragon, his brother's widow, and she had not given him an heir. For that reason (and also for his pleasure, it was whispered), he had asked the pope to grant a divorce so that he could be free to marry his mistress Anne Boleyn. According to Christian customs, it was out of the question for a king to divorce, and Clement VII agreed. Catherine of Aragon was Charles V's aunt, and in his anger he strongly supported the Church's principled position.

"You are one of the great scholars of our day," Richard Croke said to Giacobo Mantino, smoothing his long gray hair with the flat of his wrinkled hand. "You were educated at the famous university in Padua, where you studied along with Copernicus. Your translation of the commentary by Averroes on Aristotle's *Metaphysics* has had a profound influence on me."

Richard Croke leaned down over a table stacked with books and manuscripts.

"Therefore, I asked permission from His Majesty Henry VIII to come consult you about a problem that could affect the very future of England," he went on. "The pope realizes that those who know the Holy Scriptures best can be found among the Jews. Your opinion about the interpretation of the Law has great influence in the Vatican. But, as you know, the text Clement VII's advisors use to justify their refusal to authorize the divorce of the British king from Catherine of Aragon is in Deuteronomy. The Biblical text enjoins any man whose brother has died to marry his widow."

Giacobo Mantino had been standing near the fireplace. He walked over to the table and sat down on a rustic bench facing the English dignitary. Color rose in his full face, clean-shaven as usual. His washed-out little eyes stared at Croke.

"The visit of a man such as you flatters me," he said. "However, I don't think I can help you." Ambassador Jean-Baptiste de Casal had been drying his damp clothes by the fireplace where a lively fire was crackling. He, too, came over to the table.

"But my dear Mantino, you know better than anyone that the law in Deuteronomy, on which the Church bases its refusal to grant the King of England a divorce, has never been applied since the Temple was destroyed."

The comment struck home. The president of the *Va'ad* shifted on the bench, and the bench screeched. Beneath his beret, a few tufts of brown hair mixed with gray were caught by the wind as the door opened. Tobias came in, bringing glasses and a carafe of Venetian wine.

Giacobo did not reply to the ambassador's words. He filled the glasses, then raised his own.

"To the king's health!" he said dully.

It was only after he had taken a sip of wine that he asked, feigning cheerfulness, "And what, my honorable visitors, is the basis for holy legislation in this matter?"

"The words in Leviticus xviii, verse 16," Richard Croke replied.

"And what are they, in your opinion?"

"I quote: 'Thou shalt not uncover the nakedness of your brother's wife. It is your brother's nakedness.'"

"And what does that mean?"

"That His Majesty the King of England does not have the right to remain married to his brother's widow, and that he never should have been allowed to marry her."

"And what then becomes of the law of Deuteronomy?" the president of the *Va'ad* asked weakly.

"It is to be considered a corollary of the chapter in Numbers that deals with inheritance."

"But whoever could have told you that?" Giacobo Mantino shrieked, and in his irritation his cheeks got redder still.

"The honorable Elisha Halfon, a famous rabbi," said Ambassador Jean-Baptiste de Casal.

This time the doctor paled. His blood rushed from his head, leaving his face ashen. He dragged himself to his feet and began to walk nervously back and forth. It was obvious that he was furious. The three young Venetians, standing in the middle of the room, moved toward the door so he would be freer to move around.

"Elisha Halfon, you say?" he hissed, stopping suddenly by the fireplace. "Elisha Halfon, that irresponsible man!"

Giving himself free rein, he began to shout:

"Halfon is ambitious. He's a mad man who can't be trusted! He has a twisted mind, for he is a partisan of David Reubeni, that imposter who claims to be the Envoy from some non-existent Jewish kingdom."

Richard Croke got to his feet and studied Mantino carefully.

"David Reubeni? The man King Frances I praised so highly to our own King Henry VIII?"

Throwing his cloak around him, he started immediately toward the exit without even saying good-bye. Glancing at Mantino, he turned to the ambassador.

"It's time to leave!" he said. "I sense that the honorable scholar can be of no help to us."

Even when he found himself alone once more, the president of the *Va'ad* was unable to relax. Here was that adventurer David Reubeni again! Ever since the Envoy from that so-called Kingdom of Chabor had first set foot in Venice, he had been in Giacobo Mantino's way. Reubeni was mixed up in political intrigues that could only be harmful to the Jewish Diaspora!

He summoned Tobias. He asked him to clear away the carafe and glasses and then to get his friend Azari ben Salomon Dayena, rabbi of Sabionetta, whom he knew was in town.

"At this time of night? He is surely asleep," Tobias said.

"Well, wake him up! It is urgent to protect ourselves against the danger hanging over the Jewish community! Men like Elisha Halfon, Shlomo Molkho, and David Reubeni have always been the cause of all our tragedies!"

For the rabbi/doctor, there was no doubt that the Jewish community would be running a grave danger if it got involved in a debate that was none of its business. If, in order to repudiate his legitimate wife, Henry VIII broke relations between Rome and the Church in his country, then all European politics would be changed, and along with the political change would come a shift in the balance of power. But that would not change the condition of the Jews. On the other hand, if the Jews intervened in the quarrel in support of one side or the other, then they would suffer new persecutions no matter who the winner was.

Indeed, all the debate did was increase Giacobo Mantino's hatred for the Prince of Chabor. It seemed to him that his duty, as it had been the first time, was to limit the danger the Prince of Chabor represented. It was now urgent to put a complete halt to the imposter's career. He knew that Rabbi Dayena shared his views on the matter. Dayena, guided by Tobias, joined him three quarters of an hour later. They spent the night in conversation, making careful plans. They decided that the best thing to do about Rabbi Halfon would be to denounce him to the Holy See or perhaps directly to the Inquisition as a false theologian who supported Henry VIII's ungodly plans. And as for David Reubeni and Shlomo Molkho, the plotters resolved to hire some thugs from Murano who could do away with the two. Dayena agreed to recruit the thugs himself. By dawn, their plans were set. This time their machinations would work. After his colleague from Sabionetta left, Giacobo Mantino, a man of great faith and upright virtue, gave thanks to the Eternal, blessed be His name, for having inspired their plans.

Meanwhile, in the brightly-lit Contarini Palace, the dinner went on. After a variety of salads and vegetables, the servants brought game that they sprinkled with alcohol to flame. And then came venison, hares, and young rabbits, and all the meats were superbly flavored with spices such as turmeric and cardamom, along with verjuice. The man from the desert was always surprised by such arrays of food, and this time he soon gave up even trying to count the dishes, many of which he did not even try. Laughter and conversation echoed throughout the dining room, along with music from orchestras playing nearby. It was practically impossible for him to speak with the Most Serene Andrea Gritti, though they were seated side by side, until after dessert.

The Doge of Venice was indeed, as people said in political circles, an unusually handsome man. He carried the weight of his sixty-eight years elegantly, and as he began his conversation with the Prince of Chabor, he said he was thankful never to have been sick in his entire life. When the subject turned to more serious things, he asserted that David Reubeni's project seemed right.

"The Jewish people do deserve their own country," he stated. "But…"

"But what?" the Messenger asked, watching him carefully.

"As you know, Prince," the Doge said, "the territory that you claim is currently in Turkish hands. And the Turks are not about to give it up. Furthermore, Soleiman's ambitions do not appear to be limited to the Aegean. Soon, and this is no secret for anyone, the Sublime Gate will show interest in the Adriatic."

"Exactly," the man from Chabor noted. "If the Sublime Gate were weakened by a war in the Near East, that could only be beneficial to Venice."

Andrea Gritti gave a sigh.

"But Venice, alas, does not have the means to support such an endeavor."

"What we need," David Reubeni went on, "is a place, a place where we could build up and train a Jewish army. In Portugal we had the help of more than twelve thousand volunteers."

"Venice, Prince, is nothing but a lagoon…"

"That is true. But your city does have other territories, including Lombardy, the Friuli, and Venetia."

"Indeed. But where will you get the necessary funds?"

"We will collect funds throughout the Diaspora."

"And how about weapons?"

"We will purchase weapons with the money we collect."

Andrea Gritti gave a loud laugh.

"You have an answer for everything! But Venice cannot offer the slightest military training camp, particularly in Lombardy, without the prior agreement of Charles v. Does the Prince know that since the Treaty of Worms, signed in 1523, our good city has had to pay considerable amounts to the empire every year just to be able to keep our territories?"

The Doge emptied his glass, wiped his mustache, and placed his long pale fingers over David's hand.

"My dear Prince," he said, "you must realize that there are only two European powers: the empire and Turkey. King Frances i, who apparently admires you greatly, was not wrong to sign a pact with Soleiman…"

He laughed once more.

"He could also have concluded an agreement with Charles v," he added. "But it is often easier to get along with foreigners than with those who are nearby."

Before saying good-bye to the man from the desert, Andrea Gritti advised him to go see the emperor.

"As for me," he said, "as much as my feeble means allow, I will support you. But I ask you to see Charles v. Today in Europe, he is the only one who can give you what you are asking for, the only one who can allow you to take back the land of Israel. Go talk to him in your inimitable style. Promise him that he will be able to ride triumphantly into the Holy City. The idea will captivate him. But be careful. Unlike prophets, grand visionaries always make sure something will happen before predicting it."

Chapter fifty-four

Murder on the Lagoon

Davd Reubeni awoke with a start. Standing in the doorway were Shlomo Molkho and Joseph Halevy with scowls on their faces. He guessed immediately that their interminable quarrel had broken out once more. He looked over at them questioningly.

"Master, Master!" Angel Solomon cried, more feverishly than ever. "I've just come from the Ghetto. The Jews there are waiting for you to appear; the people are asking for you! I have seen all those poor, miserable, hopeless people, all with those horrible saffron-colored hats they have to wear. They want to see you face to face! They need to reaffirm their trust in our Holy Torah! Only words from the Messiah…"

Joseph impatiently cut in.

"Shlomo does not understand anything, Master, nothing at all! The Jews will wait patiently until they see you. As long as you are living with Gentiles and can speak directly to the Most Serene Doge, they will wait. And they will follow you even if you send word from here in the Contarini Palace…"

"Many more of them will follow you if you speak to them from the Campo in the Ghetto Nuovo!" Shlomo Molkho objected.

Joseph scowled.

"No, no! If David appears in the Ghetto, the community will break into at least two camps…"

The Angel pushed Joseph aside so he could be closer to the man from Chabor.

"I know Jews better than Joseph!" he claimed. "I've brushed shoulders with them in Salonika, in Avignon, and in the Holy Land."

And he looked deeply into the Messenger's eyes, quoting a psalm:

Your justice is like the mountains of God,
Your judgments are like a great abyss,
The Eternal gives you strength…

"I certainly hope," Joseph said, sighing in exasperation, "that the Eternal will give strength to our master, my friend, for…"

He paused for a moment and then went on.

"For I have learned, I who 'do not know the Jews,' that a new plot is developing on the Grand Canal. Last night a strange delegation went to see Giacobo Mantino in the Ghetto. It was that deceitful Tobias who showed them the way."

Shlomo Molkho stepped back in surprise.

"Where did you hear all that?" he asked.

"In the Ghetto."

"But I too was in the Ghetto!"

"How could you have heard anything?" Joseph sniggered. "You are always caught up in your own dreams. Whereas I am working on a very concrete plan!"

David Reubeni intervened, raising his hand to call for calm.

"We will come back to this subject after our morning prayer."

But once they had prayed, a majordomo announced Moses de Castellazzo and Mechulam del Banco. Both were eager to see the Messenger again. He welcomed them into his apartment on the second floor of the Contarini Palace. The artist was the first to come in. When he saw David, he let out a joyous cry, tossed down his beret, and rushed over to him. His red hair was flying everywhere and his face was flushed as he embraced the man from Chabor. The old banker

Shimon ben Asher Mechulam del Banco needed more time to climb the stairs and appeared a few moments later. Leaning on his cane, he stopped three paces from David and burst into tears.

"I've been waiting so long, my son!" he said, his voice cracking. "May God bless you!"

And then he drew himself up straight and pointed to Angel Solomon.

"That is him, is it not? The young preacher, the famous Shlomo Molkho?"

And tears once again began to course down his wrinkled cheeks. He wiped them away, and then turned back toward the Messenger.

"Your friend, the prophet, is astounding. Everything he predicted has come true."

"Except the Messiah's arrival!" said Moses de Castellazzo.

Shlomo Molkho looked over at David.

"There he is!" he said firmly. "There he is, standing right in front of you! As he did six years ago, when you, my friends, did not recognize him!"

The old banker's compliments had no doubt touched the young man from Portugal. His cheeks were flushed. And his eyes began to sparkle violet. To everyone's surprise, suddenly he raised his arms as if to ask the Heavens to bear witness, and his voice became that of a street preacher.

"Blessed is the man who will live to see Daniel's visions become reality for the Turkish Kingdom! Blessed is the man who will see that unclean kingdom collapse, inspired by a mad prophet!"

And then, still agitated, he began to pace up and down in the room. Finally, he stopped near Mechulam del Banco.

"'*Weighed*' and '*divided*.' Such words finally reveal their true meaning," he explained. "'*You have been weighed*.' Those are the words that will ring in the Turk's ears, for the end of his time will have come."

As he talked, he started pacing again. Soon he was standing directly in front of Joseph, and his words became a prophecy.

"Those two fateful words, whose numerical value is nine hundred and thirty-six, signify that the fall of Islam will take place when that false religion has lasted nine hundred and thirty-six years."

"So that will be soon," Mechulam del Banco whispered, awed by the predication he had just heard.

An uneasy silence settled over the room. It was broken by Joseph, more than a little disgusted with the way Angel Solomon was acting, and he took it upon himself to bring everyone back to reality.

"While we wait for that great event, and to prepare ourselves appropriately, we first need to confront current threats," he said.

And he turned toward the artist and the banker.

"Are you aware that at this very moment, in the Ghetto, a plot is being hatched against the Messenger, against our David?"

Moses de Castellazzo gave a start.

"Mantino again?"

Joseph gave them the details of the information he had gathered in the Campo market.

"So who was part of that mysterious delegation?"

"I don't know. I did learn, however, that after the visitors left, Tobias the traitor went to see the rabbi of Sabionetta, Azari ben Salomon Dayena, who lives these days in the guest house belonging to the Scuola Grande Tedesca."

"Rabbi Dayena?" asked Mechulam del Banco in surprise. "I know him. He is not an evil man. I will go immediately to talk to him."

"Our friend is right," added Moses de Castellazzo. "We need more information."

He thought for a moment.

"Let's go to the Ghetto," he said. "I will convene the members of the *Va'ad* in my studio."

Shlomo Molkho was ecstatic.

"That is what I said! That's what I suggested earlier! The Ghetto is expecting our Master! The Jews are awaiting the Messiah!"

"Fine," said Joseph, a frown on his face. "It'll be good to meet the members of the *Va'ad* in Moses's studio and find out more about the situation. But I prefer that David not come with us. That is just being prudent. He is safer here, within the walls of the Contarini Palace. Especially since our men are already in the Ghetto and would not be able to escort him to there."

"Have you forgotten this proverb of our King Solomon?" asked Shlomo Molkho. He looked inspired, and immediately rushed into quoting the proverb:

If your enemy is hungry, give him bread to eat. If he is thirsty, give him water to drink. Thus you will be heaping coals of fire on his head.

"And you will be careful not to touch his head," Joseph muttered. But the decision had already been made. David Reubeni had been quiet until then, but now he spoke.

"Since we need to find out what is being planned and what the Jews know about it, let us go to the Ghetto," he said decisively.

The Magnificent Santo Contarini, once he was informed, put two gondolas upholstered with red velvet at David's disposal, as well as two armed bodyguards. The Prince of Chabor climbed into one of the gondolas along with Joseph and the two bodyguards. Mechulam del Banco got into the second with Shlomo Molkho. Moses de Castellazzo started toward the Ghetto on foot so he could alert David's men that he was coming. He also had to invite the members of the *Va'ad* to the meeting in his studio.

The rain that had been falling since the night before finally stopped. A sea breeze scattered the few remaining clouds. A cold sun reflected off the dark water and the gilded palaces along the canal sparkled in the sunlight. Shlomo Molkho's gondola moved more rapidly because it was carrying fewer people. Soon it disappeared around the bend near the Rialto Bridge. Near the landing stage, sitting on the bow of a fishing boat painted with the Torcello coat of arms, a flutist was playing a sad tune. Suddenly, as they reached the Ca' d'Oro, several rows of gondolas appeared from San Mercuola, and, as if they were part of a parade, moved forward side by side toward the Messenger's gondola, filling up the entire canal. In the middle of the flotilla was a larger boat, mounted with a purple canopy and decorated with wreaths of flowers. Several orchestras were playing on the nearby gondolas.

"A wedding!" the gondolier cried joyfully. He was standing in the rear, using his pole to navigate.

The closer the procession drew, the more nervous Joseph became.

"It looks like they are trying to run us down!" he said.

And indeed, the line of gondolas was bearing down on them. David Reubeni could already make out the happy faces and hear people laughing and calling out to one another. Some members of the joyful party were wearing masks, for Carnival was not far off. At the last moment, just before the Messenger's gondola would have struck the wall of bows and oars, it opened to let them through, and the passengers greeted them warmly. For a moment, Joseph forgot his concerns. He stood up to greet the new couple. They answered as if they were speaking to long-lost friends. There was a drum roll, and then a second, third, and fourth, followed by trumpets. Everyone was laughing and clapping. Joseph waved a few more times and then dropped slowly back down to his padded seat.

Everything was over in seconds. The joyous group was already far behind them. David Reubeni reached over toward his faithful servant and placed his hand lovingly on Joseph's shoulder.

"Joy has no family," he said, "but sadness has plenty of family members."

When there was no reaction, he looked more closely at Joseph. Joseph's face was expressionless, and his mouth and eyes were open wide. A red spot was widening in the middle of his tunic, and blood was dripping down his leg. When the Messenger touched his hand, it did not move. David cried out in horror and distress, and it was a terrible scream.

Contarini's guards hurried to reach Joseph. The gondola almost tipped over.

"A dagger!" one of them shouted when he had examined Joseph. "Someone threw a dagger!" he said, and the man from the desert could see the bloody weapon.

Joseph Halevy was barely breathing. He tried to say a few words, but he was suffocating. David Reubeni took Joseph in his arms.

"Leave Venice," the wounded man whispered, his voice barely audible.

He was able to add a few words, but they were more like groans and difficult to understand.

"They will kill you. That is their plan. You are upsetting too many people. May the Eternal…"

He lost consciousness. His head fell back on David's shoulder before he could finish the sentence.

A huge crowd was waiting for the Messenger outside Moses de Castellazzo's house. When his men, all dressed in their white tunics, saw him coming, they organized an honor guard to help him through the crowd. People began to shout: "Long live the Messiah!" And then suddenly things got quiet, and they began to whisper worriedly when they saw the Venetian guards bearing Joseph's motionless body.

"He is hurt!" someone shouted.

"Who is it?" someone else asked.

"One of the Messenger's servants…"

"What happened to him?"

"Look at his clothing! It's covered with blood!"

"May God protect him!"

"Blessed be the Messenger!"

"Long live the Messiah!" someone shouted from down some side street.

Everybody was talking at once, asking questions, giving answers, making comments. And then suddenly all was quiet. The news had quickly run through the Ghetto: By a miracle, the Prince of Chabor had escaped an assassination attempt. But Joseph Halevy, his right-hand man, the longtime friend who had accompanied him all the way from the depths of Arabia, had been killed in his place.

After a moment of surprise and consternation, people began to speak again.

"Who could have done such a thing?"

"How did it happen?"

First they were angry, and then anger turned to fear.

"Which Christians did it?"

Shlomo Molkho had reached Moses de Castellazzo's house well before the man from the desert, and he now rushed out of the house weeping. In the surrounding streets, in the Campo, the crowd kept getting larger. The guards carrying Joseph had stopped outside the artist's house, uncertain what to do. David Reubeni had said nothing up until then, and then ordered two of his men to go inside and bring out a table to set up in the street. That is where they put Joseph's body. The Messenger walked over and tenderly caressed his friend's curly hair, and then, as if some invisible force were lifting him, he stood up straight. He suddenly seemed much more imposing. He dominated the crowd, and appeared even taller than before. However, his sharp features remained expressionless, and he did not move. But his mica-colored eyes had a strange glow.

"The *Shekhina* has descended upon him," Shlomo Molkho whispered.

People heard the words, and they were massed throughout the Ghetto and beyond the arcades of the Campo. David Reubeni raised his right hand as if he were swearing a solemn oath and began to recite the *Kaddish*, the prayer of the dead.

May the name of the Eternal be glorified throughout the earth which one day He will renew when He raises the dead, calling them to eternal life. Then He will rebuild the city of Jerusalem and re-establish His temple in its midst. And then idolatry will be banished from the earth, and the worship of the one true God will be restored. The Most Holy One, blessed be His name, will reign in all His glory and majesty throughout your lifetime and throughout the lifetime of all the house of Israel, soon, and in the near future. And you shall say 'Amen!'

Thousands of voices answered:

"Amen!"

Later, many witnesses to the scene confirmed that the crowd shouted "Amen" so loudly that the entire Canareggio, where the Ghetto Nuovo was located, shook.

Chapter fifty-five

Goodbye to Venice

Joseph Halevy was buried in San Nicolo del Lido, the Jewish cemetery located between the sea and the lagoon, facing Venice. There was a large crowd at his funeral, as if the entire Ghetto and many Jews from all over Italy had agreed to gather.

The Doge Andrea Gritti was much affected by the murder, and he asked Ramuzio, his chief of police, to take charge of the investigation himself. There were all sorts of contradictory rumors circulating among the people in Canareggio, and the Ghetto remained in a state of effervescence. Moses de Castellazzo demanded that the *Va'ad* undertake its own investigation, but of course its president refused. During a stormy meeting, Giacobo Mantino managed to have the *Va'ad* agree to the idea that it should leave the investigation to the Doge's official police. In his opinion, the Jewish community in Venice should never appear to be questioning Ramuzio's investigations, or they might be setting themselves up for trouble. His arguments were once again based on fear that there could be reprisals against the Jews, and that was typical of the doctor's thinking. What he did not talk about was that in the name of his politics he was planning other shadowy killings of more Jews.

Moses de Castellazzo and Mechulam del Banco went to the Contarini Palace on several occasions. The Messenger remained closed up in the palace, and they were losing hope of having him meet the members of the *Va'ad*. Shlomo Molkho, too, tried in vain to get in to talk to him. But until the *shloshim*, the thirty days of mourning were over, the man from Chabor would remain alone.

David Reubeni knew the price of solitude. But solitude helped reinforce memories and strengthen one's convictions. The Prince of Chabor owed it to Joseph to devote one whole month of reflection and silence to him. He remembered their interminable walks in the desert, during which they discussed everything and considered all possible failures. Curiously, they had never talked about death. It was as if they believed, without ever daring to say so, that their enterprise would accelerate time so that, according to Isaiah's prophecy, death would be *destroyed forever, and the Lord God would wipe the tears from every face.*

Shut away in his apartment in the Contarini Palace and living on bread and water, the Messenger soon lost track of time. What day followed the day before? How many hours of daylight had there been since Joseph's death? His spirit was as taut as a cord from his pain, and he was near the breaking point. And yet, outside, beyond his meditation that cut him off from the world, a new year was already appearing on the horizon: the year 1531 of the Christian calendar. He realized how much he would miss his servant. Joseph had always been the only one ready to help and protect him from danger. He felt that his companion had been right, in his last breath, to advise him to leave Venice. Hatreds in the lagoons of Venice were persistent. In the stagnant waters of the City of the Doges, history had often drowned, and hope along with it. In this city of slow death and devastating passions that had always marked individual destinies, was there even a place for a powerful, collective dream to take shape?

Suddenly, outside his windows, he could hear music. It was as if reality, with its charms but also with its duties and its demands, was timidly coming back into his room. It was the dawn of a new day. Day was beginning to break, and life was returning. He realized that he was now eager for life to come back and that the time for mourning was past. A letter arrived, handed to him directly by Count Contarini, signaling the return to action. The letter was addressed to *The Honorable David Reubeni, Prince of Chabor.* A woman had given it to Captain Campiello Pozzo as his ship was anchored in the port of Ancona. The Messenger opened it. It was from Dona Benvenida Abravanel.

The man from the desert thought back to the passage of the *Zohar* that she had quoted and commented on three years earlier in Rome: *The Holy One—blessed be His name—plants souls here on earth. If they take root, so much the better! If not, He pulls them out. He pulls them out several times if necessary and keeps transplanting them until they do take root...*

He thought briefly about Joseph, who had been unable to take root anywhere, and began to read the letter.

Dona Benvenida Abravanel expressed her concern for the Messenger's safety. She had learned of the attack, and it had brought many tears. She encouraged the prince to lose none of his determination and to pursue his goal. The people of Israel, she wrote, must return to the land of Israel, according to the will of the Eternal. She also informed the Envoy of Chabor that she would be going to Milan on business and that she would be staying in Marignanoo, a few leagues outside the city on the Lambro River, in an inn kept by Joseph de Casalmaggiore. After meetings with bankers in Milan, she was expecting to swing by Venice where she hoped to see David. She had recently completed several profitable transactions, and she was proposing to place the profits at the disposal of the future Jewish army. There was no metal so hard, no situation so bad, she said, that gold could not improve.

David Reubeni reread the letter and reflected for a moment. The Jews, at least a large number of them, were ready to follow him. The money was available. Other bankers in addition to Dona Benvenida Abravanel were disposed to provide funds. So weapons could be purchased. On the other hand, he still had no place where he could assemble and train his troops. And the fleet of ships that would be needed to transport them to the Holy Land were still lacking. For the moment, the pope could do nothing for him, nor could King Joao iii of Portugal. As for Frances i, his growing relationship with the Sublime Gate would prevent him from supporting a plan to retake Israel. And had not the Doge Andrea Gritti just told David a month before that Venice, despite its real sympathy for the Jewish cause, did not have the means to help him? So it seemed that the suggestion the Doge had made was appropriate. David needed to go see Charles v and try to interest him in his plans.

At his request, the count's majordomo brought him a detailed map of Europe. He studied it carefully and noticed that one road from Venice to Ratisbon, where the emperor's fortress was located, would allow him to go through Milan.

Someone knocked at the door. It was Shlomo Molkho. He had just learned that the Magnificent Contarini, for the first time since Joseph had been killed, had seen the Messenger. He, too, wanted to talk to his hero. When David called out for him to enter, he hurried in excitedly. His violet eyes glimmered with all the fever of his earlier days. When the Messenger said that he intended to visit the Doge, he repeated once more the way he saw things.

"Stop begging for help from kings and other powerful people!" he said. "There is only one King. Will you continue to act like Jonah, you the Prince of Chabor, and refuse to carry God's message to the people of Nineveh? Announce who you are! Millions of Jews will follow you!"

David did not immediately reply to his vehement exhortation.

"Perhaps you are right," he said finally. "But there is, however, one very powerful person in Europe who might still be able to help us. And upon reflection, it is clear that it would be in his own interest to do so."

"Do you mean Charles v?"

"Yes, Charles v."

"It will be done as you say, Master," said the young man resignedly. And then he pulled himself together proudly and added, "I will go with you, of course!"

"Of course," the man from the desert whispered. "Of course..."

Angel Solomon was overjoyed to hear his words. Now he was finally a part of the destiny of the man he venerated. They would remain united forever in history: The Messiah and his prophet!

The Messenger folded up the map he had been studying before his Portuguese associate had come in. He stood up.

"Tomorrow," he announced, "I will see the Doge. The following day we will leave for Ratisbon."

He paused for a second.

"The first stage will be Milan," he added. "I will leave before you with a small escort. You will catch up with us in Marignanoo with the bulk of the troops. I will be waiting in an inn kept by a Jew, Joseph Casalmaggiore..."

Shlomo Molkho was upset.

"I will not let you leave alone! The Eternal has willed that I watch over you..."

"You will watch over me, I promise. But only after we leave Marignanoo."

And then he added in a tone that brooked no discussion: "Go tell our men. Horses will need to be readied in Mestre on the mainland, and supplies must be purchased. Don't forget to display our banners. Ask two of our men to come here tomorrow. They must be here early. And have them bring my Chabor banner."

The next morning, dressed in his ceremonial tunic, David Reubeni took a seat in a gondola with the Magnificent Santo Contarini and several armed guards. His two servants were in a gondola ahead of them. They, too, had several guards (the count wanted to be especially careful) and were flying the flag decorated with Hebrew characters. They reached the San Marco docks without incident, and as people gawked and the bells of the Campanile rang out their welcome, they entered the Doge's palace.

Andrea Gritti kept his promises. At his request, Charles v's ambassador had come in person so that the man from Chabor could meet him. In the ambassador's presence, the Doge handed David Reubeni a letter for the emperor. In the letter, he pointed out to Charles v how advantageous it would be for him to receive the Envoy from Chabor with all the honors due a Jewish prince and to give his plans favorable consideration. After which, the Most Serene Doge presented a bag full of gold coins to David.

"For you and your men," he said. "This should be enough to cover your trip as far as the gates of Ratisbon. Please accept my modest gift. Thus is my wish."

As the Messenger thanked him, the Doge added:

"This is only a small contribution by the Republic of Venice to the rightful cause of rebuilding the Kingdom of Israel and a Jewish Jerusalem."

Later that afternoon, David Reubeni received Moses de Castellazzo and Mechulam del Banco, but once more he refused to meet the *Va'ad*.

"Of what use is it to have the fear of God as your compass if your conscience does not man the tiller?" he explained before embracing each of them in turn.

That evening, he dined with Count Santo Contarini, to whom he gave an oil lamp dating from the days of Herod. It was a gift he himself had received when he was last in Palestine.

"I would also like to entrust something else to you," he said to Contarini. "Something valuable that I cannot take along with me over the Alps."

"What is it?" the count asked.

"My ebony chest and its contents: my personal effects…"

"You may leave it all here," said Santo Contarini. "We will take good care of it."

"In the chest there is one particular document which I would not like to see fall into the wrong hands—my journal. In it, I have been writing all my thoughts and everything related to my mission ever since I left Chabor."

"Relax, my friend," Contarini answered, placing his hand on the Messenger's wrist. "Nothing will leave my house until you have come back."

"Before I leave tomorrow morning, I will give you the chest."

"As you wish, Prince, as you wish…"

Once dinner was over, the Messenger retired to his apartment, where he spent the rest of the night rereading and revising his journal. As dawn came, he put the manuscript back in the chest and said the morning prayer:

…Standing before Your grandeur, I am filled with alarm because Your eyes know every thought in my heart. What can the heart and the tongue do? What can my strength and the spirit within me do? But since You are pleased with the songs of mortal men, I shall praise You as long as my divine soul remains within me.

Escorted by fifteen well-armed men, David Reubeni rode all morning long. Only the Chabor banner—the one decorated with Hebrew characters embroidered with gold thread on white silk—waved at the head of the cortege, and they bypassed Mantua rather than riding through the city. Not far from the market in San Bernadetto Po, they had to stop. Some Jews had recognized the Messenger and were soliciting his blessing.

Through them the man from the desert learned about the legend, according to which Mantua was chosen by the poet Manto as the place to exercise her art and die. The story had a strange effect on David, and he was secretly glad that they had not ridden through the city.

The cavalcade continued on to Soncino, where their weary horses were exchanged for fresh ones. The little town, surrounded by red brick walls and towers, was nestled in a green valley. The innkeeper who welcomed the little group answered to the name of Samuel. He explained that he was a relative of those Jewish printers who, in 1483, had published the first Hebrew Bible with a Latin translation right there in Soncino.

"It is said that Luther made use of it for his German translation," Samuel whispered into the Messenger's ear.

After the sack of Rome, it was dangerous to pronounce the name of the little Wittenberg monk aloud in a Catholic area.

They continued their trip, and finally, as night was falling, David and his men finally reached Marignanoo. The fortified town clung to a rocky spur that looked out over a river. The innkeeper that

Dona Benvenida had mentioned in her letter was the grandson of another Joseph de Casalmaggiore. His grandfather had managed to get authorization to keep an inn thanks to the famous condottiere Francesco Sforza, who stopped in Marignanoo and who enjoyed the kosher food served in the inn, known then as now as a place where Jewish merchants liked to stay. There was no Jewish community in Milan, and so there was no synagogue or lodging to be found there. Hence, the success of the Casalmaggiore family.

As soon as he entered the inn, David Reubeni caught sight of the fateful Dona Benvenida Abravanel seated under the trellis in the courtyard. She seemed less attractive in the candlelight than he remembered. For a moment, he regretted having hurried so to meet her. But when he sat down beside her, he noticed once again her perfectly oval-shaped face and the fine network of tiny wrinkles around her eyes that seemed to make them larger. He found the same intelligent, dizzying look in her eyes. As his own eyes met hers, he was stirred in the same way he had been when they met in Rome. And to think, when he left Dina, that he was impervious to desire!

And indeed, the six years that had passed had in no way altered the woman's features or figure. Her waist was still just as thin, her wrists just as delicate, her breasts just as full. Once again, he felt awkward and clumsy in the presence of a cultivated society woman who was so accustomed to big cities and the ways of the nobility. Either out of awkwardness or the feeling that it was unseemly to show how pleased they were to see each other, they began talking immediately about current events. In just a few sentences, Dona Benvenida summed up the situation in Europe following the sack of Rome and the treaty between the Turks and the French. Her conclusions were the same as the Messenger's, as he confirmed with a smile. She too smiled, delighted that they saw things the same way, and she placed her long, thin fingers over David's hand. Her fingers were trembling.

Dona Benvenida's room was on the second floor, near his own. As soon as things had gotten quiet in the inn, she came to his room. The moon's pale, bluish light filled the room. She was seated on the bed, and he in a chair. Their conversation went on for hours. He spoke to her about Portugal, Diego Pires becoming Shlomo Molkho, the months spent in pirate hands on the desert island, the trip to Avignon, and the meeting with Frances i. He described in detail his last meeting with the pope and the return to Venice, and his voice saddened as he told her about the murder of his faithful lieutenant Joseph. Talking did him good, though he usually expressed himself through his silence or only brief words. She listened attentively, at times leaning forward and taking his hands to show how interested and compassionate she was.

Finally he grew silent, and she began to speak. Her voice was spellbinding, and from the first words had a soothing effect on him. He could sense all the nuances in her thought. Benvenida's perspicacity seemed to have multiplied. She talked not about herself but rather about him, about his plans, about Jerusalem and the Holy Land. And then, suddenly, she brought up her long nights of waiting, the myriad dreams that had come to her along with the desire to see him again, to be close to him just as she was now. Then, sorry to have spoken so freely, she abruptly stood up, and when she did, she tripped. David reached out to steady her. His hand slipped from Benvenida's elbow to her breast, and he could feel her heart beating like a dove in his hand. Benvenida's big dark eyes grew wide. The Messenger opened his hand and let the dove fly away.

"That is not right," she whispered. But she did not move, and her motionless body contradicted her words.

Only once before in his life had the man from Chabor been so overwhelmed by feeling. And that was in the Arabian Desert, when after a week of walking, dying of thirst, he saw water reflecting in the blinding noonday sun. Gently, quietly, motionlessly, he told her the story.

"And what did you do?" she asked, her voice choking.

"I dove in."

He realized that his own voice seemed to be diving deeply as well, taking on unfamiliar sonority. And afterward, he did not remember any of those words they spoke during the blessed hours when Benvenida's body abandoned itself to his. Where could those sentences he did not recall have come from?

She left him early in the morning and went back to her own room. After praying *Shaharith*, when he saw her again in the dining room of the inn, she was more beautiful than ever, but she had grown distant. Before leaving her, he had to promise to stop in Rosheim to ask Rabbi Joseph Josselmann for advice. Josselmann was a friend, a man she trusted, and he was among Charles V's advisors. She knew that he had a keen mind and that he understood the emperor's complex personality.

Shlomo Molkho arrived around noon with the rest of David's escorts, approximately eighty men. The twelve banners waving in the wind, representing the twelve tribes of Israel, impressed the people in Marignanoo greatly. When the man from Chabor said goodbye to the innkeeper and his family, many people came to see them off.

"Was I the reward the Prince expected?" asked Dona Benvenida Abravanel quietly when the Messenger came to say goodbye.

"God is my witness that I never deserved such a reward!" he answered in a whisper as the crowd shouted.

"But is that what you had wished?"

He had to make an effort not to wrap his arms around her. He cleared his throat.

"Do you have any doubts?"

"Will you be back?"

"A man in love is like algae on the surface of still water; even if you push it aside, it always comes back."

"Living, I hope!" she added, not really sure why.

David Reubeni's face brightened into a broad smile.

"Where I come from, in Chabor, people say that in order to truly love a living man, one must love him as if he were going to die the next day."

Chapter fifty-six

Meeting Ashkenazi Jews

Crossing the Alps was difficult. During that month of January, 1531, it rained all day, and the nights were freezing. It quickly became obvious that David Reubeni's men were suffering from the cold. Their tunics of fine white wool could simply not protect them against such weather. In Locarno, the Messenger purchased heavy greatcoats with flared sleeves for each man. He even offered fifty ducats to anyone wanting to go back home. Only ten accepted his offer and turned back.

Shlomo Molkho followed in silence. He kept a pensive look on his face and followed orders without complaining. Often, he passed orders along himself, making sure they were understood, as if he were playing the role that Joseph had played before. When they reached Basel in a snowstorm, however, he displayed his ill humor. It was Sabbath eve, and he wanted to go to the synagogue before nightfall. The escort was to be lodged in a hotel near the Rhine. Bélé de Fribourg, a money changer by trade, to whom Dona Benvenida Abravanel had recommended David, welcomed Shlomo Molkho and the Messenger into his own home. He led them to an old synagogue between Rue de l'Horloge and the bridge linking the two parts of the city. After the service, David's men could go directly to their inn, not far away.

The temple was constructed of wood. In its center, a huge stove was emitting white smoke. Perhaps a hundred of the faithful, wearing fur hats, were swaying to the rhythm of the songs. The unexpected arrival of a group of armed men speaking a foreign tongue provoked near panic. At first, the Jews in Basel had taken the Messenger's escort for followers of one of the mystical sects whose militia were terrorizing Switzerland. When Bélé relieved their concerns and explained that it was the Prince of Chabor, excitement rose to a fever pitch. Everyone wanted to get near David, look him in the eye, and touch his hands or garments.

Angel Solomon, somewhat forgotten in one corner of the synagogue, decided it was time to climb to the *bimah*, the raised platform from which the officiating priest, facing the scrolls of the Torah, leads the prayers, so he could address the audience.

"My brothers of the house of Israel," he said, "do you not know that our strength, the divine *Shekhina*, remains in exile because of your sins?"

Facing the dumbfounded Basel Jews, he lifted the scrolls of the Torah above his head and began to move as if in a strange dance. Then he abruptly stopped, seeming to stare deeply into each individual. He looked up to the heavens and exclaimed:

"O, Torah! The light that illuminates everything! So many springs, so many streams, rivers, and seas emanate from You and flow everywhere! Everything exists thanks to You! In the Heavens and on Earth, You are the source of light! Torah! Torah!…"

He lay the scrolls back down on the stand and pointed his finger at the crowd.

"Repent, Jews! Admit your sins! Prepare yourselves to be worthy to receive the Messiah in obedience to the voice of the Lord!"

The disapproving murmurs that had accompanied his initial words now turned to protest.

"Who are you to tell us what to do?" a voice shouted from the back.

"What arrogance!" someone else called out.

As the anger grew, Rabbi Samuel de Worms, an old man dressed in a black caftan, stepped up to the *bimah*. He raised his hand for silence and turned to Shlomo Molkho, still standing on the platform beside him.

"You call for us to repent and expiate our sins before the Redemption. But we have lost the power to do so. For we are staggering beneath our suffering like drunken men, unable to walk in a straight line. Our wise men have told us that Redemption will *come before* the expiation. They knew that poverty, when it is crushing, turns men away from the Creator's face!"

"Well said!" someone shouted.

A murmur of approval ran through the audience. Heads began to sway to the same rhythm as before. Just like the dunes in the desert when the wind attacks, thought the Envoy of Chabor.

"You cannot be upset with them," Bélé de Fribourg explained to Shlomo Molkho and the Messenger, when, after the service, they were having dinner at his house. "The Jews here are miserable," he went on. "And they are sensitive to the danger that false hopes can bring—the danger that they might become even more miserable."

The moneylender's house was quite modest, just four rooms—one of which was his office—for himself, his wife, and their three children. A smoky, potbellied ceramic stove in the dining room provided heat for the house as well as a place where Bélé's wife had prepared food the evening before.

Many of the Jews who had been in the synagogue came to join them after dinner. They wanted to show the Prince of Chabor their support for his efforts to create a Jewish kingdom in the land of Israel. And they did not want him to leave Basel misunderstanding their intentions.

"In Basel," said a young man with a thin, curly beard, "we have seen every form of fanaticism. The most extreme Calvinism rushed through Basel like a torrent. Likewise, the Anabaptist terror. Here in Basel, a man named Hoffman calling himself a prophet proclaimed the city of Strasbourg as the "New Jerusalem" and announced the arrival of one hundred twenty-four exterminating horsemen who, with Elijah and Enoch, would destroy the Lord's enemies with fire and sword!... And then, Luther. How many deaths there have been in the name of the Reformation!"

Then Rabbi Samuel de Worms, who had also come to greet the visitors, turned to Shlomo Molkho.

"I know, young man, that your past predictions have been confirmed by facts. But please believe my long experience. It is easier to predict destruction than liberation. Misfortune arrives without being summoned. It flows downhill like water. But happiness, on the other hand, especially when everyone is longing for it, demands will, faith, and persistence before it can be attained, if ever it can be!"

Angel Solomon shifted nervously. He adjusted the feathered hat that had slipped down over his blond hair. He was about to respond when David Reubeni, silent until then, intervened, as if to challenge his young friend's words with reality.

"When God saw that Israel's soul was sick unto death, He wrapped it in the mordant sheets of poverty and misery. But, He also spread the sleep of forgetfulness so that Israel could bear its pain. However, for fear that their spirit might completely die, He awakens it from time to time by the false hope of a Messiah, and then he allows it to go back to sleep until the night is spent and the true Messiah has appeared. That is why the eyes of the wise are sometimes blind..."

Bélé de Fribourg whistled in admiration.

Rabbi Samuel de Worms raised his arms toward the soot-blackened rafters.

"May the Eternal bless those who are capable of such wisdom!" he murmured. Then, surprisingly agile for a man his age, he abruptly went over to the Messenger, bowed down, and kissed his hand.

The next day, David Reubeni and his escort started up the highway along the Rhine. The Messenger was surprised to find no other Jewish communities. In Uffheim, halfway between Basel and Mulhouse, not far from Sierentz, some peasants, who were clearly hostile but intimidated by the harquebuses and swords, showed the Prince of Chabor a farmhouse located at the edge of the village.

"A house belonging to Jews? There it is. There is not another one until you reach Munster, not far from Colmar!"

Amschel, a cattle merchant, dropped to his knees when he saw David Reubeni riding up with one of his men holding the banner embroidered with Hebrew characters. He covered his face with his calloused hands and burst into tears.

"*Barukh haba*," he stammered, wiping his tears. "Welcome to my humble abode. Welcome to the Jewish Prince!"

And then he got back to his feet.

"It has been a long time since we've seen free Jews! Such a long time…"

He hurried off to call his family. They had taken David's group for a horde of brigands and were hiding in one of the outbuildings at the back of the courtyard.

"Jews have been expelled from most Alsatian cities," Amschel's brother explained. He was a young, dark-haired man built like a bull. "So they have moved on to Lorraine or to Switzerland. In Strasbourg, where we take our animals on market day, every evening the cathedral bells remind us that Jews are forbidden to remain in the city overnight."

"And how about Josselmann von Rosheim?" the Messenger asked. He was beginning to regret that he had promised Dona Benvenida to go out of his way to meet Josselmann.

"Oh," said Amschel respectfully, "Joseph, the son of Gershom, has indeed done well for himself! First he was simply the *parnass* of the Haguenau Jews, and then he became the representative of all the Jewish communities in the Holy Empire. Charles v receives him frequently. But the prince will no doubt smile when I tell him that in all of Alsace there are no more than three hundred Jewish families."

David Reubeni and his men spent the night at Amschel's farm. Animals were slaughtered, and the Envoy of Chabor insisted on paying for them, but the farmer gave them bread, wine, and fowl in addition to other meats. A meal for a hundred was improvised, prepared by Zlata, Amschel's wife, with the help of the entire family and the Messenger's men. When night came, they all managed to find places to sleep, some in the kitchen, some in the barn, and some on straw in the stables.

The next day the sun returned, reflecting brightly on the snow and ice that had accumulated during the night.

"Take care, Prince," said Amschel as they said their goodbyes. "Watch out for brigands, for there are many in these parts. And then, too, Jews are often associated with the Devil. So for some Christians, including the brigands, killing Jews is considered to be a good deed."

Amschel was right. Near Habscheim, not far from Mulhouse on their way to Ratisbon, David Reubeni came to a barricade. There were carts blocking the highway as if there had been an accident. Standing on another old cart, a peasant waved them forward. Instinctively, the man from the desert sensed a trap. He gave several rapid-fire orders. Quickly his men spread out, prepared their harquebuses, and aimed. They fired the first salvo. The man standing on the cart dropped. They could hear shooting from behind the barricade. A band of men surged out of the nearby forest.

"Fire!" the Messenger ordered again.

The harquebusiers pounded their attackers with lead and forced them to withdraw. Followed by fifty of his horsemen, the man from Chabor galloped after them, saber raised. The bandits were taken by surprise and fled, seeking refuge in the underbrush. The victory would have been complete if Saul de Fez, who had followed David from Portugal, had not been shot in the leg at the last moment. The wound was painful. In Habscheim, they were able to find a doctor who could treat him and calm his pain. The skirmish allowed the Messenger's men to capture several carts, one of which was filled with food. It would be enough to feed them at least as far as Rosheim, and perhaps all the way to Ratisbon. The brigands, because of their ill-conceived attack, had themselves been robbed. And in any case, a band of brigands as fearsome as Armleder's band had been routed. For the people living in the region, that was a formidable task. Even though the Jews were inspired by the Kabbalah, a satanic work surely guided by the Devil, as people around there said, they had nonetheless gone into battle with dangerous vermin and had rid the country of them. From that point on, all along the road leading to Rosheim, the peasants and merchants whom David and his men met greeted them with respect and doffed their hats when they rode by. Only Rabbi Josselmann did not seem especially impressed.

"The most brilliant victory," he noted, "is only the glow of a fire."

Rabbi Joseph, the son of Gershom, known as Josselmann von Rosheim, was a little man with a white beard, and he wore a long, black greatcoat. He was lively and affable, and he knew how to be considerate of others. He radiated intelligence and perspicacity. Josselmann received David Reubeni with great kindness and invited him, along with Shlomo Molkho, to stay with him for Sabbath.

"Do you know, Prince, why *Leviticus* uses the plural, saying 'Observe the Sabbaths'?"

"No," the man from the desert admitted.

"The plural is related to the Sabbath of On High and the Sabbath here on earth, both of which become one."

"That is what I said in Basel," cried Angel Solomon. "But the Jews wouldn't listen to me!"

"Oh," said the rabbi, and his eyes displayed amusement beneath his white eyebrows. "They surely believed in a plural Sabbath, but not in the Messiah's coming!"

Shlomo Molkho had a response on the tip of his tongue, then thought better of it.

"They did, however, believe that it is necessary to take back the land of Israel," noted the Messenger. Then he explained his plans and his reasons for going to see the emperor.

Josselmann von Rosheim listened carefully, then reflected for a moment. When he broke his silence, he spoke frankly.

"Prince, I will not mince words. I am telling you frankly not to go to Ratisbon."

"But the Emperor has been told that I am coming! He is expecting me," David objected.

"As you know," said the rabbi, "I am well acquainted with Charles v. He is impetuous, unpredictable, and deceitful. He is not to be trusted. He could be dangerous, and he is capable of anything!"

The Messenger argued and asked for details, but Josselmann was not to be swayed.

"Even if he promises his support," he said forcefully, "you cannot fully trust him!"

The man from Chabor could not ignore Josselmann's advice. The look in the rabbi's blue eyes was persuasive, for they emanated goodness and kindness.

Josselmann made a suggestion.

"Why do you insist on getting Christendom's help?" he asked. "Why not go meet Soleiman? Through him, Islam controls the Holy Land. It might be more judicious to negotiate with Islam. Believe me when I tell you about Charles v. You might obtain more from the Sublime Gate than from the Holy Roman Empire." ·

And with a smile, he added:

"You know better than anyone else, Prince, that one's word given under a tent in the desert is always respected. Whereas mutual trust proclaimed in a fortress is most often shamelessly disregarded!"

David Reubeni remained deep in thought. The idea proposed by the old rabbi echoed certain comments made by the Doge in Venice and also by Frances I, and it began to work its way into his mind. He was about to begin discussing the idea with Josselmann when Shlomo Molkho, silent up until then, spoke sharply.

"The Envoy of God should never fear a monarch!" he cried. "The honorable Rabbi Josselmann is hypnotized by a king who is only human, and he has lost sight of the one true King who is right here and who is protected by the hand of the Eternal! Does not the rabbi realize how abundant divine goodness is, and that God reserves it for those who fear Him?"

The old man pretended to ignore the Angel's comment as well as his vehemence. He spoke to the man from the desert, repeating that there was no reason to hurry to see Charles v.

"As I have said, Prince, the most brilliant victory is only the glow from a fire. And this I would add: The purest fire is no equal to God's glory. You must be careful that the fire of retaking Israel does not destroy Jerusalem. What victory would there be if you restored the Jewish people to a field of ruins? And even more, what triumph is there to be hoped for in the dubious company of the master of the Holy Empire?"

David Reubeni remained in thought. The argument with Shlomo Molkho, which the rabbi had skillfully avoided, would have little to do with his fate. In fact, he had just come to a decision. He would go meet Soleiman if he failed to convince Charles v to support him against the Sublime Gate. The Most Serene Andrea Gritti, Doge of Venice, had already sent word to the emperor that David was coming, and Charles v was expecting the Messenger. Since the Eternal, blessed be His name, had helped him, the Envoy of Chabor, to get this far, he had no right not to respect His will and carry on. So he would go on to Ratisbon, in spite of Josselmann's fears and objections. The next morning, when he was ready to set out, the old rabbi clasped him tightly in his arms.

"May God protect you, my son!" he said, his voice breaking with emotion. "May His holy light guide you, and may my suppositions be wrong! But do not forget: A conversation with Soleiman, even a harsh conversation, is perhaps worth more than a war supported by Charles v."

When the Messenger started off that morning, he did not know that Giacobo Mantino had learned about his journey and sent the following letter to Charles v by a series of rapid couriers who rode day and night:

Your Majesty,

In the name of the Jewish community of Venice represented by its assembly, the *Va'ad Hakatan*, of which I am the head, it is my duty to warn you about the dangerous activities of the imposter David Reubeni and his damned associate, the false theologian and apostate Shlomo Molkho. The plan that these adventurers will propose to you is absurd, even if it does seem to contain some attractive features. In truth, the real goal of these deceitful men has nothing to do with taking back the land of Israel. Their true enterprise is to bring back to Judaism those people who used to be Jews but have become Catholics, as well as to encourage other Christians to abjure their faith and choose the faith of Moses. As a Jew who wishes to maintain harmony and cohesion between our two traditions, Judaism and Christianity, I cannot stand by and see such deleterious and reprehensible maneuvers gain a foothold in the minds of princes. I beg you, Sire: Do not allow yourself to be fooled by the vain prestige of a so-called "Judeo-Christian pact" which they will propose to you. You will recognize the truth of what I say by this sign: At the moment they feel is opportune, the intriguer and his prophet of doom will suggest that you give up the religion of Jesus and accept the religion of Moses. That will be inevitable, because in my opinion, their goal is to conquer Europe, not Judea.

You see, Majesty, in my legitimate concern for maintaining unity and good relations between our peoples and for avoiding terrible misunderstandings, I am taking some risks myself. The sign that I have just given you will allow you to verify the truth of my words. If that does not happen, if I am wrong, then I accept, Sire, to be considered a madman and to be removed from my duties at the head of the *Va'ad Hakatan*. If the sign appears, as I believe it will, then I will leave it up to you and your justice to punish those two individuals as is appropriate. It is of the utmost importance that they be prevented from carrying out their dangerous plans, thus freeing our peoples from the perils and confusion that would otherwise await them.

May the Eternal bless His Majesty the Emperor of the Holy Roman Empire.

His faithful servant,
Rabbi Giacobo Mantino,
president of the *Va'ad Hakatan* in Venice

Charles v found the denunciatory letter repugnant. He had heard a great deal about the Envoy of Chabor, and was not displeased to counter Soleiman's expansionist plans in Europe. In fact, he was eagerly awaiting the arrival of David Reubeni and Molkho and was predisposed to look favorably on their plans. When they did reach Ratisbon three days later, he gave a lavish reception, welcoming them with all the respect due to high-ranking visitors.

Chapter fifty-seven

Charles v's Acts of Kindness

T he Emperor was unable to see his guest the day he arrived as he had initially planned. A sudden attack of the gout that had been torturing him for years prevented him from doing so. He had requisitioned the loveliest inn in Ratisbon for David Reubeni and his men, *Zum Goldenen Kreutz* (The Golden Cross), located near the *Rathaus*. The day before the Jewish delegation arrived, a lansquenet officer made the mistake of reciting some verses of a popular song to his men: *Von grossen Juden Ich sagen will / Die Schad dem Land tun in der Still* ("I wish to denounce the powerful Jews / Who from the shadows are ruining the country"). He was immediately arrested by the imperial guard, taken down into the depths of the *Reichstag*, to the *Fragestatt*, the interrogation room, and was hanged the very same day.

The city's austerity, the majestic weight of its Gothic buildings, the monumental bridge with its arches and fortified tower, and the Danube carrying along chunks of ice that could be heard grinding against each other beneath low, grey clouds were sufficient to amplify the heavy anxiety that had been eating away at the Messenger ever since his conversation with Rabbi Josselmann von Rosheim. Looking out through his window at the somber facades that closed off the horizon, he felt totally alone. And it was not that deliberate solitude he had sought after Joseph's death, but rather something forcing itself upon him. It seemed to move at its own pace, and it seemed to be relegating him to a place outside society, apart from others. A feeling of that kind was totally opposite to what a man of action normally felt, and it made him fear the worst. But what could the worst be? He thought of a proverb from Chabor: "It is better to be in a country where the stones know you than in a country where the people know you." The memory brought a smile to his face.

As for Shlomo Molkho, he had humbly withdrawn back into his role as the prince's advisor, and he said not a word.

Two days later, they were received in the room where Charles v normally gathered with his friends, across from the official room on the first floor of the Reichstag. The emperor's broad smile, though it displayed his yellowed teeth, also illuminated his large sad eyes with an almost childlike joy. He seemed pleased to meet the Jewish prince. Accompanied by several military advisors whom he introduced one by one to David Reubeni, he was dressed in the Spanish style, simply, wearing a black velvet doublet embellished with fur. When everyone had been seated in the wide brocaded armchairs and the interpreter was standing behind the Emperor, he suddenly pulled out a letter. He spoke to David Reubeni.

"This is a missive from one of your friends," he said with a smile. "A certain Giacobo Mantino, from Venice. There are some Jews, Prince, who do not wish you well!"

Charles v burst out laughing. His thin beard bobbed along as he laughed. When he had finished, the Messenger began to speak.

"The only reward for a good action, Sire, is to have accomplished it."

And then, after the interpreter had translated, he added:

"The Eternal is my witness, Majesty, that my only objective is to free my people. If I succeed, the people will forget me. If I fail, they will curse me!"

To the surprise of his advisors, the Emperor struggled to his feet and walked over toward David Reubeni.

"Speaking of rewards, Prince, you have touched my heart. Here, look at my hands. They have initiated and carried out so many grand and noble things, and they have handled weapons so well. And yet, today they do not have enough strength left to open a simple letter! Those are the fruits I have harvested for having acquired this grandiose title, so full of vanity, of Grand Captain and All-Powerful Emperor! Some reward, isn't it?"

There followed an interesting and fruitful conversation. Charles v and his advisors seemed charmed by the man from the desert. Shlomo Molkho, who had remained in the background ever since Rabbi Josselmann had scolded him, seemed overcome with happiness as he listened to the man he so venerated.

"If we needed to sketch the current political scene in Europe, what would it look like, Sire?" asked David Reubeni. "It would be quite dark, alas! Germany is torn by religious dissension. Once again, the Turk is attacking in Austria and has nearly reached your own lands. Frances I, now his ally, is taking advantage of the respite the Peace of Cambrai has given him to plot against you along with the rebellious Lutheran princes of the Schmalkalde League. Henry VIII of England has married Anne Boleyn in spite of the pope's opposition and thumbs his nose at excommunication. And the Mediterranean is at the mercy of Barbarossa, a pirate who threatens all our coasts! I see only reasons for worry, and none for celebration. And I imagine that it is the same for Your Majesty."

"Your imagination, Prince, has not led you astray," Charles v conceded. "And each of the issues you have brought up could call for a thousand comments..."

"Or one vigorous action, capable of reuniting the European powers and orienting them all toward a common goal! And the Holy Roman Empire could itself take the lead," replied the Messenger.

"Are you talking about a modern crusade, Prince?"

"That is not the right word, Sire. But it would indeed require standing firm against the Sublime Gate and Islam's expansion. In fact,

I am simply proposing to mobilize Europe to help me create and support a Jewish army. If that army were to attack the Turks in the land of Israel, that would be enough to force Soleiman to leave Austria, for example. Reinforcements from the south, the cavalry from Chabor, led by my brother the king, would force the Turks to keep most of their troops in the Orient. And that would allow Your Majesty to regain control of a Europe that has been far too splintered..."

Discussions continued for hours. The bold plan of the man from the desert had to be taken seriously, and its strategic interest was obvious. For several days, the Reichstag in Ratisbon buzzed excitedly. Travelers were consulted, as well as spies, generals, and prophets. They studied maps. Finally, on large scrolls, they wrote out the text of an agreement. The scribes included every detail. It was a pact in which Charles v committed to arming European Jews. In addition, the document stated that Prince David of Chabor was to become the commander-in-chief of the navy and army that would engage battle with Soleiman. According to the terms of the contract, the Emperor was not required to participate with his own troops, but he reserved the possibility, should it be appropriate, of coming to lend a hand to the prince and his brother, the King of Chabor.

And the solemn moment arrived. After obligingly allowing David Reubeni to sign first, Charles v was holding the quill, ready to sign the agreement. It would be the culmination of all the efforts undertaken by the man from the desert since he had reached European soil, more than seven years before. His strategy and his political views had been accepted completely. This success would open the door to other successes. From now on he would have the means to start toward Jerusalem! He had just signed the parchment. Charles v had picked up the quill. With a genuine smile on his face, he laid it back down. Gracefully, with both hands, he donned his black fur hat, as if it were a crown. And then, in three slow, distinct, calculated movements, he picked the quill back up, dipped it in the inkwell, and finally signed.

And then the unthinkable happened. Shlomo Molkho, unable to contain his exaltation, took the floor. His visionary lyricism made its inevitable mark, the mark of fate.

"The Emperor of Europe has joined the Envoy from God!" he proclaimed. "The Emperor of Europe is returning to the true faith. Through the King, through David, he is returning to Moses! Long live Charles V in the splendor of his Sabbath!"

Thus, by putting his signature on this military agreement, Charles V had apparently signed his adherence to Judaism! Mantino's perfidious but intelligent prediction had been confirmed.

For a moment, David Reubeni was unable to speak, but then he shouted:

"That is crazy!"

But already Charles V's face had turned crimson. And the Emperor of the Holy Empire flew into a horrible rage.

Shlomo Molkho, through his ill-thought extremism, had fallen into the trap the man from Chabor had been trying to avoid all along. And with him he was dragging along the person he was describing as an Envoy from God!

Rabbi Josselmann's view that the Emperor was impetuous and untrustworthy was also confirmed. Charles V tore up the parchment, tossed the scraps into the air, and without even listening to David Reubeni who was trying to rectify Molkho's words, he called his guards.

"Take them down to the *Fragestatt* and put them in irons," he ordered. "I'll deal with them tomorrow myself."

"And his men?"

"Shoot them."

"Sire!" cried David Reubeni, pulling away from the lansquenets and taking a step toward Charles V. "Sire, remember that a king's greatness is also judged by how generous he is!"

The Emperor turned toward him. His anger evaporated as quickly as it had come upon him. In his final analysis, he liked the man of Chabor, with his shining eyes and his sharp, straightforward features. His guest was standing before him, svelte and powerful, looking imposing with a Star of David embroidered on the front of his linen tunic, and he was not the kind of man to back down in adversity. "We could have done great things together," the Emperor thought. "But does an emperor have the right to change his mind so quickly?"

The man from the desert noticed Charles v's hesitation. That encouraged him to launch into a vigorous defense of his men.

"These young men, Sire, have harmed no one. They have followed me because I paid them. Does that justify their death?"

The king realized that his advisors were waiting. He turned to the head guard.

"Send them back where they came from!"

And he turned his ugly chin toward the Messenger.

"Let it not be said that to my knowledge and with my consent violence has been done unjustly to anyone!" he grumbled.

The next day, Charles v was unable to get out of bed, brought down by another attack of gout. By the day after, his suffering had lessened somewhat, but he still didn't feel like going to face the Envoy of Chabor. The look in his guest's eyes would be too direct, too deep, and too forthright. The emperor regretted what had taken place, because upon reflection, he realized that the Jewish prince's plan did seem judicious and realistic. Furthermore, he was impressed when David Reubeni intervened on behalf of his men. Those acts of generosity and courage so typical of outdoor men had always been especially striking to him, a sedentary man who ruminated over his decisions in the shadows of his fortresses.

But to his mind the Messenger had nonetheless committed a serious error, accepting an advisor like Shlomo Molkho. Charles v often liked to say that when folly was done, it was always because advice had been accepted. He hated visionaries. He had been forced to come to terms with Luther, to listen to him rage, and to accept his imprecations and filthy insults against Catholics and Jews. Luther's offenses were so serious that even Erasmus and Melanchthon, two of the Wittenberg monk's best friends, were appalled. The only reason Charles v had put up with such infamy was that the leader of the Reformation enjoyed the support of forces that counted in the empire. Led by the Elector Johann Frederick of Saxe and the Landgrave Philip of Hesse, those forces represented large cities like Württemberg, Augsburg, Strasbourg, Ulm, and Konstanz. In the face of such power, the dignity of a king could accept seeking compromises that would be necessary to hold the empire together. But without losing face, how could Charles v have accepted those kabbalistic attacks made by a young Portuguese apostate?

Now that the two men were in prison in the Reichstag, it would be his responsibility to determine their fate. He pondered the question and decided…to decide nothing at all for the moment. At that stage in his life, he did not want to burden his conscience.

Two days later, he left for Italy. The first stage of his journey would take him to Mantua. Long before, he had promised the Marquis Federico di Gonzaga that he would like to associate him more closely to the empire's future, to visit his city. He took the two prisoners with him, and when he learned that a Holy Office of the Inquisition had been set up in Isabelle d'Este's city, he decided on a whim to place the question before the court. In truth, he was happy to play Pontius Pilate and pass the responsibility of decision on to someone else. Pope Clement VII respected Shlomo Molkho and had lent his support to the Prince of Chabor's plans. So it would be up to the pope to find a way to help them!

It so happened that at that very moment the Superior of the Dominican order, Paolo Constabile, and the general commissioner of the Catholic Inquisition, Thoma Zobbio, were asking prelates to undertake a witch hunt and pursue heretics, "using all authority and power available to them." One of the prelates so charged, Francesco Bobbo, a man who was reserved but conscious of his responsibilities, had just been named Inquisitor in Mantua. The two prisoners given over to him by the imperial guard took on enormous importance, for it was the first heresy case he was called upon to deal with. Even though the charges against the two men were not very substantial, there was, however, an accusatory letter to the Emperor from the president of the *Va'ad Hakatan* in Venice, as well as a note, signed by Charles v, confirming the accusations mentioned in the letter. Yet, the feelings raised all over Europe when people heard that David Reubeni and Shlomo Molkho had been arrested were so high that Francesco Bobbo needed to be especially careful in his investigations and prudent in his decisions.

The King of France was the first to call for the Pope's clemency. He had just invited a rabbi to Paris as he had promised the Prince of Chabor. An Ashkenazi grammarian, Elisha Levita would be teaching Hebrew at the Collège des Lecteurs Royaux, which had just opened. In fact, the Messenger knew Elisha Levita since he had met him back in Rome at Cardinal Egidio di Viterbo's. Frances I, believing that the prince's misfortune in Ratisbon had been partly due to his own relationship to David, was very insistent with the pontiff. He wanted to help David Reubeni, and if necessary he was willing to lay down a substantial financial guarantee.

When Dona Benvenida Abravanel heard the news that David Reubeni had been arrested and that he was in a dungeon in Mantua, she flew into a violent rage, broke a valuable Etruscan vase, and wept for hours. Later, once she had calmed down, she sent for Abramo Luzzato, her steward. When he appeared, with a dark patch over his left eye and wearing a broad-rimmed hat, Dona Benvenida was watching the sunset. The terrace behind her house looked out over the city and an incomparable panorama. To the left there was Vesuvius, and to the right she could see the Isle of Capri.

"So much beauty for nothing," she whispered as if to herself. And then she quoted Isaiah for Abramo Luzzato: *"Beauty is an ephemeral flower."* Finally, she got to the subject that was bothering her. "Are you aware of what's happening?"

"To the Prince of Chabor? Yes, Signora."

"Is Giulio here in Naples?"

"Yes, Signora. I saw him only this morning in the port. All the brigands in the city were there."

"Send for him!"

Abramo Luzzato half-closed his one good eye.

"Does the signora wish to help the prince escape?"

"Yes."

"That is more dangerous than trying to inspect a cargo ship in the port of Naples!" her steward said.

"I know."

"And it might cost an exorbitant amount…"

"I will pay!"

Meanwhile, Doctor Joseph Zarfatti and Rabbi Obadiah da Sforno were on their way to the Vatican to deliver a petition of support for David Reubeni, Prince of Chabor. The petition was the first of its kind. One hundred important people were beseeching the leader of Christendom, in the name of Christ's mercy, to intercede on behalf of the Messenger, for he had come from Chabor as a friend, and his advisor Shlomo Molkho. Among the signatories were Michelangelo, who remembered fondly the Jewish Prince posing for his famous *Moses*, Ariosto, Raphael, and even Titian, who was busy at that very moment doing a portrait of Charles v. The Venetian painter, who normally did not like to get involved in politics, had not hesitated supporting David Reubeni as a favor to his longtime friend Moses de Castellazzo.

However, Clement vii's situation was far from comfortable. He was quite frank with Cardinal Egidio di Viterbo, who had come to the Vatican specifically to discuss the problem. The sovereign pontiff had been strongly opposed to opening a Court of the Inquisition in Portugal, because it would have been set up exclusively for Jews. But in Italy…

"I yield to your clairvoyance, my dear Egidio," the pope said when the cardinal came to his apartments, which had been redone since the ravages of May, 1527.

The pope was wearing his red hat and his white robe with the garnet hood. It was clear that he found it difficult to stand on his feet.

"I have permitted some Inquisition offices to be set up in order to combat heresies that are infecting the Church," he sighed, collapsing into his armchair. "But I have also promised to respect the independence of the justice system. How could I, without going back on my word, intervene in this procedure that affects our friends?"

The cardinal's strong face was grave. His eyes grew dark:

"But, Your Holiness," he said, his voice subdued, "we cannot allow the Prince of Chabor and young Molkho to be burned at the stake!"

"I know, I know!"

Clement vii was nearly shouting, as if he were trying to silence his conscience. Then he paused briefly and smiled through his wide mustache.

"The prince is not at risk," he continued. "He is a Jew, a foreigner, and he is loyal to his own faith. Therefore, he is not subject to the Inquisition's jurisprudence."

"Unless it can be shown that he converted or tried to convert Marranos or Christians to Judaism. There will no doubt be an investigation about that in Portugal."

"I'm not sure what to think," the pope said. "But do you know Francisco Bobbo, the Inquisitor of Mantua?"

"No, I do not. But I could perhaps speak about our friends to the general commissioner of the Catholic Inquisition and request that he free them…"

"Thoma Zobbio? He is as stubborn as a mule! He would demand a written order…"

"And His Holiness, of course…" the cardinal went on.

"…can never allow such a document to circulate," said the pope despondently.

The two men grew quiet. Clement VII was the first one to speak.

"What makes the question even more complex is that Shlomo Molkho, whom we love, is clearly apostate. He has renounced the Christian faith in which he was raised. For that reason, it would be perfectly legal for any inquisitor to send him to the stake!"

"And so?"

"So," said the pope, a crafty look in his eyes, "since David Reubeni is not in danger for the moment, we shall first save Shlomo."

Chapter fifty-eight

In the Claws
of the Inquisition

I n the dungeon in Ratisbon, and then throughout their horrible journey to Mantua, chained up in the same cage like vulgar bandits and guarded by armed soldiers, David Reubeni and Shlomo Molkho had not exchanged a single word or even looked at each other. The young man from Portugal, his eyes half-closed, was continually in prayer. The Messenger, though he did not deprive himself of recourse to prayer, kept thinking about how they could get out of their predicament. Once they reached their destination, they were thrown into a dungeon where they were chained up facing each other and tied to the same ring in the wall.

The following morning, after their jailer brought them some crusts of bread and two bowls of a strange-smelling gruel that they would not touch, they had a visitor. It was a skinny, dark-haired little man with shifty eyes and a heavy beard. As he talked, his pale hands never stayed still. He was wearing an academic gown made of gray cloth, typical of clerical dress from earlier centuries, and a wooden cross hung from his neck. A red hood and a fringed biretta completed his uniform. The man was none other than the Inquisitor Francesco Bobbo. He introduced the people who had come with him, a commissioner, an interpreter, a notary, and an armed escort, and then in his reedy voice he read a declaration.

"We, Brother Francesco Bobbo, Dominican, inquisitor designated by the Apostolic See over the lands belonging to the city of Mantua, at the request and demand of His Majesty the Emperor Charles v, after reading the letter from Giacobo Mantino, rabbi by profession and president of the *Va'ad Hakatan* of Venice, we accuse and denounce to the Church Diego Pires for having blindly abandoned the faith in Christ for which he had received the sacrament when he was baptized in the city of Evora, in Portugal, and for turning to the Jewish rite, taking on the name Shlomo Molkho. Faithful to the Holy Church, and in obedience to it, we promise and swear on the four Gospels that we will seek the truth concerning the will of the aforementioned Diego Pires to convert European Catholics to the faith of Moses. Considering that it is the responsibility of those who have been born to the true life through water baptism to root out all heresy, it is our task to show and to prove that the apostate Diego Pires, alias Shlomo Molkho, has furthermore blasphemed against our Holy Church, and…"

Angel Solomon's violet eyes stared at the Inquisitor as if he were a rare insect or some other freak of nature. Apparently the young man, whose lips kept moving soundlessly, was continuing to pray as if he were alone in the world. That butterfly who kept repeating legal nonsense concerned him not at all, except as some kind of sideshow. He would not let anything distract him from his infinite dialogue with the Eternal, blessed be His name, not even the fluttering wings of some butterfly, even if they took on the form of the Inquisitor's cape! As for David Reubeni, he scarcely listened to Francesco Bobbo's words. As the man prattled on, he did absorb that he would be able to have someone defend him, on the condition, the Dominican said, that it would be "an upright lawyer, unsuspected of heresy, expert in civil and in canon law, and a true believer." He also said that they might simply appoint someone, and that would happen when the accusation of having trying to win *Conversos* back to Judaism could be supported by witnesses and proofs. Since David Reubeni was a foreigner in Mantua and belonged to the Jewish sect, they could accuse him of nothing more than supposedly wishing to convert Christians or to bring Marranos back to the Jewish faith.

After that ceremonial reading of the charges, when the Inquisitor Francesco Bobbo and those with him had left, the man from the desert returned to his thoughts. He did not know Mantua, nor did he know anyone living there. He could not even imagine where the prison was located. Would it be easy to escape? Might his friends in Rome and Venice have the means to get him released? He had full faith in them and was certain that some of his friends would try something. Perhaps they were already working at it. In truth, the Messenger was not depressed by this latest reversal of fortune that had in a moment cast him from the brink of success to the dungeon. His faith in mankind helped him keep his sanity. Freedom was too deeply anchored within David for him to do otherwise. The cunning words of an agent of the Inquisition could never win out over his life. Nor over his life's purpose.

"The Eternal, blessed be His name, will come to our aid," said Shlomo Molkho. "You will see."

That was the first time for days that the young man had risked speaking to the man of the desert. As he didn't get the slightest response, he added:

"He will come to our aid. I know He will. I can feel it!"

And he began to recite a psalm:

My God comes to meet me, in His kindness.
He makes me look with joy on those who persecute me...
The Lord, our shield!

David Reubeni still did not respond. He was busy with something else. He was secretly checking to see how solidly the ring holding them was attached to the wall.

"My Master, my Messiah, are you still angry with me?" the Angel asked.

He tried to move closer to the Messenger, but could not because the chain was too short.

"You will succeed," he continued. "You will succeed, Master. I'm telling you! You will survive because the Messiah does not die! He cannot die! And you will liberate your people."

The sound of his own voice was reassuring. He was speaking to the Messenger, but even though David remained silent, Molkho was happy. He continued, his voice stronger.

"This setback, Master, this defeat was necessary. As it was necessary to cast Adam and Eve from the Garden of Eden. Mankind lost its home. In the days of the Messiah, mankind will again be at home in the world."

And then he quoted a psalm:
And I believe in God,
And the Eternal will save me.

David Reubeni kept working at the ring they were chained to and felt it begin to loosen in the damp stone. Now he knew that if he pulled more strongly he could tear it loose. But he would still have to break down the dungeon door and then climb the stairs to face the armed guards. He glanced over at Shlomo Molkho. In the semi-darkness, he could see that he again looked as he did as an adolescent, arms folded, his blond hair in disorder, and his violet eyes turned inwardly. The Messenger was moved at the sight. Molkho was beautiful. The worst that can happen to us poor wretches, he thought, is for the Eternal to deprive us of a sense of beauty.

"You crazy young fool," he said, hardly realizing that he was opening the door to a dialogue. "Do you know what the word Messiah means? Literally, it simply means 'anointed.' In that sense, the word appears neither in the Torah nor in the apocryphal texts. Some prophets never consider the possibility of a human Messiah, and for them only the Lord is the Redeemer. For others, the Messiah is only a collective force…"

He paused. With reproach in his eyes, he asked:

"Why did you have to speak just as the Emperor had signed? He had just given us his total support for retaking the land of Israel!

Do you realize that because of your foolishness our people will continue to wander between banishment and exile for centuries? What compelled you to do it? What evil genius?"

"God! It was God alone!" Molkho moaned. "The All-Powerful Eternal was speaking through my mouth!"

The light coming through the bars was beginning to fade. Day was almost gone.

"It was God Himself!" the Angel repeated, trying to convince David. "Did not the Eternal, blessed be His name, harden Pharaoh's heart so that Moses could outdo himself?"

The dungeon they had been thrown into was only about four feet across. Sitting cross-legged, as in the desert, David repositioned his legs before answering sharply:

"Since your path crossed mine, you've brought me nothing but trouble! You have nearly destroyed any chance for me to complete my mission!"

Molkho did not reply. The Messenger could hear only his deep breathing, and from time to time a big black fly buzzed past. The Envoy of Chabor remembered the Arabian sun and the stones in Jerusalem that sometimes were ocher and sometimes pale grey. He thought of the fine wrinkles extending out from both sides of Benvenida Abravanel's large dark eyes like streams of light...

"My Master, my Messiah!" the young man called out once again. "Speak to me! I can sense disapproval in your silence..."

"You speak!" David answered.

"Well, I just thought that...Do we not belong to the chosen people, those mentioned by Isaiah and for whom the Eternal *will bring water to the desert and rivers in solitude?*"

"No," said the Jewish prince.

"But, Messiah..."

"Don't be absurd!"

The Messenger could hardly contain his anger, and his voice shook.

"Are you still calling me the Messiah?"

"Yes, Master..."

"Do you know that when the Messiah does come, there will no longer be a 'chosen people?' Remember what the Prophet Amos said:

Children of Israel, saith the Lord,
For Me are you not the children of the Ethiopians?
Did I not bring Israel out from under the yoke of Egypt
Like the Philistines in Caphtor and the Syrians in Kir?...."

After a short pause, he continued.

"And now leave me alone and be quiet. I would like to say the evening prayer."

"But...Master, O Messiah!"

"What is it now?"

"Allow me to pray with you..."

David Reubeni, weighed down by his chains, shrugged his shoulders. But he did nod his agreement. And in unison, they recited the prayer.

"And He, full of mercy, forgives our sins. He does not carry out His destruction. Often He holds back His anger, and He does not unleash His wrath. Lord, come to our help!"

The Inquisitor appeared neither the next day nor the day following. For more than two weeks David Reubeni and Shlomo Molkho exchanged scarcely a word, as if all possibility of conversation had been exhausted. The young Portuguese kept praying. The man from the desert meditated. The verb *to wait* was at the base of his thoughts. He was waiting for an event which didn't happen. The forced inactivity, the dungeon's damp straw, the questionable bread and water they ate were wearing them down, and they could feel themselves growing weaker each day. One morning, as they chewed on some half-moldy bread, the Messenger felt some paper between his teeth. He pulled it from his mouth, and turning to one side, he was able to make out a few words: *"Keep up your courage...at the end of the next Sabbath...with the help of the Eternal..."* And there was also a signature: *"Daughter of Jerusalem."*

He thought of the Song of Solomon. His heart began to pound.

"Master," the Angel said. "Have you found something?"

"Yes," David answered quietly.

"What?"

"Hope."

Since the message had arrived, the irritating fly had stopped buzzing. Shlomo Molkho called out once more to the Messenger.

"Master, O my Messiah!"

"Yes?"

"I've been thinking. I've been thinking, and I understand why you have failed temporarily."

"Why do you think so, if it was not because of your damned tongue?"

"It was not my tongue, master! It was because you were trying to move too quickly. You tried to force the issue, to force God! You preferred looking for help elsewhere rather than from God. You forget what Hosea thought."

"And what did he think?"

"He would say: *The Assyrian will not save us. We will not mount our horses, and we will no longer say to the things we have made: 'Our God!' For it is with God that the orphan finds compassion.*"

David Reubeni was silent for a moment before replying.

"My young friend, I too have been thinking..."

"Yes, Master?"

The Angel's voice was sonorous, suddenly almost joyous. The Messiah, his Messiah had called him "my young friend." So he had been forgiven!

The Messenger continued.

"Remember, Shlomo. You are the one who was trying to force God's hand. You are the one who insisted that I was the Messiah. But I am only an army general, a fighter. I know how to lead men to victory, but to defend *their* cause, not God's! Although I believe in the Eternal, blessed be His name, with all my soul, it is because I believe in His mercy. I believe, as it says in the Scriptures, that: *He strengthens man's steps, and He loves to hear his voice. Even if a man should fall, he is not overcome, for the Eternal takes his hand. I was young. I have grown older. And never have I seen the righteous forsaken...*"

"No, Master, no!" the Angel cried. "You have been seeking God to put Him in your service. Whereas I place myself in His!"

His voice broke.

"But you are right. The Eternal will deliver us. And if we were to fail, it would be because He has so decided. And then our death will redeem the sins of the people, and the people, absolved by our martyrdom, will finally reach the promised land of Israel!"

This time, David Reubeni gave full vent to his anger.

"Stop spouting nonsense! Our death will redeem nothing, for there is nothing to redeem. Because death is blasphemy, a sin against God! *'You will choose life!'* says the Eternal. Yes, it has been because of your madness that the trouble we are now in won out over victory. Because of your damned tongue, yes, failure replaced success. Be quiet and pray!"

The cell door screeched open. Four jailers came in, escorting the notary. David recognized him by his obese figure, only partly hidden behind the guards, and got to his feet.

"Not you!" shouted the obese man, and he turned to Angel Solomon to read a document he had prepared. "I, Augustin, notary of the Holy Inquisition, I come to summon Diego Pires the preacher. He is also called Shlomo Molkho, an apostate, accused of speaking heretical and scandalous words in public. I am to take him before the court of the Holy Office and the people of Mantua so that he may hear the complete charges and witnesses against him and the well-known proofs of his misdeeds. And then he may try to defend himself…"

When the jailers removed his chains, Molkho tore away and ran over to the Messenger.

"My Master," he cried, throwing his arms around David's neck.

He had just the time, before the guards seized him once more, to place his blond head on David's chest, the man whom he continued to venerate.

"I have loved you so much!" he stammered. "So much!"

The guards then dragged him out of the dungeon.

Alone, the man from the desert began to weep.

Two hours later, the notary and one guard came to get David. He didn't even listen to the words the notary spoke. He was thinking only about the way in which he would conduct himself in the courtroom. He brushed his hair back with one hand and dusted off his tunic. He intended to present himself in a dignified manner. A prince of Israel does not appear before a judge like some ordinary bandit.

In a dark corridor where resin torches were flickering, he met Shlomo Molkho, whom they were bringing back to the dungeon. He slowed.

"*Alleluia!*" the Angel shouted, his emotions at a fever pitch.

"What is happening?" the Messenger asked worriedly.

"Master! My Messiah!"

"Speak!"

"I will be sacrificed as a burnt offering, Master!"

"What?"

"Will the smoke from the fire that consumes me be agreeable to the Eternal?"

The guards pulled them roughly apart, prohibiting their conversation from continuing. David Reubeni lost sight of the young Portuguese, who was chanting a litany of victory and joy on the way back to his cell.

The courtroom was large and bright. A huge crowd had pushed its way in. The harsh light pouring through the windows half-blinded the Messenger due to its sharp contrast with the darkness of his dungeon cell.

When he came in, there was a stir in the room. He looked at all the people in surprise. There were rich burghers on the lookout for something unusual. There were also some poor wretches attracted by the show that the Inquisition would put on. He even thought that here and there he could glimpse Jews with their saffron yellow hats. He knew that anyone who aspires to a goal beyond the reach of most men commands a certain fascination. He wondered if that were the only reason so many people had come to the courtroom. The room was so crowded that many had been unable to get inside, and through the windows he could see large numbers of people massed on the square. He was convinced that people had gathered in much the same way that flies swarm in with the smell of carrion. Torture and death fascinate people more than kindness.

"May the Eternal bless you, my son!" a voice whispered as he walked by.

He would have recognized that voice anywhere. He turned and saw old Rabbi Obadiah da Sforno.

"You are here?" he replied in a whisper. "But that is dangerous!"

"At my age," the old man replied, "the risk is not great."

"What day is today?" David asked.

"Thursday."

"Two more days...," the Messenger murmured.

The guards pushed him forward to the stand.

There was a large, unadorned cross hanging on the white wall at the back of the platform. Francesco Bobbo was seated at a long table, along with the commissioner and two men dressed in black. The notary sat to one side. When the Prince of Chabor was facing the Inquisitor, Bobbo got to his feet.

"In nomine Domini, Amen," he chanted, his voice cracking.

He looked at the Messenger, but was unable to hold his gaze. David had gotten used to the light and was looking him in the eyes. To the Dominican, it was as if they burned into him. The eyes held a strange power, like a dark fire burning behind his pupils, ready to burst forth at any moment. Francesco Bobbo avoided his gaze and turned to the crowd. He tried once again to meet the prince's gaze, but then had to lower his eyes and pretend to study the dossier. Bent over the dossier, he prepared to read the charges. He cleared his throat, but that only seemed to make his voice worse. He began his speech.

"In the year 1531, on the nineteenth day of March, I, Francesco Bobbo, Dominican, doctor in theology, Inquisitor for the territory of the city of Mantua, in the presence of the city's notary public, the commissioner and scribes from the Holy Office of the Inquisition, I accuse the man David Reubeni..."

When he reached that point in his text, the Dominican was suddenly interrupted in Hebrew by the man from the desert. In a loud voice, he began to speak.

"In the name of the Eternal, God of Israel, I challenge the authority of this court. It has no right to judge me!"

The interpreter, a skinny, bald man, translated, rolling his eyes in fear. But his voice was strong, as loud as the Messenger's, and everyone could hear his words. An uproar filled the room. People were calling out to each other, arguing, shouting, and the raucous sounds echoed back down from the vaulted ceiling. People began to push and shove, and Francesco Bobbo could do nothing to bring things back under control. Finally, David Reubeni himself raised his hand, and the room grew silent. He stepped toward the Inquisitor, placed his hand flat on the table, and stared at his accuser. The crowd waited with bated breath.

"I am the Prince of Chabor," he continued, his voice strong. "I am the brother of Joseph, King of the Jewish Kingdom of Chabor. I was sent on an official mission to Rome, carrying a letter from my brother the king to His Holiness Pope Clement VII."

He paused for a moment so the interpreter could translate. All eyes were focused on the platform where he stood. Facing him, not more than an arm's-length away, the Inquisitor's face was dripping sweat. His little rodent eyes looked from right to left, unable to peer directly into the eyes of the man from the desert.

"There is no jurisdiction over me except that of my brother, the King of Chabor, and the ever-present Eternal! Furthermore, I have been invited personally by the pope. Only he, if he judged my conduct against my Christian brothers reprehensible, could ask me to leave Italy and go back to my own country!"

Throughout the room, people began to murmur when the interpreter had finished. Then the Messenger concluded his remarks, and his eyes bore into Francesco Bobbo's, who had even more trouble holding his gaze.

"Your honor, I have nothing further to say to this tribunal. It is null and void, since it has no jurisdiction over me. Therefore, I will answer no questions that your Inquisition presents to me. The Eternal, God of Israel, is my witness."

And out in the crowd, someone shouted, "Amen!"

David Reubeni once again recognized Obadiah da Sforno's voice.

Chapter fifty-nine

A Miracle at the Stake

The uproar in the crowd was so great that the Inquisitor Francesco Bobbo decided in his fright to suspend the proceedings and begin again the following morning.

When the Messenger got back to his cell, he was surprised to find that Shlomo Molkho was no longer there. Instead, there was a stranger struggling with his chains, tied to the same ring.

"Let me go!" he was shouting to the guards. "I will steal no more. I promise! In the name of our gentle Savior Jesus, I beg you to let me go…"

But the guards just whacked him in the ribs and told him to calm down and shut up.

When they were alone, the man from Chabor questioned him in his rudimentary Italian.

"Who are you?"

"I am Marcello Locato. My friends call me *Il Ladrone*."

"So you are a thief. But why are you here?"

"I stole a purse from a nobleman from the house of Gonzaga. But how could I have known that he was a nobleman belonging to the court of the marquis?"

"So you got caught?"

Il Ladrone rubbed away a tear of frustration with the back of his hand.

"Yes, sir," he sniffled. "I tried to run and slipped, unfortunately…"

"And then?"

"Then? The duke's guards caught me and began to beat me. Then other guards showed up. Strange men. They put a sack over my head and brought me here. When they pulled off the sack, I saw a young blond man, like me, who was chained up. They took off his chains, led him out, and put me here in his place."

He looked fearfully at David.

"Where are we, sir?"

"In a prison, young man."

"But you aren't from here, are you, sir?"

"No."

"Where are you from?"

"From far away. From very far away."

"Have they harmed you?"

"No."

"Are they going to torture us?"

The Messenger did not answer. He was lost in thought. Someone had substituted this young thief for Shlomo Molkho. The only thing the two had in common was their blond hair. *Il Ladrone* was just unlucky. He had slipped, as he said, "unfortunately," and now he was in danger of being burned alive in place of the young man from Portugal. It was a simple plan and had been carried out quickly. But who could have come up with the idea? If the subterfuge worked, Angel Solomon's life would be saved, but what would David's own fate be? Would the plot that Dona Benvenida Abravanel was organizing to help him escape be helped or hindered by the death of the false Shlomo Molkho at the stake?

Young Marcello seemed comforted by having a fellow prisoner, and he fell asleep like a child worn out from too much crying.

The Messenger tried to calculate what time it was. It must not be late, for the sky through the bars was still grey. So he still had a lot of time ahead of him, even though he needed to stay ready to escape, and he confidently waited for Sabbath to end. If such were the divine will, he would soon be free once again. If on the other hand, the Eternal refused to save him, it could be for only one reason: It would be because he could no longer do anything useful. Once he escaped, he would be pursued like a fugitive. He would no longer be able to go into any Jewish house for fear that some innocent person might pay for that visit with his life. How, in such conditions, could he work against History? How many hopes and dreams would be lost if in his pride he insisted on persevering, if he refused to admit his defeat? He came to no specific conclusion. In fact, he wondered if he should even escape...

Now the dungeon had become completely dark. The man from the desert shivered. He feared daylight's coming. What would happen if the guards realized the subterfuge when they came to get young Marcello? If they noticed nothing, would not the death of that innocent man be on his own conscience? David Reubeni could feel the humidity from the walls penetrating his body. He tried to move away from the wall with his chains clanking. And what about Angel Solomon, he wondered suddenly. Was changing his religion really a crime? Was he not innocent as well?

Just before dawn, the cell door screeched on its hinges. Along with the notary and ten guards, one of the Inquisition's scribes came in. Marcello woke up.

The scribe was dressed in black. "My son," he said, "the charges against you are heavy..."

Il Ladrone, in tears, broke in.

"I'll never do it again, Mr. Judge, I promise. In the name of the merciful Savior..."

But the scribe wasn't even listening. He continued his speech.

"Therefore, as you have brought it upon yourself, you will be delivered over to the secular authorities to be executed."

"No! Have pity!" the poor man cried.

But his shouts were already muffled by the sack the jailers were placing over his head. They removed his chains and started down the sinister corridor. Toward the stake.

The adolescent's moans died away in the distance, and David Reubeni felt compelled to say the *Kaddish*, the prayer of the dead.

May His great name be magnified and sanctified in the world He created according to His will...

The death of Shlomo Molkho, burned at the stake, caused many different reactions. That was the first time such a sentence had been applied in Lombardy. Marquis Federico di Gonzaga was indignant and concerned about his city's reputation. He demanded that the General Commissioner of the Inquisition, Thoma Zobbio, send his representative in Mantua, Francesco Bobbo, away immediately. Apparently, Shlomo Molkho had twisted and turned in the flames, asking for mercy and forgiveness. When the Emperor Charles v heard about those tragic circumstances, he was so upset that he immediately withdrew his complaint against David Reubeni. And he did even more. He sent a letter by imperial courier to the Dominican Paolo Constabile, putting in question the reliability of all the witnesses for the prosecution, including the Duke of Urbino and Ambassador Miguel da Silva. He reduced to nothing the accusation brought against the Prince of Chabor by a certain Tobias, his former servant. Tobias had revealed the existence of a secret journal in which the man from the desert wrote heretical statements accompanied by kabbalistic signs. And the traitor Tobias claimed that the journal was hidden in a chest filled with amulets. The chest had been entrusted to the care of the Count Santo Contarini by the Messenger before he left for Ratisbon. The Magnificent Contarini, when he was interrogated in Venice by special emissaries of the Inquisition, flatly denied those accusations by someone he called an untrustworthy valet. He did not hesitate to swear under oath that he had never seen such a chest or journal. So the two of them, the count and the emperor, helped destroy the charges against David Reubeni.

When Shlomo Molkho's death became public knowledge, Dona Benvenidae Abravanel was sick with worry, and she decided to move to Grazie, not far from Mantua, to be closer to the Messenger. She quickly gathered together some friends. They needed to come to a decision, but what would it be? Everyone had a different opinion.

Giulio, the brigand leader from the old port in Naples, thought they should go ahead with their plans. In his opinion, they needed to help David escape. The reward promised by Dona Benvenida required as much. But Abramo Luzzato didn't see things in the same light.

"Given the new situation, since Shlomo Molkho was killed, Signora," he said, "I'm not sure that we should help David Reubeni escape."

"You prefer that he stay in prison?" Dona Benvenida asked.

"Or go to the stake, like his friend?" Giulio added.

"Good Lord, no! But a man who escapes from prison remains a fugitive, an outlaw, a man whom everyone considers guilty, and the police are always looking for him. That is not a situation our friend deserves."

"And so?"

"So, Signora, I believe that helping him escape is not the appropriate thing to do at the present time. On the other hand, if he is released after an inquisitorial decision and they publicly declare him innocent, then he will be free to continue working to re-establish a Jewish kingdom in the land of Israel. And it is even probable in that case that he would receive more support. If he is freed officially, then there will be a new wave of enthusiasm among those who love and follow him."

Dona Benvenida thought for a moment before speaking to Giulio.

"I believe that Abramo sees things clearly," she said. "We must put off our plans for his escape. But I want you and your friends to stay here in Grazie, ready to intervene in case of emergency. I will pay you whatever is necessary, have no fear of that. And in the end, even if things go the way Abramo suggests they might, you will still get your money."

However, David Reubeni could not leave the Mantua prison unless the pope agreed. And only Thoma Zobbio, general of the Catholic Inquisition, would be able to get the pope's agreement. General Zobbio's pride had been hurt by the abortive trial, and nobody knew how long it would be before he would approach the pope. But in the meantime, at least the worst had been averted for the Jewish prince, and the conditions of his detention were clearly improved.

When the death of the young kabbalist was announced, the Jewish communities all over Europe, including those dependent upon the Ottoman Empire, declared a day of mourning. In Venice in particular, the Jews were in despair. At first the Ghetto was in deep sorrow, but then, as the role of Giacobo Mantino in the whole affair came to light, they grew more and more angry. Even his most faithful friends would no longer shake his hand. So, in fear of the people, the rabbi resigned his position as president of the *Va'ad Hakatan*. He left the City of the Doges with his whole family and settled in Bologna, where a doctor was needed.

For the pope, things were now looking better. The damage done during the sack of Rome and the floods of 1530 was slowly being repaired. He was busy bringing back all those who could use their talents to bring glory to this new era of his papacy. Now that there was peace again in Italy, young artists from Tuscany and Flanders, artists like Salviati, Vassari, and Martin Heemskerck, returned to Rome. And even Michelangelo, whom Clement VII asked to undertake in the Sistine Chapel "something that would mark the end of a tragedy by a symbol as powerful as the events themselves." The pope was showing his years, but not without dignity.

Shlomo Molkho, since he had been secretly freed by the pope's agents, was living hidden away in the Vatican. He was delighted that the pope had chosen Michelangelo. Only an artist who knew Israel's history the way Michelangelo did, he said, would be able to express the tragedy of the modern world, because he himself had experienced it and understood it from the inside out. He remembered that the sculptor had used David Reubeni's face as the model for his Moses and that he had supported the Prince of Chabor's plans to restore a Jewish kingdom in Palestine.

Clement VII liked to ask the young Portuguese for advice. Since the young man had been hiding in the Vatican, their close friendship had picked up where it had left off. Angel Solomon, however, was worried. In spite of the fact the Emperor's complaint had been withdrawn and the witnesses against David had been declared null, the man from the desert remained in prison. The Inquisition had sent no request to the pope for his release. And each time Shlomo Molkho brought up the question with the pope, Clement VII repeated that he had to wait. But waiting is not a visionary's primary virtue.

On that particular day, when Angel brought up the matter again, Clement VII tried to explain.

"My dear son," he said. "God is my witness that I sympathize wholeheartedly with the prince's misfortune, but the pope cannot take a position in this matter unless he has been asked specifically to do so by the Holy Office of the Inquisition. A conflict between the Vatican and the Inquisition would only make David's situation more difficult! Our friend Cardinal Egidio di Viterbo is at this very moment negotiating with the Dominicans..."

And he laid his hand tenderly on Molkho's shoulder before continuing.

"You see, my son, recently you both were in danger of being burned at the stake. Today, thanks be to God, here you are with me, and David, though he is still in prison, is no longer in danger. Surely you have not forgotten the Psalm you quoted me yesterday:

They laid a snare beneath my feet,
My soul was bowed.
They dug a pit before me,
And they fell therein.

Believe me, my son. Things will end as it has been written!"

But the sovereign pontiff's display of friendship was not enough to bring peace to Shlomo Molkho. The pope seemed to be thinking only about going down in history as the pope of peace. Only serious pressure from the people could compel such a man to take risks. And who better than Angel Solomon to stir up the crowds in support of David Reubeni?

It is true that he didn't always agree with his hero, but he did love him and believed that he understood David better than anyone else. The Messenger thought that basically men acted out of self-interest; even those who devote their lives to learning are interested in finding out how wisdom can be helpful to them. Freedom, he insisted, is in everyone's interest, and that is why people are ready to fight for their freedom. Shlomo Molkho couldn't accept those arguments. For him, love alone can push men from the beaten path so they might take real risks. And first of all, love for the Eternal. And then, love for all those whom He has created in His own image. And he, the Angel, he did love the Eternal, the God of Israel, with all his soul. And he loved God's Envoy, the man whom He had sought out in the far-off Chabor desert in order to give renewed hope to the Jewish people. He was the only one, he thought, who loved David so deeply, the only one who venerated him so appropriately! He remembered that he needed to act as it is written: *And You will bring a Liberator to their children's children for the glory of Your name, out of love...* Yes, who other than Molkho could set the Messiah free?

It was the month of *Sivan* in the year 5291 after the creation of the world by the Eternal, blessed be His name, just a few days after *Shavuot*, near the time of the Giving of the Law, *Zeman Matan Toratenu*. In that particular year, the Jewish festival corresponded with Christian Pentecost that commemorates the descent of the Holy Spirit on the Apostles. On that day, in spite of all the safety precautions that had been imposed on him, Shlomo Molkho slipped out of the Vatican without letting anyone know. He walked so quickly that he felt he was almost flying through Rome.

During that season every year, a fair was set up by the Theater of Marcellus, near the Jewish quarter. The weather was lovely, and waves of customers washed through the fair daily. A few years before, this was the place Shlomo Molkho had chosen to give his prophetic warnings to the Christians, the sons of Esau. This time, he needed to move them deeply. He wanted to touch their hearts and incite them to move en masse to Saint Peter's Square, where they would pray for David Reubeni's life and demand that Pope Clement VII grant him pardon.

"My Roman brothers!" he cried.

A few heads turned in his direction.

"My Roman brothers!" he repeated. "Christian brothers and Jewish brothers, look at the sun!"

He raised his arms.

"The sun shines for everyone. Tomorrow, it will shine once more. The Eternal has willed it thus. But the day after tomorrow, it will rain, and the world will seem sad to you, painfully sad!"

Conversations stopped. Nearby, all was quiet, and like a rock rolling down a hillside, the silence brought everything to a halt. Soon, all that could be heard was the Angel's voice gaining strength and urgency, and sentence after sentence hypnotized the crowd.

"And you will discover that your salaries are meager, that your children are sickly, that wars are killing your brothers, and that disease is carrying off your loved ones! Not knowing whom to turn to, you will turn to the Lord of the Universe and you will ask for His protection and His love. However, the God of mercy has already sent a man to help you, my brothers, a man to help protect you from evil, to limit the ugliness, to free the sun!"

"Say," a vegetable seller whispered to a woman near her stand, "that looks like that Portuguese preacher, the fellow who predicted the destruction of Rome and the floods!"

"Nonsense!" said an old man standing nearby. "Everyone knows that the man was burned alive on the public square in Mantua on the Inquisition's orders!"

"The woman is right!" exclaimed another man. "That is him, I recognize him! I was right here at the Theater of Marcellus when he came to speak three or four years ago. I'm sure. It's him! That's the man who was burned at the stake in Mantua!"

The news spread like wildfire. Shlomo Molkho was alive! The advisor to the Messenger of Chabor had come back from the fire!

Angel Solomon continued to harangue the crowd. It kept growing larger, crowding in to where he stood and filling the whole marketplace and the streets around the theater. Ottavia and Foro Piscano streets were jammed. The Jewish quarter was bubbling, and people were nervously chattering all the way down to the banks of the Tiber.

"Come quickly!" Obadiah da Sforno shouted.

The old man was almost running, and he pounded on every door to alert the people living there. Finally he reached Doctor Joseph Zarfatti's house, and the doctor invited him in. His sister Dina was there as well.

"Come quickly!" the old rabbi panted, refusing to come in.

"What is happening?"

Chapter sixty

Angel Is Martyred

Don Miguel da Silva, in the name of Queen Catherine of Portugal, had written several times to the General Commissioner of the Catholic Inquisition, Thoma Zobbio, encouraging him not to give in to Vatican pressures and to go on with David Reubeni's trial. And he did even more. He came to Rome in person to defend the cause he believed in—purifying religion in Europe. His discussions with Thoma Zobbio and with Paolo Constabile, the Dominican General, seemed to be bearing fruit. Diego Pires the apostate had been burned at the stake, and the Portuguese ambassador was hoping for the same punishment for the adventurer from Chabor. For him, the risks were high. Another execution would be the prelude to establishing a permanent Office of the Inquisition in Italy. And in Portugal, in addition, special courts would be set up.

As the ambassador was passing near the Farnese Palace, he heard people shouting in the streets. So, he stopped his carriage to ask a passerby who was running toward the Octavian Portico and the Orsini Palace.

"He has risen!" the man was shouting.

"What?" Miguel da Silva called out. "What are you saying?"

But the man was already lost in the crowd rushing from Piazza Navona toward the Octavian Portico.

The ambassador began to call out to anyone who would listen. "Who has risen?"

But everyone was in a hurry to see with their own eyes the man who had come back from the dead, and they paid no attention to the Portuguese dignitary. Finally he climbed down from his carriage and grabbed an old man by the sleeve.

"Who has risen?"

"Well, by God, it's that young Molkho! You know, the man who had prophesied that Rome would be destroyed!"

"He was burned alive!" replied Miguel da Silva. He was incredulous, but worried nonetheless.

"I know, I know," said the old man, pulling away in irritation. "Why else would I be telling you that he has come back to life?"

Back in Sant'Angelo Castle, Cardinal Egidio di Viterbo was the first to notice that Shlomo Molkho had slipped away. He immediately called the commander of the papal guard, Luciano Mascherone. The commander said that he had indeed seen the young man leave the Vatican. But there had been no orders to keep him from going into the city. So he hadn't seen any need to tell anyone. When the cardinal alerted the pope, Clement VII sent his guards to look for Angel Solomon and bring him back immediately in any way they could. They needed to find him before the Inquisition spies and agents could do so. If the Inquisition found him first, they would discover the subterfuge that had allowed him to escape the stake. If they got their hands on him, it would be difficult to save him a second time...

"Lord of the Universe!" proclaimed Shlomo Molkho, "I have come to this place only out of love for heaven, as Your glory knows..."

The papal guard had to leave their horses near the Caetano Palace, because the crowd was so thick that they could only move on foot.

"Let us through! In the name of his Holiness the Pope! Let us through!" the commander shouted.

Luciano Mascherone was a powerful man, but he could hardly work his way forward. In spite of his physical strength and the lances of his guards, it was almost impossible to push through that human sea. Its tides seemed to roll in and out uncontrollably.

"Ask for David Reubeni's freedom! Demand his freedom!" Shlomo Molkho kept repeating, just a few yards away. "Lend your support to the man who answered the Eternal's call and came because he loved you so much! And the pope, in his infinite kindness, will listen to you. He will hear you and understand your pain. He will see how right you are to demand the Messiah's freedom. And then the Inquisition will have to relent! And death will be vanquished!"

Followed by his lancers, Luciano Mascherone had to maneuver his arms like a swimmer to get through the crowd. Finally, he spotted the young preacher standing on a market table. Bareheaded, his blond hair blowing in the wind like the words he was speaking, Shlomo Molkho was still haranguing the crowd. Immediately, the commander of the papal guard ordered his men to form a wall with their lances. With the direct threat of the lances, people did finally move aside. There was much pushing and shoving. A woman fell to the ground with a cry. People shouted out their complaints. But now Luciano Mascherone had finally almost reached the Angel.

And just then, from the direction of the San Nicola in Carcere Church, twenty men suddenly appeared. They were dressed in long black capes and their hoods hid their faces. The commander of the papal guard leaped toward Shlomo Molkho, but he was stopped in his tracks, struck by a dagger from the hands of one of the men dressed in black. Blood poured from his mouth as he coughed. He caught a glimpse as he fell of the young Molkho struggling in the grasp of the black forms. They dragged him away through the crowd. Swords glistened in the sun. Luciano Mascherone had been dealt a blow of death, and he would never get up again.

After the initial surprise, Rome spent the rest of the day numb. Contradictory rumors and information kept circulating. As the day came to an end, the Romans did indeed have more information, but there was still much they could not understand. Some facts appeared to be true. First, there had been no miracle, no rising from the dead. And people realized that the pope himself had been behind the whole business. People were astonished to learn that to save Shlomo Molkho from the Inquisition, the sovereign pontiff had not hesitated having him removed from his prison and replaced by an ordinary thief. A poor innocent, or at least he was almost innocent, had died instead of an apostate or a prophet (according to one's point of view) to please Clement VII! The notion was surprising, even scandalous. And the exploit ended unexpectedly, for instead of staying hidden away in the Vatican, Shlomo Molkho had gone out into the city, on a campaign to free his master David Reubeni who was still in prison in Mantua. Little good it had done, for when the Dominicans of the Inquisition found out some way or another that he was out in the city, they sent their private militia to whisk him away before the papal guard could arrive there to protect him.

Though people began to understand the various events, they could only conjecture about what motivated the different actors. For example, why had the head of all Christendom given protection to an apostate? Why had Emperor Charles v withdrawn his accusation against David Reubeni? Why had Frances I offered to pay a large ransom if the Jewish prince were freed? And even more surprising, why had the Sublime Gate suddenly taken an interest in the affair? Why had Soleiman the Magnificent, the very person the man from Chabor was proposing to fight, intervened on his behalf?

All around the Mediterranean, even far away, these questions were the subject of long discussions and vigorous debates. When the decision of the Holy Office of the Inquisition was announced, sending Shlomo Molkho to be burned at the stake, riots broke out all over Europe. In Rome, thousands of the faithful streamed toward the Vatican, singing songs to obtain his pardon. They were turned back at the Sant'Angelo Bridge by the pope's Swiss guards.

In Cardinal Egidio di Viterbo's vast library, several of Clement VII's closest cardinals gathered around him. The situation inside the Church was explosive, and the confrontation between the Vatican and the Inquisition was no longer a secret for anyone. The Holy Office of the Inquisition claimed that it was free to decide and act in complete autonomy. Joao III, King of Portugal, now simply a puppet of Queen Catherine and her "Spanish clan," was demanding papal authorization to set up special courts in his country to try the *Conversos*. And even Luther had accused Clement VII of being the "Jewish pope!" Among the many insults and affronts that the Church had suffered in Germany, this last blow seemed the most serious and the most dangerous.

Shlomo Molkho was alive, but once again he was destined for the stake. Those two pieces of news were deeply distressing to Dona Benvenida Abravanel. She immediately gathered her friends together, and, with a first-rate escort, went to Mantua so she could evaluate the situation directly.

The city was in a state of siege. From the San Giorgio Gate to the edge of the lake and all around the duke's palace and the Buono-colsi Palace, the duke's guard and the Inquisition's militia were patrolling everywhere with weapons at the ready. On Piazza Sordello, in the shadow of the cathedral with its imposing Romanesque façade, workers were stacking wood intended for the ordeal. Soldiers were checking the barricades around the piazza to be sure they could hold back the crowd. On the rooftops, there were harquebusiers with their weapons aimed downward. And the prison where David Reubeni was incarcerated had been placed under the exclusive guard of the Inquisition's police.

Dona Benvenida's heart ached. She was sorry she had not helped the man from the desert escape while it was still possible. It is true that her actions would have been interpreted as the work of a woman in love, and she would have preferred his escape to be seen as a patriotic feat of the developing Jewish army. But nothing had happened, and she felt guilty for not having evaluated the situation correctly.

"I kept the cause in mind," she confided to Abramo Luzzoto, "instead of thinking about myself! What is the name of the Arab poet who said: '*Drink some wine, since you do not know where you came from. Live joyously, since you do not know where you are going?*'"

But Abramo had no idea who the poet was.

Benvenida's big dark eyes filled with tears.

The ceremony of the *Auto pubblico generale* started at dawn with a mass recited in the central nave of the Duomo. The crowd that filled the Romanesque cathedral, with its five naves separated by tall columns, was strangely quiet. It was as if the faithful were not yet awake or forced to be there against their will. Each was holding a candle. At about noon the procession set out, with soldiers on both sides. Piazza Sordello, Piazza Broletto, and all the nearby streets were jammed with people. The barricades and three rows of soldiers held back the thousands of people eager to see the "risen one" die once more. On Piazza Sordello rows of seats had been built. People had rented the windows and balconies of nearby houses, some at exorbitant prices. The main stage held the loggia of the duke and places for the local nobility and dignitaries of the Inquisition in Mantua, and it was built up against the duke's palace. That was where the court's sentence would be read.

All the Jews in Mantua, protégés of the Gonzaga family, stayed away. On the other hand, hundreds of others had come from the Marche province, from Padua, and even from Venice. Moses de Castellazzo made the journey alone. With the Messenger's arrest and Shlomo Molkho's inevitable death, a part of his own life was disappearing, and he preferred being alone with his pain. In Venice, it was often said that collective ruin makes each individual's suffering less. But what could be more intimate and personal than suffering? That is what he had said to Titian with a sigh before he left Venice. Once in Mantua, he found a place near a barricade, near the Santander Church, far from the crowds of Jews.

At about two in the afternoon, with the sun beating down, the trumpets blared. The procession was on its way. Before it, came sergeants of the duke's guard, recognizable by their leather breastplates and their yellow shirts. Then came the cross, draped with a cloth and accompanied by children tolling out their steps with little bells. And then came the penitents. Silence lay heavily over the square. One could even hear the wind fluttering the cloth that covered the cross. Suddenly, the suspense was broken by the clatter of hooves. Officers on horseback, members of the Court of the Inquisition, appeared holding banners high. Moses de Castellazzo realized that nobody was even talking about the show. Everyone was quiet, as if mesmerized by anxiety. The stake in the center of the square awaited its moment. The only thing lacking was the victim. For a moment, as the bailiff read the sentence, the artist had the crazy idea that Shlomo Molkho might once again escape his executioners. But alas! Soon he was led into the square, head bare and wearing a white tunic with a golden star stitched into the front. Quickly, the fire was lit and the Angel became partially hidden by the flames. A burning stick fell to the ground. The crowd stepped backward and Moses could hear murmuring.

And then he thought he must be hallucinating. He could hear someone singing. The wind had risen just as the inferno had been lit. It carried away the words of a song he recognized, and then when it changed direction he could hear them again.

"The Jew is singing!" said a little girl perched on her father's shoulders.

The song grew louder. The voice was almost crystalline, and it seemed to rise higher than the flames themselves.

"It is as if he is speaking to the angels of heaven!" the little girl added.

"Who is singing?" asked a woman who was clinging to the artist's shoulder to avoid being trampled by the crowd.

"It's the Jew!" somebody answered nearby.

"But, isn't he burning up?"

"He is burning and singing at the same time!" a female voice said with a sob.

Moses de Castellazzo turned around and recognized Dona Benvenida Abravanel. Their eyes met. He tried to speak to her but she jumped in ahead of him.

"He is singing Psalm 57," she said.

And she, too, began to chant softly.

My soul is among the lions
I am lying in the midst of men who are spewing flames from their mouths…

The artist picked up the psalm, his voice louder.

In the midst of men who have lances and arrows for teeth…

Abramo Luzzato, who was protecting Benvenida with his powerful escort, joined his voice to theirs. Suddenly, all around the square, other voices joined in, singing along with the victim.

And their tongue is a sharp sword...

A movement ran through the crowd as if it were a giant millipede, for everyone was trying to see where the songs were coming from. And then Moses heard some Latin words, and people were singing the very same psalm in Latin.

Be Thou exalted, O God, above the heavens!
Let Thy glory be above the earth!

The soldiers, holding back the crowds behind the barricades as best they could, did not know what to do and were beginning to lose their composure.

"Make them be quiet!" shouted a man dressed in purple from the stage.

But it was in vain. The singing grew louder. A few burning sticks collapsed to the ground in a shower of sparks. Moses and thousands of others watched through the whirling flames as the Angel raised his hand and pointed in the direction of the people on the stage.

"The Jew is loose!" someone shouted.

"An angel of the Lord has delivered him!" cried the little girl perched on her father's shoulders.

Instinctively, the crowd drew back. Fire had just caught the Angel's white tunic. The young kabbalist's voice grew louder still, more sonorous, brighter, and it became almost unreal.

They prepared a snare under my feet;
My soul was bowed down.
They dug a pit before me:
They themselves fell therein.

He paused for a moment, as if to look out over the crowd that was watching him. His two arms were dripping with golden flames as he raised them toward the heavens. And then, in a stentorian voice, he gave one last shout.

"Lord of the Universe, You are One!"

His arms fell. His head dropped, and he collapsed into the inferno.

"Amen," the crowd sighed.

Moses de Castellazzo was weeping. Weeping from sympathy. When he dried his tears, he noticed that Dona Benvenida and her escort had disappeared.

During the entire trial ceremony, Dona Benvenida had been thinking only about David Reubeni. She could not stand the idea that someday soon he, too, might be burned at the stake before a crowd eager to see another mad spectacle. Even if it meant she must die with him, she needed at all costs to try to free him.

The prison was near Lago Superiore, on the road to Cremona. Giulio knew that he would be undertaking something dangerous, perhaps the most perilous task he had ever undertaken. Most of the army and the ducal guards had been mobilized to prevent any problems in the city. Giulio hoped that the prison would have fewer guards. One of the walls around the prison extended out into the lake, and fortunately, water was Giulio the sea pirate's favorite domain.

A hundred men were waiting for him down in the crypt of the San Sebastiano Church. The priest, also from Naples, was a friend. Weapons were distributed, and a dozen of the men put on uniforms like those worn by the ducal guards. An hour later, everything was ready. Giulio was hoping to use trickery to get into the prison. But they were forced to wait. Suddenly they heard the noise of galloping horses, with shouts and whinnying. Dona Benvenida hurried over to the exit. But just then, the priest came in.

"The Emperor's lansquenets!" he announced.

"What are they doing? Where are they going?"

Dona Benvenida's voice reflected her worry.

"I'll tell you in a moment," said the priest. "Let me go see what's happening, Signora."

A few minutes later, he was back.

"The Emperor himself is leading them!" he shouted.

"Are there many of them?"

"Thousands!"

"Where can they be going?"

"It looks like they are going to the prison…"

"My God!" cried Dona Benvenida, raising her hands to her face. She began to sway and fainted away in the arms of the priest who hurried to help her.

The priest of San Sebastiano Church had been right. Charles v, leading a large contingent, was indeed heading toward the prison in which David Reubeni was held. On his way to Spain, he had heard about Shlomo Molkho's supposed resurrection and then how he had been killed. He wasn't bothered much by that, because he had never liked the young preacher. He found madness despicable, and for him, Angel Solomon was crazy. On the other hand, he liked the Prince of Chabor, and he thought that his project was noble and just. He regretted having turned him over to the Inquisition. And he did not want the prince's death on his conscience. He remembered the sea metaphor David Reubeni had used during their conversations back in Ratisbon: *Of what use is it to have the fear of God as your compass if your conscience does not hold the tiller?*

That occured just a few days before *Rosh Hashanah*, the Jewish New Year, in the year 5292 after the creation of the world by the Eternal, blessed be His name.

Epilogue

Five years after these events, in the year 1536, a rumor trickled through Venice: Several reliable witnesses claimed that David Reubeni was back. They swore on the Holy Torah that they had seen him entering the palace of the Magnificent Santo Contarini. More and more curious, they had waited near the canal on the *documenta*. A short time later, the Prince of Chabor left the count's luxurious dwelling in the company of two of the count's servants who were carrying a heavy ebony chest.

When Moses de Castellazzo was interrogated by the members of the *Va'ad Hakatan*, called into session by the new president, Shimon ben Asher Mechulam del Banco, he refused to deny or confirm the rumor. David Reubeni's friends from Rome would also say nothing, claiming that they did not know anything about it. *The world subsists only through secrets*, is all old Obadiah da Sforno would say, quoting the Kabbalah.

However, that very year, just a few days after Passover, Azari ben Salomon Dayena, the rabbi in Sabionetta, affirmed that he, too, had seen the Messenger in Padua. With four servants dressed in their distinctive white tunics, David Reubeni had crossed the wide

Piazza del Santo, then walked past the Oratorio di San Giorgio. The rabbi had even tried to follow him, but the man from the desert had slipped into the Palazzo del Bo and disappeared behind the walls of that famous university still marked by Dante's presence. And so, the imposter who should still be languishing in prison was freely moving around all over Italy! Azari ben Salomon Dayena thought it was urgent to inform Giacobo Mantino about this new scandal. He did so in a letter dated April 15, 1536.

When Mantino left Venice, he practiced medicine in Bologna for three years, but then he was living in Rome. As soon as he received the letter informing about the reappearance of the man from Chabor, he hurried to see Thoma Zobbio to find out more. The general commissioner of the Holy Inquisition answered that according to those highly positioned in the Spanish Inquisition, David Reubeni had died in the year 1533. He had undergone torture in Spain in the Badajos prison, where he had been moved from Mantua.

Giacobo Mantino made haste to circulate that information in Rome. But according to his own friends, he didn't believe the news himself. Soon another rumor, this time from Alsace, added to his doubts.

In Rosheim, Joseph Josselmann had confided in his family just before he died. In 1531, he had fervently pleaded the Messenger's cause to the head of the Holy Roman Empire. Charles v, judging that the dreams of the man from the desert should not disappear forever in the Inquisition's dungeons, had decided to remove the Jewish prince from his Mantua prison. Not to take him to Badajos, in Spain, but rather to put him on a ship leaving for the Holy Land, for that land of Israel of which he so fervently dreamed...

Author's Note

Though four centuries separate us, I find that I am still fascinated by the enigmatic figure of David Reubeni, the Prince of Chabor who claimed to descend from the tribe of Reuben, which out of the twelve original Jewish tribes was one of the ten that disappeared from history.

I discovered him as I was doing research for the book *La Memoire d'Abraham*, and even included him in that book. Already then I was surprised by historians' lack of interest in the man. Was it because there were insufficient texts, documents, and witnesses? Or was it because the man did not fit the archetypes preferred by Jewish historiography? For example, even the most famous Jewish historians, Joseph Hacohen and Gershom Scholem, devote only a few lines to him, and those few lines are critical. That very silence concerning Reubeni and the suspicion that seemed to surround him were enough to attract me to him.

He was a contemporary of Michelangelo and Machiavelli, two symbols of the Renaissance. More than four centuries before another David, David Ben Gurion, he had planned to create a Jewish state in the land of Israel. His plan had diplomatic, political, and military components. The key to his strategy was a Judeo-Christian alliance that could counter the growing influence of Islam on both sides of the Mediterranean. In exchange for the support of European kings for his Jewish cause, he was ready to concede control of the Christian holy places in Jerusalem to the Vatican.

That was enough to compel me to want to know more about David Reubeni. At the very least, I wanted to find out exactly who he was and why over the centuries his name alone had been enough to cause people apprehension.

As I began to read about his era, I had the strange impression of *déjà vu*—as if the sixteenth century kept reminding me of the twentieth. For the sixteenth century, like our own, was marked by an unrivalled cultural, artistic, and scientific apotheosis, but also by an unleashing of barbaric activity, the like of which had not been seen before. The Inquisition wiped out Sephardic Judaism in the name of religious purification. Four centuries later, the Holocaust tried to destroy Ashkenazi Judaism in the name of racial purification. Both tragedies were followed by a resurgence of Jewish national conscience. The sixteenth and the twentieth centuries both saw an increased number of civil wars and watched Islam's surprising progress. And finally, both eras have been marked by the end of universal hopes, and consequently, by the increase of popular mysticism, expressed most clearly during the time of David Reubeni by the feverish expectation of the Messiah's coming.

So for more than seven years I followed the trail of the "Messiah from Chabor," visiting the countries he had visited, staying in the cities where he had stayed. I read every document and witness account I could find about him. I met most of the contemporary historians who have written about him or even simply mentioned his name. And I went from surprise to surprise.

For example, the most famous and accurate chronicler of the day, the Venetian Marino Sanuto, mentions that David Reubeni appeared in the City of the Doges in November of 1530. But the texts that I was able to consult, as well as David Reubeni's *Journal* itself, date his arrival in Venice in 1524.

Between the sixteenth and the nineteenth centuries, no one even suspected the existence of the *Journal*. Written in Hebrew, it suddenly reappeared in 1848 in the library of Khaim Michael, a collector of rare books. The discovery caught everyone's interest, and the manuscript was purchased by the Bodleian Library at Oxford, copied in 1867, and then translated into German. The copy of the Oxford text has been preserved, and I was to able study it. On the other hand, the German translation made its way by some means or another to a rabbinic school in Breslau (Wroclaw today) in Poland. And since then nobody knows where it has been. Nor does anyone know where the original is, for it, too, mysteriously disappeared! However, the Messenger's banner, with its Hebrew letters stitched in gold, has been preserved. It can be found today in the Jewish museum in Prague.

Appearing out of nowhere and then disappearing, for seven years David Reubeni did, however, make his mark on the politics of the great courts of Europe and nourished the dreams of an entire people. If history is a lesson—as the creator of Hassidism, Rabbi Israel ben Eliezer whom people called Baal Shem-Tov, would claim— then those days of the sixteenth century, so similar to our own era by their violence, loss of values, and interest in the irrational, are worth reflecting upon. Through the evidence and the depth of analogies between the two eras, we must surely be observing the united power of reason and passion at work in history!

About the Author

Marek Halter was born in Warsaw in 1936. When he was five, he and his family escaped from the Nazis by crawling through the sewers under the Warsaw Ghetto. He has lived in France since 1950. In addition to being a writer, Marek Halter is also an artist and a human rights activist and has served as president of the European Foundation for Science, Art and Culture. His book *Le Fou et Les Rois*, which recounts his experiences working for Middle East peace, won the *Prix Aujourd'hui*.

His bestselling novels *The Book of Abraham* and *The Wind of the Khazars* are also available from *The* Toby Press.

The fonts used in this book are from the Garamond family

Other works by Marek Halter
available from The Toby Press

The Book of Abraham

The Wind of the Khazars

The Toby Press publishes fine writing,
available at leading bookstores everywhere. For more
information, please visit www.tobypress.com